THE POSSIBLE WORLD

Also by Liese O'Halloran Schwarz

Near Canaan

THE POSSIBLE WORLD

LIESE O'HALLORAN SCHWARZ

HUTCHINSON
LONDON

Published by Hutchinson 2018

1 3 5 7 9 10 8 6 4 2

Copyright © Liese O'Halloran Schwarz 2018

First published in the USA by Scribner in 2018

First published in Great Britain in 2018 by

Hutchinson
20 Vauxhall Bridge Road
London SW1V 2SA

Hutchinson is part of the Penguin Random House group of companies whose addresses can be found at global.penguinrandomhouse.com.

www.penguin.co.uk

Penguin
Random House
UK

A CIP catalogue record for this book is available from the British Library.

ISBN 9781786331182 (hardback)
ISBN 9781786331199 (trade paperback)

Printed and bound in Great Britain by Clays Ltd, Elcograf S.p.A.

Penguin Random House is committed to a sustainable future for our business, our readers and our planet. This book is made from Forest Stewardship Council® certified paper.

MIX
Paper from
responsible sources
FSC® C018179

With gratitude to all the doctors and nurses and patients
who taught me what I know of medicine

and

In loving memory of my parents, Jacquie and Paul,
who taught me everything else

The invariable mark of wisdom is to see the miraculous in the common.

RALPH WALDO EMERSON, NATURE

CHAPTER ONE

Ben

MY MOM HAS THREE FRECKLES, light brown and almost perfectly square, two on her right cheek and one on her nose. She has an up-and-down line between her eyebrows that gets deeper sometimes. Like now, when the car has parked and she's gotten out, and I still haven't moved.

"We're here," she says, opening the back door. "Hop out."

I put my thumb on the seat belt button beside my booster seat. Nobody else in my class still uses a booster seat. In two months, when I turn seven, I can use just the seat belt. If I grow.

"How long will it be?" I ask.

She looks at her phone.

"I'll come back for you at seven. So, four hours."

"What are you going to do?" My thumb still on the button.

She purses her lips in a thinking way. "I will go out dancing. I will put on an electric-blue gown that goes all the way down to my toes, and silver high-heeled slippers."

"No you won't." She doesn't *have* a dress or shoes like that.

"No I won't," she agrees, smiling. "I will probably do some grocery shopping and clean the kitchen." She puts a hand on the top of the car door. "Or do you want me to stay?"

I sneak a look at the house beyond her.

"Why does it have to be so many people?" I ask.

"It's not so many. Four is not so many."

Her phone burrs from her pocket; she takes it out and looks at the screen, then puts it to her ear and turns away, talking. She pushes the car door almost closed and leaves her hand on it, like I might jump out.

How she looks: she has yellow hair that comes down to her chin, eyebrows darker than her hair and brown eyes, a black speck in the right one the shape of a bird with only one wing. One tooth is slightly forward from the others in her mouth, just a little bit, and her smile goes up more on the left than the right. There's a white line under her chin from a roller-skating accident back when she was a little girl. Two holes in her earlobes where the earrings go, usually the little pearls, but sometimes dangly ones; none today.

How she sounds: her voice brisk in the mornings, telling me to *get a move on,* softer in the evenings, and when she laughs I think of a brown velvet ribbon falling through the air. The nonsense song she sings to me when my tummy aches: *lavender blue dilly dilly, lavender green.* I told her once that lavender's a kind of purple, and purple can't be blue or green; she paused and then said, *But the song's still good* with a question in it. Yes, the song is still good just the way it is. Other things she says: *I love you more than pizza, or Bingo, or caterpillars.* Last week she asked me, *Do you really have a stomachache?* while I lay with my head on her soft lap, ear down. *You're having a lot of stomachaches. Shhh, I'm listening to your tummy,* I said. *Sometimes my stomach hurts when I'm worried about something,* she said. *Are you worried about something? Sing some more,* I said, and she did.

The way she smells. In the morning like hand cream and shampoo. She brings a different smell home with her from the hospital. I said something about it once and now she washes her hands and changes her clothes right after work. Until her next shower, though, there's always still a trace of that chemical smell.

How she feels—when I go to her room after a nightmare she lifts the covers and it's warm and she puts her arm over me, across my chest, and it's warm and solid and she pulls me against her and I can feel that warmth spreading through me and the bad dream melts away. *I love you more than bunny rabbits and Jell-O. More than Gorgonzola and crayons.* Her long fingers, their smooth unpolished curves of fingernail.

Before is sliding away. I barely remember it. The tall woman with the water-blue eyes, like a mother but not my mother, I know there was a time I saw every detail about her in my mind, but now I see her only in flickers: standing in a kitchen paring the skin from an apple into a looping red curl, or kneeling in the dark spring dirt. I feel the wet on my knees too, and the grainy earth, but as soon as that comes it's gone again. She lives there now in that warm slice of time before I sleep, and even that is getting smaller, closing like a door.

"Buddy, you're so serious," Mom says, putting her finger on my nose. She's off the phone now. "What are you thinking about?"

"I'm memorizing you," I say, and that warm brown ribbon unspools and falls around me. I close my eyes and breathe deep to pull the noise in with my ears.

"You are so funny." She bends down a little bit and looks me in the eyes. "Honey, there's no law that says you have to go."

"I want to go." Kyle is my best friend and I got him the toy he wants most and I can't wait to see him open it. But I don't know how it will be with the other boys there.

She knows what I need to hear. She puts her hands on the top of the open window and rests her chin there, so she sounds like she's chewing when she speaks. "You'll go inside," she says. "Maybe Kyle will open the door or maybe his mother."

"And Scooter."

"Uh-huh. Scooter will bark at first, and then he'll see it's you and he'll wag his whole butt."

Kyle's dog with the flat face, whose mouth doesn't ever close all the way, his pink tongue with brown spots on it always showing, moving when he breathes. Scooter's kind of gross. But it is funny how he wags his butt because he doesn't have a real tail.

"You'll take your shoes off in the hall. Remember, they have those wood floors. You'll line your shoes up with the other shoes."

Now I can see the wood floor in my mind, long and shiny. Scooter's toenails *clack clack* on it, and when he runs to the back door to greet Kyle's dad he sometimes can't stop and slides right past into the laundry room.

"Then you'll pet Scooter." He'll slobber on me and I'll need to wash my hands; it'll be okay, though, there's a little bathroom on the first floor that Kyle's mom calls the powder room. "Then you'll probably play some games."

"Kyle has PlayStation." I can see the basement room where the games are, the blue bouncy sofa and the Lego corner where Kyle and his dad are working on a castle. They've been building it for months and it's taller than me.

"Then you'll have cake. I don't know what kind," she says before I can ask. "Maybe chocolate. You'll sing 'Happy Birthday' and he'll blow out the candles, and then he'll open his presents and there may be some time to play with them before the movie."

"What movie?"

"I don't know."

I weigh this—the maybe-chocolate and the unidentified movie.

"Then you'll come?" I ask. "Right after the movie?"

"Right after."

"Okay." Now I can see it, the afternoon ahead into the evening, and finally the *want to go* defeats the dread. I push the belt release button with my thumb and the bands across my chest and tummy suck back into the holder. Mom straightens herself up and swings the car door open.

"I can stay for a while," she says, taking the wrapped box from the back of the car.

"No." No one else's mother will be there. I'm the smallest kid in my class, the youngest by more than a year. The only one with training wheels, maybe the only one who's never been to a sleepover. I can't be the one whose mom stays with him during a birthday party.

I hold her hand until we get to the front walk and then slip it out, just in case someone is watching from the window. When we're on the doorstep, she gives me the present to hold.

"Ben!" cries Kyle's mom when she opens the door. She's holding a coffee cup with a big yellow smile on it. "It's great to see you."

"Thank you for inviting me," I say. Kyle's mom raises her eyebrows, makes a nodding smile at my mother.

"I bet I know what this is." Kyle's mom takes the present from me with her free hand. "The boys are downstairs in the playroom. We'll be having pizza and cake in a little while."

"Where's Scooter?" I ask.

"He's on a doggy playdate," says Kyle's mom. "He gets a bit too enthusiastic around pizza."

"You okay, buddy?" Mom asks. She puts a hand under my chin; my heart pulses once, twice, against her fingertips where they touch my neck. I nod.

"Go on downstairs. I'll let you know when the pizza comes," says Kyle's mom.

My mom drops her hand. She looks at me hard and I nod again; she smiles and follows Kyle's mom toward the kitchen.

I rip the Velcro straps on my shoes and line them up in the hall next to the others. I am careful not to slip on the wood floors. It's easier when I get to the living room; there's a carpet with a tasselly fringe. The door to the basement is around the corner.

"What a little gentleman you're raising, Karen," I hear Kyle's mom telling my mom as I open the basement door and the music of the PlayStation game swells out. "Can you stay for coffee?" I step down onto the first step and pull the door closed behind me.

WE HAVE TO take turns. There are four of us, but only two can play at one time. I get pretty far on my turns; I'm good at shooting things. In between it's fun to watch Kyle play; it's his game so he knows all the tricks.

"I'm going again," says Charlie when he's finally Game Over. That's not fair, he's had a long turn with Kyle while Elliot and I watched. Charlie keeps the controller and presses the buttons to start a new game.

"It's my turn," says Elliot. Charlie pretends not to hear him.

"Who's playing with me?" says Charlie. He's one of the biggest kids in class. Some kids say he already did third grade at another school, and when he came to our school they made him repeat. So he should be fourth grade and I should be second grade, but we're both in third. He and Kyle are on the same soccer team.

"It's my turn," Elliot repeats. I really can't believe he says this. Neither can Charlie; he turns his head slowly, like a robot. "It goes Kyle, then you, then me, then Ben."

"Lemme go. You can go next," says Charlie.

"It's my turn," repeats Elliot, and I want to tell him to shut up. Charlie hands the controller over, but I know that's not the end of it.

Kyle offers me his controller, but I shake my head; he shrugs and presses Start.

So it's Elliot and Kyle jumping through the Dragon Kingdom while Charlie and I watch. Charlie's next to me on the sofa. He's the kind of person who does something mean and then says, *What, you can't take a joke?* when the other person is crying.

"That's the doorbell," I say. Are more boys coming?

"Probably the pizza," says Kyle, jump-punching the serpent

that killed me on my last turn. There's heavy walking on the floor above. "Elliot, get that power-up right in front of you."

"Pizza!" says Charlie. "I'm starving."

"No green peppers, right?" says Elliot, collecting a trio of stars on the screen, boosting his health bar. "I'm allergic."

"I don't know," says Kyle. "My mom ordered."

"Smelliot's allergic," says Charlie in a whiny singsong.

"I get hives," says Elliot. "I swell up."

"Like your face swells up?" says Charlie. "Or what?"

I can see that Charlie is hoping there will be green peppers. A part of me almost hopes so too. I've never seen someone swell up before. I'm allergic to cats, but when I get around them I don't swell up, I itch and sneeze.

"Everywhere," says Elliot. "No green peppers or pecans," he tells Kyle. "My mom must have told your mom."

"Pay attention," orders Kyle. They're at a tricky part.

"Who puts pecans on pizza?" says Charlie.

"Not on pizza," says Elliot. "Just any pecans. In anything."

"She usually gets pepperoni," says Kyle. "Jump now, *jump*!"

"Smell-i-ot," says Charlie. "Smelliot can't eat pee-cans. What else can't Smelliot eat?"

And just like that we're on the edge of something. I can feel it, Elliot can feel it. Kyle, who's concentrating on the game, is unaware.

"Just green peppers," says Elliot. His voice is blank, like he's making a wall with it, trying to stop what's coming. His avatar takes one hit, then another. He flails, runs into a wall, tries to jump away from it, but his lifeline is pulsing red. "Ben, it's your turn next."

"I have to go to the bathroom," I say.

"Use the one upstairs," says Kyle. He's still trying to shoot them out of the dead-end Elliot has brought them to. "The one down here has spiders."

The word is electric. He has to know what will happen next. Or maybe kids like Kyle, kids everyone likes, don't have to see what is obvious to kids like me and Elliot. We can see what's coming: Charlie sitting on one of us, dangling a spider *Open up* while pinching nostrils shut. Chest burning, mouth finally gasping open. I can almost feel the spider legs tapping my tongue.

"But it's your turn." Elliot is almost pleading; he's looking at me instead of the screen. Kyle yelps disappointment at the dying whine of Game Over.

"You can take my turn," I tell him, pushing away the shame. I shouldn't leave Elliot to risk the spiders on his own. "I really have to go."

I am quickly up the stairs, safe at the top. Behind me, I hear a thud and an *oof*—Elliot hitting the floor. I hesitate for a moment, but then turn the doorknob, step through, and shut the door behind me. I cross the hallway into the powder room and close that door too. I didn't actually have to pee before I went in, but suddenly I find I do. I turn on the fan and run the water in the sink. I'm careful, but I miss just a little bit, and I tear off some toilet paper to wipe up the drops from the floor. It's the end of the roll, though, and when I pull the remnant off and the cardboard is naked, I've got only half a square in my hand. I open the cabinet under the sink, where Mom keeps the toilet paper at home, and there it is, a soft white pyramid. I'm not careful enough reaching into the cabinet: I jostle things and a plastic bottle tumbles out onto the floor and rolls away from me, spilling a thin line of oil.

I retrieve the bottle, find the cap and screw it on, put it back into the cabinet. Then I crouch and try to wipe up the floor with toilet paper, but the oil spreads into a big shiny patch. It's obvious that I spilled. Steps go by outside the door; is someone about to knock? My heart is going fast.

I wind off lots of toilet paper, wet it in the still-running tap, pump *one one thousand, two one thousand* hand soap on, use the clump of it like a sponge to wash the floor. Too many bubbles; a bigger mess. I use several wet-tissue-clump sponges with no soap, and then some dry ones. When everything is finally back to the

way it was, more than half the toilet paper roll is gone. I rub my
hands under the water for two alphabet songs and sniff them to see
if the oil is gone, but I can't tell. Hand soap and two more alphabet
songs, and then I dry them on one of the hanging towels, using the
part that's behind, next to the wall, so the wet doesn't show. I turn
off the tap and the overhead fan and take one last look at the floor.
I can still see the shiny place, but maybe no one else will notice.

Doors are always risky—you can never tell what's on the other
side. I use both hands to turn the doorknob and open the door
just a bit, then a bit more, then finally take a breath and push so
it swings wide open. Half expecting to see Charlie looming in the
gap: *you've been in there forever.* Laughing, *Eww you smell like a lady,*
maybe all the boys laughing, even Kyle, who's never laughed at me
before. But the hallway's empty.

I was in there a long time, long enough for Kyle's mom to have
called everyone up for pizza, but the basement door is still closed
and there's no sound from the kitchen. I should go tell Kyle's mom
that Elliot can't eat green peppers. She probably knows that, though.
I could tell her instead that I'm hungry, so she'll call the boys to
come upstairs and eat, move us all to the next thing on the list of
pizza and cake and presents and movie.

There aren't any lights on in the hallway and it's gotten dark.
I make my way by feel, one hand on the wall, toward the living
room; the kitchen's on the other side of that. When I step onto the
fringey living room carpet it squelches. Uh-oh, Scooter probably
peed and now it's on my sock. It's a whole lot of pee—my sock's all
warm and wet—and I step back and lift my foot to peel the sock
off. Something in my brain knows that it's not pee; there's something flashing *Warning* in my head, but I've already got the alarm
there from Charlie and Smelliot and the long, panicked bathroom
cleanup, so I take another step onto the carpet, holding my sock
in one hand. Almost to the kitchen. Why aren't there any lights
on? There's a smell of coffee, and a metal taste in my mouth, and

a weird distant noise I can't identify, like a faraway siren. Suddenly I hear another sound, very nearby, that some place deep inside me recognizes—a short gurgle that makes the hairs on my neck stand up.

Instantly I'm dropped onto my belly and scrambling backward, stopping only when my feet hit a wall and I can't go farther. I'm under a table, eyes wide open. The blackness in front of me shifts and I realize that what I thought was just more darkness is a standing person, and the person is turning. Toward me? I can't see details, just shapes. I stare as hard as possible; I hold my breath. My heartbeat shakes my body and I try to press myself into the floor. There's a voice in my head keeping me still, saying, *Bark on the tree, buddy, you're bark on the tree.*

A motion-detector light comes on suddenly outside the upper windows, making slanted boxes of light across the room, and in one of them I can see Kyle's mom lying kind of sideways. She's mostly on her stomach with her hair across her face, and the smile from her coffee cup is on a broken piece beside her. She lifts her head a little and looks at me, hair stuck down across her face so that only one eye is showing. She swallows and coughs and blackness rushes out of her neck.

There's another sound right above my head and I look up, into the face of a man who's bending over me, his face glowing in a stripe of light from the window.

"You're not gonna say anything, right? You're gonna shut the fuck up?"

I am nodding like a puppet, like a woodpecker, so fast and automatic *yes-yes-yes.*

"Thank me," he says. "You need to thank me for saving you."

My jaw feels frozen. I open my mouth but nothing comes out.

The outside light goes off, leaving the room even darker. Is he gone? I stare hard into the black, not moving.

After a long time, or after no time at all, everything goes white and there's a *shhhhh* in my ears like the ocean and far away someone is screaming.

CHAPTER TWO

Lucy

PATIENTS LIE. EVERY DOCTOR KNOWS it. They lie innocently, or out of embarrassment; they lie to get something they want, or to avoid something they fear. Good lies and bad lies, meaningless lies. There must be a limited number of lies in the world, because I hear the same ones over and over again.

I only had two beers.

My car got broken into and my Vicodin (codeine/Demerol/Percocet) was stolen.

I was just walking down the street, minding my own business, and some dude came up and stabbed me.

Some Dude really gets around. He steals the pills, he stabs and shoots, he sails through red lights and stop signs and smacks into law-abiding cars. Sometimes he blooms cohorts: he is Two Dudes, or even Three.

I don't care about the lies or the dudes; I don't need or want the whole truth anymore. I want to know only the part that matters, that will guide me to discover what needs to be found and fixed.

In Trauma 2, an ambulance team is transferring a patient to the stretcher.

"Thirty-five-year-old restrained passenger, car versus tree." One of the paramedics reads from his run sheet as the other snaps the belts back across the now-empty ambulance gurney. "Prolonged extrication, some delta MS but awake and talking, vitals good." Delta MS means altered mental status, anything from confused to somnolent to psychotic. "Driver's on the way."

"Hello, Doctor?" from the woman on the stretcher.

"I'm your nurse," Dennis tells her cheerfully. "Doctor's right behind me."

Scrabbling fresh gloves from the box on the wall, glancing at the EMS note for a name. "Hello, Crystal. I'm Dr. Cole. Does anything hurt?"

She tries to shake her head but the hard collar around her neck prevents that. "Where are my shoes?"

"Probably still in the car. Take a couple of deep breaths for me, okay?" Hooking the stethoscope into my ears, I press it against her clothing, then lift it to let the tech's trauma shears scissor by. The clothes fall away and the patient lies briefly naked, a length of pale gooseflesh, before the tech flicks a hospital gown open over her.

"Any medical problems?" I ask. Lungs clear, abdomen normal to palpation. "Do you take any medicines every day?"

"Um, thyroid." Crystal lets the tech lift her hand and guide it through one of the armholes in the gown. "Where are my shoes?" She puts her other hand through the other hole.

"She's been asking that the whole ride here," says one of the paramedics as they trundle the gurney out of the trauma room. "It was *all* about the shoes."

"What's the last thing you remember before being here?" I ask Crystal.

Furrowed brow, pause. "Today is what?" I have to think for a moment myself.

"Saturday."

I look at Dennis, who nods.

"Okay, breakfast," says Crystal. "I made chocolate-chip pancakes."

A concussion can wipe out everything for a variable period before the trauma, leaving retrograde amnesia—a blank space in recent memory that patients sometimes fixate on trying to fill up. They may say the same thing again and again. *Did you let the dog out, I'm late for work, my birthday's tomorrow, please help me.*

"Let's roll her."

The tech puts firm hands on either side of the head to keep it in-line, the nurse takes hold of her hip and shoulder, and they pull her—*one, two, three*—up onto her right side, with her back to me.

"No pain here? Or here?" I ask, pressing my fingers down the spine, pushing hard against each vertebra in turn, pausing briefly to hear each no.

"Where are my shoes?" says Crystal as they roll her back down.

There's a ruckus outside the room, the doors sliding open at the end of Trauma Alley, the voices of paramedics and the overhead call for *surgical team to Trauma 3*.

"Tell me if anything hurts," I say, rocking the pelvis and moving down the extremities. Bending the joints, checking the pulses. Intact, intact, intact. Scraping my thumb up each sole, watching the big toe point on each side. Normal. So just a concussion then, no other injury. Lucky: from the noises next door, the driver isn't doing so well.

"Do you have any allergies?" I ask Crystal.

"Not that I know of," she says. Strange how precise most patients are about that—as if allergies are stalking them, and it's just a matter of time before one leaps out from behind the bushes and reveals itself. A fleeting pucker at her brow and she adds, "I was wearing my purple dress."

"That's right." The dress lying in pieces on the floor is purple.

She shivers, an involuntary ripple that knocks her teeth together. Dennis looks up from his charting, gets a blanket from the warmer, and tucks it around her.

"Oh, thank you," Crystal croons. "Thank you so much."

The X-ray tech approaches with the orange metal-jacketed plate in her hands. "Trauma series plus a head CT," she sings out, like she's leading a call-and-response prayer. "Okay, this plate will be cooold, I'm sorry," she tells the patient.

"Where are my shoes?" The question is whispered now, urgent.

"Oh my God," says Dennis, under his breath. "Enough with the shoes."

X ray—the call to evacuate the room. Everyone goes into the hall, the tech dragging the thumb control on a long, curly cord. She presses it and there's a dull click from the mechanism; then she and Dennis dart back in to place the next X-ray plate.

Trauma 3 is not doing well; that's clear from the doorway. Bad sign number one: the entire trauma team is in there, from chief resident (long white coat), through junior resident and intern (scrubs, no white coat), down to medical student (short blindingly white coat). Bad sign number two: the sound of the vent, chuffing breaths down the ridged plastic ventilator tube that snakes through the air and disappears into the cluster of personnel around the stretcher. The worst sign of all: the Level One rapid-infuser has been rolled out of the corner of the room, and it's running blood. That's a Hail Mary right there.

"I've got the passenger next door," I tell Kim, the documenting nurse. "How is he?"

"His GCS was five when he came in," says Kim, looking up at the monitor above the stretcher, then down again to copy numbers onto the chart. "His pressure's dropping."

Tame words to contain such disaster. The Glasgow Coma Scale boils brain function down to eye opening plus verbal response plus limb movement, and predicts prognosis after head trauma. A normal GCS is fifteen, meaning alert and responsive, opening eyes spontaneously, following commands. You get a point in each category even if you do nothing: a doorknob has a GCS of three. But GCS is a luxury for this patient at this moment, an unnecessary frill: *pressure dropping* in the setting of blunt trauma means imminent death.

"We need to take him," says the surgical chief resident, striding to the foot of the stretcher. A *crack* as he steps on the brake there, releasing it. "We need to take him *now*." He puts a hand on each stretcher siderail and begins to pull.

The cluster of white coats breaks apart as the stretcher rolls toward the door. Hands jerk monitor leads from the patient's chest; more hands snap open the Level One and pull out the bag of blood inside, hold it up high in a two-fisted squeeze. An instant piercing shriek of alarm from the ventilator as the connection is detached, and then other hands are there with the Ambu bag, puffing manual breaths down the endotracheal tube. I get a glimpse of a purpled bleeding face, the eyes swollen to slits, as the stretcher goes by. It accelerates down the hall toward the OR elevator in a tense, tight company, a nurse running alongside and fumbling for the elevator key hanging around her neck.

Trauma 3 is now empty, its floor littered with the detritus of rescue: wads of bloody gauze, wrappings from the central line kit, the Foley kit, the endotracheal tube, the nasogastric tube, the IV bags. The monitor whines from the wall, leads drooping down, all of its lines flat. The ventilator still screams from the corner. I walk over to punch all the power buttons off.

"They musta been going a hundred," says a voice behind me. I turn to see one of the paramedics. He takes a cell phone from his front shirt pocket. "I got pictures."

"Jesus," I say as his index finger pushes the images by. For all the ER trauma I've managed during my residency, I haven't seen too many accident scenes. My EMS ride-alongs required back in internship were three years ago, and most of those were nontrauma runs. Dizzy old people, chest pain, asthma attacks.

"Took twenty minutes to get his door open," he says. I can see why: the vehicle in the pictures is impossibly compacted.

"Passenger's okay."

"She was belted. He wasn't." He lowers his voice. "And look at this." Pushing his fingers apart on the phone screen and homing in on an area behind the car. "No skid marks."

That meant the driver hadn't stepped on the brakes before the crash; he wasn't trying to stop. March in Rhode Island swings between stolid midwinter and the earliest fringe of spring; the recent thaw means that the ground in the image, between tired filthy fragments of snow, is soft enough to have taken tire marks.

"He could have been unconscious," I say, looking at the clean twin impressions, unblurred by skid. "Maybe he passed out before the crash."

"Nope." He swipes to the next photo. "See?"

It's hard to tell what he's showing me. The car isn't even in this picture.

"*Turn* marks," he says, and then I see them. Curved gouges in the ground. "Like you get when you make doughnuts on a lawn?" He traces an eight in the air with his index finger. "The road went straight, but the car turned. About fifty yards from the tree." He sees that I'm getting it. "So he stepped on the accelerator until they were going a hundred miles an hour, then he cut the wheel hard. Aiming for that tree." His voice is thick with disgust. "Unbelted, trying to die. With his fucking wife in the passenger seat."

"She doesn't remember anything. Although I don't know how long that will last." Postconcussion amnesia will usually lift after days or weeks, but sometimes blank patches remain forever, the events right around the trauma never completely restored. "Maybe it's best if those memories don't ever come back."

"Wouldn't you want to know if your husband tried to kill you?" He clicks the phone off and drops it back into his pocket.

Would I? There are a few things my husband did that I wish I didn't know.

"Lucy, I need you in room 19." Grace, the charge nurse, comes up to us. She adds, seeing my expression, "No, it's not that." Nineteen is one of the pelvic rooms, the one usually used for rape cases.

"Thank God," I say, wishing my relief were purely compassionate. Rape kits once begun have to continue until they are finished, to preserve the chain of evidence. Forty minutes of evidence collection can totally torpedo a shift.

"Don't speak so soon," says Grace. She offers me a chart. "It's a kid."

"Okay," thinking *so?* The nurses, most of whom are mothers, can get weepy about kids. Childlessness has its benefits for an ER doc. Not something I can say to the people who are forever telling me, *You'll never know what love is until you have a child.* I want to tell them: *Okay, got it, I'll never know.*

"Brought in from the scene of a multiple homicide, needs a medical eval before he goes to Psych."

"Psych? Is he the perp?"

"Perp?" says Grace. "Somebody's watching too much cable. No. He's a child, maybe five or six. It's not clear what he saw, or if he saw anything. He's not talking. We don't even have his name."

"Is he injured?" Looking over the front sheet of the chart I see there's no triage note, just vitals and in the name field, Johnny Doe.

"We didn't find anything. We've already taken pictures for evidence. If you clear him, we can send him up to the floor and Psych can see him there. Social Work's on the way."

Outside room 19, two male detectives are sitting in chairs on either side of the closed door, one a tired, tweed-suited sixty, and the other a tall, pink-faced blond who cannot be as young as he looks.

"Dr. Cole's gonna see him," Grace tells them.

"Psych?" says the older detective, perking up.

"ER," I say, and he slumps disappointedly back into his chair. "I'm going to medically clear him so he can go upstairs. You can talk to him there."

"I'm gonna need coffee," says the cop. He scrubs a hand over his face. "Listen, get his name if you can. We don't know if he lived at the house, or if he was one of the party guests." I raise my eyebrows at *party* and he adds heavily, "There was a birthday cake in the dining room."

"Any more vics on the way?" I ask.

The younger detective, who's been leaning forward with elbows on his thighs, staring down at his shoes, lifts his head.

"He was the only one alive," he says. The horror of the scene is stamped onto his face. The older cop rolls his eyes and turns away. Probably thinking what I am thinking, some version of yes, this is awful, but seriously, dude, reconsider your life choices; there are a lot of bodies ahead of you.

"We need to find next of kin ASAP," says the older detective. "I don't want the family getting the news from Twitter. Seriously, get his name and I'll bring you Dunkin's your next shift." In New England, Dunkin' Donuts is king. Distances are measured, and driving directions given, by the pink and orange stores.

"I'll try." I tuck the chart under my arm and go through the door.

He's small, even if he's only five or six, and looks even smaller here. Room 19 is the largest room in the Department. It has space for a pelvic table and ultrasound machine, for counselors and chaperones, for a counter with a sink, cabinets above and drawers below to hold a stock of rape kits, plus its own private adjoining bathroom. Grace has dimmed the overhead light and turned on the one in the bathroom. The boy is lying back against the pillow, and at first I think he's asleep, but as I close the door he turns his head toward me. I roll a stool over. Patients relax and give a better history if the doctor is seated, rather than looming over them or seeming poised to flee.

"Hi. I'm Lucy." It feels good to sit down; the popping sounds my spine makes as I do are somewhat alarming. Is this normal for thirty-three?

The boy doesn't react; it's as if I haven't spoken. His pupils are so large that his eyes look like dull black buttons; his dark hair is spiked up on half of his head and slicked down on the other. What weird hairstyles little boys have now. Immediately I chide myself for the thought; maybe after a few years of parenting I too would be driving through McDonald's for dinner and fauxhawking my kid along with the rest of them. I'll never know.

"Does anything hurt?" I ask. He blinks but says nothing. So much for history. "I'm just going to check you over, okay?" as I unloop the stethoscope from around my neck and stand up.

He doesn't resist as I listen to his heart, and when I put my hand on his shoulder he leans forward without being told, to let me listen to his lungs. I run the circular glow of my penlight over his back. A small healing bruise there, green already so maybe five days old, not an unexpected finding for a typically active boy; otherwise nothing.

"I had a dog when I was your age," I say, putting a hand on his shoulder while ratcheting the back of the table down to lay him flat. "I'm going to check your tummy, okay?"

His lack of response is as good as consent. Small children are not polite; they'll tell you they hate you if they feel it. They'll kick you, bite you, whatever it takes to make you and your hurty nasty self go away. Which makes their occasional expressions of trust so moving: a small hand put out to take mine on the way to X ray, or both toddler arms, one dragging an IV, upraised in the universal signal for *pick me up*.

I lift his shirt. His narrow chest has a short scabbed scratch on it, nothing worrisome, nothing fresh. "My dog was the color of straw," I say. "Do you know what straw is? Like in a barn, what the horses eat." Or is that hay? No matter, keep things going, a river of story can break up a shy-child logjam. "His coat was really fluffy." When I palpate his abdomen (soft, normal), he doesn't squirm or giggle, even at the end, when I try to make it ticklish. "Unless he was dirty. He was dirty a lot of the time." No change in the boy's expression, but are his eyes focusing on me now? "He loved to swim—in the creek, in a lake, in a swimming pool—but he hated baths. Isn't that silly?"

When I pull back the sheet to look at his legs and feet I am stopped for a moment. His feet are washed in brown, up to the ankles on both sides, and up one calf and thigh to his buttocks, where the side of his little-boy underwear is dark and stiff. The sour-penny smell of blood is unmistakable.

I've presumed *taken from the scene of a homicide* meant he'd been found in a house where a domestic dispute had ended in gunshots—that he'd been hiding in his bedroom or ensconced terrified in a closet. Not close enough to the action to be soaked in blood. So much blood—what must the scene have been like? A twinge of guilt at my judgment of the young cop outside. I drop the sheet again and stand, glove up from the box on the counter, then examine the feet more carefully. No cuts or abrasions there, nor any on his legs. I run a gloved finger under his waistband and pull the fabric away. No signs of injury under the crusted cotton.

He opens his mouth to my *say ahhh*; I train the penlight beam briefly onto his pink tongue and the arch of his palate, then move it upward, over his face. As I've begun to suspect, the spikes in his hair aren't a hairstyle. His hair is molded with coagulated blood, pushed up on one side and lacquered down against the skull on the other. He must have been lying in a pool of blood. I push my gloved fingers over his scalp, chasing them with the light beam, seeking a gap or a clot that might signify a laceration. Nothing: this is not his blood. I strip the blood-smeared gloves off, hold them drooping inside-out in one hand, and go to the drawer under the counter that holds the evidence bags. Where is Social Work? He shouldn't have been left alone in here.

"What was his name?" The whisper from behind me sets the hair up along my arms.

"Whose name?"

"Your dog."

"His name was Moses." Very casual. I keep my back to him, drop the inside-out gloves into the bag and seal it, sign the label, put the bag into my pocket, and turn around. "I called him Moze. My best friend called him Gross."

"Was he fat?"

I take the chart from the counter and reseat myself on the rolling stool. "Fat? No. She called him Gross because he was stinky." Success; the tiniest smile.

"Gross means fat in French."

"So it does." What little kid knows French nowadays? I'd loved studying it, but often I wish I'd learned Spanish in school instead—my ER Spanish barely meets my needs. "*Tu as un chien?*"

"*Un chat.*"

"Lucky. I always wanted a cat. Does he have stripes?"

"He's orange."

"Orange cats are the best."

He gives me a long, estimating look. I hear my idiotic words. *Orange cats are the best.* Really? I'm so tired; I left my house sixteen hours ago.

"Do I need a shot?" he asks.

"Nope. No shots today." I hold up my empty hands, the open chart balanced on my knees. "I just want to ask you a couple of things. First, what's your name?" I uncap my pen, poise it over the name field. He says nothing. So much for matter-of-fact. I try an appeal to fairness, which can be a strong instinct in kids: "You know *my* name. I even told you the name of my dog." Nothing.

Sigh. With an adult you'd just ask, they'd just answer. They might lie, but they'd say something. With children, obstacles rise up unexpectedly; you have to presume that even kids old enough to talk might not say one word.

"Should I guess?" Not even a blink. "Is it . . . Geronimo? Nostradamus? SpongeBob?" He just stares, not a trace of humor in his expression. "All right, I give up. What is it?"

He presses his lips together so that the skin around them goes white and shakes his head, hard. It's such exaggerated obstinacy that it would be comical if the situation were different.

"You don't know your own name?" A direct challenge, maybe difficult for a little boy to resist.

Not this boy.

"Hm," I say. "What am I going to do? I don't know what to call you." And wait. A child strong on empathy might want to solve the problem for me.

He's staring down at his hand, where it's flat on the stretcher.

"If I tell you," he says, pleating the fabric of the sheet between two fingers, "you might send me back." Pleat, unpleat.

"Back where?"

He looks up, stricken.

"I don't know," he says with an edge of panic.

I put the chart on the counter behind me and scoot the wheeled stool close to the bed.

"We just want to get you home," I tell him, looking him right in the eyes. "We need your name to get you home."

His eyes move over my face as if reading a message there.

"Leo," he whispers finally.

"Great!" I scoot back, retrieve the chart and pen from the counter. "Leo what?"

But that's all he'll say. I wait him out for minutes this time, leaning my back against the counter, my legs extended and toes braced against the bottom of the pelvic table, arms crossed. The silence stretches out between us until my head suddenly jerks down and then up and I realize that I've fallen asleep. He's asleep too, his little spiky head against the pillow and his mouth slightly open. I get up as quietly as possible and go out into the corridor.

"Well, I got a first name," I tell the detectives. "Leo."

"We can work with that," says the older cop. "Thanks." He takes his phone out, taps on the screen, and a minute later, without preamble, "Check the class roster for a Leo. Try second and fourth too."

"We know what school the kids went to," explains the younger detective, accepting the bag of bloody gloves from me. He takes the pen I offer and signs the label below my name. He looks a little less dazed now. "We're guessing third grade, from the number of candles on the cake."

I begin documenting the physical exam, backslash backslash backslash on the template.

"He's pretty scared," I say. Scribbling a small X on the child-shaped outline for the old bruise, another for the small scab, shading the dried blood. So much blood. "Do you think he saw anything?" *Anything*: a limp stand-in, but he knows what I mean.

"I hope so," he says. "But I also hope not."

His words have the fervent quality of a prayer: may this child be quickly returned to the tight embrace of his worried, living mother; may this terrible day become a bad memory shrinking smaller over the years as he grows up.

"Look again," the older cop barks into the phone. "Leo. It's three fucking letters." I know that impatience, that harshness. He doesn't have the luxury of sorrow right now, he can't indulge in dewy eyes or prayer; this boy is depending on him. He can't make the dead children alive again, but he can locate this one child's family and get him back home. I hear his voice as if it is my own, and I recognize: he's doing what he can do.

I sign the chart and give it to Grace, who has come back down the hall. "He needs a serious scrubdown," I tell her. "He's medically clear, though."

"I'll send him up," she says.

BACK IN TRAUMA 2, Crystal's cervical collar is off and the back of the stretcher has been raised. Her eyes are closed.

I put a hand on her forearm and she opens her eyes, pupils springing tight under the overhead light. Tiny cubes of windshield glass sparkle from the dark mass of her hair. "How are you feeling?"

"Okay," she says. A throwaway answer to a throwaway question.

"Your husband's in surgery."

"He's not dead?" Her voice is sharp with surprise.

"He has internal bleeding. They're doing what they can."

Is it my place to tell her what the paramedic deduced? If the husband dies, would Crystal want her memories of him clouded by the knowledge that he tried to kill them both? If he lives, she'll eventually find out. Does she need to know right now?

"You may not get your memory back for a while," I tell her. "You may never get it all back."

I could say, *I know what it's like to have the rug pulled out from under you.* But do I? Divorce—even infidelity and divorce—are relatively bland horrors. *My husband cheated on me* is anybody's story. Murder-suicide is on a whole other level. But it's all loss, isn't it? Loss and betrayal.

"Is everyone okay in the other car?"

"There wasn't another car," I say. "Your car hit a tree."

To my surprise, she bursts into tears.

"Oh thank God," she says on a ragged exhale. "Thank God."

And somehow I know that there isn't any need to tell her about the paramedic's photographs or about what her husband had tried to do. She'd been part of it. She had dressed up in her purple dress and best shoes; she was ready. The driver had been drunk as hell, but Crystal's blood alcohol was zero; her urine tox screen was negative. She'd faced the act clearheaded. Does that count as courage?

Then I remember: chocolate-chip pancakes this morning.

"Who's got your kids?" I ask.

"My mother."

She really begins to weep now, in long, tearing sobs. I know she wants comfort, but the doctor who could have comforted her is on a distant shore now, on the other side of the six-year-old with his spiky bloody hair and his Jesus feet, who'd possibly watched his whole family die.

"Someone will take you upstairs to the surgical waiting room." I can hear the change in my own voice; it's brisker, less kind. "We'll get you a phone so you can call your mom."

I dial down the overhead light, pull the curtain closed, and leave the room.

It'll be an eighteen-hour shift by the time I get to sleep, but I've done longer before without feeling this spent. Age isn't the culprit. The culprit is the *why*. I didn't sign up for the why. I specialized in emergency medicine to deal with the *what*, and the *how*, and the *how do I fix it*. I'll sic Psych on poor Crystal and Child Protective Services on her kids; I'll leave Leo to Social Services and pedi-Psych and the cops. Let them cope with the why. I've had enough of it for today.

PATIENTS ASK DOCTORS, *How's he doing?* Meaning, *Is he going to die?* They say, *What did the tests show?* Meaning, *Am I going to die?* They say, *I don't remember,* meaning, *I can't live with what I know.*

And doctors tell patients, *Just a little pinch.* Meaning, *This is going to hurt like hell.* They say, *It won't take too long.* Meaning, *You'll be waiting for hours.* They say, *She didn't suffer.* Meaning, *I know that's what you need to hear.*

People say to each other, *Tell me the truth.*

Which can mean anything.

CHAPTER THREE

Clare

THE VISIT FROM THE MAN in the cardigan breaks the afternoon wide, a thunderclap on a sunny day. Not that he is loud, or tall, or commanding. He is none of those things. He is meek and mumbly, and diminutive enough that the whole shape of him is obscured by the aide who precedes him through the corridors of Oak Haven, coming toward me where I sit in the east sunroom with my large print biography of Cleopatra.

"Well *here* she is," cries the aide (Wendy? Linda?), appearing in the doorway. "Miss Clare, we have a wonderful surprise for you."

No, this is Margaret or Melanie, something like that. One of the big ones, tall and wide. Always a source of wonder—people didn't used to come in that size. As I look up, she seems to double, pulling apart like a cell dividing. A blink abolishes that magic, and I see that a short man has stepped out from behind her. From the raveling blue cardigan (not dark enough to be navy, not light enough to be periwinkle), to every scant hair on his head, to his eyes obscured behind round gold-framed lenses, his whole affect is an apology.

"Well, now," he says, holding up a finger, his smudgy spectacles flashing in the sun from the window. "Well. We can't say that yet."

"This is Mr. Barclay," says the aide, beaming, as proud as if she'd birthed him right there, sweater and spectacles and all.

They don't really expect me to speak. I am just delicate furniture to most people now, something to be moved from one place to another, put into the sun, taken out of the sun. Like a plant. I consider Mr. Barclay, deciding whether or not to reply. Silence can be a powerful weapon. Keep quiet and others will rush in to fill the empty spaces.

"What is it?" calls Mrs. Donovan from across the room. "Who is that?"

"Miss Clare is getting the Cup!" the aide (Molly? Polly?) cries in answer.

The effect is galvanic. Or what passes for galvanic in Oak Haven—something like a shot of electricity worming through a vat of honey. The knitters look up from the fleecy clouds in their laps; the card players collapse the fans in their hands to slim bricks; the reader-nappers jolt awake from their dozing. A low querulous rumbling starts up: *What is it, who is that, what did she say?*

"*What's* happening?" That is Mr. Simonetti, deaf as a stone, from one of the card tables.

"The Cup!" repeats the aide, ignoring Mr. Barclay's protestations, which to be fair are easy to overlook, consisting as they do of a soundless slow head shaking and that still-upraised finger, now quivering.

"They still do that?" says Mrs. Burgess, one of the knitters, sounding cranky. No doubt annoyed to have her stitch-counting interrupted.

"What?" Mr. Simonetti again.

"*The Cup!*" in a chorus from around the room.

Mr. Barclay is still shaking his head; he begins folding and unfolding his lips as if preparing to speak, and raises his index finger higher as if trying to catch someone's attention, but no one is looking at him except me, through my half-shuttered lids.

"That can't be right," yells Mr. Simonetti after the news has been shouted to him a few more times. "*I'm* older than her."

"You're not, Mr. S," says the aide. "You're only ninety-two."
She turns to Mr. Barclay. "We heard about Maude Nummly over
at Gardens, of course, rest her soul. But she was one hundred and
four. Clare's not *that* old." She looks at me, her eyes squinted, as if
looking me over for a mint mark.

"Well," says Mr. Barclay. "That's just the thing." But the babble
has begun again; it surges up around his next words and swallows
them, a dozen monologues rippling out from the subject like water
in a pond, in widening, increasingly irrelevant circles. *Clare's a
hundred? She doesn't even use a walker; oh that fellow looks just like
the man who lived in that big red house on Prospect Street; who, that
television person?; no, you know, that one with the little dog; is it banana pudding for dessert today?*

"Shhhh," says the aide, with no effect.

*We never have banana pudding; you always say that; well we never
do; you mean the one who did the weather?; now I've lost my place, I'll
have to rip out two rows; the one with the little dog, you remember; is
it four o'clock already?*

Suddenly, one voice cuts across the bedlam.

"Everyone *hush*."

It isn't terribly loud, but something about it, some quality of
pitch or timbre, allows it to penetrate the din. Everyone seems to
hear it, even Mr. Simonetti. They all turn toward the speaker, who
sits in the doorway in her wheelchair with a grabber stick across
her lap.

Gloria Esperança Pereira. She arrived just a week ago. I'd heard
her name loud and clear as she spelled it out carefully the first day
for her doorplate. She is a youngster by Oak Haven standards, only
seventy; her hair is still partially dark, worn bunned at the back of her
head. She has the room next to mine (once Ellie Schlosser's room,
before that Marjorie Beam's room, and back and back, a dozen or
more ghost neighbors breathing that air on the other side of my
bedroom wall during the time I've been here), but what with the

fuss and flurry of settling in—there's a lot involved in cramming a whole long life into a two-room suite with attached bath—we haven't formally met.

She nudges her wheelchair forward with an electric *rrrr*.

"What is all this commotion?" she demands.

That voice. Mr. Barclay stands a little taller as he answers.

"I'm Wallace Barclay, president of the Barclay Foundation," he says. "We handle the Barclay Cup of Winfield."

"The Barclay Cup of what now?" says Gloria.

"Winfield," says the aide. "That's the town we're in. Oak Haven's in Winfield."

I remember when Winfield was an outpost, a hinterland. Now it's treated as a suburb of Providence, along with Cranston and Warwick and a dozen other towns, as though the capital city has flung its skirts out and annexed every bit of civilization it could.

"For more than a hundred years, the oldest resident of each town in the state is presented with a Barclay Cup." Wallace Barclay addresses Gloria alone, as though she has been elected our representative.

"I've never heard of this," says Gloria. "And I worked for the *ProJo* for thirty years. Both Features and News."

"Oh, it's not in the *cities*," says Mr. Barclay. "Only the towns." He warms to his topic: "At one point, more than twenty towns participated in the tradition. Now it's just six."

"What happened to the others?" Gloria asks. She cocks her head interrogatively, the picture of a Lady Reporter; she lacks only a little pad of paper and a pencil.

"Theft or damage or simple carelessness. Winfield's Cup, I'm happy to say, is one of the last remaining originals."

"Who would steal a cup?" Gloria asks. "Is it made of gold?"

He looks pained.

"It's made of sterling silver with ebony inlays. But the historic value far outweighs . . ." And he's off on a lecture.

As he speaks, Gloria's eyes behind her glasses move to me. The thick lenses make her eyes look enormous, cartoonish. After a good long minute, they move back to Mr. Barclay.

"So yada yada yada, you still have your cup, good for you," she says, cutting across his disquisition. "And someone died, and now it's time to find the next victim."

"It's a local *honor*," says Mr. Barclay after a startled pause. "Winfield's Barclay Cup tradition has been bestowed in an unbroken chain of succession for more than a century."

"Unbroken," Gloria repeats, and there is a challenge in it. "Unbroken?"

Mr. Barclay looks vexed. "Almost unbroken," he concedes. "There was a brief time during the 1980s when the cup was put into a storage unit by the family of the former honoree." How had Gloria guessed? She's pounced on the one weakness in his narrative. "It was returned to us in 1992, and we've had close control of it ever since."

"So where is this thing?"

While Gloria spars with Mr. Barclay, attention in the room is drifting. The knitters are starting to knit again; the card players are peeking at their hands. And of those who are still watching, it isn't clear how many are following anything of the discussion or just happen to have their heads turned this way.

"Well, I don't have it with me." Amusement at the thought. "We're hoping to present it at the sestercentennial of Winfield, next summer."

"How exciting," the aide says. "There'll be a place in the shade, won't there? For the sester—for that event. There needs to be a place in the shade. And easy access to a bathroom."

The Barclay index finger goes up again.

"There's a, there's a wrinkle."

Mention of the bathroom is having its typical effect on this group—around the room, walkers and canes are being deployed and their owners getting up.

"For the first time in the history of the Cup, we have two contenders," says Mr. Barclay. "Both nearly one hundred. And neither one has a birth certificate." He puts his finger down. "Not unusual, for, ah, for persons of such vintage. That's not the issue." He turns to face me for the first time. I drop my eyelids again, deliberately relax my mouth muscles, and let my jaw drop a little. Old lady camouflage. "The issue is that there isn't any kind of record of her. Not in Winfield, not in Providence. Not anywhere." I peek up at him, his smudgy spectacles and downy head. "And we've looked."

"We all know Clare. She's been here for twenty years," says the aide (Andrea? Annette?), putting a hand on my shoulder.

"She had to come from somewhere," says Gloria. "She didn't spring from Zeus's head." I almost laugh at this reference; does she notice? I look down again.

"We haven't been able to find out where," says Mr. Barclay.

My father used to say, *Look people in the eyes, let them know you're someone.* But of course, his battle was different, against the strong anti-French prejudice of that time; he didn't live long enough to become invisible.

A chime flutes through the air; the lights go on and off three times. Immediately there is a great clatter of walkers and canes, and a welter of grumbling rises around the room. The aide excuses herself, crosses the room to help Mr. Simonetti up from his chair.

"What's happening?" says Mr. Barclay, but he can barely be heard.

Where's my scarf?; we need to get there before they run out of banana pudding; will you carry my water, dear?; they never have banana pudding; I'll know if you changed the cards, I've got a system; that's 'cause they run out; no they've never ever had banana pudding; that's why we have to get there early.

"Dinner bell," Gloria tells Mr. Barclay. "They're like Pavlov's dogs."

After a good five minutes of noisy exodus, they are all gone, leaving only Gloria, Mr. Barclay, and me.

"You were saying," says Gloria.

"Oh—yes," says Mr. Barclay, as if startled from a reverie. "It's rare that a person is completely undocumented. There's always *something*. A tax record, a mention in the obituary of a loved one, a lease, a census, a hospital bill. Church records are the mainstay, of course. We have more churches per capita than any other state in the Union." As if that is something to be proud of. "But this time we've been through all available records, and there's nothing."

"She's off the grid," Gloria says. "Very forward-thinking."

"Now, people do change their names," Mr. Barclay continues. "Through marriage, adoption formal or informal, out of personal preference, to cover up a crime—"

"That's an idea," Gloria interrupts. She turns to me. "Are you an escaped criminal?"

Finally someone addressing me, but not sincerely. She doesn't expect an answer. It is a bit of comedy, as if she's talking to a ventriloquist's dummy.

"I didn't mean to suggest—" Mr. Barclay barely suppresses his annoyance. "I just meant that a person will take on a new persona for any one of a number of reasons. It was easy to do, back in the day. Before centralized records a person could take a new name and just live his life out, no questions asked."

Brief silence now, from both of them. Should I speak up and rupture the illusion of being lost in a fog of senility?

Gloria speaks before I can decide. "From what you've told us," she tells Mr. Barclay, "it doesn't matter what her name is. It only matters what her age is. She knows her age, or at least she did at one point. So unless you're saying she's a liar . . ."

"I'm not suggesting any such thing," he says. "But documentation is important. My great-great-great-grandfather started this tradition. He commissioned the Cup, he designed the engraving. Each generation of my family has appointed a member to oversee the Cup. In my lifetime, my grandfather had the duty, then my uncle, and now me. I won't entrust the Cup to just anyone."

"Aha," says Gloria. "*You're* the one who lost the Cup in the eighties."

He closes his eyes, as if willing her to disappear.

"I'm right, aren't I?"

"I didn't *lose* it," he snaps. "The honoree's family misplaced it. I'm the one who *found* it." He slips a hand into the patch pocket of his cardigan and takes out something, holds it up in front of himself.

Seeing it, my heart starts up, a clapper in a bell. I hold out my hands.

They both look startled, as though a tree has reached out toward them. Mr. Barclay recovers first, and hands the item to me. I accept it from his soft, uncalloused fingertips.

It is a reprinted photograph from a newspaper article, mounted on a bit of cardboard, marked at the top with a black pen: 11/1/1936. A slim girl in a long dress, a spray of flowers in her hair.

"From the archives of the *Providence Journal*," he says.

"Fan-*cy*," says Gloria, who's rolled her chair up beside me to look.

I remember the feel of that dress, gray in the picture but sky blue in real life, of a heavy cool satin that slipped against my skin as I moved. My Best Dress.

"Is that you?" he asks.

You can see the jacketed elbow of my companion at the edge of the frame, the rest of him lost forever; I can almost smell the candles burning, hear the breathy truncated moans of the orchestra tuning up.

His voice, a coaxing whisper now: "Is that you?"

I tear my eyes away from the image to find him unsettlingly close.

"No." My heartbeat shakes extra syllables into the word: *no-o-o*.

"Are you sure?"

Is it the rattlesnake that mesmerizes its victims? I stare back at him, breathing in his smell: clean laundry with a hint of liniment.

I open my hands, let the photograph slip to the floor. He pounces and recovers it, holds it up in front of me again.

"Asked and answered, young man," says Gloria, *chrrr*ing back from her place at my side and then forward again, toward him. "Asked and answered."

"Excuse me, ma'am," he tells her, not looking away from me. "This is a private matter."

But the spell is broken now: I see him again as he is, soft-handed and ineffectual. No doubt he's had someone else making his dinners his whole life, doing his laundry. Left alone in the world, he would surely starve. He is no match for me.

"Wasn't private a minute ago," Gloria says. "You know, we don't even know that *you* are who you say you are. We haven't seen any identification."

She brings her wheelchair right up to him, bumping the footrest against the sides of his legs. He sidles away a few steps, still holding the picture, fumbling in a pocket with the other hand and pulling out a silver card case, a foppish item to come from under that ratty cardigan. Gloria lifts the grabber stick, and with a surprising delicacy closes its pincers over the business card he draws out. "Let me see that." She brings it very close to her face and tilts her head back to peer through the bottom of the trifocals at it. "*Wallace Barclay, Barclay Foundation, President.*" She drops it into her lap with a dismissive air. "You could have gotten that made anywhere."

"What?" he says.

"Is this identity theft, is that what this is?" She is clearly enjoying herself. "Are you one of those Nigerian scammers?"

"I assure you—it's not—it's a well-established honor." Fluster is bringing out his accent. *Nawt. Awnuh.*

"Do you watch the obituaries? Hightail it to the bedside to be there when the death rattle comes, Johnny-on-the-spot to snatch your Cup back?"

"People are usually *thrilled.*"

"You're like a vulture." She pokes at him with the grabber stick. "This woman is almost *one hundred years old*." Poke poke poke while she advances her chair.

"That's the point," he protests as he backs away from her.

As she passes me, I can see that her bun is made of a very long braid coiled up and pinned. That won't last; she'll soon have the easy-care, sexless bob of white fluff around her ears that we all have here.

"Angela," cries Gloria. That was the name, Angela.

And the aide is there, stepping between the two of them.

"You won't get much from old Miss Clare, I'm afraid," she tells Mr. Barclay. "She's in and out."

"Any kind of documentation would be helpful," he tells Angela, putting the photograph back into his knitted pocket, allowing her to draw him away. "A marriage license. A family Bible."

"Miss Clare's never been married." The ooze of pity in her words. "She's a charity case, doesn't own a thing except what's in her room. She's never had a visitor." As they cross the room I can still hear them. "Might as well give the Cup to the other lady."

Mr. Barclay turns his head back toward me one last time, spectacles flashing, before he goes through the doorway. And then he is gone, and my heart is settling down again and the muffled soundtrack of Oak Haven is closing quickly over his visit, the coughs and murmurs and the clicking of cutlery from the dining room swelling and the photograph receding already, the whole thing nearly forgotten.

Not by everyone, though.

"I must say I didn't expect such intrigue in a retirement home," Gloria says. There is a bloom across her cheeks, and her eyes behind the lenses are huge and bright. "I think Mr. Hawkins may be running numbers out of his room, and now you, a potential outlaw. Is that it, are you *on the lam*?"

"Young lady," I say, calling up the spirit of every nun who'd ever held me in her steel gaze. My voice feels rusty with disuse, and I clear my throat. "You should be ashamed of yourself."

The cartoon eyes go even rounder with surprise.

"You are mocking me," I say. "Mocking all of us."

"I didn't mean—"

"You said, 'We're like Pavlov's dogs.'"

"It was just—"

"Dogs."

We might be equivalent in the eyes of the world—two old, unimportant ladies—but she is thirty years my junior. By the time she was born I'd already lost my whole world, not once but two times.

"It's not your job to pry into people's lives anymore," I tell her. "You *used to be* a reporter. Your life before is gone." The mirth drains from her expression. "And you're not just visiting. You'll see." I fumble in my lap blanket for the call button. "For one thing, that ridiculous hairstyle. You won't find anyone to take care of it here." A hand goes up to touch her hair. "Where do you think you are?" I find the button and give it a vigorous squeeze. "This isn't a cruise ship. This isn't a spa." Squeezing again, as hard as I can. "This is the place you've come to die." I can feel the air go still before my next word. "Alone."

For that is really the only reason she would be in Oak Haven at her age: sickness advanced enough to require care, and no one loving her enough to be willing to provide it.

We sit a moment in the echo of my cruelty before an aide appears in answer to my bell.

"Nellie, there you are," I say.

"What's wrong, Miss Clare, what's all the ringing, did you have an accident?"

She isn't Nellie, of course, Nellie was a dozen girls ago.

"No, no, just help me up. I want to go to my room. I want some peace and quiet."

"What a shame," she says as she helps me up from the chair and puts my cane into my hand. "And here I thought you'd gone and made a friend."

THERE IS NO knock on my door at bedtime, for I don't require a sleeping medicine. Sleep is my reward for each day; it's where my memories live. I slip into it effortlessly, an otter sliding into a warm current. I long for it so greedily that I have set myself strict rules: two naps a day totaling no more than three hours, and bedtime no earlier than nine o'clock. The soft steps in the hall of the aides coming around to the others tells me it's time. I put a bookmark into my book and slide my feet down below the covers, switch off the bedside lamp, and close my eyes.

AND IT'S SUMMER, the blazing green and hand-over-your-mouth heat of August, the air so dense that not even the flies are buzzing. In my sleep, I am smiling: this is a good day, a good memory.

I'm in the cemetery, which means that it is afternoon. In summer, I did the harder garden work in the morning, starting early and keeping ahead of the sun as long as I could. Summer days split themselves like that: mornings in the garden weeding and watering, replacing the coffee cans full of drowned slugs and re-tying the tomatoes that were forever shifting their weight as they grew and threatening to touch the ground. After noon I went into the cemetery—one day to mow and the next to edge the fringes left behind after the mower, and daily care for the rose bushes that grew up against the stone wall on all four sides of the green. Two or three mornings a week were devoted to canning, the little stone house a fog of steam as the glass jars *pop-pop-pop* sealed up one by one, a bounty against the winter. Winter was always at the heart of everything then, even the hottest day.

Those long summer days were hard, but at the end of each as the sun finally began to slant toward setting, what more satisfying sight than Roscommon. I would sit on the front step of the house with a glass of cool well water and look down over it all, admiring the white markers parceling the cemetery into neat green rows, the gray stone perimeter clotted with blooms of yellow and red and white and lilac. And on the near side of the stone wall the garden, with its fenced-in glory of harvest: the netted tomatoes fat on the vine, the beans tied primly to their poles, the flat bitter furbelows of beet greens spaced against the soil, the pale curling fists of lettuce like a row of French knots. I loved that quiet hour looking out over my piece of the world when the sun was sinking. Everywhere I looked was evidence of my labor, of my mark upon the earth. I did not own Roscommon legally, but it was mine all the same.

In my dream, I'm edging a plot near the middle of the cemetery, and when I hear the rustling beyond the stone wall, I don't pay any attention at first.

I'M JOLTED AWAKE by sounds from next door, Gloria's growling alto and the higher, younger voices of the aides.

"Of course I was assigned the *woman's angle*." That is Gloria. "How was the widow coping, how were the children doing without their dad? They never gave me anything meaty."

"Men are jerks," says one of the aides. "Okay, next one is big, plenty of water."

A pause—Gloria is swallowing a pill—then she continues.

"No one expected the story I brought back." The next bit is drowned out by the rumbling of the motor as the bed is being adjusted. "No lie," cries Gloria. "She *showed me the murder weapon*." For nearly a minute her alto wheezing mingles with the *Are you serious!* and *She did not!* and light pealing laughter from the aides.

"They had to print it in the News section." Triumphant: "And that was my foot in the door."

The aides stay in Gloria's room much longer than they need to, longer than they ever do in Mr. McHenry's room on my other side. Since his stroke, Mr. McHenry doesn't speak well; it can take him a long time to find each word. His bedtime ritual is much quieter, the aides talking to each other as they work together to get him tucked into bed, treating him like I am so often treated, as if he isn't even there. They're in and out of his room in an eyeblink, giving him no time to eke out a sentence. Their trilled *Do you need anything else?* is followed immediately by the door clicking closed. The aides never wake me by joking with Mr. McHenry.

When more laughter erupts next door, I knock on the wall. Three raps. The voices stop abruptly.

"Oops," says one of the aides. "Shhh."

Activity resumes more quietly amid whispers. A giggle—maybe they are laughing at me, maybe just another story. More pills, more murmured conversation. Then the voices stop and the door closes.

A full minute. I can hear her breathing, and I recall the long ritual of pills. For such a relatively young woman, she really must not be well.

"I do know where I am," says Gloria clearly. "I suppose I was indulging in a bit of denial. You're right, that couldn't last. Nothing does." Her voice is calm. I hear a click of the bedside lamp. "Good night."

AN HOUR LATER, I am still wide awake, my right hand lying over the area where a fragment of my history makes its secret beside my heart. The overlying scar is ragged, like a half-spoonful of pink jam smeared across my skin, numb in the center but sensitive at the edges. My fingertips move over the painless, painful place, that survivor's wound.

Nothing lasts. Though I lie here breathing, remembering, though I have existed and still exist, there is no proof of any of it. The years have poured through me; I am a vessel, nothing left of all I have known and felt except a photograph I won't claim and this sediment of memory; soon that too will be gone. And what after? No matter what the nuns promised, I fear that this is the only world there is. I am aware of how generous my lifespan has already been, yet I am galled at how ephemeral is all our suffering, all our loving and our hope. Nothing, nothing comes of it; nothing that won't be snuffed out in an instant by death, leaving no trace.

The nuns would be horrified at these thoughts; so would my mother. They would tell me *hush,* they would remind me of Heaven's glory, and of the miracle that saved me, once upon a time. *God has His reasons,* they would say. There was a time when I would have believed this too. But that was a long time ago, and now I see it differently. To me, it seems more than possible that not all miracles come from God.

CHAPTER FOUR

Leo

NOBODY GETS ANGRY HERE. NOT the lady with the fluffy sweater and the half glasses, not the police officers. They don't even raise their voices. Everyone does a lot of crouching and looking me in the eyes, and their voices are soft, soft, like I am sick and they're really sorry.

They give me cookies, four in a packet that crumble into sweet dust in my mouth and make me cough; they give me grape juice in a plastic tub with the foil peeled up on one side, and they don't get upset when I spill. The first night, one nurse washed me for a long time, bringing a chair right into the shower and letting me sit down and close my eyes while she scrubbed and scrubbed at my hair. They give me a pair of yellow pajamas with trucks all over and metal snaps up the front, and in the morning they bring a big brown tray and lift off the top, releasing a plasticky smell from compartments filled with scrambled eggs, two short tubes of sausage, two sweaty triangles of buttered toast, a tub of orange juice, and a carton of milk. A lady opens the milk and cuts up the sausage for me and then lays the fork down on the tray and says *eat up*.

The questions begin after breakfast. There are a lot of them and a lot of different people asking. They want to know how I'm feeling, they want to know if anything hurts, they want to know *anything—just anything you remember.* My mind is empty, a big shiny bowl holding nothing.

They show me pictures, black-and-white photos of faces on a piece of cardboard, six of them. *Do you recognize any of these guys? Just point if you've seen one of them before.* The men are wide-eyed, like they're surprised to be photographed. *Look again, just take your time and look carefully.* I don't know any of them. I can tell the policemen are frustrated. The old one with the hair on the rims of his ears pushes his gray eyebrows together every time I shake my head.

Once when the fluffy-sweater lady leaves for a minute, the two policemen are alone with me and I think *uh-oh.* The hairy-ear man comes forward, and I get ready.

"Kid, give us a break, okay?" he says.

The tall blond man behind him starts to say something, and the old one puts up a hand, just shows him the back of it, like *stop.*

"We want to get the bad guy who hurt your mom," he says. "Don't you want to help us get the bad guy?"

A flicker of something in the emptiness. "You mean Clyde?"

"You see," says the old guy to the blond one. "Clyde who? What's his last name?"

"Did Clyde hurt Mama?" *Mama.* The word comes naturally, but brings nothing with it: no face, no feeling.

"That's what we're asking you. This is very important." His face is really close now. "You must have seen the guy who hurt Mrs. Wasserman and your mom. You were right there. Just tell us." He brings out the cardboard with the photo faces again. "Is it any of these guys? Don't be afraid, he can't hurt you now."

I don't know the faces on the cardboard. I don't know Mrs. Wasserman. I do know Clyde. It's fleeting and flapping around the corner of my memory, a blue shirt on a wash line, a pair of black boots inside the door. A bad feeling licking up around the sight of the boots—*he's home*—but then draining away just like that, out of my mind. I hold my breath and try to coax it to me—*the boots, the boots*—but then the lady comes back and she shoos the cops out.

When everyone's gone and it's quiet, I hold my breath and the flickering expands into snatches of thought: Clyde would have backhanded me for talking too little or talking too much; Brother Timothy's face would have pinched up with disgust and I would have to hold out my hand, or both hands, if he'd *had enough of your insolence, young man.* So the shiny bowl isn't totally empty after all; there's Clyde, and Brother Timothy. But they're mere flecks swimming around, and if I try to look directly at them they swirl away, leaving just the peaceful emptiness, like a blanket of new snow over a landscape.

I know it's a hospital but I don't feel sick. They haven't told me what's wrong with me, but I guess it's bad because everyone's very, very sorry. They're sorry to move me, to wake me, to ask me questions. The sorrow is in the cookies, the juice, the rough towel they dry me with after the bath, but mostly in their eyes, all of their eyes that don't look right at me. It's as though I'm the sun, too painful to look at, I am something too hugely sad to behold.

CHAPTER FIVE

Lucy

WHAT WAS THE NAME OF that pasta we liked

How is he able to do this every time? His texts carry so much with them, like tiny digital icebergs, and seem impossible to answer. Is he reminiscing about the early days of our courtship, or planning dinner with his new girlfriend? Does he presume that six weeks is far enough past the immediate turmoil of breakup to chitchat and share recipes, or is this a way of reaching out? It feels like a test.

Which one

There, put the ball back in his court, matching his lack of affect and punctuation. Make him explain himself. The answer comes quickly.

The one with the capers

The memory telescopes out from his words, taking my breath with it. Like a punch in the chest. Of course he'd meant that one. The one he'd labored over for my birthday our first year together, settling me with a book and a glass of wine and barring me from the kitchen for hours while he cooked, that little apartment filling with aromas: garlic, browning butter, rosemary. Finally leading me to the table, making me keep my eyes closed until the big reveal. The first thing I saw when I opened my eyes was the heap of dirty pots and pans in the sink behind him, before seeing his huge smile and then, looking down, the plate of linguine. He must mean that pasta. So what should I reply?

The one you made when we lived on Mott Street? No, that sounded sentimental. How about I don't remember? Too obviously disingenuous. I could say Ugh, that one—I hate capers. Although true, that would be just nasty to tell him now, after all the years of pretending that it was a delicious meal instead of one cherished primarily for the love and the effort. It seems very much in keeping with what I am beginning to understand about him that he remembers the pasta, but not the rest.

Why

The single word throbs on the screen like an accusation. *Don't ask a question unless you're prepared for the answer.* Don't I remember that from some television courtroom drama? He might say Making dinner for new girlfriend or Missing you. I'm not prepared for either of those. I tap the Delete key three times, leave the screen blank, drop my phone back into my pocket.

I'M A WEEK into a Nights Month, the twice-yearly dreaded block of night shifts. Also known to the residents who suffer it as Death Month. Each shift starts at 11 p.m. and ends at 7 a.m., officially a mere eight hours but always bleeding well over the finish line. In a Death Month, I go to bed midmorning and rise again after sundown, the day swallowed by unconsciousness, and life is made into a speeding night train, all the color and sound flashing by the window in segments: one night, two nights, three. Hold your breath and count them, six in a row and then a day off; after four weeks of this, the disconnection from society will feel like a mild psychosis.

Tonight, judging from the waiting room, things are under control. Scattered patients waiting, no one moaning or crying or vomiting. A child leans into its mother, neither of them visibly ill, both of them training their eyes on the television suspended near the ceiling. But who knows what is behind the locked doors to the urgent area? Sliding my ID badge through the security scanner, I steel myself for the first glimpse of what kind of night it might be. The double doors *chunk* open to an almost-empty triage area—only one patient there, a man on an ambulance stretcher. At bedside, the charge nurse, Sheila, and the intern, Alice; at the foot of the gurney, the two paramedics who brought him in.

"Hiya, Doc," says one of the paramedics.

"Hey, Bill."

Big Bill must work nearly every day. Tall and bowling pin shaped, he reminds me of one of those inflatable clowns with sand in the base that my cousins and I used to punch when we were kids. The first time I heard the gravelly shout of his voice I laughed out loud, thinking it was a joke.

"Found Down," Sheila tells me, pumping the rubber bulb to take his blood pressure. The patient lies still, eyes closed, no response as the cuff tightens around his biceps.

"Just layin' there in the middle of the sidewalk," says Bill.

"We're trying to figure out if he needs a trauma room," says Alice.

Sheila thumbs the wheel on the bulb, hissing the air out, and takes the stethoscope out of her ears.

"Normal vitals," she says.

"Did he respond when you put the IV in?" I ask Bill.

"Nope."

He doesn't look like the usual Found Down. Clean clothing, neatly dressed. He's maybe forty, just a few strands of gray in the hair that's cropped to a tidy level above his ears. I lean forward: no eau de street comes up from him, no alcohol, urine, vomit, or ripe sweat; instead, a faint whiff of aftershave. Apart from the scissored sleeve of his jacket and shirt, where EMS has gotten IV access, he looks as though he could be peacefully asleep on his sofa at home.

"Maybe it's a whaddyacallit, designer drug," brays Bill.

"Dextrostick was ninety-six," says Bill's partner. Not diabetic coma then. "No track marks, so we didn't give Narcan." His tone a bit anxious, seeking approval.

"Makes sense," I say. It still could be heroin—no need for needle marks, it's easy to snort an overdose—but nothing about this guy looks like heroin. It was wise not to give Narcan if there's not actually an overdose; the medicine's effect is highly unpleasant with a reaction that often includes violent vomiting, and unconscious patient plus vomit equals aspiration and possible death.

They all stand there looking at me.

"Well, by definition he's comatose," I say. *Coma: unresponsive with eyes closed.* "I guess he needs to go to Trauma."

"Can I help?" Alice asks. I nod. As an intern, she works urgent care in the Big Room only; she won't get to Trauma Alley until next year, when she'll junior on critical cases. In two years, Alice will groan at the sound of a trauma call over the PA, and play Not-It with her colleagues; but for now, she is excited by the prospect of caring for one of the sicker patients.

"Trauma One," directs Sheila, and we roll him there while Bill and his partner stay in the triage area to write out their paperwork.

In the trauma room, we get to it. Sheila brakes the stretcher and goes to retrieve the neat coil of wires looped over the monitor on the wall, flips off the plastic tabs and adheres the leads to his chest, while Alice cuts his clothes off and I listen to his lungs. Both sides clear. The pulse oximeter clamped to his index finger reads 100 percent.

"Nice shoes," I comment, tucking the socks inside them and dropping them into a plastic patient-belongings bag. They're expensive-looking loafers, unscuffed, not your typical junkie footwear. Curiouser and curiouser.

"Okay, what now?" asks Alice.

"Airway's good," I say. "So—?"

"Breathing circulation," she finishes, pulling two gloves from the box on the wall and snapping them onto her hands. She puts her stethoscope against the skin of the patient's axillae, left then right, and reaches under the gown to press two fingers over the femoral canal at the top of his leg. "Good pulses," she says.

"So he doesn't need CPR," I say. "Let's finish the exam."

We go over him head to toe, looking for occult signs of trauma, checking the webs between his toes for injection marks, ending by rolling him to look at his back, doing a rectal exam while we're there—normal tone, no blood.

"Nothing," says Alice when he's supine again. "This is weird."

"Now a good coma exam. First, a noxious sensation."

I show her how to use a Q-tip to tickle his nose. Cruder options are nipple pinching or knuckles rubbed hard along the sternum. Nose tickling is just as effective, and a more elegant choice, one that doesn't leave bruises. The cotton bulb twirled lightly around the inside of each nostril provokes no reaction: the patient doesn't raise his hand or even grimace. I uncap a sterile needle and touch it lightly to the soft area between his first and second toe on each foot, then march the point up the spinal levels: the side of the foot, the calf, the outer thigh, inner thigh, and then up the torso left right left right, all the way to the collarbone. Zero response of any kind, at any level. But he's not paralyzed: his reflexes at knee and ankle and biceps are normal.

"What tests are you going to do?" I ask Alice.

"Um," she says. "Tox screen. Definitely head CT. ABG?"

In reply, I take an arterial blood-gas kit from a drawer in the bank of cabinets that line the side of the room and hand it to her. This will kill two birds—not only the measurement of gases in his blood as a clue to metabolic or respiratory dysfunction, but the provision of a stronger pain stimulus than any other one thus far. An ABG is notoriously *uncomfortable* in doctorspeak.

Alice sinks the needle into his right wrist. He's still as a rock.

As the bright arterial blood pulses up into the slender syringe barrel, Sheila pulls a bigger, darker sample from a vein in the other arm and then distributes that blood into various tubes for routine tests.

"Should we intubate him?" Alice asks, pulling out the ABG needle and taping a pressure dressing over the puncture site.

"No. He's breathing fine, and there's nothing to suggest cerebral edema."

We stand for a moment looking at the patient, who lies completely placid, naked under the thin cotton gown, no injuries or abnormalities evident except those that we have inflicted, the bandages from the blood draws and the tiny drops of crimson along the path of my needle. Sheila says what we are all thinking:

"What the hell is wrong with this guy?"

It's been a good while since I've been completely flummoxed. Of course, at the beginning of my training, I was constantly baffled and overwhelmed, but at some point in the second year of residency, the ratio of unfamiliar to familiar dropped into a more manageable zone, and it's continued dropping ever since. Human physiology and behavior can always surprise, but there are some axioms too, some deep consistencies so basic they are immutable, like the laws of physics. This patient is like something falling *up*: he simply does not make sense.

He doesn't smell like alcohol. His pupils are too big for an opioid OD. His breathing is normal: not fast to indicate metabolic acidosis, nor slow from carbon dioxide retention. His normal heart rate rules out almost all other overdose types. He could have a brain bleed, but that's unlikely without neurologic deficits. I can't shake the persistent impression that he is merely sleeping.

"We still need the tox screen," says Alice.

"How're you going to get that? It's not like he's going to pee in a cup for you."

"Oh, Foley, of course. I'll do it."

A few minutes later, she's poised with the catheter at the tiny pout of his urethra, her other hand gripping his penis at its base.

"Okay. A little pressure now." She's nervous; although this might be one of the simplest medical procedures in existence, she hasn't done it very many times yet.

"Just go for it," says Sheila. "He's obviously not feeling anything."

"Right," says Alice. She dips the tip of the catheter into the sterile lubricant jelly and leans forward.

Just then, the curtain at the entrance to the trauma room is pulled back with a shriek of metal rings. Two men stand in the doorway, gawking at the tableau before them.

"Jesus, Dave, what the fuck," exclaims one of them. "Let's go."

The patient's eyes open.

"What the *hell* took you guys so long?" he says, leaping from the stretcher, Alice jumping aside. The Foley tray falls to the floor, the pool of disinfectant spilling in a long brown stream down the sheet.

"Whew," Dave says, looking from Sheila to Alice to me, clutching the balled-up cotton gown against his groin. "That was close."

"Sheila, call security," I say.

"Not necessary, Sheila," says one of the men in the doorway, grinning. He flashes a police badge.

"I'll explain later," says Dave, grabbing the plastic bag with his clothing and following the others at a run.

I have to be quick to get to Trauma Alley before the three of them are through the double doors at the end of it. Police lights outside the ambulance bay spill red, then blue, then red through the glass, then move away.

"Never a dull moment," says Sheila, standing behind me. Shaking our heads, we go back into Trauma 1, where Alice stands, still holding the bladder catheter aloft, instinctively keeping it sterile. "You can throw that away now," Sheila tells her.

Alice goes back out to the Big Room, and Sheila and I stay to finish the documentation. The chart will be filed as an *elopement*, the term for a patient who leaves the ED without official discharge, but how to record the details? I decide on a straightforward telling: *patient absconded before Foley catheter placement; he appeared alert and oriented with good mentation and speech.* I see again the white buttocks disappearing through the ambulance bay doors. *Normal ambulation.*

"It's gotta be a full moon," Sheila says, pressing the button on the wall to alert Housekeeping. "We better get ready for some whackadoo shit tonight." It's such a common theory that it actually has been formally studied. And conclusively debunked: the phases of the moon are not associated with bizarre Emergency Department presentations. "Speaking of which, did you hear about that resident?" Her voice gets low and serious as we walk together toward the door to the urgent area. "She goes to a birthday party last weekend with her kid and some psycho breaks in and murders everyone in the house."

"What? A resident was killed? How did I not hear about that?" It's no mystery, actually. I don't keep up with local news, and my social life could best be described as vestigial. As the dust has been settling and sides taken, all *our* friends turned out to be *his* friends. Why not? He was the one who went for drinks or dinner or barbecues or Game Nights while I worked or slept. I remember a handful of bleary brunches, some movies I dozed through. *They call you my imaginary wife,* he told me once. Why hadn't I paid more attention to that?

"He killed two moms and three kids," says Sheila. "I think she was Dermatology? I didn't know her."

"I can't believe I didn't hear about it." I pull my phone out, tap a text to Karen, an anesthesiology resident and also my first fragile postmarriage friendship.

WTF a derm res was murdered?

We'd met a month ago while grabbing a coffee during the break on ACLS recertification day, and giggled like bad children through the afternoon small-group session. We'd texted intermittently since then, and managed to meet for a couple of lunches, always meaning to get together more often, but schedules hadn't sorted that way yet. A hard fact of not-so-young adulthood: making new friends is harder. Deep friendship is generally born out of lazy time, and there's no lazy time in this stage of life, the period during which most people are coupled and parenting, when every minute is spoken for already by work and family. I had old friends, of course, but they'd been sidelined by residency. A passive act, a product of circumstance; I suppose I'd fully expected to bring them back into my life when the furor of training was done. Now abruptly uncoupled and nearing the end of residency, I've got patches of free time I didn't have when married, but I'm in a strange town now (*it's only four years,* I'd told Joe when ranking residency choices at the end of medical school; *after this you'll get to choose where we live*), and all those sidelined friends are far away and also busy, the Lucy-shaped holes I'd left in their lives closed over long ago.

"They all died, except one kid," says Sheila. "Turns out it was *her* kid, the resident's kid." Then, impatient, "Come on, you heard about this." I shake my head. "Wow. Okay, well, they caught the guy. They think it was totally random; he didn't even know them."

They all died except one kid. A bell is ringing in my memory.

"I saw a child from a murder scene last weekend," I say. "He was the only one left."

"That must have been the survivor. I heard he came through here on the way to Psych." She swipes her ID badge through the sensor, and the doors between Trauma Alley and the Big Room swing open. "How'd he look?"

"Bloody." No response to my text yet. Oops, it's nearly midnight, Karen's probably sleeping. A double infraction, since she has a child. When she'd mentioned that, I'd felt both impressed—how brave to go ahead with single motherhood, especially during training—and also ashamed of the selfish thought that crept beneath my admiration, that her free time would be limited. I remember her fond voice. *My little guy was reading at two; that genius-only sperm bank wasn't kidding.*

I pull up a search and poke terms into the browser, trying *doctor stabbed birthday murder.* The news reports spring up with a shocking speed. The name makes my mouth go dry.

"That's my—" My what? Not my friend, not really. My acquaintance? But it had been more than that; there had been the spark of friendship, of a kindred feeling that I have only recently begun to understand as rare.

"You knew her?" Sheila's interested.

I feel a jarring sadness, and an accompanying feeling of fraudulence: I have no right to claim this loss.

"Not well." Which is the truth, and also not. I remember the boy alone, drenched in blood (Karen's blood?), his button eyes staring.

Shake it off, shake it off: the hours ahead have a claim on my full energy and focus, nothing to spare.

FIRST STOP DURING the relative lull: the Tank, the corner of the Big Room that serves as our holding spot for overdoses and EDPs, emotionally disturbed persons. A euphemism for what is most commonly intoxication—crack or meth or bath salts or good old alcohol. An EDP with health insurance gets a regular urgent-area bed and a pysch consult; for the rabble it's the Tank, a no-frills cluster of three rooms, ten stretchers, ten sets of leather restraints hanging ready on the railing outside, and a security guard on a rolling stool in the hall. Best to give the Tankers a good once-over before the shift gets wild.

We have six drunks in various stages of sleep and foulness; I shake each of them awake, interview them, and do a quick check-over for injury. They've all been Breathalyzed (if cooperative and capable) or had their blood drawn (if uncooperative or too slack-mouthed drunk), and the Tank nurse has entered the blood alcohol number on each chart. From those, I calculate the "sober time"—the time each patient will reach legal sobriety and will need to be reassessed and discharged. The theoretical drop is twenty milligrams per deciliter per hour, but for these hard-core drinkers with their highly tolerant livers, it's closer to thirty—they'll sober up faster than the textbooks predict. Like *The Price Is Right,* it's important to get the sober time right without going over, since the main goal with Tankers is to get them outside on the street in time to find their next drink and avoid the DTs. Delirium tremens has a high mortality rate, even when fully treated. Once when I was an intern, I let a Tanker sleep through his deadline, and suffered the poisonous hate-eyes of the ICU resident who had to admit him, her whole tight-lipped affect radiating disgust at the waste of a critical bed on a drunk. What a difference three years make: now I fudge the numbers upward or downward according to the indicators at hand (odor, filth, depth of sidewalk-suntan, number and condition of teeth) with easy confidence; my drunks will be ambulatory but not tremulous or hallucinating when they go out the door. I write their sober times on my forearm with a ballpoint pen; as I discharge each one I'll wipe the numbers off with alcohol. In between initial evaluation and discharge, unless they become obstreperous, I can basically ignore them.

The last Tanker is wide awake. He's not a drunk, but a frequent flyer. More than that, he's a B&B'er—one who presents multiple times a week with various ailments, as a way to avoid the shelter and get a sandwich and a bed for the night.

"Hey, Freddy." He doesn't smell as bad as usual tonight; he must have gotten a shower somewhere. "I like your hat."

He puts a hand up to the orange ball cap, as if to confirm that it is still there.

"I just got it," he says.

It is bright and stiff with newness, a contrast to the dingy hodgepodge of layers on the rest of his body: a quilted hunting vest over a T-shirt over a long-sleeved shirt, camo pants cinched with a belt over blue jeans that peek out in a raggedy, dirty fringe above his sneakers.

"Nobody hurt me, and I don't want to hurt myself," he says, unprompted. He knows the drill. "My knee's bad, though."

"Bad as last time?"

He considers that, looking down at the skinny cylinder of muscle swimming in the fabric layers.

"I think it's got worms in it."

"Well, we'll take a look." There aren't going to be any worms, of course; there never are. I've examined that knee so many times I know it better than my own. "Did you get a sandwich?"

"Uh-huh. And cookies." His face splits into an Oreo-blackened grin.

The worm delusion argues an intrinsic thought disorder, but he's also got a divot in his skull, a caved-in area the diameter of a golf ball, spanned by a well-healed scar. I've asked him for details, but he can't or won't share them. God knows what his life was before the injury, where his family is, or if they know where he is. *Some people don't belong in houses,* he'd told me once when I asked.

SORE THROAT, PNEUMONIA, punched a wall, angina, groin lump, ran out of meds, infant rash, something in my eye: the puttering mix of urgent-area patients makes a droning backdrop to the critical cases. At 3 a.m. when the overhead bells go off again, Sheila and I go to Trauma Alley and wait. When the doors open, we can see that the patient is fighting, nearly twisting off the stretcher, despite the straps and the paramedics holding her down. It's an EDP, too wild for the Tank.

"She's a biter," cautions one of the paramedics as they go into Trauma 2.

"*Vete a la verga,* bitch," the patient says without opening her eyes.

I put my stethoscope to a bit of chest wall accessible between the straps: clear breath sounds, rapid heartbeat.

"Called in for peeing in a flower bed," says the other paramedic. She's sweating but cheerful. "This is definitely my cardio for the day."

"*Cuero del diablo,*" the patient hisses at her.

"Now, now, you don't mean that. One, two, three," and we pull the backboard onto the trauma room stretcher.

"You speak Spanish?" I ask the paramedic. I know conversational gems like *Have you vomited, Was there blood,* and *Show me where it hurts.*

"Yeah, but that's not Spanish," she says. "That's the universal language of crack."

"*Maldita cuero,*" the patient spits, kicking a leg out. Her feet are bare and dirty.

Sheila holds up the spray of monitor leads. "Can we Haldolize her, please?" she asks me. Toneless. She's hit her wall tonight, already over this shift and ready for 7 a.m. "I don't feel like going MMA to get these on."

"Did you get a D-stick?" I ask the female paramedic.

"Hundred and twenty."

Damn. Hypoglycemia would have been so easy.

"*Vete a la chingada,*" the patient shouts. "*Menca cabrona.*" She shakes her head violently side to side, an oxygen prong slipping from a nostril, and twists a hand where it is pinned at the wrist by one of the straps. With a mighty grunt she pulls it free.

"Five IM Haldol and two of Cogentin," I say, stepping back from the waving hand, the pinching fingers. Sedation will make getting information from her impossible, but it seems that will be impossible anyway.

The miracle of vitamin H: in minutes she is unconscious. We unbuckle the straps and roll her onto her side, sliding the backboard out. The tech scissors clothes off and attaches monitor leads; on the screen above the bed the waveforms flutter and catch. I examine her while the nurse slides an IV catheter into one of the now-limp arms and attaches the Vacutainer.

"Hooray for Haldol," Sheila says as the blood pulls silently into one specimen tube, then another. "Good for what ails you."

But what exactly ails her? The monitor shows normal sinus at eighty-five; she's breathing regularly. No evidence of trauma: pupils reactive, no dark cloud of blood behind the tympanic membranes, face not swollen or bruised, teeth intact. Neck, abdomen, pelvis, and extremities all unremarkable. Her clothing, now puddled in ruined strips on the floor, is basic East Providence housewife, yoga pants and a clean cotton sweater. Her hair, though disheveled, looks as if it has recently been styled. Her skin is soft, smooth: no junkie-acne or bruises or scars, and the veins in her arms are healthy hoses, no knotting from needle tracks. Some of her fingernails are broken, but her cuticles are nicer than my own. The grime on the soles of her feet is enough only to account for a couple of blocks' stroll down a city sidewalk. From the looks of her, she has a home of her own, and a toilet in it, somewhere not far from where she'd been found. Why then had she been squatting on a neighbor's lawn? She could be a psych patient off meds, but that kind of slide is gradual, not abrupt, and this woman looks like she went crazy in one short minute tonight. Another puzzle, like Coma Cop from the start of the shift.

"We're running a special," I tell Sheila.

She gets the reference immediately. "Yeah, maybe this one will pull a badge out of her vag and run out the door."

Perhaps she has epilepsy, and this is simply the confused, combative state that can follow a seizure. That would be the best scenario. In that case, she'll be waking up in a little while, embarrassed, after a lot of negative tests. I hope for that outcome, but my job isn't to presume the most benign situation, it's to imagine the worst. *You must believe that each patient you see, no matter how mild the complaint, is trembling on the precipice of death.* How many times have I told medical students and junior residents that? I can't remember now who first taught it to me.

It could be poison. She's sweating, though, so nothing anticholinergic. No excessive oral secretions, so not organophosphate. Could be a spontaneous rupture into the brain from cocaine or congenital aneurysm. Or a brain tumor; although they grow slowly, they can present with sudden symptoms.

"Could it be a cockroach in the ear?" ventures the tech. "That was a question on one of our practical exams."

Theoretically, an insect in the ear can make a person berserk. However, every case that I've ever seen, and I've seen plenty, has been completely unmysterious, the triage note reading *cockroach in ear* and the patient grossed out but totally rational. If only this patient could be cured that easily, a little mineral oil in the ear canal to drown the culprit and then a few tedious minutes with tweezers pulling out the corpse in soft, oily pieces. I've already checked her ears, though; no varmints there.

"Not this time," I tell the tech.

"Usual suspects?" Sheila asks, labeling the tubes of blood with a felt-tip pen: Juanita Doe 756755001.

"Add a thyroid panel and a tox screen and a head CT. Get an LP tray too." A spinal tap will rule out encephalitis.

I am turning away from the stretcher when I see it: a tiny area on the scalp where the black hair is a little blacker than the hair around it. I bend for a better look. It's a clot of blood, smaller than a dime, just above the hairline on the left temple. I pull the curls up and away, carrying the flattened clot with them, revealing a stellate wound underneath. Four lines meeting at a single point, the whole thing not much more than a centimeter across. The lines buckle outward in the center of the X, an ooze of ivory-colored material bulging through, minutely veined.

No more mystery. No need for a spinal tap. This one won't be waking up with negative tests, embarrassed.

"Cancel the LP tray," I tell Sheila, who's hanging the Foley bag on the edge of the stretcher. "Let's make that CT stat."

"What is that?" she says, coming over and looking down at the scalp.

"Gunshot wound." The escaping gases in the blast from a muzzle pressed right against the skull can lift the skin in flaps, making an X like this one. I roll the patient's head away to look: no exit wound. "Ancef, tetanus, load Dilantin, call Trauma and the Providence PD."

"What's that stuff coming out—oh no."

"Oh yes. That would be brain."

Her CT scan shows a ragged streak of white running from the thin temporal bone on the left side straight toward the other ear. The rough oval of skull on a head CT should properly be filled with gray and black: gray walnut of brain, black of cerebrospinal fluid. White means blood, or metal, or bone. The bright-white track on this scan crosses the posterior frontal lobes in a diagonal so shallow it is almost horizontal. Move it just a few inches forward and this could be a Dr. Walter Freeman classic, the barbaric transorbital lobotomy from the 1950s, performed without anesthesia. He'd tip the head back, insert an ice-pick-like tool under the upper eyelid, and use a mallet to tap through the thin plate of bone. Then a slice left and right to disconnect the frontal lobes from the brain. Ten seconds to maroon all passion, all rage and joy and lust, in the anterior frontal lobes forever.

This CT shows the exact opposite of a lobotomy: the posterior, not the anterior, frontal lobes are destroyed. The posterior lobes are the home of conscience, decorum, shame. Without their inhibitory function, the impulsivity in the anterior lobes can run unchecked, setting the darker, angry side of the person free.

The bullet rests innocently just behind the ear, an irregular chunk of dense white, like a comet with a tail of destruction behind it. Smaller than my fingertip.

"I heard the yelling." I turn. It's Giles, the psych resident on call. He looks at the monitor. "Yikes."

He's doing a wise resident's preemptive strike, trolling the ED for potential consults before he's called, in the hopes of getting the paperwork done early so that he can get some sleep tonight.

"Am I terrible to be relieved that she's not coming to me?" he asks.

Giles and I met as interns and jumped straight into a light chumminess from the moment he'd looked at my ID badge. "We both have the names of British children in postwar children's books," he'd said. "Riding railways and carrying rucksacks and forever telling each other to keep our chins up." His mother is Chinese; he'd lived in Hong Kong until he was nine. In that first conversation, I learned his biggest regret (being brought to America just young enough to lose his accent), his biggest grudge (against his parents for same), his short-term goal (a hot boyfriend), and his long-term goal (a hot husband). He's funny and sharp-witted, the kind of person who knows every phlebotomist and tech and housekeeper in the hospital by name. When I'd told him about Joe, for once the sparkle had dimmed, and he'd hugged me. *Chin up, Lucy,* he'd murmured, and it had been unexpectedly bracing.

"When are you done with nights?" he asks. "We should get a drink." A surprising invitation—we've always been strictly hospital friends.

"April."

He winces. "Brutal. Well." He taps the counter, two brisk knocks. "Maybe we can have an early dinner before then." He grins and is gone.

A HISPANIC MAN in a windbreaker is there when I get back to Trauma 2 after reading the CT. I see that the chart now has a name: Ortiz.

"Rosa," the man is saying, bent over the stretcher. He has one of her limp hands in his. "*Abre los ojos. Mírame.*" He sees me. "What's wrong with her?"

"It looks like she was shot."

"She was shot?" His accent gets thicker suddenly: *chot.* "Where?"

"In the head," I say as gently as I can. How could anyone say that gently?

"*Pedazo de mierda,*" murmurs Rosa. Mr. Ortiz looks shocked.

"I think we're ready for more Haldol," says Sheila. I nod and mouth *five.*

"*Vete a la verga,*" Rosa says, pulling her hand out of her husband's grasp; lightning-quick, she slaps him across the face.

"She's not herself right now," Sheila tells him, sneaking the Haldol into the IV port.

"*Vete,*" Rosa says, slapping the air as he backs away. "Asshole."

"Rosa," says Mr. Ortiz, staring at his wife, his hand still over his cheek. He turns to me. "She's—you know? *Callada. Reservada.* She makes, you know, pictures with sewing. We have children, five and seven years. She's always *tranquila,* you know, she never yell."

"Are your children okay?"

He nods. "They were sleeping. They didn't wake up." The tears come into his eyes. "I was at my cousin's house." I can smell the cousin's beer on him. "I should have been home."

You'd be shot too, I want to say. *You'd be in Trauma 3.*

"She need surgery"—miming, an open hand moving vaguely around his head—"to take it out?"

"Maybe. It depends on what the neurosurgeon recommends."

"When she is going to be better?"

He means when will she be back to normal. How can I say never?

"It's not clear how she'll heal," I say, sidestepping. "There's damage to the part of her brain that has to do with personality." I'm not sure how much he understands, but he's nodding and I press on. "She'll need to stay in the hospital for at least a few days. Then she'll probably go to a different hospital for a while, in case she has trouble with things like walking."

There are antibiotics to prevent infection, anticonvulsants to prevent seizure, the ICU and then the rehab facility where Rosa can be nursed back to health. And odds are good that she will heal, every part of her except the shattered brain tissue.

"*Culera,*" mutters Rosa. Her voice is slurred, the Haldol booster beginning to take effect. "*Vete a la chingada.*"

He blanches, takes another step back.

"My wife is a Christian," he says. "She doesn't even know those words."

His meaning is clear: *this is not my wife.* He's right. The quiet, religious needlepointer is no more. This profane, irascible woman has replaced her.

Who could blame him if he leaves her after this, in a month or a year or a decade? When she goes home, if she is ever able to go home, her children will not know her. The younger one may grow up without any memory at all of the person she was before. This injury has already taken Rosa from her family; in the years to come, it will take them from her too, driving away everyone who has known and loved her before tonight.

When I pass the room a while later, I see a spare tableau: Rosa lying back with eyes closed and a middle-aged woman standing alone at the side of the stretcher, holding her hand.

I have often thought that if you're going to have a child, have a daughter. She'll be the one by your bedside in the ER and in the ICU waiting room, sleeping on the hard chairs around the clock to be allowed in to see you for fifteen minutes every four hours. She'll be the one arguing with your doctors about your medicines or your diet, talking to you in your coma, encouraging you through physical therapy. Looking at Rosa, I can see that the child is only half of the equation. In the end, there might be only one person by Rosa's side, one person who will still see the baby, the girl, the

Rosa-ness in the coarse, vituperative stranger. It will take more than this to drive a mother away.

NO ONE KNOWS the hospital like an ER resident. We rotate through every specialty and become familiar with every unit and floor. That knowledge has come in handy recently, every morning when my shift is over and I've needed a place to sleep. Of course, I could just go home, but each day I consider it briefly and decide no.

The internal medicine call rooms scattered around the building are off-limits; they're strictly assigned. I could easily find an empty pallet in one of the surgical bunkers filled with the breath of unwashed napping interns. But I know a secret, so I get into the elevator and press the button for eight. The doors slide closed and eight levels above they slide open again on Obstetrics.

I badge into the doctors' lounge, empty now, everyone at rounds or in the OR, and go past the espresso machine, past the comfy armchairs and flat-screen TV. Push through the door at the back, and there it is: the OB call suite. Six clean quiet rooms snuggled into the corner of the building. No bunk beds here; these call rooms are plush. One room each for an attending, resident, intern, and student still leaves two unoccupied; I've staked one of them out with a toiletry bag on the nightstand and a jacket over the desk chair. Knowing no one will challenge it—who would sleep here voluntarily if she could be home?

As I'm falling asleep, entering that delicious interval of loosening, my joints and spine melting into the mattress, my brain disengaging and wheeling free before the plummet into unconsciousness, I suddenly see Karen. Laughing, shaking her head. *Life is too damned short.* The way she says it, it's a quip, the end of a funny anecdote, not a prophecy. Her face bright with amusement, just another afternoon of another day in the long domino series of days we're all so foolishly sure we have ahead of us. Is it memory or dream? Impossible to tell.

CHAPTER SIX

Clare

WHEN I FINALLY NOTICE THE new pill in my morning cup of medicines I wonder how long I've been taking it. I've gotten into a lazy habit of swallowing the pills without inspecting them. Nearly twenty years in this place means I've seen a lot of changes. The waxed, gaily patterned Dixie cup has shrunk into a soft fluted paper thimble; the colors and sizes of the pills themselves have varied too, as one medicine goes generic, or as another stops being manufactured. A new one gets added for a while twice or three times a day to treat a minor infection; then that one goes away and it's back to the familiar quartet: vitamin pill, calcium pill, stomach pill, laxative.

"What's this pill?" I ask the nursing assistant, pointing to the cup.

"Which one?"

I turn the cup over into my palm and poke my finger into the pile of tablets, chasing the green oval one away from the others.

"That one. I've never seen that one before."

"I think that's antacid," she says, but not with any conviction.

"It's not. This one is the antacid." I chase a different pill to the rim of the bowl my cupped palm makes. When did my hands become so hollow?

She looks at the two pills balanced on the edge of my hand. "Maybe a water pill?" she guesses. Her phone buzzes and lights up her pocket; she darts a glance down. She'll be in trouble if any of the nurses notice. Phones are supposed to be off during a shift.

"I don't need a water pill," I tell her. "I have never needed a water pill."

"Maybe the doctor added one." She looks down again into her pocket, straining to read the message there. "Almost everyone here takes a water pill." She adds in a stage whisper: "Mrs. Pereira takes *three* different water pills." Really, this one should be fired.

"The doctor didn't talk about a new medicine the last time he visited. Surely he would have said something." Her expression tells me how bizarre that statement seems to her: Who would bother discussing medical decisions with doddering, ancient me? One doesn't inform the shrub when it's being pruned. "Well, he *should* have said something. Anyway, nothing about me has changed, so why would my medicines need to change?"

"I don't know," she says, her impatience no longer subtle. She holds out the cup of water. "Here you go."

"You expect me to take a mystery pill without any explanation?"

Still holding out the cup of water: "Miss Clare. You need to take your medicines."

"Or what." I close my hand over all the pills.

She's not looking; she's scooped her phone from her pocket with her free hand and she's frowning at it, tapping at the screen with one thumb.

The arrogance! It reminds me of my former neighbor Ellie Schlosser's story from the Anschluss—the booted Nazi tossing a command at her as she was walking out of Vienna. *Go back, he said, without even stopping. He didn't even look to make sure I obeyed. He just presumed I would obey; he presumed we were all that beaten.* She didn't obey. She didn't go back; she kept walking and she escaped, and lived until ninety-seven and died surrounded by generations of descendants, just next door here at Oak Haven, in the room Gloria has now.

"Are you kidding me." The aide has noticed at last that I have not taken the water from her. "You will not win this," she declares. "I have a toddler at home."

She drops her phone back into her pocket and shifts her weight to her other hip, and we stay like that for a while, her holding the water out, me with my geriatric fist clutching the pills. Her eyes are focused in the middle distance, over my head.

"I have other residents waiting," she says finally, breaking the standoff.

"Don't let me keep you."

She mutters something, sets the cup of water down on the bedside table, and leaves the room. I rest my hand on my knee.

Now I'm thinking about Ellie. She'd been the subject of an oral history project; a student had come every day with her recording equipment, and for some weeks snatches of monologue, in Ellie's deeply accented English, floated out from her room. *I had to choose between my husband und my mother. My mother made me go.* Her voice matter-of-fact about everything else but her mother and the peremptory Nazi. She returned to him again and again. *The arrogance! The arrogance of that man!* The outrage lancinating across the decades, fresh for a few seconds before her narrative subsided again into a composed recitation of fact.

Belinda, the heavyset Liberian nurse who's been at Oak Haven about as long as I have, comes into the room.

"Belinda," I say, shaking away the ghost of Ellie. "That girl is trying to kill me."

"No one is trying to kill you, Miss Clare. My goodness. What's the trouble?"

"She's giving me someone else's medicines." I open my fist to show her, the pills rattling in the valley of my palm. My skin so dry that the pills aren't sticky, not even a little bit. How could I need a pill to rid my body of water?

Belinda gives me a long, hard look.

"Why do you treat people like that?" she says. "You know her name."

"Her name doesn't matter. She'll move on in a year."

"Everyone's name matters," says Belinda. "She knows *your* name."

"Well, she's paid to," I say. "And it's written on my door."

She waits.

"Tanya then," I say. "Tanya is giving me the wrong medicine." I hold my hand out higher. "That's not my pill."

"It's Mariah," she says. "Not Tanya. And you *knew* that."

She squints through her reading glasses at the pills. I touch each one with my forefinger.

"That's my vitamin, and that's my antacid, and that's my calcium, and that's the laxative. So what's that one?" I push it to the rim of my hand again, bring the hand up closer to her face.

"That's a nerve pill," Belinda pronounces.

"What?"

"Green oval with a D on it? Mmm-hmm, that's an antidepressant." She straightens up.

I can't make out the D, but it is green and it is oval.

"I don't take a nerve pill. That's not my medicine. Someone mixed it up."

Belinda lifts the top page of the clipboard she's carrying and scans the page below.

"It's your medicine all right," she says. "Started on Monday. Dr. Evans's orders."

"Why in the world," I say, staring at the little green pill.

"His note here—" She struggles to make out the handwriting. "He says Mandy's reported you're withdrawn." She looks over her readers at me. "You do spend a lot of time on your own."

Mandy is the recreational therapist, whose spirited intrusions we all have to bear. She pops into my room each Monday and reads the offerings from the list clipped to her brightly stickered clipboard, lifting her voice at the end of each, so that she sounds like she is reciting a list of questions: *Senior Jazzercise? Mall walking? Ceramics?* She entreats me with a special vigor to join in, as I am more mobile than most, despite my near-centenarian status, and despite the titanium rod in my thighbone. When I demur, she makes a mock frown and puts an X on her list. Apparently she also confides in the doctor.

"You are always reading," continues Belinda. "Even when you're in the dayroom, it's always with a book. You don't talk to people. You don't come to Bingo."

I bend the index finger that's been holding the green pill at the edge of my hand and flick the pill away, in a long arc across the room.

"That's what I think of Bingo," I say.

Belinda shakes her head. "You know I have to pick that up."

"I'm sorry," I tell her, and I am. "But I don't need a pill to make me go to Bingo."

"Dr. Evans is just trying to help you," she says, squatting to look for the pill. "He thinks you'll be happier if you socialize a little." She goes down to her knees to sweep a hand under the dresser. "Miss Clare, you are naughty. Look what you are making me do." Her voice is a little squashed. Success—she gets the pill and lumbers to her feet. She slaps invisible dust from the thighs of her scrubs. "Mandy worries about you. We all do."

"I won't take that pill," I warn her.

"I'll write that down so the doctor knows," she says, and hands me the cup of water, watches me chase the other pills down one by one. "Good girl," she says, and from her somehow it's tender, not condescending.

When Mandy next visits, although I feel like I'm making hostage negotiations, I agree to a mall walk on Thursday. She puts a tick against my name on the list with real delight.

WHEN THURSDAY COMES and Mandy appears in the doorway of the breakfast room, I'm already regretting my decision. Wouldn't the day be better spent the usual way, with a series of naps and a book? Maybe I should have opted for ceramics: the messy bad-child feeling of the clay might have been fun. But at least mall walking will be a chance to evade Gloria, who's been persistent as a terrier, always at my table for dinner, rolling up to me in the dayroom and striking up a conversation about whatever book I'm reading. She's read everything, it seems, and has an opinion about it all. It's gotten so that the noise of her wheelchair starts a dull headache behind my eyes.

We need to be ready by 8:30 a.m., Mandy reminded us all twice the day before. Breakfast is served at seven, so that shouldn't be a problem, but there's the meal itself and then the slow scramble of preparation, each one of us in our room fussing over dress, hair, handbag contents. The *wheres* ripple from room to room. *Where are my glasses, where is my wallet, my lipstick, my tissues?* And then the debate: Where to carry cash? A purse, a wallet, a pocket? In a purse, it can be zippered in safely. But then the whole bag might be so easily pulled from one's grasp. Mr. Simonetti's preference is for a front trouser pocket. *Coat pockets are shallow, you see, no depth to them.* Mr. Tuttle boasts about his jacket with snap pockets—no rough zipper teeth to cut the back of your hand. Mrs. O'Meara has a bag with a strong interior compartment that zips. There is no detail too trivial when you're old.

I sit waiting, listening to their declamations. I have little to prepare once I am dressed; I am bringing nothing with me. Mandy runs from room to room, zipping here, knotting a shoelace there, dispensing reassurance: *Fine, fine, you look fine,* and *Here it is, right here.*

Finally, a whisker before eight thirty, we are all at the front of Oak Haven, waiting for the transport van. There are six of us: Mrs. Donovan, Mrs. Bentley and Mrs. O'Meara, Mr. Simonetti and Mr. Tuttle, and me. As we are loading the van, Gloria Pereira appears in her wheelchair in a steady, motorized version of bursting onto the scene.

"I changed my mind," she says. "May I come?"

"The more the merrier," cries Mandy.

The mall opens early for mall walking twice a week; after the short ride across town, our van joins a stream of similar vehicles from the various senior facilities in the area. We travel in a kind of convoy, collapsing into single file for the last mile or so, then snaking up into the parking structure, inching along to the double doors where one by one each van disgorges its occupants, the skylighted middle level of the structure filling with a palsied throng. Walkers, canes, wheelchairs. It looks like a march to Lourdes.

The section Mandy has chosen for us is no more than a quarter mile of smooth indoor boulevard, with benches at intervals. There isn't a lot of conversation as we move ourselves bench to bench, each of us going at a different pace, Mandy loping among us like a border collie, her voice encouraging and soothing by turns.

"You're doing great, Clare," says Mandy, dashing by as I am approaching the next bench, only three more to go. "I hope I'm half as fit at your age," she says. "You have to tell me your secret. I'll bet you were a dancer."

She dashes off again without waiting for a reply.

I lower myself to the bench and lean my cane against my legs. It's been a while since I've walked so far, or been able to look up and see sky. Although the sun is shining down through a glass barrier high above our heads, I fancy that I can feel its warmth. There's a potted plant beside me, a welcome spray of green. I rub a thumb and index finger over a leaf: plastic. I get up and move to the next bench at a tortoise pace, feeling the pleasant pull in my muscles. I'm not sure which is more incredible, the memory of the physical labor in my past, or the fact that nowadays creeping twenty feet under my own steam before resting is an accomplishment.

The stores are blinking their lights on and unlocking their doors. Across from where I sit, a smartly dressed woman fills the jeweler's window with sparkling trays; on the corner of the row is a very large store apparently devoted solely to the sale of brassieres. That storefront display would have been considered pornography not so long ago. A smell of cinnamon sneaks into the air. Customers begin to appear, some of them solo, fast and purposeful, but also slower-moving pairs and trios, sipping coffee from white paper cups, chatting and laughing and sometimes stopping to look at items in the windows. There's something bright and colorful and inexplicable almost everywhere I look.

I don't know how long I've been sitting here, observing the customers drifting in and out of shops, trying to puzzle out what a store called LIDS might sell—I'm too far away to see more than the neon sign—before I see Gloria exiting a shop just a few feet away. She's putting a white paper bundle into the huge handbag on her lap when she looks up and sees me. I sigh as she *chrrrs* over.

"Look what I got."

She opens her handbag and angles its maw toward me. It gapes a crush of tissues, eyeglass cases, paperback books, pens, and I don't know what all.

"Heavens," I say. "You carry all that around with you?"

She holds it up closer to my face.

"Close your eyes," she commands. "Take a deep breath. Can't you smell it?"

I close my eyes and inhale. First just more of the same: a cool wash of chemical interior air, polluted by a blend of cinnamon and artificial florals. And then something else. The water rushes into my mouth, surprising me. I haven't had much appetite for a while; lately everything's been tasting of the same dull flat nothing. I figured it was my taste buds failing, another county heard from in the relentless progressive decrepitude of age.

"Sausage?" I say. It's all I can manage. I am fairly drooling.

"Not just *any* sausage." Her face seems lit from within. "Hand-cured linguica." She brings the handbag under her own chin and breathes deeply. "Just like that, I'm back in my grandmother's kitchen."

"I'm just guessing," thinking of the *three water pills.* "Against doctor's orders?"

"Ab-so-lutely." She's grinning. She snaps the clasp of the purse and wedges the bulky thing beside her in the chair. "What's *your* madeleine?"

"What do you mean?"

She knows I know what she means; she blinks once, slowly, as she explains. "Is there a particular smell that brings back your childhood?"

So many things come to mind, tumbling over themselves, pushing to be first: *choose me, no me.*

"I don't dwell in the past," I say. I don't think I have ever told a bigger lie. I almost expect the God I turned away from eighty years ago to reach down and rap me on the forehead, knock me dead where I sit.

"Nonsense," she says. "We're all of us obsessed with our own story. Especially those of us near the end of it. We go over it and over it. But guess what, Clare." She leans forward, mock whispers at me. *"We're still writing it."*

She is addled. She's the one who needs a nerve pill.

"Are you ready?" she says, hand on the knob that controls her wheelchair, and I realize she means for us to proceed together.

My little shadow again. How did this start? How can I end it?

"I'm fine. You go ahead."

"I don't mind waiting," she says. "You can give me the lowdown on our fellow citizens. What's up with Mrs. Donovan? Is she demented or just deaf?"

Both.

"You're not still mad about the other day?" she asks. "I thought we sorted that out." When I don't answer she rolls her eyes, magnified to the size of hard-boiled eggs by her glasses. The effect is impressive. "I don't understand you," she says. "You're alive. You're *walking*."

The words rise up in me and dam at my lips, pressing there for a moment before ebbing back down my throat.

"You know nothing about me," I manage to say.

"No one does," she says bluntly. "I see you sitting alone, day after day. There are some very nice people at Oak Haven, Clare, and not one of them knows anything about you."

"You've been *asking* people about me?" How intrusive.

In the distance, I can see Mandy coming toward us. She must be collecting the stragglers.

"For goodness' sakes," says Gloria. "I'm trying to be *friends*. Who doesn't want a *friend*?"

"We have nothing in common." It's a flat statement of fact, empty of invitation, but apparently she hears a challenge in it.

"We're both readers," she says. "That's something in common. We both seem to have most of our marbles. *That's* a pretty significant thing to have in common, considering."

"How are you ladies doing?" Mandy cries, reaching us.

Gloria gives me a look. "Your loss." She turns her head away from me and smiles at Mandy. "Coming." She juts out an elbow, uses it to tuck her bag up against herself like a mama hen gathering a chick, and then jams the wheelchair controller knob forward.

We proceed, Mandy chattering and Gloria and I silent, through the thickening mall crowd, to the large glass double doors at the exit. When the van comes, Gloria is loaded last, and though her wheelchair ends up locked in beside my seat, she doesn't say a word to me. No one talks on the ride home except Mrs. Donovan, who reports on everything we pass. *There's a Dunkin' Donuts, mmm, I'd love a chocolate glazed,* and *There's the Big Blue Bug, he's got Easter Bunny ears on, is it Easter again already?* and *Look, another Dunkin's.*

By eleven we are back. We disband exhaustedly into our rooms to rest before lunch. The midday meal marks the beginning of every day's slowdown; afterward, there's an hour to digest before an onslaught of personnel: for some, the physical or occupational therapists, for others the nursing assistants who prick fingers for sugar levels and administer snacks or insulin as necessary. The afternoon passes with books or television or card games or knitting or napping, and before long it's dinnertime.

I delay my entrance to the dining room, giving everyone else a chance to get there before me. No, not everyone—Gloria. I want Gloria to commit to her seat. She's been sitting at my usual table, and tonight I will sit somewhere else.

But when I finally enter the dining room, Gloria is not at my table. Scanning the room, I see her seated near the window, with some of the group from our outing, engaged in an animated conversation. The new clique has caused a shakeup in habitual seating, and my regular table is filled with knitters, who take me in and dismiss me with a glance. They're correct to do so—I can knit, but only in a lumpy, serviceable way, and I never did it for enjoyment. While they discuss the best way to set a raglan sleeve, I watch Gloria shout-chat with Mr. Simonetti and Mrs. Donovan. I suppose that's a match made in Heaven: those two can't hear well enough to be bothered by her nonsense.

The tossed green salad from the menu is disappointing—flaccid cucumber slices and hard pale wedges of tomato scattered over chopped iceberg that was kept in a too-cold refrigerator, so that its cells are packed with grainy ice.

Were vegetables really as I remember them, each speaking individually and boldly on the palate, tomato and cucumber fully distinguishable from each other? They differ solely by texture now. I have read that the soil of those big farms is drenched in chemicals. Maybe that's the difference. I never ate anything but homegrown in my life before coming here.

"This whole meal is unnatural," I say. "I bet these bacon bits never saw a pig."

The knitters stop talking, but none of them responds. Am I speaking too softly?

"These tomatoes are terrible," I say, a bit more loudly.

"We used to grow tomatoes in the summer. In the backyard," says one of the knitters.

"That's right," I say. "In summer. Tomatoes in spring are a perversion of nature. Not that seasons matter anymore." In every one of my memories, the weather is predominant, like an extra sense or dimension. Nowadays, living in climate control, the present is a rhythmless slush, and I'm hard-pressed to know the month without looking at the calendar. "They could be feeding us anything." I point my fork at my plate. "Maybe this isn't cod. It could be an amazing simulation."

"Mine's cod," says the knitter, touching her fork to the flaky half-eaten square on her plate.

"I meant—" I begin, but her blank expression stops me.

There are a few moments of silence as if to honor the death of that conversation, and then the knitting discussion starts up again.

There are peas, frozen of course and overcooked to a khaki mush. I eat some in silence and then go to my room. Doze for a while and dream of peas thumbed raw from the pod, crunchy and sweet. After a while I hear Gloria's door open and the noise of her chair, then some drawers opening and shutting. At least she's not a television watcher. Some earlier occupants of that room had the thing going night and day.

I should apologize. Belinda's right, I shouldn't be so rude. And Gloria and I really may be the only ones here with *all of our marbles*. I acknowledge now the humor in that turn of phrase, picturing Mrs. Donovan with one lonely marble skittering around inside her skull. I lift my hand to knock on the wall, but as if she's heard my thoughts, Gloria's television goes on.

CHAPTER SEVEN

Leo

THERE ARE A BUNCH OF kids here, but no one my age. A little girl with tangled hair who smells of pee and doesn't talk, and a very thin teenager who sucks her thumb. A pair of ten- or eleven-year-old girls who wear matching T-shirts they made with puffy paint in OT and are always whispering in each other's ears. The only other boy here is much bigger than I am. He looks like that boy who used to sit behind me in chapel and spit into the space where my collar gapped away from my neck. A name floats up to me: Bedrick. I haven't seen this kid spit on anybody, but he has the same hoarse voice and barrel-bellied walk and I stay away from him. He's easy to avoid: he spends most of his time in his room, playing a game on something called a Nintendo, which is a television set on a rolling cart. I'm intrigued by it, but it stays in the big kid's room and it never seems to be anyone else's turn.

After breakfast I am expected to wash and dress as if I am going to a classroom, even though I just sit at the desk in my room and do worksheets. I copy the alphabet and color in pictures of the American Revolution and do easy math problems: one orange plus two oranges equals three oranges. Each day has a workbook section, and when it's filled in, school is over. Sometimes I do everything slowly and carefully, keep the color inside the lines and make my letters perfect; sometimes I draw faces on the fruit outlines, or doodle designs in the empty spaces around the pictures of patriots. It doesn't seem to matter what I do; as far as I can tell, no one checks my work.

The tangle-haired girl is named Missy, and she's too young for school. Sometimes she brings her tablets and coloring books into my room and draws pictures silently while I do school. Her drawings are mostly flowers and houses, but the ones with people have black cross marks across the faces. She'll draw three people next to a house under a sun, and put in all the grass and the flowers, and then just when you think she's finished with the drawing, she puts big Xs over the heads. When I close my workbook, she jumps down from her chair and we go together down the hall to the playroom and look out the big window at the buildings below and the people walking. We're in the tallest building so there are a lot of roofs. There's a store across the street, Garibaldi's, that has a sign for frozen lemonade in a green-and-white-striped cup. Missy puts her tongue against the glass and licks it like ice cream.

At first the police came every day, but then that stopped. Maybe they finally believed that I didn't recognize the photo faces, and couldn't tell them more about Clyde or Mama or the day I came here. No one has told me what's wrong with me, but it must have something to do with the emptiness in my memory. I know that it should be different, that there should be a long story like a book I'm in the middle of, with pictures and words filling the pages. When they ask me to open the book of my story, every page is blank. But then when I'm not trying to remember, things swim up in the corners of my mind, like bright fish that dart out of view when I look.

Miss Meredith is the name of the fluffy-sweater lady. She calls me Ben; they all do. She comes to get me today as usual, and when I go down the hall toward the room where we always go from eleven to noon, she steers me past it, toward a different door.

"Let's talk in here today," she says, and pushes the door open.

It's a bigger room than the one we've been using; it has a big mirror on one wall and smiling brown monkeys hold hands in a chain just under the ceiling, all the way around. There is a bookshelf with some books on it and a dollhouse and large toy box in the corner, and in the center of the room there's a round table surrounded by plastic chairs. Miss Meredith sits down in one of them.

"You can play with anything in here," she says. "You choose."

I stand next to the toy box and look down into the jumble. Rubber snake, dolls, metal cars, airplanes, army men.

"Anything you like," she says.

I pull out the snake, wiggle it. It's got rings of color around it. A coral snake, you can tell from the colors. *Red touching yellow, kill a fellow.*

"Ooh, you're brave. I hate snakes."

Silly: a rubber snake doesn't require courage. I drop the snake back into the bin and take up a soldier. His plastic feet are frozen to a plastic disk, in a half lunge forward with his gun aimed. I drop that back into the toy box too.

"Let's draw," she says, as though it's a new idea. She asks me to draw every day.

I climb onto the chair across from her, although I don't feel like drawing. There are tablets of off-white paper, one in front of each of us, and a box blooms crayons in the middle of the table. It's a sixty-four box, with the gold and the silver and the sharpener in the middle, and it must have just been opened, all the crayons pointy. She hovers her hand over the box, finally choosing brown, and starts drawing.

I pull two crayons from the box.

"This is magenta," I say. "Not"—I read from the paper covering—"Jazzberry Jam." Her head snaps up, but when she speaks her voice is casual.

"You read very well." She chooses a light green and makes some grass.

The air in here is dry. My eyes make little sounds when I blink.

"I'm drawing a park," Miss Meredith says, making blue waves, a pine tree, some things that could be ducks. "It's my favorite place. My family goes on picnics there." She puts another pine tree in, jagging the edges.

I reach across to the crayon box. I touch a fingertip to an orange crayon, rocking it back and forth; a cat arches and stretches in my mind.

"Can you draw your favorite place for me?" She is coloring a yellow sun.

I pull out the dark green and the orange and the gray.

"What are those things?" says Miss Meredith after a few minutes. "They look like—wheels?"

I look up; her eyes are on my paper. She blinks and I see Brother Timothy blinking, fluttering his short lashes and wrinkling up the skin around his nose like a rat. I blink too, and chase that image away.

"They're headstones," I say.

"Head . . . stones." She pulls up the chain around her neck; there are the half glasses. She unfolds them and puts them on. "Headstones?"

"There should be names here." I put a forefinger on one of the humps. It really does look like a wheel; I am not good at drawing. "And sometimes carvings."

She points to Archie. "Is this a dog?"

"My cat."

"I like his tail."

She's no longer drawing; she's just watching me.

I flip to a fresh page in the tablet, choose colors for the big window over the doorway: red the color of cherry juice, bright orange, robin's-egg blue. When that is finished I pick up the gray crayon—Timber Wolf—again and fill in the stonework, peeling away the label as I need to. When I am done, the crayon is mostly gone, and the label says only *olf*.

"What is that big building? Is that your school?"

"My church," I say, and as I say those words, I smell the cold air inside the thick walls, just one breath; by the next inhale it's gone.

"Very nice," she says, peering through the glasses perched half-way down her nose.

I have colored so thickly in places that the crayon has left waxy crumbs scattered across the paper. I touch one of them, roll it under my fingertip. The crayons lying beside the paper are Cerise and Sunglow. The robin's-egg blue is Robin's Egg Blue.

"These crayon names are stupid," I say. "This is *red*, and this is *orange*."

"I suppose the people who own the company that makes the crayons thought it would be fun to use different names. Does it bother you?"

"Renaming something doesn't change it."

"We need to talk about something. Okay?" Her voice is serious, says, *We're done talking about crayons.* "Do you remember coming here?"

I nod.

"Your mom was hurt."

She waits; she seems to want me to say something.

"Okay," I say.

"I know it may be hard to talk about what happened." She looks me straight in the eyes, no blinking now. "It was a really confusing day, wasn't it." I nod again. "You've told me that you don't remember anything. But that may not be forever. The memories may start to come back."

"Okay."

"Will you make me a promise?" She goes on without waiting for an answer. "Will you tell me if you do remember anything? Even just a little bit, like a color or a sound or a smell. Even something really small can help."

That lingers in the air, begging me to say, *Help what?*

"I don't remember."

"I know," says Miss Meredith. "But if you do. It's really, really important." She takes my silence as agreement. "Okay." Like we've settled something. "Now, do you have any questions for me?"

No one has asked me that yet. I think for a minute. So many questions crowding up like feeding fish. I choose the nearest one.

"Are there any more books?" I ask.

"Excuse me?"

"All the books here are for babies. Are there other books?"

"Not here," she says, after a pause. "There's a public library a few blocks away. Maybe one of the aides can take you."

Like a kick from inside, a singsong chant goes through me: *What do you say?* A familiar voice, but whose?

"Thank you," I tell Miss Meredith. "Thank you very much."

I OVERHEAR HER talking in her office later that day, when she doesn't know I'm in the hall. She must be on the telephone, because she talks and waits and then talks some more, and I don't hear anyone else.

"He hasn't said a thing about her," she says. Her voice isn't as soft and slow as it usually is. "Not one word. It's been a week." Pause. "No, it's not that. He talks. Not much, I'll grant you, but he isn't *mute*. I haven't gotten him to put together one coherent memory. You'll see on the video. He volunteers nothing." She gives a little laugh, but it doesn't sound happy. "Oh, except that he wants to be called Leo, and he wants to go to the library." That's when I know she's talking about me. After a pause: "Leo. I don't know. We have his birth certificate. He's definitely Ben." Another pause. "Nope. None. Dad's Donor Number Whatever and Mom was an only child, no living parents. Who *does* that? Who brings a child alone into the world like that?" Pause. "Yeah, well. Either he was a sociopath before it happened or he's completely dissociated because of the trauma. Anyway, we're making zero progress and he can't stay here forever." She stops talking for so long that I think maybe she's hung up, but then she says, "I know, but we have no choice. All right. All right. You have a crack at him then." She has a getting-off-the-phone voice and I slip back down the hall to the dayroom as quietly as I can. When she looks in there a few minutes later, I'm frowning over a jigsaw puzzle with Missy, as if I have been working on it with her all along.

IT'S MUDDY, AND *hot, and there are bugs crawling on my face. They swarm there in a paste of blood and sweat. That's the worst part, almost—not being able to wipe my face. They're stinging me, but with my hands bound I can't shoo them. I can only shake my head, and that does nothing.*

I wake up shaking my head, and there's a moment where I'm not sure where I am. My cheeks and forehead sting, and I rub my hands over them hard: nothing there. Slowly the shapes of the room pull out of the darkness and I recognize the hospital. I can feel that I'm not alone, though—there's someone else here. I hold my breath; do I hear breathing? My heart is still thumping and I half think my pursuers have come out of the dream with me.

"What's wrong?" Tiny, squeaky, the voice comes from near the door. A figure creeps forward; light from the window falls across its face. Missy. Her forehead glows white below the haystack of her hair.

"Bad dream," I say.

"Was it the rope monster?" she whispers.

"I was lost. And bugs were biting me."

She nods, stands chewing her lips. It's my bad dream, but she looks scared. Maybe her own nightmare brought her in here.

"Come up," I say, and move over a little on the bed. Not that she needs much room: she's so light that when she climbs up the mattress hardly dips. "I'll fix your hair."

I use the plastic hospital comb from the drawer. It'll snap if I try to pull it through any of the tangles, so I hold one of the knots in my hand and tease at the bottom of it, bit by bit, with the teeth.

"I used to comb my sister's hair," I tell her, and then there's a full sunny flash of memory: scraping Sally's blond hair into ponytails, twisting the elastic. When was that? I can see the speckled kitchen floor and her feet swinging, a mosquito bite on her shoulder. And then it's gone.

Missy's head drops forward and jerks back, then drops forward again and stays there; she's fallen asleep. I put the comb onto the table beside the bed.

"I'm awake," she mumbles.

"It's okay." I pat the pillow and she puts her still mostly snarled head there. I sit up against the wall and pull the blanket over her, causing a warm puff of pee smell to rise up. She curls up, her back to me, bending her knees to meet her elbows; the sound of her thumbsucking tails off as she falls back asleep.

My feet still ache from my dream; I remember tight, hurting boots and walking. Walking where? I push the memory of the dream away, but with a sense that it won't help much. It's like poking a feather back into a pillow and seeing the tiny hole it leaves, knowing another will work its way through soon enough.

CHAPTER EIGHT

Clare

WHEN I HEARD THE NOISES beyond the wall, I was edging a plot near the middle of the cemetery, and at first I didn't pay any attention. The boys from the school next door occasionally took their amusement by paying the cemetery surreptitious visits. There weren't any of the typical country diversions to draw them: no water to fish or swim in, apart from a small swampy pond that shrank to a puddle in a dry spell, and it was a couple of miles down the hill to the nearest store, in the tiny town of Waite. It was the mid-1950s, and the interstate not yet put in; we were up in the rural northwestern corner of the state, and most of the roads were dirt or gravel with farms strung skimpily along the miles. Only a few hard-topped two-lane roads swung through on their way north to Massachusetts or west into Connecticut. There was nothing near the school grounds but me, and uphill a tangled half acre of berries; the rest was farmland.

I don't think they have anything like St. William's Priory School now. It was run by monks, and was more of a reform school than an orphanage. There wasn't the same concept of childhood then as there is now, no parental or societal outrage to act as a check on institutional grimness. The prevailing attitude seemed to be that these children were unwanted for a reason; they were treated a bit like criminals, uniformed and regimented and harshly corrected, schooled and churched and put to work to learn a proper trade.

The crops grown in St. William's fields fed the boys and the brothers, but the lion's share went to market for sale. There was also a laundry service, started in the late forties to replace the forge, after the wartime boom was over and it became clear to the monks that the motor had more or less permanently replaced the horse. The laundry serviced the hotels and restaurants in Providence, at rates cheaper than anyone else could match. A van brought bales of linen up the hill each afternoon, and shuttled clean ones down just after dawn. The boys worked the fields and the factory machines.

I'd seen a stealthy party of boys earlier that day, climbing the hill. They didn't officially have free time, so they had to be shirking some duty to be there. It was late for berries, and the hot rainless spell we'd been having would have cooked any remaining fruit on the bushes, so I knew the boys would find their way back downhill soon enough. When they reappeared, sneaking behind the low stone wall like commandos, I ignored them, working my edger around the pitted flank of a headstone without looking up. In the twenty years I'd been at Roscommon, these visits had never amounted to more than a puppet show of heads over the wall and maybe some catcalls.

I was edging the Dolans, a cozy family of five who had been carried off by influenza during the Great War. As I peeled away the beard of weeds left behind by the latest mowing, the engraved numbers emerged: 1918 . . . 1918 . . . 1918 . . . 1918 . . . 1918—a sad litany. The infant first, and then the two-year-old. The father had held out longest, watching his wife sicken and die, hoping against hope for the five-year-old, George. How he must have despaired when the little boy began his rusty coughing. The Great War had been less harrowing in some ways than the influenza—the war stayed in Europe, while the influenza came to us at home, a scourge like the plagues in Exodus, the frogs dropping from the sky, the rain of blood, the Angel of Death. Only it wasn't just the firstborn sons this angel took; it was all the sons, all the daughters, and their parents too.

I wasn't prepared for the apple that struck Cathleen Dolan. Mushy fruit that must have been last year's, wintered over in a cool St. William's cellar. This year's apples were still in midswell on the tree, and would have been hard as baseballs. I looked up to see four heads jerking out of sight behind the wall.

I sighed; I would have to scrub the headstone right away, before the sun cooked the fragrant bits of apple into a brown cement that would be tenacious as a barnacle. I went across the cemetery, through the gate, and up the path to the house. As I came back down into the cemetery with a scrub brush and a bucket of pump water, I expected that the boys would be gone. But as I knelt before Cathleen and dipped the brush into the water, another apple struck me on the forearm, bruising the muscle.

I scrubbed Cathleen's stone quickly, reckoning my options. Chasing the boys would likely only make them scatter, and they'd be able to pelt me from all sides. It might be most prudent to sacrifice the afternoon's work, go back up to the house, let the boys wander away. But something in me balked at giving these hooligans sway over my day's plan. I rose to my feet and looked around, pantomiming annoyed confusion, turned in a circle and stared in the wrong direction, lifting a hand to shade my eyes. An eruption of giggling from behind the wall while I placed the edger against Seamus Dolan's headstone and stepped on the blade, forcing it into the sod. I removed and replaced the blade at an angle, stepping again so that the two cuts met and a wedge of earth came away from the headstone. The same movements I had made countless times that day already, except that now each time I lifted the metal crescent I swung it over the bucket of water, dropping its burden there instead of into the wheelbarrow.

There was a short interval filled with scrambling noises, the boys moving along behind the wall, and then murmurs of conference coming from a new spot. Keeping my head down, I heard: *it's your turn, Leo, go on,* and then an exasperated, *coward.*

Another missile struck me square in the back, driving a sticky wetness through the layers of cloth. I looked up, making a dramatic show of looking all around, this time stomping a few steps toward the wall, a ploy to keep them in hiding while I tiptoed back toward the Dolans. I could almost feel the boys' exhilaration, their heart-beats racing with delighted panic as they duck-walked to another ambush point. I propped the edger against a headstone and took up the bucket.

I had to be quick now. Had they gone left or right? I chose left and went that way, running on the balls of my feet, holding the bucket full of muddy, weedy water with a stiff arm, to minimize sloshing. Since the wall was only three feet high, they were obvious to me, their knees and feet showing while they sat with their backs to the stone. There was a small pile of apples next to their feet, and a deflated canvas bag. They were arguing in hisses. *You go. No. It's your turn.* Three pairs of legs right in a row, grouped together, and another pair a little apart. *Leo, look. What's she doing?* I lifted the bucket, and just as I did, the boy sitting apart from the others leaned forward and twisted his trunk, putting one hand on the ground and one on the wall and shifting his weight, preparing to peek over the wall. He looked up, and our eyes met.

We looked at one another in a strange, timeless moment. Me with the bucket upraised, him crouched on the ground with his eyes lifted and wide. I expected him to squeak some alarm, to kick his legs out and crabwalk a retreat from the wall, but he made no sound or motion. He kept his light brown eyes on mine without changing expression.

Is she looking? hissed one of the other boys. *Dummy,* and a foot kicked out to get his attention. My co-conspirator said nothing.

Do you see her? What's she doing? just as the bucket's contents came down over them, a thick brown slurry now, the wedges of sod having married with the water. It was a perfect surprise: one of the boys even looked up, mouth open, and caught a choking swallow. They all sprang to their feet, coughing and shaking their heads, clawing their fingers to clear the mud from their cheeks and eyes. *Bitch,* they spat, and *Jesus Christ.* One of them had the courage to scrape a handful from the front of his tunic and toss it across the distance between us. I watched it fall harmlessly at my feet, then looked up again. That small movement frightened them: like a covey of startled birds they burst away, making a clumsy rush toward St. William's Wood, stepping on twigs and stumbling, cursing and spitting, disappearing among the trees.

The smallest boy had not moved. He was still crouching there with the wall between us; it put me in mind of a begging animal. I didn't move either, and after a few more moments he rose to his feet. His eyes held nothing: no satisfaction or amusement or guilt. Then he turned and ran off in the direction the others had gone. I stood there with the empty bucket swinging from one hand, listening to their fading calls. *Leo, you son of a bitch. Leo, you're gonna pay for this.*

I kept the apples. They made a fine sauce.

I LOVE THIS dream, the summer of it, the pure nostalgia of youth and my capable, limber body, not yet even forty years old. I usually awaken from this reverie happy. But this time the dream ends abruptly, and when I check the bedside clock it's the middle of the night. It takes me some time to fall back into a restless sleep. Perhaps I can blame some lingering effect of that green pill, or Gloria's loud television detective programs, for injecting a sinister element into my sleep; whatever the cause, after I rise in the morning the dream nags me all day, a wound that won't close.

Leo's face hangs before me, accusing: *you've forgotten me*. I shake my head: never. *It's like I never lived at all.* Newly urgent although deeply past, Leo's lostness tugs at me. He's right. When I'm gone, Leo will be erased. As though he'd never been. I will sink out of memory myself, but I've chosen that; is it fair to take him with me?

IT TAKES ME two days of arguing with myself, but I make up my mind, and when the next evening's dinner bell goes, I am ready. I wait inside my room, hungry and attentive, listening to the sounds from next door. She's taking a long time. I hear a door open, but it's a false alarm, just a cupboard. At last I hear the click of her room door, and the *whirrr* moving into the hall. I watch the long hand on my big-numbered clock. Two minutes to get down the hall and two more to cross the large common room. After four ticks of the minute hand, like a sprinter exploding out of the blocks I exit my own room and follow in Gloria's wake.

I've timed it well: when I get to the dining room, Gloria is just rolling herself up to a small table occupied by the married couple, Mr. and Mrs. Barlow.

We get couples at Oak Haven from time to time. They are of three basic varieties: ones in which the men are ancient and crumbling while their wives are still bright-eyed; ones in which the wives are direly ill and the husbands are comparatively healthy; and others in which both spouses are of roughly equal disability. The first type tend to go everywhere together, the wife a tugboat for the sinking vessel of her spouse; the second type usually have separate rooms, the ailing wife cared for intensively by staff while the husband lives a bachelor life, participating in activities solo; the third type clings together, eating in their quarters and venturing out only as a twosome. The Barlows are of the crumbling-husband type.

When I settle myself into the remaining chair at the table, Gloria flicks a glance in my direction, her magnified eyes unreadable, and then looks away. An attendant rolls a cart up to us and reads from the diet sheets Scotch-taped to the tray covers.

"Kidney diet."

Mrs. Barlow raises her hand and gestures to her husband, who may or may not be awake beside her. "He's kidney, I'm diabetes," she says. When the trays are placed in front of them, she attends to her husband's first, gathering up the cutlery and putting it in reach of his age-spotted, trembling hand, opening a napkin over his chest and tucking it into his collar.

"Low sodium, low fat, jeez, low everything," says the attendant, setting a tray in front of Gloria. "Yum."

My tray is the one remaining, no dietary restrictions.

"*Bon appétit*," says the attendant, mangling the language of my childhood and lifting the cover, releasing a limp waft of steam. I sneak a peek at Gloria's tray: she has vegetable lasagna and a bowl of carrot coins.

"Not carrots again," says Mr. Barlow. Not asleep after all.

"What?" says his wife.

"We had carrots last night."

"No, we didn't," she says.

"What did we have then?"

"I don't remember, but it wasn't carrots."

"All I'm saying is why not a nice bread pudding?"

"Bread pudding isn't a vegetable. Oh I remember, we had string beans last night."

"Well, that's no better," he says. "I don't like string beans either."

"But they're not carrots."

"Of course they're not carrots," he says.

I watch Gloria picking out the lima beans from her square of lasagna, winkling them out one by one with her fork and scooting them over to a small growing hill on her plate. I know what she is doing—she's hoarding them for a full mouthful. I have always liked lima beans myself, and they can't be properly tasted in dispersal.

"How is it?" I say.

She takes her time chewing, swallowing.

"Like damp toilet paper," she says.

"Mine's not too bad," I say, suppressing a reflexive wince at the word *toilet* at the table.

"They left the food in yours."

"Well, maybe we'll make another trip to the mall soon." I inject some heartiness into my voice. "You can acquire some more contraband."

She swallows, then sets her fork down.

"All right, what is it, why are you talking to me?"

"Just being pleasant."

"Why now? You took such pains to be *un*pleasant before."

"You're very direct."

"Neither of us has a lot of time to beat around the bush."

"I'm feeling cheerful today." Maybe my idea isn't such a good one after all. I lie: "Nothing more than that."

She lifts her fork again, puts the last bite of lasagna into her mouth, and chews suspiciously, her eyes on me.

"Aw, you don't like lima beans?" the attendant says, appearing at Gloria's elbow and reaching for her plate.

"I—" starts Gloria, but the food in her mouth goes down the wrong way and she starts coughing. The attendant doesn't notice; not even looking at Gloria, she has the plate and is drawing it away. I reach out quickly with my fork. The attendant cries *ow* and the plate clatters back onto the table.

"She's *saving* those lima beans," I say.

The attendant leaves, her hand in her mouth, mumbling around it *crazy old bat*.

"Are you all right?" I ask Gloria.

"Drink some water," orders Mrs. Barlow.

"Water's no good if she's choking," corrects her husband. "Raise your arms over your head, that's good for choking."

"She's not choking," says Mrs. Barlow, and then to Gloria she says, "Are you choking?"

Gloria, coughing, shakes her head no.

"Drinking water's about the worst thing you could do if you're choking," says Mr. Barlow.

"How is it the worst thing you could do?" argues Mrs. Barlow. "The worst thing you could do is *choke*."

And they're off again, drawn away from us into the current of their bickering.

Gloria's coughing subsides, finally.

"That was impressive," she says. "You've got reflexes like lightning."

"I learned from the best," I say. "I got my own knuckles rapped a great deal as a child."

"Me too."

We say it together: *nuns*.

Her laughter catches in her throat and dwindles into a cough, a burbling leftover of the previous fit.

"Uh-oh," I say, and deadpan: "Quick, drink some water."

She fixes her cartoon eyes on me.

"That's about the *worst thing I could do*," she says. Then she lifts her eyebrows and rounds her mouth into an O of exaggerated surprise. "Why, Miss Clare, I did not know you were capable of a smile."

For a moment we sit there grinning at each other, and then her expression frosts over again.

"So tell me: What do you want?" The no-nonsense voice is back.

"All right, I do want something. Two things." It's the beginning of the speech I have been preparing. "First, I want to apologize. I was very rude."

"Well, that's true," she says. "Although the etiquette books might say it's rude of *me* to point that out. So we're even, and we're forgiven. What else?"

"I wanted to ask a favor of you."

She raises her eyebrows, but her expression otherwise doesn't change. She waits, neither encouraging nor hostile.

I open my mouth and the words push out of me in a chaotic rush. Nothing like I'd planned. "I want to tell you my story. It's not just mine. You'll see. I mean, if you agree." I've never sounded so awkward. "There's a tape recorder here we can use. They used it for Ellie Schlosser. You didn't know her. A student recorded her talking. She died, but. They still have the tapes."

Gloria listens very seriously.

Finally, finally I stop babbling, and there's a beat of silence.

"I'll bet it's been a long time since you asked for something," says Gloria.

CHAPTER NINE

Lucy

THE KEY TURNS. A MILD surprise: he hasn't changed the locks. That doesn't mean anything, except that he hasn't bothered. He doesn't expect me to come back. Or maybe he just doesn't care if I do.

I push the door open with a guilty frisson, although I'm not officially trespassing; my name is on the lease along with his. But of course nothing about this has been official. We're not officially anything. He's here, I'm there, we're halved, or at least halving.

Was the entryway always this dingy? The beige paint is chipped along the molding. The air smells different too—something missing. Had I contributed some personal chemistry to the household? I stand on the threshold and close my eyes, breathe it in—the smell of my marriage, minus me. Cooking odors from the downstairs neighbors who seem always to be poaching onions, plus Joe's deodorant, coffee, a hint of cigar. Cigar? He quit smoking years ago—or maybe he hadn't. There was a lot I hadn't known about what he'd been doing while I had been at work.

The apartment is neat; he's a tidy person. There's a spoon on the drain board and beside it, a coffee cup rinsed and upside down. Not the coffee cup I gave him, but one of the set of anonymous white mugs from the cupboard. The spoon is cheap flatware from

the drawer. They've recently touched his lips; it seems almost unbelievable that they look so ordinary.

He might be back anytime; I want to be gone before then. I'm
here with a purpose, to get the things I left behind, to drag every
bit of myself out of here. I go first to the hall closet and slip my
letterman jacket from the hanger. Joe had ordered it in secret from
his high school and sewed his varsity letters onto it during evenings
while I was at work. There were a lot of letters: lacrosse, baseball,
football. He'd been captain of his football team, MVP twice; the
black-and-white photos in his yearbooks show him more often than
any other player, flying through the air in a tackle or standing on the
field postgame, helmet under his arm and hair soaked with sweat,
the muscles in his neck so thick he was barely recognizable as the
same person I married a dozen years later. He'd dated cheerleaders
then, of course, the popular girls. If we'd gone to the same high
school, we never would have spoken.

"Now you've always been my girl," he said when I opened the
Christmas box.

There had been men before him—I'd even been in love before
him—but he was forever for me, and I knew it fairly soon after
we'd started dating. So the jacket was perfect, rewriting history,
marking the beginning of a shared path, the rest of our lives. I wore
it everywhere, although its boiled wool was scratchy and raised
hives on my skin.

I carry it with me now as I go around the apartment, gathering
the meaningful and the mundane into the shopping bags I've
brought. The carved rose soap I store with the linens to perfume
the bedsheets; my hairbands; my favorite travel mug. I strip scarves
from hangers, pluck shoes from the back of the closet. It all goes
into the bags. Thus far it's rote and pangless, a preamble to what
I really came back for.

In the bedroom, the bed is neatly made with a blanket we'd
gotten as a wedding present. I'd never used it—it had always been

on the shelf at the top of the closet in a crackly zipper bag, too nice for everyday use. Did he think *fuck you* when he'd taken it down and shaken it out of its folds, tucking the soft clouds around the mattress? Has he slept with *her* under that blanket? I go around the bed to the far side, trying not to look too closely. I don't want to see a dent from her head on the pillow. My pillow.

A lone navy-blue men's sock lies curled on the floor. I gather it into my hand. I don't know how long I've stood there, clutching the empty cotton shape of his foot, my mind an aching blank, when the landline rings from Joe's nightstand. Its shrill sound is startling. I'm unsure what to do. It's my phone too; the bill is actually in my name. But who would be calling me here? Everyone who wants to reach me uses my cell. The ringing stops and voice mail picks up. I lay the sock on the floor again and turn toward the nightstand on my side of the bed. Finally, what I really came here for.

For the last few years, Joe and I have been keeping opposite hours—I'd leave for a shift at the hospital before he came home, and when I got back he'd be sleeping; then he'd be gone to work before I woke the next day. Often I'd find a chain of Post-it notes making a paper trail in his distinctive half-capitalized handwriting, cartoons and short notes leading me with love through my morning routine. He knew me so well. Bedside table, bathroom mirror, kettle, teacup, tea canister, milk carton. A note curled into the hole of a pumpernickel bagel in the bag in the pantry: *I hope you slept well, sweetie*; another under the cardboard lid of the box holding the cream cheese brick in the fridge: *I'll miss you all day*. When I'd had to travel out of town to clinical rotations at other hospitals, he'd sent me actual mail—postcards, greeting cards, an origami package folded around a white pebble in the shape of a heart. I kept them all: every note, every card and letter, every silly doodle. Nine years of love crammed into an overflowing envelope, brought along with each move and put into my bedside drawer in the new place as part of making it home. It's what I've come back to get, the only really irreplaceable thing I left behind. I'm not sure what I'll do with the collection now. Stuff it into a bigger envelope and keep it just in case this is all going to blow over and become something in the rearview, a *rough patch* that we'll mention with a rueful smile in years to come? Burn it, a ritual to give closure to our ending? Cherish it, as evidence that I was loved once, in case love never comes to me again? I don't know, but I want it. I want to take charge of the history of us.

When I pull open the bedside drawer, it's empty.

At first I am so shocked I doubt my vision. I put my hand in, touch the naked wood of the drawer. Had I taken the envelope with me on the day I left?

It had been a Sunday. A rare weekend off. Since I'd been on overnight that Friday and would need to sleep much of Saturday, it would really work out to a day and a half off. But we had dinner plans on Saturday evening that could turn into a late night, maybe even wine, maybe even sex, since I wouldn't have to go to work the next day. Joe wasn't home when I got home; probably at the gym, I figured. He'd be home soon but I went to bed, determined to get in a solid block of sleep so that I could for once be well groomed and alert, fully present at the impending social occasion. When my alarm went off at 3 p.m. he wasn't back yet. I texted, but got no answer. I showered, then checked my phone; still no answer. Texted again. We've got dinner at Nelson and Millie's where are you The notation *Delivered* appeared below each text but not *Read.* I phoned; voice mail. Was his phone off? Maybe he was jamming with the band that kept breaking up and re-forming, renaming itself so often that I couldn't keep up. They called it *rehearsal,* although there was no performance in the offing.

By six, near the time we'd need to leave for dinner, I phoned our friends to tell them we'd be late. That's all I meant to say, but *I don't know where Joe is* spilled out. *He's not answering his phone.* Nelson was remarkably calm, told me not to worry, you know Joe, he always lets his battery die. He'd poured soothing words over my anxiety: no need to panic, he'll be home, you two can come on over whenever, we're totally casual over here. And an afterthought, probably prompted by the feminine murmuring I could hear in the background of the call: you're welcome to come over by yourself if you like. *I'll just wait for Joe,* I said. *Thanks.*

Later I realized that he must have known. Everyone knew everything, it seemed, but me.

By 10 p.m. I was pacing the apartment, jumping every time I heard the click of the downstairs entryway door echoing up through the building. But it was always a false alarm, footsteps going by our apartment door and on upstairs while my heart rate decelerated. I told myself that the explanation would turn out to be simple: Joe had forgotten our Saturday plans, he'd mixed up this weekend with another and thought I'd be sleeping and then working, so he'd made plans of his own, with other friends. At midnight I realized that that excuse was losing validity. Even if he had been out with friends, even if they'd gone on to a club after dinner, he should be coming home by now.

I wondered if I should call the police. Could he be considered officially missing? I hadn't seen him since the previous evening, when I'd left for work. Just about twenty-six hours before. An involuntary slide show played in my mind's eye: his truck wrecked against a barricade on I-95, the EMTs cutting into the cab to extract him. I surrendered to that vision, let it play itself out. EMS would get him into the ambulance, boarded and collared, and then go through his wallet for ID. They'd find the card I'd put there long ago, grim benefit of my experience, "Next of kin:" printed on it and my mobile number. *Now* they'll call me, I thought, lying on the bed and holding the phone. *Now.* I tried to replace the car-crash reel with others: Joe at a downtown club, standing right in front of the speaker the way he'd do, his head down, listening to the music intently as if straining to hear a subliminal message. I could almost see it, but then the red and blue lights of police and rescue would wash over the scenario and take me back to the roadside, looking at a twisted hulk of metal and a sweep of shattered glass.

After three phone messages, I confined myself to texting. Texts of one word or two, some magical-thinking attempt to jolt the preceding ones out of a clogged virtual pipeline. They all said *Delivered* but never *Read*. Had his phone run out of charge? But even if it had, where would he be at two in the morning? The thing I simply didn't have an answer for: *Where was he?*

Seeing Joe unconscious behind a spiderweb-cracked windshield for the hundredth time, I went to the bedside landline, holding the mobile like a talisman in my other hand.

"Hi, Sue," I said to the secretary who answered. "It's Lucy."

"Hey, Dr. Cole. You joining us tonight?"

"No, I'm not on. How is it there?"

"Knock on frickin wood, we just ordered out. Don't say it." She didn't want me to utter any of the verboten words: *quiet, calm, slow.*

"Any traumas tonight? I'm—" I swallowed. "My husband's truck is gone. He's not answering his phone. And it's raining."

"I'll check." Snapping out of her social languor, voice crisping up, computer keys clacking. "Nothing since I got here at eleven. We had an MVA earlier—oh, that was a motorcycle." Tap tap tap. "A COPD exacerbation, an MI, an overdose." Her voice lingered on the last word. Then she added, "Okay, the overdose was female." More typing. "Nothing under Cole."

"I kept my name," I said, and spelled Joe's for her, R-E-I-D-Y. "I last saw him Friday evening around ten."

"Nothing," she said after some more clacking. "I checked all the traumas and admissions since Friday, including all the Does. He's not here. Did you check Pawtucket? Or could he be down at Newport for any reason?"

I phoned all the hospitals, and in between texted him, an anguished digital shout, Where are you I'm really worried

The rest of that night was a sleepless tunnel clutching my phone, opening my eyes to every notification that flared light through my eyelids: Instagram: jb16v liked your photo and MicroWeather: rain stopping in six minutes!

Finally, finally, at dawn Sunday morning I went hunting. First his desk and the drawers of hanging file folders. I looked at the joint credit card statements he had neatly filed, the ones that I had paid each month without even looking. Fanning the papers out, scanning the itemized charges, I found restaurant names I didn't recognize, concert tickets for a show I hadn't heard about. Those were not clearly damning: he could have told me about the concert and I'd forgotten, and the restaurants could have been innocent outings with coworkers.

I lifted the lid of his laptop, and held my breath as I clicked into his email.

And there she was.

Tucked in among the subscription emails and receipt emails and spam, a personal email with a title beginning "re: re: re: re:" A long thread. No salutation in any of the individual messages, and the email address did not contain a name. Nothing sexual in the message body, but there didn't need to be. The intimacy breathed out from the words; I could hear his warm voice in them. That the content was so humdrum made it obscene. The small details of his day, the things he used to say to me. I steeled myself, then scrolled to read her reply.

I'd read only one line of it—*you're definately right about that, I never thought about it that way*—when my phone vibrated with his text:

On my way home

I shut the computer, stood up from the desk chair, went to the closet, and pulled down my overnight bag from the top shelf. Like a game show contestant with the prize clock ticking down, I ran around the apartment filling up the bag with the things I would need immediately, the white coats and socks and underwear and scrubs, phone charger and toothbrush. I burst through the door, not pausing to lock it behind me, running down the steps and out to my car. More desperate to be gone before he returned than I had been desperate for his return, throwing the bag into the backseat and driving away fast. That was six weeks ago; I haven't been back until now.

Perhaps in that blur of exodus I had scooped the notes into my bag, or maybe I'd moved them somewhere else—a different drawer or a box—sometime before that? I can't remember the last time I opened the drawer to add a note to the collection. This is a new thought. I pull the drawer all the way out now, and like a fool pull out the drawer below it too, as if the notes had come to life and one by one shimmied through the crack at the back. Nothing, of course. Under the nightstand, nothing; the space behind the nightstand, nothing.

I know I didn't move them; I'm increasingly sure that I left them behind.

In the weeks since I left, he hasn't gotten rid of anything else. I've just been through the whole apartment and found it all—my shampoo, my clothing, my tampons, everything I left—still in their places. But he chose to move this. They're just notes, just paper, but the loss of them, not knowing where they are or what happened to them, makes me breathless. They are the landing lights for my past, until so recently my present.

I recall the email I read, and make the belated connection: *those* are what he's writing now. His love notes have been upgraded, from analog to digital, from an old, too-familiar recipient to a new one. Probably younger, less judgmental, less tired and cranky. Someone who smiles admiringly up into his face. Someone who misspells *definitely*. Someone totally unlike me.

Abruptly I am brimming with rage. I turn over the shopping bags I've been carrying and drop everything out, my scarves and my shoes and my shampoo. The beloved letterman jacket and the volume of collected Dorothy Parker. I shake the bags hard and things fall out messily, the shampoo cap cracking open against the stainless steel travel mug and sighing a blond ribbon out over everything. I step over the mess and am out of the apartment empty-handed, locking the door behind me, and before I can change my mind I twist the key off the ring and push it through the crack under the door. With a defiance I don't completely feel: *keep it, keep all of it, keep our past and my memories. They don't mean anything now.*

Nowhere to go but back to the hospital; halfway there, I pull over on a side street and take out my phone. I could call Nicole, a friend from medical school who's an abdicated surgeon, home full-time with her first infant in upstate New York. I'd talked to her right after the split, and she was gratifyingly horrified. I know she'll be enthralled by the latest installment and I hover my finger over her name on my phone screen, marshalling the story, anticipating the warm unstiffening, like bands breaking across my chest, of sharing it. There's nothing like talking to a friend, the feeling of being known and understood. Nicole will get it, she'll vilify him for me, she'll say the terrible things I've been thinking, and it will make them less terrible somehow, being brought into the open air.

I hesitate: it's nine o'clock on a Monday morning. She's not at work, but maybe her husband's taken the day off and the two of them are sleeping in, the baby between them. Or maybe he is at work but she's gone back to bed after a difficult night with a fussy infant. No way to know. I scroll down the contacts screen in my phone. Mike, a high school friend who now lives in Hawaii; it's only 4 a.m. there. My stepmother will be home and she's been very kind, but I know it frustrates and baffles her that Joe and I are frozen in this limbo, that we haven't spoken at all since I left; I need someone to hear me, not argue with me. Emma, my best friend from college. It's been so long since we've talked, though;

how awkward to make this bomb our first contact in years. I keep scrolling—*at work, at work, triplets*—until I reach the Zs and realize there's no one to call.

IF YOU'D ASKED me two years ago, I would have said that a person can live happily alone, that one doesn't need to be partnered to be complete. But now I feel the lie in it. Haven't I always felt dimly sorry for the patients who come to the ER alone, no one at home, no one by the bedside and no one to call? Last year, when taking the history from a patient, an old woman widowed and without children, I'd been blindsided by the thought surging up from my unconscious: *What was the point of your life then?* Why would I think that? I'd never wanted children. Had I changed my mind subconsciously?

It seemed like a message from the universe when a few days after that, Joe came home and showed me photos on his phone of a coworker's new baby. *We have to have one of these,* he'd said, and for the first time I had not recoiled at the suggestion. Yes, I'd breathed, looking at the tiny feet, the rosebud mouth. Yes, okay, we will.

And just like that, at thirty-two, I'd re-formed my life course, changed the arc of my ambition to enfold a child. Not Harvard then; not department chair or residency director. Although I'd always planned to go into academic medicine, I began to cut down my hours at the lab and tidy up my projects there. Making just a few degrees of adjustment now that would result in a large correction a few years hence. When residency was done I'd be thirty-three, with a family-friendly schedule ready to deploy, eleven or twelve shifts a month and a stay-at-home husband. We'd have enough with my salary alone for a modest but privileged life, freedom for Joe to pursue his music, good schools, and a couple of exotic vacations a year; as much as we needed, and better than either of us had known growing up.

My definition of happily ever after had turned on a dime. I'd thought Joe was turning with me, but we'd never actually had a discussion about it. For me that single harmonic moment looking at the photos had had the strength of a mandate. I'd thought we'd been pulling together toward a common goal, but apparently while I was going to work and back and we were meeting in the shreds of time between my shifts, he was brooding. How had I missed that?

I'd had a glimpse of it, one night last November, as I'd slung the stethoscope around my neck and taken my keys up from the table in the entry hall, preparing to leave for a 6 p.m. to 2 a.m. shift. I'd turned to say good-bye and seen him impossibly far away, his expression impenetrable. *Are you okay?* I'd said. He'd brought cold eyes to mine and said, *I can't live like this anymore.*

Would it have changed anything if I'd dropped the keys back on the table and walked to him then, if I'd braved that space between us? If I'd reached out and made my voice soft and nonurgent and loving, if I'd sat down and taken the stethoscope off? If I had done anything that night but what I did do, which was check my watch and say *I have to go*? Like a damaged robot unable to adapt to the situation, already halfway to work in my mind, I went through the door and left him there, our dissonant words hanging in the air. I'll never know what might have happened if I'd stayed that night.

But of course that simply had not been possible. Medical residency doesn't have personal days. There's no slack to the roster; staffing is skeletal on late shifts and a missing doctor means the ER will spin out, patients in the urgent area waiting longer and longer to be evaluated while traumas roll in. Delay under those circumstances can be fatal. Staying with Joe that night would have meant abandoning those patients. Walking out the door had been my only possible choice. Perhaps to Joe it had been a test. One I'd utterly failed, demonstrating that my real loyalty was to strangers, not my husband, that their needs came before his, even before I'd laid eyes on them.

I left that night, I failed Joe's test, if that's what it was, and we never talked about it afterward. I intended to, but that resolve evaporated when Joe had seemed his normal self the next day. I said nothing. Partly denial, partly selfishness: I didn't want to open a can of nasty worms. I put it off, put it on a list like the ones I used to make as an intern on the wards (*recheck potassium—draw Vanco peak and trough—review post-op X ray*), to keep from forgetting a critical task. To do: have children, have a social life, talk to husband about his unhappiness.

And something occurs to me now, sitting in my car pulled over with no destination and no home, a saying I heard first as a medical student. *You have to love medicine—it won't love you back.* Back then, it had seemed to be a challenge: Do you love this job enough to do it well? Now I hear it differently, with the emphasis on the second part: as a warning. It seems so obvious now.

CHAPTER TEN

Leo

DURING SCHOOLTIME ON FRIDAY, A new man appears in my doorway.

"I'm Dr. Jellicoe. May we talk for a while?"

I close the workbook and get down from the chair. I don't know why they pretend everything is a choice here. *May we talk* means *we're going to talk*.

Dr. Jellicoe is tall, with white hair and eyebrows like caterpillars. Instead of a doctor coat, he wears a dark-green sweater that buttons, with twisted panels crawling up the front. He takes me into the playroom, draws two chairs up across from each other, sits down on one, and leans across to pat the seat of the other; I climb up.

"Miss Meredith tells me you don't remember anything about the day you came here." There's a sticker on the toe of my sneaker; I scrape at it with the other heel, but it's stuck down very flat. "And you may have even forgotten some other things." I'm peeling the paper up with my fingers; I notice he's paused, so I nod. "She also says you want to be called Leo." I've gotten the whole thing up now, a creased purple flower on my fingertip. "So you're Leo. Who's Ben?"

"I don't know." The name is dull, meaningless. It doesn't even sound like a name. I crumple the flower into a tiny sticky ball and smear it off my finger onto the seat of the chair.

"Miss Meredith also tells me you're having bad dreams," he says.

There are lights in the soles of these shoes; they flash when I walk. They flash when I tap them together too. I realize that Dr. Jellicoe isn't saying anything, and I look up to see him watching me.

"Sometimes," I say.

"Can you tell me about them? Your dreams?"

"They're all different." They drain out of me quickly after I wake, vanishing all day until just a little bit remains, single sand grains left by the tide. "Sometimes I'm walking." Telling this, I feel the breath of the jungle in my face, my painful boots.

Mm-hmm, he says, *mm-hmm.* When I don't say any more, he leans forward, rests his elbows on his thighs, and clasps his hands together.

"Sometimes we have scary dreams when we're trying to remember things," he says. "There may be a way to remember that isn't as scary. Would you like that?"

I would.

I HAVE TO go downstairs for a scan, what Dr. Jellicoe called *a picture of your brain.* I lie in a loud clanging tube while a voice tells me to *hold your breath—don't move—now breathe,* and when it's done no one shows me the picture. Then I'm wheeled to a different part of the hospital and a thin perfumey woman glues a lot of wires to my head and I have to *hold very still* again. There's also a blood test, which doesn't hurt because they put numbing cream on my arm an hour before. The man who does the blood test has little gold butterfly earrings in both earlobes. Just look at the butterflies, he says. Keep an eye on them. All done, he says, pressing a sticky bandage across a cotton ball in the crook of my elbow. You were super brave.

I don't see Miss Meredith anymore. Instead I see Dr. Jellicoe every day in his office, and we *work on feelings.* He shows me a line of faces, from smiling all the way on the left to frowning with tears all the way to the right. I have to choose one of the faces after looking at a cartoon, after a story, after playing a game. The face with the line straight across is the one I choose most.

"It's okay to feel sad, or scared," he says. "Everyone has those feelings sometimes." It's hard to imagine what would make a grown-up like Dr. Jellicoe sad or scared.

He gives me a poster for my room, with three stripes of cartoon faces for each day. The poster goes on the inside of my door, and in the morning and again after lunch and then at bedtime, I am supposed to put an X over as many feelings as I'm having, confused or silly or happy or angry, sad or surprised or worried or scared. I use a squeaky black marker; the X'd-over faces remind me of Missy, who's gone home from the hospital now. My marks get wiped off sometime during the night; every morning the poster is clean again.

After a week of the Xs and cartoon faces, Dr. Jellicoe says we're ready to try the new thing he talked about, the way to remember that isn't scary. I thought the faces were the thing, so I'm a little surprised.

"It's a relaxation technique," he says. "Do you know that word? Relaxation? It means making yourself calm." He presses one of the light switches on the wall, so the only lights left on are the ones around the edges of the room, and I get into the blue squishy chair. "Are you comfortable?" I nod. "It's okay if you go to sleep."

He puts a fingertip against my forehead, right above the space between my eyebrows, then takes it away and tells me to look at that spot. Of course I can't see it, you can't look at your own forehead, but he says to look up at the place and I try. He talks slowly; he keeps talking. When my eyes close, he says *that's okay, that's good.* And he keeps on, the words collapsing into one another until his voice becomes a long drone *you'rebackhomewithyourmomhomewithyourmom*

GETTING SALLY READY for school, coaxing Tad out of bed and to the breakfast table. Sally has such yellow hair, the color Mama says hers used to be when she was young. I hold each soft tangle in my hand and pull the teeth of the comb through in short yanks.

"Ouch," says Sally. She is whiny these days, quick to cry; her way of testing love.

"Hush." I draw the comb over the crown of her head, divide it into a gold double waterfall and braid each half, behind her ears like she likes. She puts her hands up to make sure I did it right.

"Look." I take two lengths of ribbon from my pocket. They're new; I bought them last week with money a neighbor gave me for helping her carry groceries home. "Don't let your dad see." I tie them onto the ends of her pigtails. He'll want to know where they came from, and if he knows I held back pocket money he'll be mad. Not that he'll be awake anytime soon.

She nods, feeling the ribbon ends with her fingers, then jumps down from the chair and runs off to see herself in the mirror.

I harass Tad through his eggs. He's always slow in the mornings, and he's purposely delaying today. He's started to hate me already.

"You're not the boss of me," he says.

"I'm older than you." I almost said *I'm bigger*. I shouldn't teach him to value that. Plus I won't have that card to play for much longer. He'll soon be as tall as I am. His father, Clyde, is tall. Clyde calls me The Runt.

I hate being late to school. It's embarrassing walking in when everyone else is seated already. If I get another tardy I may have to stay after. Who knows what consequences that might bring.

"Stop fooling with them," I tell Sally, who can't keep her fingers off her bows. She's pulled one of the loops small already, and I retie it. Tad finally finishes his breakfast and I put his dishes into the sink. No time to wash them now.

Mama comes in then, surprising me. She isn't usually up when we leave for school, but today she's fully dressed.

"There are some dishes in the sink," I tell her, buttoning up

Sally's coat. I open the front door. "Come on, we're going to be late."

"Look," says Sally, pulling her braids forward. "Mama, look."

"Leo, wait," Mama says. She looks tired, and she has the low gargly morning voice she gets sometimes. "I'll take them. You're not going to school today."

"I'm all right," I say quickly. It's true. Last night wasn't so bad. She shakes her head.

"You wait here. Answer the door if someone comes."

"Why?" I say, but she doesn't answer. She herds Tad and Sally out. I watch through the window as they walk down the path. Sally is chattering up at Mama, Tad is kicking stones with his new shoes. None of them looks back.

I go into the kitchen. Who might be coming to the door? Maybe a doctor. Maybe Clyde's sick. I push down the leap of hope. Or maybe last night was the last straw and she's called the police to take Clyde away. Although I wish for it, I suspect that would be a bad idea; men with guns might get him out of here, but he'd come back. And he'd come back angry.

I have washed the dishes and put them away, and am wiping down the table, when the knock comes at the door.

I DON'T HESITATE to get into the van with them; they are monks, after all, men of God. I recognize the vehicle as one I have seen before, making deliveries in Waite. There's a boy in the back when I climb in.

"Hello," I say.

He looks at me. He's dirty, not like playing-in-the-dirt dirty, but really filthy. There are tear tracks on his cheeks, although he is an older boy, maybe fourteen. His eyes linger on the swollen place over my cheekbone.

"I tripped," I say, bringing up the lie easily, the one I had had

ready for school, the one I always had ready, although hardly anyone ever asked.

His expression changes from mild curiosity to contempt.

"Liar," he says.

The doors slam as the monks get in.

"Where are we going?" I ask the boy as the van pulls away.

"Shut up." He shoots a glance at the monks in the front, but
they haven't heard over the engine noise.

The van bounces over a bump, turns right; I slide across the
metal floor.

"Get off," the other boy says, kicking me. I scramble back to
my place, brace my hands on the floor of the van to keep my place
when we take the next turn. There aren't any windows back here,
so I can't see out, but after a while we are pulling up a long hill and
then leveling out and finally coming to a stop.

One of the monks opens the rear doors, and the boy goes through
them. I follow and stand blinking in the sunlight for a moment,
wiping my hands against my thighs to get the black from the van
floor off them.

We're beside a large gray building. There's an unfamiliar smell
in the air; I wrinkle my nose. The other boy is already crossing the
swath of gravel, and I start to follow, but a monk stops me.

"This way." Putting a hand on my shoulder, steering me toward
a little door beyond some bushes.

We climb some stairs, turn and turn, and then we are in front
of a closed door. The monk raises his hand and knocks, then opens
the door and pushes me in.

The man behind the desk looks up.

"I got Bedrick," says the monk behind me. "I put him on stalls."

"Good," says the man behind the desk.

That means nothing to me—stalls—although later I will feel a
reflex nausea hearing the word.

"I'm not Bedrick," I say. "I think this is a mistake."

The man looks at me. He is a monk too, but some kind of fancy one: while the others' robes were dusty, these brown folds fall clean and new, like velvet, and he wears a silver cross.

"No mistake." He looks up at the monk behind me. "Thank you, Timothy." The door shuts. He takes a book from a drawer in his desk, opens it to a page. "Leo."

"Yes." I realize then that Bedrick must have been the other boy.

"I'm Prior Charles. This is St. William's School. We have rules here. First among them is that boys don't speak unless spoken to. Is that understood?" I nod. "Prayers three times a day, finish the food on your plate, give an honest day's work to the Lord." He gives me a closer look. "And it should go without saying that there is no fighting."

"I wasn't fighting," I say, my cheek throbbing. When he scowls, I add, "You were speaking to me."

"Impertinence is a habit you'll unlearn." He notes something down in the book. "You're from Waite, correct? Any experience with animals?"

"I had a dog once." Before Clyde.

He closes the book, rings a bell. A minute later, the door opens behind me. I turn and see a boy standing there; he's huge, with a soft face like a pudding.

"Gregory," says the prior. "This is Leo. Get him outfitted. He'll start in milking."

"Come on." Gregory puts a hand on my shoulder, but I shrug it off and turn back to the prior.

"Why am I here?"

Prior Charles leans forward, his hands together on his desk. "You're here to make something of yourself," he says.

Gregory takes my shoulder again firmly and steers me out, pushes me ahead of him down the hall to the foot of some narrow stairs and prods me up them.

"You'll want to take these stairs," he says. "And you can't use the big front door ever; use the little one on the side to go in and out." We come to a landing and go down a long corridor. He turns a doorknob, pushes a door open. "Here's where you'll sleep."

It's a big room with damp-looking cots spaced in two rows.

"Bring anything with you?" he says. I shake my head. "That's good. They'd only take it anyway." I don't ask who *they* are. "There's the bathroom," he says, pointing to a door down the hall. "Piss before bedtime even if you think you don't have to, because you can't get up during the night." He takes me down the stairs again, and then outside. I have to run a little to catch up.

We go around the back of the building, to another large building about a hundred yards away. Inside, the air is steamy and bleachy, and there is a racket of machines. We pass open doors: a large room filled with tubs, others filled with noisy equipment. Boys are swarming purposefully everywhere. Gregory stops in front of a half door, the top half open showing shelves and shelves of soft-cornered beige bundles. He puts his head into the opening.

"New boy," he calls.

The top half of a monk appears in the space, sizes me up without speaking, turns away. He comes back in a minute and passes over a bundle and a pair of shoes. Gregory takes them and goes down the hall to another door, opens it and beckons to me. I follow him into a tiled room, humid like the rest of the building. He twists a tap on the wall, and a spray of water sputters from a showerhead in the corner.

"Hurry up," Gregory says. "Chapel in twenty minutes."

I strip down and get under the water, scrub myself using a hard bumpy lump of soap I take from a recess in the wall. It doesn't lather well. I am embarrassed to have Gregory watching, but he pays no attention, unwrapping the bundle to reveal a pile of folded clothing. I turn my back to him to rinse off.

"You're what, nine?" he says.

"Eleven." He hands me a flannel from the pile and takes it back from me when I have dried off. Then he hands me underwear, undershirt, shirt, trousers, and a pair of thick socks. He tosses the wet flannel into a bin as I dress.

"You're lucky. Milking's easy." He yanks my collar right side out and does up the top button for me, mashing his thumb hard against my neck as he does; then with two fingers he tugs the trouser waistband away from my stomach. "A little big but they'll do. We used to have suspenders, but too many boys got clever. Come on," he says as a bell tolls from somewhere outside.

"Gregory," I pant, stumbling after him in the new shoes, which are too big too. "How long have you been here?"

"Seven years."

Seven *years*. He must be joking, or lying. But why would he lie about that?

"Why did you come here?"

Gregory wheels around, anger distorting his pudding face.

"Never, *ever* ask anyone that."

"I'm sorry," I stammer.

"Come on," he says, and I stumble after him again, toward the building with the tolling bell swinging back and forth in its tower, and the boys streaming in through the doors below.

NOW YOU'RE WAKING *up, you're feeling refreshed, like you've had a nice long sleep.*

When I blink my eyes open, it does feel like waking from a dream.

"How do you feel?" says Dr. Jellicoe.

"Okay." The shiny bowl isn't empty anymore. There's so much in there now, a hive of boys, the dirty floor of a van, a kitchen table, the long vibration of a tolling bell. Weren't there other people too? "I don't remember everything, though."

"We're just getting started," he says.

CHAPTER ELEVEN

Clare

*I*T'S ON NOW, I CAN *talk? It's recording?*
We've tested it three times. Go ahead. Start at the beginning.

I WAS BORN the youngest of eleven, the only girl, and when I emerged into the light of day I was quite unmistakably dead.

The omens hadn't been good from the start. My mother was no longer young. She'd given birth every other year for two decades, losing three in infancy along the way, and then five barren years had followed my brother Michel. She quite reasonably thought the whole business was done; she was looking forward to grand-children. Then in one terrible year, war took the two eldest boys and influenza snatched away two of the others. She'd given birth to ten children and had only three left. When she learned I was on the way she wept: another baby meant another opening of her bruised heart, a new opportunity for loss.

She didn't weep long, though. She was both devout and de-termined, believing in *God's will be done,* but also in *God helps those who help themselves.* She dried her tears and took herself to the church, made a scrupulous confession, and then wheedled the priest into blessing me where I lay bean-sized in her womb, as a sort of advance baptism to capture my prenatal soul. Then she went home and told my father.

"This time, we'll call in the doctor," he said.

"Absolutely not," said my mother. "I will not have a man in the room." Coming from a normally gentle and compliant person like my mother, her statement had the air of a royal fiat; my father did not argue. "We'll use the midwife who brought Auguste." My cousin. She added, "And you know it may not get that far." For the reality was then that not all pregnancies became babies, just as not all children lived to grow up.

Despite the odds, I grew under her mourning clothes; I provoked terrific heartburn and kicked her at night when she tried to sleep. She used to say I was more trouble to her than all the boys put together, before I ever drew a breath. Not that it looked like I was going to do anything of the sort, when after a prolonged labor I slipped into the world.

"A girl," said the midwife in an appropriately disappointed tone.

"A girl?" cried my mother, sitting up despite her exhaustion. After ten sons! She hadn't really dared to hope. She beckoned the midwife. "Bring her to me."

The midwife dried me off and flicked the bottoms of my feet. I lay pale, unmoving. Still, she was not overly worried—she had coaxed many an infant back from Limbo. She turned me over and scraped a rough towel up and down my back. She dealt my buttocks a firm slap. Nothing. She gave a *tsk*.

"What's wrong?" cried my mother.

"*Ne t'inquiète pas,*" growled the midwife. She was a stubborn woman, proud of her skill; she would not, would *not* fail, would not lose the soul of even a girl child. While my increasingly anxious mother watched, she pinched the tender flesh between my white toes and blew with her own mouth into my nostrils.

"What are you doing to her?" my mother demanded.

They were alone in the room. There had been no progress for

hours, and the sisters-in-law who had been in and out of the birthing room all day had thought it safe to leave temporarily, one going next door and the other downstairs, to feed their own families breakfast.

My mother prayed silently, watching the midwife, who'd now turned her back, and tried to guess from the movements of her elbows what was happening with me. Never more than at that moment had my mother wished for her own mother, slumbering beneath the Canadian ground more than twenty years by then.

"There's no use," said the midwife at long last, turning around. She brought the damp unmoving bundle of me over and laid me on my mother's chest. My mother stared down at my pale dead face. "It's probably best," the midwife told her. "You're far too old for a little one."

My father was drowsing just outside, in what would be called in modern homes a living room, and indeed it was the room we lived in. We gathered near the fireplace in winter and at the large table for schoolwork and meals. My father read there, and my mother did her sewing. Two of my brothers slept in that room at night. It was rarely empty, but that day my father was alone. The older boys were one in school and the other at work; Michel, the youngest, was with my father's sister on the floor below, having breakfast. Uncles had kept my father company for a while, bluff and helpless, smoking and trading stories, watching the women pass in and out of the door. At dawn they had drifted away to their own breakfasts and their jobs, leaving my father to keep the vigil by himself. He knew his role well by this time: sit and wait, for the kitten cries and the opening door, and in the meantime accept food and cups of tea conjured by the various women of the family. He would no sooner have entered the birthing chamber than he would have run naked down the street.

He came awake suddenly to the sound of my mother screaming, and though still half-asleep he understood immediately that it was not one of the expected noises of labor. He leapt to his feet, opened the door to the birthing room, and charged across the threshold. He stayed just long enough to see my mother keening over my body before he wheeled around and ran back out.

He returned in a few moments with a glass of water. My mother, clutching my corpse and wailing, struck out at him when he approached the bed.

"*Attends,*" he told her, fending her off with one arm, holding the water glass high in the other hand, out of her reach. "*Ce n'est pas pour toi.*"

He dipped his forefinger and thumb into the glass, brought them to my forehead. Telling the story later, my mother always said that at that moment, it was as though a hand came over her mouth. She couldn't make a sound as she watched him trace a wet cross on the tiny plain above my eyebrows. After my father took his dripping fingers away, there was utter silence in the room.

Then she said I went a slow dark red, like a coal when you blow on it and awaken its heart of fire. My face gathered in a bunch, and I opened up my mouth and howled. Not the kitten mewl of a newborn, but a six-month-infant holler.

My mother said it was the Holy Ghost who called me back into the world through my father's fingers, and I believed it for a time. But now I'm not sure; it might have just been the cold of the water, or the ridges on my father's fingertips against my tender new skin. It could have been the rush of air that entered the room with my father, or the power of a mother's prayer, or simple coincidence. In any case, I hollered and I lived. I had a proper christening a few months later. Which means that in the end, I'd been baptized three times: once in the womb, a second time by my father, and finally officially, in the church. My soul was pinned firmly in the care of the Lord.

WE LIVED THEN in Woonsocket, in one of those shaky three-family houses that fill New England. We were a solid block of French on the street, and all family in our building: my father's sister below, my mother's brother above. My father's brothers occupied two levels of the house next door. It was years before I knew that it amused others how we described that—we lived on top of my aunt, my uncle lived on top of us. Two houses next door to each other we called *side by each*. Not all the families in the neighborhood were French; there were scatterings of Italians and Irish in Woonsocket, even some Jews. But each group kept mostly to its own kind; that was the way things were then. The school I went to was taught by nuns, in both French and English.

We moved out of Woonsocket when I was eight. We didn't go very far—just a few miles down to Providence, to live above my father's new bookshop—but it might as well have been to a different country. Providence was much busier than Woonsocket, and it had no French community. In Woonsocket, all the shopkeepers spoke French and my brothers ran in and out of all the houses on our block as if they lived in them. In Providence, we knew none of our neighbors, and not a soul spoke French. My mother, who knew very little English, was marooned. She had to take one of us, usually me, with her to do the shopping. Such embarrassment I felt, seeing the scorn on the grocer's face as my mother plucked at my sleeve *qu'est-ce qu'il a dit?* I hate remembering how impatient I was with her.

I don't think I was really sad to leave Woonsocket; a child never understands what is being lost. I liked the new house. I had a little back bedroom on the very top floor. More like an alcove or a closet, just an extra bit of space barely big enough for a bed shoved under a dormer. I had to be careful not to sit up quickly or I'd bang my head. But through the deep-set, wavy-paned window I could see across to downtown Providence, the collection of clapboard buildings fringing the black water of the river, and the spire of the Protestant church on Westminster Street.

Our new church was around the corner from the bookshop.

It was an imposing building with a big carved wooden door and velvet curtains on the confessionals—so grand, so full of strangers, that I was surprised at how bravely my mother entered it. But as she said, Catholic is Catholic—whether French, Irish, Portuguese, or Italian—and at Mass, the Latin served everyone.

The new shop, at the foot of College Hill, would be a real bookstore. There hadn't been much walk-in custom in Woonsocket, the locals there too newly trickled into this country to waste money on books, and most of my father's income had depended on the rare books he bought and sold, pictureless volumes that looked very dull to me. Now we'd carry all sorts of books. Brown-wrapped parcels arrived every day, our new inventory. My brothers were conscripted to build shelves to hold them, and the first days in the shop were filled with the noise of sawing and hammering. Then the sanding began, generating clouds of sawdust that floated everywhere. Turning over in my bed at night, I could feel particles carving gruff messages on my skin, and when I combed out my hair, bits of wood showered my blouse. I was glad when the boys were done with that part of it and moved on to applying the dark-brown stain.

Meanwhile, my mother was setting up the living quarters, which meant lots of hot water to clean every surface. Stoking the fire in the kitchen, calling for my brothers to help her lift the huge pot, calling to me to help her scrub. I think we got up dirt that had been in those floors for fifty years. There was no school for me for a week while we cleaned the shop and the apartment and unpacked everything.

My father catalogued books long into the night; he wanted to open for business as soon as possible. On the third or fourth day after the move I woke up in the middle of the night, sat up and banged my forehead on the dormer, then slid out of bed and crept downstairs to find my father sitting at the front counter with a stack of ivory cards.

"*Chou-fleur*," he said without looking up. His nickname for me. I thought it was magical of him to know who it was without seeing, but of course I realize now there was no mystery about it. I was the only inhabitant of the house small enough to make such a light pattering on the steps and such a short shadow across the floor.

"What are you doing?" I asked, moving closer when I realized he wasn't going to send me right back to bed.

"Making labels for the shelves. They must be legible, you know this word?" I shook my head. "Easy to read, for the customers. But more," he said, rolling the thick dark bead of ink off the nib. "They have to be beautiful." He looked over his spectacles at me. "There is nothing worth doing that is not worth doing beautifully."

I nodded, vowing silently that I would always do everything beautifully, so that my father would look at me with his heart in his eyes. The way he looked at Michel when he brought home good marks from school; the way he looked at my mother every day.

He finished *Biography* with a flourish, two curling switchbacks under the word, then blotted the card and set it aside to dry.

"May I try?" I asked.

"You haven't used a fountain pen before," he said, eyebrows raised.

"I can do it, I know I can." I always got the highest mark in my class for penmanship.

He considered me for a moment, eyes narrowed and lips pursed, then smiled and patted the chair beside him. I climbed up and he slid an ivory card in front of me.

"Geography," he said, showing me the word on a bit of scrap paper. "You must keep the pen moving right through the word. Do you hear me? Do not stop. Keep the pen moving."

I curled my fingers around the cool shaft of the pen. Brought the point to the soft surface, moved it into the loop at the top of the *G*. The first letter went well, and I felt a warm spot of joy begin in my heart. I redipped the pen and tapped the extra ink from it, as

I'd seen him do a thousand times, then tackled the rest of the word: -*eogra*. He was nodding. Birds were singing in my chest. Now the difficult open European lowercase *p*, just the smallest of notches to hint at the closure, before ascending to join to the *h*. Perfect! I was thrilled to see the black cursive appearing under my hand, and the warm self-congratulatory spot spread into a sunburst: *I knew I could do it.* But alas, I sneaked a look at my father, wanting to see the approbation on his face, and for just a heartbeat, I left my hand still. When I looked back, it was to see destruction, the *y* having leaked all over the rest in a giant stain of failure.

I burst into tears. My father slipped the pen out of my hand and placed it back in the inkwell, pulled me onto his lap, and put his arms around me.

"You are my darling," he said, his beard scratching against my forehead. "And you are very good at many things. You will become good at many more. But you must avoid the sin of pride." He held me away from him so I would see his seriousness and pay attention. "You must learn humility." I nodded, the tears still falling, and he enfolded me in his arms again.

Pride goeth before destruction—was that the first time I encountered that lesson? It seems I was always being taught it, while never learning it at all. There was a mark on the counter forever after, no matter my mother's efforts with boiling water and lye.

WHEN THE SHOP was finally ready, the books went up into their places. My brothers and I made a line in front of my father, who would hand off a book with instructions—American History, Colonial Period—and we would run to put it on the appropriate shelf. Soon I didn't even have to look at the cards in their brackets in order to get a book to its correct place. That Saturday made the bookshop ours. Well, perhaps not my mother's. She stayed outside all day during the shelving, working on the patch of earth behind the shop.

In Woonsocket she'd planted herbs and vegetables in boxes on the second-floor terrace. The Providence plot was not large, but it was much bigger than those boxes. It was filled with trash and weeds when we got there, but over several weeks she turned it into a garden. She cleared the rubbish and tore out the weeds and dug out the rocks, revealing a pale, packed oblong of weak city soil; then she knelt and turned her fork into it, nourishing it with pucks of horse manure from the street.

Once she had the soil ready, she brought out the paper twists she'd carried from Woonsocket, containing seeds from previous harvests. She planted, weeded, and watered; she culled the seedlings, selecting the strongest and nurturing those, pinching pests from their leaves and feeding them with a tea she brewed from food scraps and grass clippings in a bucket in the sun. Before long, we had spring strawberries racing their runners across the ground between fat red clusters, then later peas and beans twisting their vines up the poles and melons swelling on the ground, followed by squash and winter lettuces coddled behind cold frames. At the bottom of the property stood a neglected cherry tree on which she lavished attention; two summers after the move to Providence, it stood heavy with fruit. Under her care, that small urban plot produced as well as an acre.

As the only girl, I was pressed into service as apprentice, but her skills had not come down to me. My weeding was haphazard and incomplete, my housework slapdash.

"You need to learn to manage a household," she scolded, finding me reading among the shelves I was supposed to be dusting. "You'll have to know these things when you have a husband and children."

"Maybe I don't want a husband."

"You don't want children? Don't be silly."

I supposed children might be nice, but I wasn't sure about the husband. How the two related was closely guarded information in those years.

"When I'm grown, I'm going to read all day, and no one will tell me what to do."

My mother found that very amusing.

"If that's your goal, you'll need to marry well, so you can have servants," she said. "But then your rich husband will tell you what to do. So. Up with you and back to work."

More than weeding or cleaning, I disliked cookery. I resented squandering effort on a meal that was consumed and forgotten so quickly. I schemed to avoid it. My mother couldn't tolerate waste; I used that virtue against her, making deliberate errors (salt for sugar in a pie, a spiral of yellow yolk staining egg whites intended for meringue) that produced reliable results: she'd cluck and dismiss me.

When I look back on that time it seems an idyll, marred only by weekly Confession. My friend Mariette and I used to go together on Saturday morning, discussing our sins nervously on the way: *I didn't say a swear word, but I thought one, does that count?* We fretted about transgressions that we practically had to invent in order to be forgiven for them. Trivial things: I said a bad word, I had an unkind thought, I talked back to my mother. We didn't know about sin, but we were trained to feel guilty.

My brother Michel told me stories of thin-porridge mornings and bread-and-dripping evenings from the years of his childhood, but the bookshop prospered in its new location, and I was shielded from want. The only daughter, personally invited back from death by the Holy Ghost, I was fussed over and indulged. There was no talk of my leaving school at twelve or fourteen the way my brothers had before me. I expected to sit for the entrance exams to the girls' high when that time came, and I dreamed of more:

university, a career as a scientist. Madame Curie was a woman, but she'd achieved two Nobel prizes. And as my father reminded me, she might have been born Polish, but she'd chosen to be French. The world seemed very wide.

THAT'S ENOUGH. THAT'S *enough for now.*
   You were just getting going. You sure?
   I'm sure.

CHAPTER TWELVE

Lucy

I BRING CAPTAIN UNDERPANTS BOOKS AND a foam-dart-shooting gun, a sphere made of plastic chain that expands and shrinks with a touch, things that Google told me were *good gifts for a six-year-old boy.* He doesn't seem surprised to see me; not as surprised as I am to be there, sitting cross-legged on the carpet across from him in the playroom.

Google's mostly wrong about this six-year-old boy—he wrinkles his forehead at the books and inspects the gun politely, laying it aside without aiming or shooting it. He likes the sphere, though, pulling it open and collapsing it again over and over, examining the plastic links closely, as if he'll be called upon to reproduce the item later.

"They said we could go for a walk," I say.

Actually what the nurse had said was *That would be great* in the exasperated voice of an overwhelmed mom. *Just have him back for hypnotherapy at four.*

"Hypnosis? For memory recovery?" It's been proven fraught with error: subjects can be suggestible and provoking false memory a significant risk.

"They're thinking DID."

Dissociative identity disorder, the current name for multiple personality disorder. For a while after the 1970s blockbuster *Sybil* came out, doctors were finding in every neurotic or psychotic adult a traumatized child who'd splintered off personalities in order to cope. Overdiagnosis can kill even a real disease; the pendulum has swung far the other way, and now whether DID exists at all is a matter of controversy.

"Jellicoe's taken him on as his personal patient," the nurse said. She lowered her voice. "You know how they get." She meant how doctors can behave when there's potential for publication. "Don't forget to call him Ben," she said as I went down the hall toward his room. "That's part of his treatment plan."

I sneak looks at him now as we push through the front doors of the hospital (I half expect an alarm to go off). Can I see Karen in his little-boy features? My memories of her are only a handful, really—a strong jaw and a slash of white teeth when she laughed, no perceptible makeup, and the crow's-feet just starting at the corners of her eyes. How was it that she hadn't had a husband or partner? Why had she been forced to have a child on her own? Our conversations had been mostly about work, hadn't touched on men or relationships at all. Surely they would have at some point. I feel again a sense of mourning, for the friendship we might have had.

I've never walked on these streets before, only driven through. Only a couple of miles from the historic homes on College Hill, the area's pretty bleak. Chilly sunlight glares off broken glass in the parking lots of a long strip of marginal enterprise: liquor store, check-cashing store, a windowless building with a sign saying Hot Wieners. I'm aiming for the ice cream parlor two blocks over that I've seen from the highway exit. But as we pass a scrubby-grassed little park, Ben slows down, looking through the fence. A set of swings and a slide, some children around Ben's size chasing each other, and a perimeter of benches occupied by women holding to-go cups and cell phones.

"Want to swing?" I ask.

He steps through the gate, but instead of the swings he goes toward the slide, an old-fashioned metal one with a tall flaky-painted ladder that screams tetanus. There's a short line of kids waiting at the foot of the ladder, and he joins them.

He has barely said two words to me. It's my fault, of course. I don't know what to say, or how to say it. I don't have a lot of interaction with children, apart from patients. With the children of friends or relatives, activities have always been clearly delineated and goal oriented: peekaboo, story time, diaper change.

He's anxious, I remember Karen saying. *They wanted to give him meds but I said* no fucking way. *He manages fine, as long as he knows what to expect.* He hasn't seemed particularly anxious to me, just withdrawn. Cautious. As if he's not sure whom to trust. I can only imagine what Karen would have said to the current putative diagnosis of DID. But of course if Karen were here, the point would be moot.

I talk about death all day at work, and even consider myself rather good at dealing with the subject, but I haven't been able to say anything to the boy about his mom. Is it because I knew her, or because he's a child, or because I haven't been to sleep yet, after my sixth overnight shift in a row? Maybe a combination of all those things. Maybe also without the white coat and the voice of authority, without established protocols, I'm unsure what I have to offer.

I've asked myself what I might have wanted to hear after my own mother's death. My situation had been very different: I'd been four years old, and the death had taken the form of a progressive absence, my mother getting thinner and sleeping more, then going away to the hospital, until one day there was the funeral. And I'd had continuity otherwise: my same dad and the same house, the same bedroom. Not long afterward had come a stepmother, Marybeth, with whom most of my childhood mom-memories had been made. I was left with early, fleeting fragments that might or might not have been connected to my mother—a window with a sunflower nodding below the sill, a warm hand dipping into the collar of my dress and pulling it straight, a bedsheet flung up in a laundry-fragrant bell of fabric. In my teens, tracking one of those memory pieces, I asked my dad who had made my birthday cake with the checkerboard pattern inside. I remembered the cake well, but not the mom or the party or even which birthday it had been. He'd looked stricken as he'd answered, *Your mom.* In a flash, I could see a grown-up hand pressing a biscuit-cutter into the center of a layer and lifting out a chocolate circle: *Watch now, here's the secret.* Was that a real memory? My dad's stark expression told me that more questions weren't welcome.

Had anyone even told Ben that his mother had died? I don't recall how I was told. What I do remember is the day my stepmother decided to clean out my mother's closet. It had been closed tight for two long years, and when she pulled the door open, the interior breathed out a delightful, nearly forgotten smell. Enveloping me, starting me crying, the snot flowing and filling up my nostrils so I couldn't smell it anymore, which made me cry even harder. Marybeth putting her arm around me, pulling a tissue from somewhere. *Oh honey, oh. Why don't you choose something of hers to keep?*

I hear kids yelling, and look up to see Leo—Ben—at the top of the slide. He's seated there like he's going to slide down, but he's not moving. His eyes are closed and he looks like he's going to be sick.

I've doubted the anxiety diagnosis? Well, here's proof.

"Hey," I call up to him. "Are you okay?"

He shakes his head hard *no*, and then his whole upper body ducks forward suddenly. Did someone *push* him?

"Hey! Did that kid just push you?" I look around for the mother.

The women on the benches are staring, but no one makes eye contact or offers help. One of them holds up her phone in landscape orientation, filming. Their expressions are so unengaged that it's as though we're already in a video that they're watching.

"Can you close your eyes and slide?" I call to Ben, trying for a casual, encouraging tone, but even I can hear the wheedle in it. "It's really safe. I'll catch you."

Niñera estupida, one woman says into her phone, a heatless narration to the person on the other end: I'm watching this idiot babysitter who let this little kid climb up the big slide and now he won't come down.

I'm not sure if Ben hears me pleading with him. He's got his eyes squeezed shut, frozen ten feet above the ground, and—a chorus of *eww* breaks out from the kids clustered around the bottom of the slide—so terrified that he's lost control of his bladder.

Well, this was a genius move.

CHAPTER THIRTEEN

Leo

Y OU CAN SEE A LOT from up here. There's a tangle of sticks tucked beside a window on the second floor of a building across the street—a bird's nest. I crane my neck, but I can't see any birds in it. My body lurches forward suddenly and I reach up, grab the handrails. The kid behind me has pushed me hard on the back.

"Fucking *go*," he says.

I hold the rails, resist him. I look over the side and my stomach swoops. A coldness breaks over me. It's too high, I'm going to fall. It's like I'm already falling, in midair with nothing above or below me and the wind rushing past.

"What are you waiting for?" The kid pushes me again, and my head dips forward; my jaws clack together. A burst of pain—I've bitten the side of my tongue.

"I want to go back."

"Nuh-uh," he says. "There's kids behind me. Just. Slide. Down." The last three words are thumps, his kneecap between my shoulder blades.

My eyes are closed, but I can feel the blue sky all around. Someone bangs on the slide and the metal vibrates beneath me.

"Are you okay?" Lucy's voice from below.

"I want to get down," I manage to say.

"Just let go," she says. "Just let go, and you'll slide right down."

I shake my head. Even that small movement sends a wave of panic through me: I'm going to fly off, I'm going to fall. I don't open my eyes. I just keep holding on to the rails; I grip very tight, the cold metal numbing my hands. My whole body is buzzing and light. There is a *ping* sound, a pebble on metal. Everything stops for a moment, cold terror squeezing my heart. And then— humiliation—I feel a warmth, and wetness.

"He peed on the slide!" A girl's voice.

A refrain of *eww* and *nasty*.

Oh for God's sake. The scolding from below is so brisk and bossy I don't realize at first that it's Lucy. She's not talking to me. A series of small jerks reverberates through me: the children are getting off the ladder. Now a measured *jolt-jolt-jolt* shakes the whole slide. Someone big is climbing up. The jolting stops and I hear Lucy's normal voice, very close behind me.

"Hi," she says.

"Hi," I whisper.

"Do you think you can climb down the ladder if I'm right behind you?" she says. "I won't let you fall."

A couple of minutes ago, I wanted to climb back down, but now I am frozen.

"I can't."

"Okay," she says. "Well."

The slide shakes again, and I feel a solidness on either side of me. I peek, see two legs in light green doctor pants sticking out in front of mine.

"We'll go down together," she says, her breath warm in my ear. "Is that all right? I'll hold on to you. We'll go slow."

"Okay."

She puts her arms across my chest and drags me up onto her lap, my legs straight out on top of hers.

"You're going to need to let go." Like it's no big deal, just the next thing to do, and I peel the fingers of one numb hand, then the other, free. For just a moment there's panic—I am holding on to nothing—but she puts one warm hand over both of mine, holds them tight against my tummy.

"Okay," she says. "One two three."

On *three*, we are moving, my eyes shut again. She is right, we go slow; it feels like a long time that we are squeaking and shuddering along. There's a lot of giggling from the ground. Finally we stop, and I open my eyes. We are at the bottom, the part where the slide flattens out, and there is a ring of kids staring at us.

"Good job," says Lucy. I scramble off her lap and stumble a couple of steps on wobbly legs. She stands first on one leg and then the other, shaking down the cuffs of her pants that have bunched up from sliding.

I can't believe she went down the slide. Right through my pee.

"Your pants," I tell her, pointing to wet patches on the fronts of her thighs from where I was sitting. She looks down at them and laughs.

"These scrubs have seen much worse." She talks just to me, as if no one else is here, although everyone in the park is watching. "I think we need some ice cream before we go back, what do you think?" She holds out her hand and I take it, and we walk through the parting crowd of kids.

"I don't remember the right things," I say when we're walking back with our cones. Chocolate for me, mocha chip for her. I wanted the frozen lemonade in the green stripey cup, but they don't start selling it until the first day of spring. That's next week, Lucy said, and it was almost a promise.

"Memories can be funny," she says.

"I'm *trying*."

"I know."

"What if I never remember?" I murmur it into the cold ball of ice cream.

"Well," says Lucy. "Sometimes that's how it goes. If you remember, then you remember. If not, then you just go forward."

"Why am I staying in the hospital?"

A pause, then: "They're just trying to find the right place for you to live." She stops, crouches in front of me with a napkin. I close my eyes for the rough brush of the paper. "There's chocolate *up* your nose, how did you do that."

"Why can't I go back to Clare?" Her face blooms in my mind.

"Who's Clare?" The napkin slowing down, then moving away. I open my eyes; Lucy is looking puzzled.

"I live with her. Lived." I know this is true, both *live* and *lived*. "I can go there." It's the first memory that has pulled me like a magnet, the first one I've wanted to keep. Somewhere there is a home, a place where I am loved and wanted.

"Clare who?"

"She lives on the hill near my school." I can see the stone buildings, the fields. "She'll be worried about me."

"Good to know." Lucy stands up again, her voice brisk and happy. "I'll tell them that they need to find Clare."

CHAPTER FOURTEEN

Clare

GLORIA AND I ARE ON our way to our doctors this morning, sitting next to each other in the transport van. Everyone at Oak Haven uses the same cluster of specialists. Mrs. Donovan, who has a neurology appointment, is across the aisle.

"Another Bed Bath & Beyond," Gloria comments as we jolt over the potholes on the highway. "Have you been in one of those? Just between us, *beyond* means the kitchen."

Roscommon is not ten miles from here, and yet it might as well be ten thousand; the van never takes us in that direction. I wonder if the cottage is still there, if it's occupied, and if any of the things that I left are inside. The things I'll never use again, the iron pots hanging on their hooks and the shed full of gardening tools. I like to think of them being used, but I suspect they are rust-flaked and woolly with cobweb, and that the house stands dark and empty. Eighteen years can cause a lot of ruin.

I shut the door that last day like it was any other day, without a hint of good-bye. Isn't that always the case: we never know when things are ending. I was pulling on my gloves as I went down the front steps, and almost immediately slipped and broke my hip on the icy path. It was only luck that brought the postman by an hour or so later, toiling up the hill toward the just-built clump of houses at the top, his white truck jammed with Christmas catalogs and packages, or I might still be lying there.

"This was all wilderness," says Gloria. "Remember?"

Indeed I do. Roads that used to be rude paths, that used to be nonexistent, are now orderly concrete thoroughfares populated with doughnut shops and nail salons. The Depression-abandoned factory buildings that hulked empty-eyed on the horizon for decades have now been torn down or rejuvenated into condos and offices. There are businesses that didn't exist back when I was in the world: shops for mailing packages, stores for cell phones.

I'd been chopping firewood the day before I fell, but all anyone saw in the hospital was a little old lady. The social worker who evaluated me after my hip replacement had made no secret of her surprise that I'd been living on my own. Her voice was slightly curdled with reproof, as if I ought to have packed up my things and relinquished my care to the state when I turned eighty.

The doctors' offices are in one of the converted factories, rough brick outside with the name of the mill painted in fresh white below the unused chimneys. Funny how certain words take on an undeserved cachet: this was probably a foul-smelling, deafening, asphyxiating place to work, but now Stewart Mills sounds posh.

"Industrial chic," says Gloria, as if she's reading my mind.

Inside, the building is all plastic and carpet and chopped-up spaces; from the doctors' waiting room, you can hear a dentist's drill through the thin partitioning wall.

"About the same," says my doctor, reviewing my latest ultrasound. She turns the computer monitor to show me. The first time she'd shown me an ultrasound picture, I'd expected color and, well, a picture. Now I know better. She brushes the screen with her finger, naming the structures: *here's your heart—and this is your aorta.* The image is grainy black and white and meaningless to me, but I understand the basics: that tunnel of black is a big artery, and the lakes of black are the chambers of my heart, and the mottled brightness on the shore of one of the lakes, cozying up to the wall of the tunnel, is the thing that doesn't belong.

It's not that the thing has moved; it's that my body has expanded to embrace it. About the size of my little finger, it is part of me now; it's been there much longer than my time on earth without it.

"Still no symptoms?" says the doctor. "No pain, shortness of breath, cough?" I shake my head. "Well, so far so good then."

She's made it clear, in a gentle but unflinching way, that this two-inch piece of wood will probably be the thing that takes my life. She's explained that it's embedded in the wall of the main artery coming out of my heart, and that someday, very likely without warning, the weakened vessel will burst. All my blood will spill into my chest cavity, in a few quick pumps of the heart muscle, and I will die. She's kind; she doesn't use words like *burst* or *spill*. But she couldn't quite hide her excitement the first time she found it, a restrained doctorly thrill at the oddness of it, the diagnosis of something she hadn't imagined possible. She hadn't expected anything like it, although she'd seen the scar on my chest and I'd told her the story. *You've had this in there* how *long?* she'd asked me twice after the first ultrasound. *Well, it's a bit of a miracle, isn't it.*

Everything else about me is stable too. No medication adjustments.

"You're the healthiest patient in my practice, Clare," the doctor pronounces. "If you'd never had this—event—I think you'd live forever." She knows the *event* in its barest details. "See you in six months," she says as the nurse leads me out to the waiting room.

Gloria's cranky, nearly silent, on the ride back.

"That teenager told me I'm killing myself with salt," she says, finally, when we are about a mile from Oak Haven. "It makes the fluids back up into my lungs. He said I'm drowning myself from the inside."

The bus takes the corner hard; Mrs. Donovan's walker skitters a few inches toward us across the aisle. Gloria puts a hand out to stop it as the vehicle straightens out.

"Is it too much to ask that the person telling me I'm going to die have one gray hair on his head?" She answers herself. "I don't think so."

We pass another doughnut shop, with its orange and pink sign. We have two more of them to pass before we reach Oak Haven. I tried one of their glazed doughnuts once; it had a pretty good taste, but was full of air and made the inside of my mouth slick, as though I had sucked on a spoonful of lard. But the Oak Haven staff can't get enough of these doughnuts; there is always an open box in the common room.

"What does he expect me to do?" Gloria demands. "Throw away perfectly good food?" She's had sausage at every breakfast in the last week, sneaking it in and dropping it onto her cardiac diet plate of scrambled egg whites.

"Well, maybe you could eat just a little at a time," I suggest. "Sausage keeps."

"I try." She is close to tears. "But it reminds me of home."

I know all about things that remind you of home, and the longing for them. I pass her a tissue from the folded mass of them I keep in the cuff of my sleeve.

"Drowning from the inside," she says, removing her glasses. "What a thing to say." I take the glasses from her lap before they slide off, and hold them while she blots her eyes. "What did your doctor say?" she asks, muffled, into the tissue.

I haven't told Gloria about the splinter, and we haven't gotten to *the event* in my oral history.

"No change." I see she is fumbling on her lap for her glasses, and hand them to her. "I'm just really old." She snuffles a laugh.

Is it worse or better that I'm not coasting down the long hill toward the end of life but instead could flick off like a light switch and die at any minute? I could go in the middle of a conversation.

Probably better for me, worse for anyone who might be with me when that happens. Or for anyone who is aware it might happen: that foreknowledge would be an unpleasant burden to confer on another person. I'm not sure I'll tell Gloria that part at all.

WHERE DID I *leave off?*

You were preparing for the high school entrance exams. You wanted to be Marie Curie.

Ah yes.

THE YEAR I turned ten, the country plunged into a dark tunnel. The Great Depression. Rhode Island had been sliding into it for a while—a mill closing here, a factory shutting down there—but when the real collapse came it was all at once and it was terrifying. Businesses of all kinds closed in a great rush, and day by day everything and everyone looked a little poorer, a little shabbier. Even with the four boys lost the year before I was born and the three that stayed babies in the stiff brown photographs on the mantel, that left two brothers and their wives and children, Michel, my parents, and me. A lot of mouths to feed. No one had an extra penny, and what pennies there were did not get spent on books. After a year or so of hanging on and spending savings, my father had to shutter the shop, and for the first time in my memory, he went out to work. He stayed away all day and came home dirty and taciturn.

In this bleak era my mother's garden stopped being an indulgence. She'd always reaped huge harvests that far exceeded what even our large family could consume, and what she didn't cook or give away she'd bottled, against my father's protests at the prospect of what steam might do to the books. She simply opened the kitchen windows to let out the clouds of vapor, and each harvest added more rows of jars to the crude shelves along the walls in the basement. They stood a dozen deep on the wood, and then when the shelves were full, lined up below them, a friendly battalion along the cool earthen floor.

I can see now that it was a gift driven by sorrow. Thrust into a strange place surrounded by a language she did not know, she'd poured her grief and loneliness into that bit of ground, anointed it with her magic tea and transformed her sadness into bounty. And then when the world collapsed, my mother's garden saved us. My brothers dug clams at the shore, and joined other men and boys fishing the river, but still some days we ate only from the cellar. We were humbled by the Depression, but we would not starve.

IT'S ODD THE things I remember, while so much else has slipped away. The dim jewel glow of the jars in the dark cellar. The shape of my father's boots, cracked softly over the arch, where he used to leave them just inside the door. The cobbled street that ran in front of the bookshop, the stone domes washed by rain into a gleaming pattern. The cloud of lint rising from my brother Michel's sweater as he pulled it off over his head, home from a long day at the mill. The bone-deep misery of cold from winter days and nights without wood or coal. That particular memory not so random. The body doesn't forget cold like that.

INTO THAT LONG tunnel went my girlhood. Went all of us, trudging forward without knowing when it would end, if it would end. My father's clean, soft hands hardened, collected and kept dirt under the fingernails, and all of us grew thinner and our clothes more threadbare, mendings done over previous mendings until the garments were as much darning thread as fabric. I stayed in school as long as I could, longer than I should have, until shame drove me away. What had seemed important before—my mother's worries about my headstrong nature and my chances of marrying well, my own dreams of scientific discovery and academic glory—was meaningless in this new gray world. There could be no plan, no future. There was just today, and then the next today, and the next, like a string of dirty beads.

It seemed that one morning I was parsing sentences and the next I was at the bobbin scramble in front of the mill, crowding with the hopeful hordes as the foreman threw handfuls of hard cardboard bobbin tubes into the air. If you were lucky enough to grab one, and if the one you got had a paper curled inside with an X on it, that meant you worked that week. When the foreman began tossing, the crowd erupted. Boys dove and fought for the tubes. I was tall and caught one in midair; it was slapped out of my hand. I went home empty-handed from the first scramble, but rarely again after that.

I started as a doffer, replacing bobbins on the spinning frame, quick enough at that to be hired on as a regular. Weave room work paid a higher wage, but that was a lofty goal: grown women worked there, not girls. But one morning as we streamed into the mill, a foreman pointed to me and waved his arm toward the weaving-room doorway. I looked around and didn't move—he couldn't mean me. I was fourteen, had been there only a few months. I couldn't see his expression behind the kerchief he wore over his lower face to keep from breathing the lint. He waved his arm again in a more emphatic arc: he did mean me. A current of grumbling broke out, audible even over the machines that had started up. *Don't mind them,* said one of the back-boys as I passed. *They're jealous is all.*

I was by far the youngest in the weaving room. The women didn't greet me; the one who trained me demonstrated once, speaking rapidly without meeting my eyes, and then left me there. *Old biddies,* said the quill boy who'd been watching. He took the shuttle from me: *Just push this out like so, push in a full one, hold here hold, now break it off and get the other ready.* Although he could have been fired or docked for it, he stood with me and showed me the timing, until I could do it myself. Then he winked *keep your eye out* and ran to pull a quill from the loom beside me.

From then on I worked in the *clackita-clackita-clackita* roar of the machines, you can't imagine how loud, turning between the two looms assigned to me, watching the shuttle, mist showering down from pipes above to dampen the lint. A workday lasted all day, fourteen hours, and it was mindless, thoughtless work. It needed to be: the body did the work, and a thought could impair the rhythm. A dropped stitch or *smash* would mean the fabric would be classed as a second, which paid half as much as a first.

When a group of weavers took a meal break they huddled together, gossiping and laughing; they did not look at or talk to me. Some of my old schoolmates worked in the spinning room, but they were cool to me now that I was a weaver. I began taking my shift break outside the back of the mill, on a tiny exterior staircase there. I would sit on the landing with an apple and a book. Many days there was no apple. I often found myself staring out over the open pages of my book, not reading or thinking, watching the traffic move along the streets while the sound of the mill thrummed through me.

A year of that, and then another. I was no longer the bookseller's cherished daughter, snatched back from death by the Holy Ghost for an important purpose in the world. My father was a laborer, laying stones in Roger Williams Park for the Works Progress Administration. My oldest brothers had joined a CCC camp in Indiana. Michel and I were millworkers, working and sleeping, nothing more. I turned sixteen without celebration, another workday.

Walkouts and strikes were sweeping the nation that year, a froth of violence starting in the Deep South and roiling toward us. Many workers wanted a strike at our mill too. Michel was one of them. His voice floats to me across the years: *We have to take what we need, instead of waiting for it to be given.* And my father's answer: *When you have children to feed, you don't have the luxury of ideals.*

We leave shadows of ourselves in the places where we change. I left a girl in the classroom, and another with her chin on her hands, gazing over downtown Providence from the dormer window. Another thin ghost stands in the mill, blinking in the fall of lint. They're all with me still, an abandoned regiment flickering separately in the back of my mind, as if I am still living all those lives at once. They won't die until I do. Or maybe they never will. Maybe the places they inhabit are their own, in a timeless void sealed away from me and from each other, where they go on forever.

THE MILL MIGHT have been the end of my story, the place I stayed for twenty or thirty or forty years, breathing in the killing, choking fibers, before the coughing started. But that's not what happened.

ONE SUNDAY AFTER Mass, I was passing the upstairs window above the bookshop and happened to spy a man standing across the street. Just standing, staring at the shop. Tall and healthy looking, in a wool jacket buttoned up to a bright blue knot of necktie, a parcel under one arm. He stared for another minute before seeming to come to a decision. As he stepped off the curbstone I moved closer to the window, looking straight down through the glass as he climbed our step and became a foreshortened cap with children clustered around below, calling up to him, *Mister, hey, mister, you got a nickel? Whatta you doing here, mister?* The cap moved and fingers ran over a blond head, then the cap was replaced. Finally, the bell rang.

I heard my mother shooing my nieces and nephews into the back room, then calling up to me. "Coming," I answered, but I stayed at the window, watching the cap pulled away again from the blond head, tilted to speak down into the opening door and my mother's no doubt baffled face. Then the blond head disappeared and my mother called up to me again. I went down the back stairway and through the long bookshelves to the front of the store, where the man was standing, holding his cap.

"There you are," he said, seeing me.

My mother's eyes communicated a flurry of messages: *Manners,* and *What have you done to bring this enormous American to our door* and *Your hair!* I put a hand up to my head, feeling the flyaway strands, too many to conquer without a mirror.

"Do I know you?" I said.

He frowned, and then turned to my mother, who was wearing the neutral pretending-to-understand expression that she adopted during conversations in English.

"May I?" he asked, gesturing. She gave him the cloth she was holding, and he held it up across the lower part of his face. "Now do you know me?"

Yes, of course, it was the shift foreman from the mill.

"I'm sorry to disturb you at home," he said, taking the cloth down. "I wanted to let you know that you probably shouldn't come to work tomorrow."

"You're firing me?"

"No, no. There's a rumor." He leaned forward, whispered it: *strike.* "You heard about Saylesville." Of course I had—the National Guard called in, shooting into the unarmed crowd, four dead. "I have reason to believe . . . it won't be safe tomorrow."

My mother was watching, her eyes darting to mine and back to him: *What is he saying?*

"All right," I said. "Thank you." I reached out, took the cloth from him. Ignoring the soundless push from my mother *Why haven't you offered him tea?*

"Well, I won't keep you," he said, going through the door.

From the doorway, I called, "Are you visiting all of the workers at home today?"

He turned at the bottom of the steps. "No," he said. Waited a beat, long enough for me to notice that his eyes were exactly the same shade of blue as his necktie. Then he turned again and walked away.

"How does he know you?" cried my mother when I shut the door. "Why were you so rude to him?"

"He's one of the foremen at the mill," I told her, watching through the front window as he crossed the street, his collar turned up against the wind.

"What did he want?"

"He said that the weaving room will be closed tomorrow." A lie to tell the priest next week.

"He came all the way here to tell you that?" She looked at the place where he'd stood, then back at me. "*Bien sûr.*"

OH, THIS IS *a love story, isn't it?*
   Shush. I'm not finished.

HIS NAME WAS Hugh. He'd been right about the strike; it began the next afternoon, and the response was violent, one worker killed and a dozen others injured.

The following Sunday after Mass, the doorbell chimed. My mother caught my arm as I went toward the stairs. She touched my hair, pushing a stray bit back into its wave. "Ask him to stay for lunch," she said.

"I don't want to encourage him, *Maman.*"

"Why not? He's handsome, and so young to be a foreman. Is he not Catholic?"

"He's a boss."

"So?"

"Michel and I are workers." Michel had gone to work on the

day of the strike, although I'd warned him, but he'd escaped injury. He'd been on the picket line every day since.

"*Tssst.*" A dismissive noise. "*La grève*, it's nothing. It's between men. The heart is important. The heart is women's business." *Le coeur, c'est l'affaire des femmes.* "Ask him to stay for lunch."

Hugh handled himself well at the table, discussing general news with my father, avoiding controversial topics, and speaking slowly enough, without being obvious about it, so that my mother could follow. I didn't say much. He chewed my mother's bread (a week's worth of flour for that loaf!) with appreciation.

"Tell him you made the fish stew," my mother urged me.

"I will." While she smiled, I told Hugh quickly, so she would not understand, "My brother and father dug those clams at the shore."

"Point Judith Pond?" said Hugh. "I do some fishing myself."

My father brightened; fishing, although it was a necessity more than a pastime these days, provided him great satisfaction.

"Have you tried the shallows at Rocky Point?" he asked, leaning forward. And they were off, discussing their favorite spots for clams, for scup, for bass.

"I THOUGHT WE'D have more time," said my father after Hugh had left and my mother and I were clearing the table. "She's just sixteen."

"I was sixteen when we married," said my mother.

"Chou-fleur, if Hugh speaks to me, what would you have me say?"

"Why would he speak to you?" I asked, taking up the soup tureen. It had been scraped empty, not even a spoonful left. "He barely knows me."

"He has the look," said my mother. "He'll ask."

"Do you not like him?" asked my father.

"There's nothing wrong with him," said my mother.

No, there was nothing wrong with Hugh. He was both pleasant and pleasant to look at. Why then did I feel so cornered?

"He won't like it when he finds out about Michel," I said.

My mother went quiet for a minute, wiping down the long table.

"You won't tell him about Michel yet," she pronounced. "Once he's in love with you, he won't care."

"MY BROTHER IS one of the ones who started the strike," I told Hugh at the next opportunity. He'd invited me for an afternoon walk.

"The mouse speaks." He smiled. "I know about Michel." And at my look of surprise, "Before I was made foreman I was a worker. I know the stretch-outs are onerous, and the hours are long. But the wartime demand has dried up, and the mill is struggling to stay open. It can't give all the things the strikers want. All it can give is work. Hard work, I know, but it's work."

"If everyone strikes, we would win."

He raised his eyebrows at the *we*.

"If everyone strikes, everyone will starve," he said. "There are plenty who walk over the picket lines now for the jobs." He tucked my hand a little more tightly under his arm. "You're an idealist, and I'm a realist. Which makes us a good pair."

As he spoke, I realized that somewhere inside me, I'd cherished a fantasy: that someday, somehow, time might loop back on itself and deposit me where I'd left off, a girl on the cusp of high school and college and the future. I'd sent a mannequin, a husk, to the mill, while my real self had curled up inside, waiting. For something that could never happen.

The reality was that I would need to marry. I didn't want the life of a spinster, gathering whispers and smirks as I aged, suffering pitying looks at christenings and confirmations. If I waited too long, my best hope would be a grizzled widower who might have me to raise his brood.

"You're so quiet," said Hugh approvingly.

The girl who arrived home that day was not the one who'd left. I let myself into the bookshop, walked between the shelves that my brothers had built, half empty now and dusty, the calligraphed cards faded and soft with age. I stepped over the bedrolls near the back stairs where some of the cousins slept. The beloved bookshop of my childhood was a shabby place. I would not finish school, or be a scientist, or travel the world.

"Good, you're back," said my mother when I came into the kitchen. "Start the fire, please."

"Was it a nice walk?" asked my father.

We'd lately been burning a copy of collected Shakespeare. I ripped the first act from *Othello* and fed the brittle onionskin pages into the stove. A line of typeface brightened against its paper backdrop—*Let heaven and men and devils, let them all*—before blackening with the rest.

"If Hugh does ask," I said, feeling my mother tense, waiting for my answer, "you may tell him yes."

CHAPTER FIFTEEN

Lucy

WHEN I AWAKE FROM MY day's sleep, Giles has sent me a Google Maps dropped pin and a peremptory text: Dinner 7 p.m. It's six now, five hours until my shift. I hate last-minute plans. *You need to be more spontaneous* I hear in Joe's voice, and my retort: *I get all the spontaneity I need at work.* I send a thumbs-up emoji and then, with a sense of anticipation that surprises me, I shower, dress, and navigate toward the gray teardrop on the GPS screen. Driving past the electrical plant painting its reflection onto the dark, still water beside the hurricane barrier, then turning onto the cobbled streets of Downcity. When I get there, it turns out to be one of the quirky eateries that spring up all around the city each year as the culinary school sporulates another crop of graduates. They settle in widening circles: the arty blocks around Rhode Island School of Design, the gentrifying Jewelry District, the still-edgy West End. Even Elmwood, the neighborhood that provides most of our gunshots and stabbings, now has spots of haute cuisine.

A listless waiter with gauges in his earlobes and a plump samurai topknot takes our orders, brings seltzer for me and a vodka tonic for Giles.

"All right, you." Giles pokes a straw into his glass, freeing a cataract of clinging bubbles from the floating lime wedge. "What have you heard from Bad Hubby?"

"A text about pasta."

"Meaning?"

"No subtext, just text. Pasta."

"What an ass."

"He was always quiet," I say.

"Like you," says Giles, surprising me. My real friends would never describe me that way. "Okay, let's talk stalking. Does he Instagram or Snapchat?" He makes a moue. "Facebook?"

"He doesn't use social media."

"Not old enough for Facebook, not young enough for anything else." Giles takes a spray of fries from his plate. "Part of the Lost Generation."

"We're the same generation," I point out. Giles is the same age as I am.

"Only chronologically. Singlehood keeps one fresh." He doesn't add *You'll see.*

"Enough about Joe," I say. "I need a consult." Giles raises his eyebrows and I tell him about Ben. "So what do you think? Is DID even a thing anymore? Is hypnosis considered a viable treatment?"

"Dr. Jellicoe is well respected," Giles says with professional caution. "And I'm not a child psychiatrist." He takes a bite of hamburger, speaks around it. "That said, it does seem rather a reach."

"He's totally alone in the world." The boy's rumpled brow, his earnest voice: *I'm trying.* "I feel like he needs my help." It sounds so stupid, I wince hearing myself say it, but Giles nods.

"He does. They all need our help. Helping doesn't always mean fixing, though."

"Tell that to an ER doc."

We move on to talk about other, lighter things, a book we've both read and enjoyed, a movie he recommends. The conversation migrates naturally. He's talking about his most recent boyfriend when I look at my watch: nine thirty. My shift begins in ninety minutes. The thought brings the anxiety buzzing back, like a swarm of gnats: *get ready.*

Giles drains his almost-empty drink, the ice cubes sliding in a rattling clump against his lip and then rattling back down again when he sets the glass on the table. He puts an index finger up to signal for another.

"The night is young," he says. He scans the throng at the bar at the front of the room, lifts an eyebrow. "Who knows where it will end."

He is truly single, not faux single the way I am. When I was last single, people actually went on dates before having sex, not the other way around, and monogamy was presumed. A moment of vertigo: Am I really going to be entering this world?

When we get up to leave, Giles kisses me on the cheek with a pleasant breath of lime. He takes my chin between his thumb and forefinger, waggles it. *Chin up.*

CHAPTER SIXTEEN

Leo

I'VE SORTED IT OUT NOW, during the hours of chores, during the long Latin prayers in chapel. This must be Clyde's doing. He's told them lies about me, told them I need punishment. The monks would believe him, a grown man; he can be charming when he wants. I remember liking him myself, a long time ago. One thing I am certain about: my mother must not know where I am, or she would have come for me. The van ride wasn't that long. It feels strange to know that home is so close. She must be worried; does she believe I've run away?

I have learned a lot in ten days: how to grip the rubbery teat and roll my fingers down without pulling, until the milk jets into the pail with a tinny ring. How to dress quickly in the dark, how to eat fast before someone spits on my plate or grabs it away. The chapel bell makes the rhythm of life here; it goes nine times a day. Six of those are for the monks only. The other three times the bell is for everyone, and we all automatically stop what we are doing and walk toward it. I don't know what the Latin means, but I learn the responses. Murmuring them in the candlelit chapel, I am thinking a different prayer: *find me*.

By now, I know that *stalls* means mucking out the spaces where the cows stand at night dropping their filth, and that it is a pun-

ishment. I know what a *runner* is, and that Bedrick is one. I know
what a *toad* is, and that I am one. Being a toad means I have to
withstand all kinds of pranks, short sheets in my bed and piss on
my pillow. This morning my toothbrush bristles were stiff with
soap. I don't know specifically who does these things, but it doesn't
matter. I know that whoever it is will tire of it in time, just the way
my stepfather's rages played themselves out if I didn't fight back.
Besides, I won't be here long. I *can't* be.

Seven years, Gregory had said. But maybe he has nowhere else
to go.

"Really applying yourself," says Brother Thomas with approval
as I empty another foamy pail into the funnel-topped metal can
at the end of the barn.

"Suck-up," says Bedrick when Thomas has gone. He shovels a
fragrant load onto my shoe. He's still on stalls, which means I see
him every day.

The first few days I fell asleep immediately, black nothing between lights-out and the morning clamor, but in the week since then
I've had some time in the dark before unconsciousness overtakes
me. Lying awake and listening to the sounds of the monks going
to and from Compline, I've made a plan. Milking will be the best
time, just two or three of us in the large barn, in the dark before
dawn. Brother Thomas will leave as he always does before the bell,
to see to the boys who are feeding the hogs and the sheep.

When Thomas leaves this morning, I whisper, "Bedrick."

"Don't talk to me, toad."

He hates me. He says it is because I am weak, because I am
stupid. But I think it has more to do with my having seen tears on
his face when we were in the van.

Still, he is my best hope. He's the only runner I know.

"I'm leaving," I whisper. "Today. Do you want to come with me?"

He stops his shoveling, turns, and looks at me.

"Where you planning to go?"

"Home," I say. "My mother—"

His features thicken with scorn. "Your mother doesn't want you." He turns away again and pushes the shovel into the heap of dung. "You wouldn't be here if she did."

"She doesn't know I'm here. My stepfather—"

"For Christ's sake, shut up. I don't care." He heaves another shovelful toward me; I jump my feet apart, so that it mostly misses.

I abandon the hope of getting help from him; I am on my own.

This is what I do: at the bell's toll, I stumble purposely and kick over the bucket, bend to right it as the other boys make their way past me out of the barn. I go through a minute after they do, but simply turn the other way, push through the bushes and into the forest, aiming blindly toward the gravel path that we drove up when I came here. Ten minutes' fast walking and I feel the gravel crunch under my feet. I am in the open now, and in the rosy-gray light I can see houses far down the hill: the outskirts of Waite.

How long will it take to miss me? The milking barn is the farthest building from the chapel; slow milkers sometimes come late (once means a missed meal, twice gets a whipping). Matins and then breakfast are both just a jumble of boys, no one taking attendance. So I may have until the beginning of morning lessons, a good hour and a half at least. I head down the hill in the breaking dawn.

The town is just waking up, storekeepers unlocking their doors and turning placards from Closed to Open. The school uniform feels like my own conspicuous sign: Runaway. My heart thumps whenever I pass anyone on the sidewalk, expecting the hand on my shoulder. But their glances brush over me without interest. I pass the diner as a man pushes the door open to go in; an aroma of bacon wafts out. My mouth waters.

We live off the main road, two turns and then straight for three blocks. I stand at the corner of our street, looking toward the house. Clyde's probably in there. They're probably all in there: it's too early for work, too early for school. The door opens and I freeze, but it's my mother, getting the morning newspaper. She doesn't look up, just takes the paper from the step and shuts the door. I go down the sidewalk and then around to the back of the house, to the kitchen with its mullion-paned back door.

She's there, spooning coffee into the percolator. He must be home; she wouldn't make a pot just for herself.

"Mama," I say, but it is too soft and she doesn't hear me. I tap on the glass, two sharp tinks. She startles and looks up; her eyes widen. She comes to the door and out onto the back step, and shuts the door quietly behind her.

"What are you doing here?"

No *Leo, thank God you're all right.* No *Leo, where have you been?*

"He sent me to prison," I say.

"It's a school, not a prison."

This is a shock: She has known where I am?

"I don't want to be there," I say. "Why did you let him send me? Why didn't you come to get me?"

"Leo," she says. "*I* sent you there."

"Why?" I say when I can manage words.

"Are they feeding you? What is that smell?"

"Cows. Mama, I don't belong there. I haven't done anything wrong."

"It's not just a place for bad boys." She is earnest. "It's a good school."

"But I don't want to be there," I say.

"You'd rather be here?" She sounds really surprised. I don't even have the words for *yes,* but she sees it in my face. "Well, we can't always have what we want."

It's something I've heard her say before to Tad or Sally when they ask for a toy. She never said it to me that I can recall. Then again, I've rarely asked for anything.

"Are you hungry?" she asks, and I nod. "Wait here."

She slips inside. I sit down on the back step, and a few minutes later she comes out again with a sandwich and a glass of milk.

"You don't know how much better it is now," she says, watching me eat. Her voice sounds like pleading. "A whole week with no fights, no shouting."

"I don't shout," I say, my mouth full. But I know she means Clyde isn't shouting. I'm not there to shout at. I swallow. "Why can't *he* leave?"

She lifts a corner of her apron, dabs milk away from my upper lip. "I have Tad and Sally to think of. You're strong, Leo; they're little."

"He wouldn't hurt them."

"They need peace. We all do. You too."

"Why does he hate me?" I don't mean it to sound as babyish as it comes out.

She takes a big breath in, blows it out again. "It's not you. Not really. It's just—you remind him that he wasn't the first man in my life." That's stupid; my father is dead, no threat at all to Clyde. "Anyway, he's got a job now. You know he's happier when he's working."

"I don't remember that far back," I say coldly.

"If we can just get ahead of the bills. Maybe by Christmas."

"Christmas." It's May; Christmas is impossibly far away.

"It isn't so bad there, is it?" She is imploring. "You can bear it for a while?"

My throat is sore from what feels like a big ball of tears gathering there. I choke down the last of the sandwich and nod, my eyes on the ground.

"Good boy. Finish your milk and I'll walk with you as far as the grocer. I'll tell Clyde I had to go out for eggs."

Before we leave, she takes four eggs from the icebox to make her lie true, and drops them as we walk through the morning. One by one, they smash softly into the grass, the orange yolks sliding out like ruined suns.

CHAPTER SEVENTEEN

Clare

HUGH AND I MARRIED IN the Woonsocket church of my child-hood, the pews filled with faces from the old neighborhood. Everything was smaller and more drab than I remembered, except my mother, who was more animated than I'd ever seen her, every-where after the Mass, talking, joking. I hadn't heard her laugh so much since I was a child. On the church lawn, my parents kissed me. "Be a good girl," my father said.

And then Hugh and I went home, to the second floor of a triple-decker frame house on one of the short streets off Hope, no more than a mile and a half from the bookshop. And I was suddenly a wife.

Which meant all of the things my mother had always said: cleaning and cooking. Laundry and mending. Keeping a budget. All the skills I had resisted as boring and pointless. They were boring, but I could see their purpose now: to create a home. The quiet— no factory machines, no lint—was almost like a paradise. We had small luxuries: an occasional evening concert or a moving picture in the gorgeous theater on Weybosset, and we had our own radio. I didn't play it while Hugh was at work—I couldn't get enough silence at first—but he liked to listen after supper, and I began to enjoy it. Radio was not as overwhelming as moving pictures; you could make the faces up in your mind.

There wasn't the love that I'd always expected to be a part of marriage from watching the tenderness between my parents, but as the quiet days passed and slowly the girl I'd been uncurled within me, I felt a growing affection for Hugh. Maybe love would come.

We had friends, an American couple from the first floor who came up to supper once or twice a week, or we went downstairs to them. "Hugh said you were pretty, but he didn't mention how tall," the wife, Mary Johnson, told me when we first met. She was a petite thing with tiny hands and feet.

The Johnsons came up to listen to the radio with us some evenings, leaving their children sleeping on the floor below and staying late for *One Man's Family* or *Kraft Music Hall*. One night when the program was over, I got up to serve cake and tea.

"Turn it off," said Hugh as I passed the radio.

"It's a quiz show!" cried Mrs. Johnson. "The newest thing. Let's listen?"

Hugh nodded, and I took my hand away from the knob and went to the kitchen.

While I served the tea, the announcer explained: a panel of experts would answer questions sent in by ordinary people. Two dollars for any questioner whose submission was read on the air, five dollars if the experts failed to answer correctly.

"Five dollars!" said Mr. Johnson, accepting a large slice of cake. "They had better be experts or they'll bankrupt the radio station."

Would it be possible to know, after having felled a tree in a forest, whether there was a good alfalfa harvest back in 1911?

"What in the world?" said Mrs. Johnson, putting a lump of sugar in her tea.

"The rings of the tree stump." Bringing my own cup from the tray and taking the chair beside her. "A dry season makes a narrow ring."

"What an odd thing to know," she said after we'd listened to the science expert explain it.

Who had two vast and trunkless legs of stone?

"Ozymandias," I said.

I thought that silly—hadn't everyone memorized Shelley's poem in elementary school?—but the Johnsons were impressed.

"You should submit a question," said Mary. "You could get two dollars."

"Can you answer the next one?" asked her husband.

If the North Star was suddenly snuffed out, how much time would elapse before its absence would be noted in the night sky?

They all sat silent, watching me as I considered.

"Perhaps fifty years," I said.

Many thousands of years, said the panel expert.

"That one caught you," said Hugh, and there was pleasure in his voice.

"Not thousands!" I said with a laugh.

You're off by a little, said the announcer. He was laughing too. *Light from the North Star travels for forty-five years to reach Earth.*

"You're amazing!" cried Mary. "Hugh, did you ever know your wife was so smart?"

"Perhaps our guests would like more tea," Hugh said. His lips were thin and pressed together, his eyes like blue stones in his face. I noticed with shame that Mary's cup was nearly empty, and I jumped up to retrieve the pot.

After the Johnsons left, Hugh didn't say a word while I cleared the table. He followed me into the kitchen and watched me scraping the dishes. I'd made a cheese soufflé, and there was a little bit left.

"Do you think this will keep?" I asked him, showing him the portion. "It seems a shame to waste it."

"Why ask me?" he said. "I don't know anything."

"What?" I put the ramekin down, reached for a wooden spoon.

I'd keep the remainder for lunch tomorrow. "What's the matter, Hugh?"

"You should know." His voice sarcastic. "You know everything."

"What in the world. Are you upset? About that quiz show?"

"You embarrassed yourself." A hiss. "Showing off like that."

"They just happened to ask some questions that I happened to be able to answer." Using the spoon to lever the soufflé away from the scalloped wall of the dish, trying to get it out in one piece. "*You're* the one who's embarrassed. I can't imagine why."

At that he took the soufflé dish from the counter with both hands, knocking my spoon away, and dropped it from chest height onto the floor. It had been my grandmother's, one of the few things I had brought to the household. It shattered into pieces, spraying bits of egg and pottery everywhere.

"That'll need to be cleaned up," he said.

I stood there for a minute, utterly blank. What had just happened?

"Clean that up," he repeated.

I got the broom and pan from behind the door. Under his eye I swept up the damp clumps of cold soufflé and the fragments of dish, and dropped everything into the bin in a tinkling rush. The sweeping made smears across the clean floor; I leaned the broom against the wall and filled a bucket, then knelt with a cloth, feeling my legs shaking as I did. Who was this person standing over me? I'd seen him angry before, but never like this, never at me. I was his *darling mouse,* his *sweet mouse,* his *prettiest girl.* Invisible slivers of china needled my hands when I wrung out the cloth into the bucket, and my blood tinted the water.

He watched me for a while, tapping his cigar ash a couple of times onto the damp surface so I had to wipe again. I kept my head down. Finally, the floorboards shifted under his weight and his shadow moved away, his footsteps going out of the room and down the hall. When I heard the front door open and close, I

sat back on my heels and waited for the shake of the house from
the downstairs entry door. After I heard that, I dropped the cloth
into the bucket, untied my apron, and lifted its loop from around
my neck.

I got as far as the sidewalk, rehearsing how it would go. *He
broke Nana Cirette's dish,* I would tell my mother, and she would
put her arms around me. She would summon my father, and—I
stopped short. I could see their disappointed faces in my mind.
What did you expect, chou-fleur, my father would say. *What have I
told you about pride?* And my mother: *all couples argue; you don't
make a marriage in a day.*

Like a flash I saw the evening as if it were a moving picture playing before me; I heard my own smug voice giving the answers, saw
my pleased expression as I basked in the Johnsons' astonishment. I
had been showing off. Apparently, the girl who had uncurled from
her slumber inside the mill drudge was a conceited know-it-all.

A force turned me around on the sidewalk then; it pushed me
back through the front door and up the steps to the apartment.
The bucket stood in the middle of the floor of the kitchen, dumb
witness. I donned the apron and tied it behind me, tipped the
bucket out into the sink and filled it again, knelt and cleaned the
kitchen floor meticulously. Then I washed the dishes and dried
them and put them away and moved the chairs back to the table
from their semicircle around the radio. Methodically returning the
apartment to the way it had been before supper, as if unmaking
the evening.

Hugh came in very late. I pretended to be sleeping but lay awake
all night at the very edge of the mattress; in the morning, I was
grainy-eyed with fatigue.

"I'm sorry," I told him as he was eating breakfast. "I didn't mean
to be a know-it-all."

He nodded. "I know you didn't." Then: "I just want my little
mouse back."

I kept my eyes down, accepting his kiss.

Was that the bargain we'd made? I would stay timid, and Hugh would be gallant and protective? I wondered about the wives in the couples we knew. Did their marriages involve similar pacts? Conversation, even when we were "just girls" without our husbands, touched only lightly on the difficulties of domestic life, and usually in a humorous way. *But are you happy?* I wanted to ask. *Does he actually like you?* I imagined their heads turning to me: in puzzlement, or in relief, or in disgust.

A year into my marriage, I ventured back to Woonsocket, to the old church, where I unburdened myself to the now-ancient priest, the one who'd baptized me twice. He listened as I said what I hadn't told anyone: *I think my husband hates me.*

"Does he strike you?" he asked after a wheeze-filled, contemplative pause.

"No." There hadn't been any actual blows. "But—he speaks unkindly."

"Are you not willing? That can sour a man's disposition."

Blushing. "It's sometimes painful, Father."

"You've been more than a year together. You're not—*taking steps?*"

No, I told him once I understood his meaning, I wasn't doing anything to avoid having a baby. I wouldn't even know the first thing about that.

"Good." He cleared his throat. The sound that had always signaled the conclusion of confession; he was ready to absolve my sins and prescribe penance. "My child," he said. "I have known you since you were born."

My shame began to ebb as I waited to hear the rest: *You should be honest, be yourself, don't be afraid, the Lord will help you learn to love each other.*

"I always suspected you'd be a challenge to your husband," he said.

It was as if I'd opened my mouth for the Host, eyes closed and trusting, and instead a stream of scalding water had been poured onto my tongue. The shock of it made me mute.

"You were always selfish. And proud." His voice stern. "A man marries to gain a helpmeet, to give him comfort and children. He goes out into the world, and he comes back weary. Are you a comfort? Is your home a respite for him?"

"But, Father." When I could manage words. "I'm not happy."

His laughter purred behind the screen. "Happiness is something that children want. You are a grown woman now. You are a wife."

"He doesn't love me, Father," I whispered.

Did he not hear it, or did he simply dismiss it?

"He must be anxious for children. God grant him patience, and may He bless your union soon." A shadow moved across the oblong of latticed light falling into the confessional booth as he lifted his hand to the screen. "I absolve you from your sins in the name of the Father, and of the Son, and of the Holy Spirit. Give thanks to the Lord, for He is good."

"His mercy endures forever," I responded automatically.

"You must turn your heart away from selfish concerns. Pray to Saint Anthony of Padua for humility, and for the strength to be a good wife."

The door slid shut.

He was right. I could be arrogant and selfish and impatient; I wasn't willing in the bedroom. Hugh wasn't violent; he kept me fed and clothed and safe. Shouldn't that be enough? A tiny voice inside me protested: *no.* But of course that selfish voice was proof of all that the priest had said. For the first time in my life, I left the confessional more burdened than when I'd entered it. I knelt in a pew and prayed to Saint Anthony of Padua to grant me humility.

During the months that followed I prayed regularly, to various saints and to Jesus Himself, but it was as if my words went out to a vast emptiness. I felt no comfort from prayer as I had in years before. My soul, untouched by grace, shrank to a stone.

WE DIDN'T SEE much of my parents, although we lived so close. I made various excuses, but the truth was that Hugh disliked visiting them, how the conversation sometimes slipped into French and excluded him. When he did concede to spend an evening there, he'd be stiffly angry for days afterward. It was far easier not to go. *We miss you, chou-fleur,* my father told me after church one crisp autumn Sunday. *I'll see you soon,* I said, but I didn't. He died that next week, falling from a height at work and breaking his neck. He wasn't even known by name there; he was documented as *French laborer* in the ranks of their dead. When he didn't come home for supper, my mother sent Michel out to the job site, where the night watchman told him about the accident and directed him to the nearest undertaker. When Michel went there, interrupting the undertaker's supper, he learned that the body had been refused for lack of guaranteed payment. I can't even think of it now, how strangers squabbled over my father's broken body. Luckily someone thought of the French undertaker; that's where Michel found him.

I stayed with my mother through the funeral, the bliss of being home mixing into my grief and regret. I remembered the last words I had spoken to my father, the insincere hurried promise while Hugh tapped his foot at the bottom of the church steps.

As a widow, my mother would normally have come to live with me, the only daughter, but Hugh did not offer and of course she would not ask. My older brothers offered to take her back to the Midwest, where they'd settled their families, but she demurred. She would not be imposing on them, nor on Michel, who was

blackballed now at the mills; his new job as custodian of a downtown building required him to live in a tiny basement flat there.
She announced to us all that she didn't want to leave her garden;
she'd be staying on in the bookshop alone. The boys could all
contribute a bit every month to keep her. It was an unusual arrangement, and I burned with shame as the puzzled eyes of the
family kept darting to me.

That night when I made my evening prayers, I first asked a
blessing for my father, then the usual request to Saint Anthony
for humility. My knees on the cool wood as I waited. After a few
minutes without any glow of response, I bent my head over my
braided fingers again.

Blessed Mary, I prayed. *Grant me strength.*

She was the mother of God, but she'd been a woman first. And
of the two, humility and strength, the latter seemed a far better bet.

BRADLEY WAS BORN on a spring morning, six months after my
father's death. Hugh was delighted. He'd been sure it would be a
boy, and from the moment he learned I was with child he treated
me like a delicate casing around an important jewel.

My mother visited daily after the birth, giving me lessons in the
simplest things, the diaper pinning and how to test the bathwater,
how to trim the little fingernails. For the first month she kept two
households, housecleaning and cooking for Hugh and me, then
leaving in late afternoon, our supper warm on the stove. I hated
to think of her eating alone—what a thing, for a woman who had
borne eleven children!—but when Hugh's tread came on the stairs
she'd wrap her scarf around her head, issue last instructions, *two
minutes on the hot fire before serving, don't forget to whip the cream
for the tart*, and be gone.

"You've been such a help, Sophie," said Hugh as my mother
was slipping past him one evening. "I don't know what might have

happened without you." He turned to me. "Maybe your mother should come live with us."

Qu'est-ce qu'il a dit? To me. She'd understood the sentiment of gratitude, but not the rest.

I was struck dumb by his words. What did he mean, *what might have happened?* Did he think I was incapable of caring for our child? I remembered the terrible shame when he hadn't offered my mother a home after my father had died. *Now* he wanted her, when it was of benefit to him? I felt then what I had not felt before: hatred.

My mother touched my elbow, and I turned to her.

"He thinks I should come to you during the weekdays," I told her in French, keeping my tone bright. "He says I can help you to reopen the shop. We can sell the remaining books."

"What a nice idea," she said, smiling at Hugh.

"She can't leave the garden," I told Hugh. A frown on his face at the reminder of how we lived, without a yard or even a balcony. "It's almost cherry season." Hugh loved my mother's cherry cakes; everyone did. I didn't say anything more; Hugh needed to make the idea his own.

"She can teach you how to make the cakes," he said. "You'll take Bradley there during the daytime, and be home before I return from work."

It was a gigantic reprieve, but with a sickening underside: cherry season was brief. But then there would be tender haricots. And then tomatoes, and eggplant for the ratatouille Hugh fancied. I couldn't string harvests together forever, of course: winter would come. But I wouldn't think about that until I had to.

THOSE NEXT FEW months are softly lit in my memory, the sun striping the wide-planked wooden floor of the bookshop, Bradley asleep in a basket while my mother taught me basic tasks. How to get out the yellow stains from under the arms of Hugh's undershirts, how to handle a pie crust without toughening it, how to slit the belly of a fish and lift the bones out in one piece. If she was surprised at my eagerness to learn all that I'd spurned before, she didn't mention it. She must have believed that motherhood had made me a woman at last.

I had worried that it might be unbearably sad to be in the shop without my father, but we felt his presence in the silences there. Sometimes it seemed like he would step out of the back room, holding a book in his immaculate hands, reading out a bit, *choufleur, listen to this*. The man he'd been when I was a little girl, not the broken WPA laborer of his last years, the one who took his suspenders down with hands scarred and permanently discolored, bending over the kitchen sink to wash his face and neck before coming to the table.

I managed to keep the arrangement in the bookshop going through a lovely summer. Meanwhile, I was a newly terrible wife, lying beside Hugh at night in a bed of secret loathing, wishing for his subtraction from my life. Somehow. Somehow.

SEPTEMBER BEGAN WITH rain, starting in the wee hours each morning and carrying on most of each day. Hugh decreed that Bradley and I would stay in the house, that even the short distance to the bookshop was too far to walk in the downpour. He carried a note to my mother, to let her know not to expect me.

"The garden must be nearly harvested now," he said. "We'll move her here when the rain stops."

It seemed it would never stop. Every day for a week, and then another week. I hated the rain that kept me from my mother, but I loved it too for putting off the day of reckoning. Would she agree to Hugh's offer? He would be furious if she declined. But if she agreed—I hated to think of her coming under Hugh's thumb. And no more garden! How would she bear that? Each day when I awoke to the drumming of rain, my heart sank, then rose, then sank again.

At last a clear day dawned.

"You'll stay home today," Hugh decreed, scraping butter across his breakfast toast. "It might yet rain." He thought me such a mouse, so completely cowed, that he didn't even look to see that I acquiesced; he delivered his mandate and got up from the table. "We'll move your mother on Saturday."

Bradley cooed in his basket while I washed the breakfast dishes. I'd need to do the laundry. It had been impossible during the long rain to hang anything on the outside line to dry. The thought came to me: if it was weather fine enough for laundry, wasn't it fine enough to walk to the bookshop? I could go and be back before Hugh ever came home; he'd never know. The more I thought about it, the more sense it made.

I couldn't go out in what I was wearing, though, a housedress with an apron on top. I left the dishes to dry on the drainboard, went into the bedroom, and opened the wardrobe. Everything needed to be laundered, except for two dresses: the first a long sky-blue satin sheath that I'd worn for my wedding and that I'd worn only once since, to an evening concert. The other was my second-best dress. My mother had made it for me out of one of her old ones, unpicking the old-fashioned dropped waist and taking out all the seams, and putting buttons down the front. The fabric was a plum stripe that she cleverly turned, the stripes meeting at the front placket to make chevrons; she'd added a belt and a little white collar. It suited me very well.

I stood in the bedroom, looking out of the window at the shiny streets, fighting with myself. I wanted to go to the bookshop; I should do the laundry.

I decided I would do both.

I made a bundle of three of Hugh's shirts, one of my stained everyday dresses, and a pair of his trousers, and pinned on a hat.

I swept Bradley up and kissed him, laid him in the pram—*we're going to see Mummum*—took an umbrella from the stand, and hung it from the pram handle. After a moment of consideration, I took Hugh's long black oilcloth slicker from the peg and draped it beside the umbrella. Just in case.

I wheeled the pram down the long drive feeling like a criminal, but once on the sidewalk I felt a flush of triumph. The laundry bundle rode nicely between the pram handles. I was so happy. I remember singing a little to Bradley as we went along. The sky was the weirdest hue, almost yellow. *Red sky in morning, sailor's warning.* There isn't any rhyme for a yellow sky. There should be.

When I arrived, my mother kissed me and fussed over Bradley (*Oh là là, he's gotten so big in just two weeks*), and made me a cup of tea. A shadow girl still stands there with my mother, watching her strong, age-spotted hand with the veins standing out on the back, tossing the leaves over the endlessly just-boiling water.

She helped with the laundry; together we pinned it to the line in the yard. Then an hour in the garden, in the humid still air while she weeded the crops of leeks and squash and I pulled late tomatoes from the vines, holding Bradley on my hip, telling him the words for things in French and English. When it was time to open the shop, I went inside and turned the key in the front door, then sat in a chair and read a picture book to the baby, getting up to help the occasional customer find a book, or to ring up and wrap a purchase. My mother's singing drifted in from the garden.

The sky darkened around noon, and not long after that a light rain began, striking the glass of the bookshop windows with insistent little taps. I went out and helped my mother pull the laundry from the line; we rehung it on a cord that she stretched across the kitchen and wound around a cleat on the wall. Showing me: *a good knot like this, et voilà. I have some cord you can use to make your own.* She waved me away from the lunch dishes, saying *There's a seam coming apart in that blue shirt. Better get to it now, before it makes a hole.* I got her mending basket out and began the repair, but the thread wouldn't behave and the fabric kept bunching up. *You've threaded the needle the wrong way*, my mother said, drying her hands on her apron. She held the thread up, showed me the fibers standing away from it like tiny branches. *It's like pulling a tree through—one direction smooth and easy, the other direction disaster.* She rethreaded the needle and handed it to me: *comme ça.*

The shop was nearly empty, for a long while no one with us but a student type who stood in the depleted art history section in the back of the store, thumbing through the colored plates in the heavy volumes there. After him there was a young woman in fashionable clothing who must have been caught outside without an umbrella and just pushed through the nearest shop door. She made several circuits of the store, her dismay obvious every time she came to the front and saw that the rain hadn't stopped. When she finally left, she didn't pull the door fully closed behind her and the wind slammed it right back open, blowing in a fat, cold slash of rain. My mother got up quickly to shut it.

I knotted the thread and snipped the end, slid the needle into the pincushion. I held up my work to examine it, but the light was too poor to see well. When had it gotten so dark?

"I should go," I said, bundling the shirt into a ball and standing up. I needed to get Bradley home and dry and changed, get the laundry dry somehow, erase all evidence that I'd gone out, before Hugh came home.

"You should stay for supper," said my mother as I came back down from the kitchen with the damp laundry in my arms. She was looking out at the rain, which had intensified, the sound of it enveloping the house. "Hugh will know to find you here." She turned to me. "I worry about you."

I almost told her then. *I've started to hate him. I don't know if this is how it's supposed to be.* I parted my lips to speak, but just at that moment Bradley awoke crying from his nap.

"It's the wind rattling the windows." I took him up and jiggled him against my shoulder. "He's frightened." He cried more loudly.

My mother took him from me. "*Pauvr'enfant*," she said into his squalling, contorted face. She clasped him against her and turned at the waist, swung him around with her body, back and forth, and he calmed down.

"You used to love this," she told me. She transferred him, beginning to wail again, into my arms. "Hold him like this, against your chest," she instructed. "One hand here"—she placed my hand behind his warm head—"one here." On his bottom. "And round and round."

I turned in a slow circle with the warm solid mass of my infant pressed against me in my arms, and he soothed again almost immediately and gave that little hiccup he used to give after a crying spell.

I had forgotten that hiccup until just now.

The moment for confession was past. I was newly shamed by my mother's competence. How good she was at everything! Nearly sixty and arthritis starting in her hands, she'd take my tortured needlework from me and replace my mess of awkward stitches with a perfect seam. I couldn't even comfort my own baby without guidance. Hugh was right: I was a sham wife, a sham mother.

I swallowed the words I had been about to say; I tucked Bradley into his pram and took the slicker from the handle and put it on. My mother raised her eyebrows.

"It's raining too hard," she said, watching me roll up the coat sleeves and work the toggles down the front. "Think of the baby."

"He won't melt," I said, and kissed her good-bye—at least I have that—and went out into the late-afternoon downpour in that old oilcloth coat with the bundle of laundry crammed against my side beneath it, Bradley in the pram with the hood stretched over him and buttoned down, and the umbrella opened over us both.

The street was empty; no one else was stupid enough to be out in such weather. The rain was coming down in a pelting sheet. Despite the pram hood and the umbrella, within half a block Bradley and I were very wet. I walked faster, and as if in response, the wind came up harder. It blew sideways, backward, forward. One moment I was struggling against it, as if against the powerful breath of a giant; the next I was practically running along as it pushed me from behind, each step carrying me a great distance. I turned the pram with effort, crossed the street leaning into the wind. It blew us across the road, then died down just long enough for me to stand, then blew again, skittering us backward. It was like an enormous cat batting us with its paws.

Suddenly a button on the pram hood popped off, and then another. The hood whirled around crazily for a few seconds, held by one last stubborn button, and then broke free and went sailing off down the street. The wind blew a drop of rain right into one of Bradley's eyes. He screwed up his face, and I scooped him out of the pram. He must have been howling, although I couldn't hear it over the wind. He was already soaked through. The pram, unhanded, bucked in place a couple of times before being blown onto its side and scraping across the sidewalk and bouncing off a wall. I felt a pang of fear—it had been expensive, Hugh would be terribly angry—but the wind came up harder as if to say, *I'll show you what to fear.*

I opened my coat, the laundry falling out, and tucked Bradley underneath the oilcloth, clasping him with one arm across my body. I was still holding the umbrella with the other. I turned and turned, trying to give my back to the wind, which was coming from all directions.

We were six blocks or so from home. Six blocks! No distance at all—and yet it had already taken so much effort to get this far. More than halfway there, so it made no sense to turn back. In Woonsocket, I could have knocked at any door to be taken in, but I didn't know anyone on this street. Nonetheless, I struggled toward the row of houses. As I did one of them gave a great tearing sound, audible even over the shrieking of the wind, and then astonishingly, its third story ripped free from its second, lifting right off, scattering debris in a rain all around me and leaving a decapitated structure where the gable-roofed house had been. It was unbelievable, like something from a bad dream, and I stood there amazed as the pieces of wood flew around us. Then I came to my senses, lowered the umbrella, and held it close like a shield over Bradley's head, retreating back to the gutter. Where was I going, though? Where could we find refuge?

The church! It was huge and heavy and made of stone. It wasn't far—two blocks away, on one of the streets that ran uphill off Wickenden. I turned in that direction and the umbrella belled out, nearly carrying me off my feet; its wooden spokes splintered and I opened my hand, fed it to the wind.

The air was now dark with suspended grit, and filled with dancing, hurtling objects. I remember a man's hat, a flowerpot, what seemed like a million pieces of glass. I struggled forward, head down, coat closed over Bradley, both arms over my chest to hold him there. A chunk of something caught the side of my head, taking my hat with it. My hair blew around my face, plastering wet tails over my eyes. I scraped them away with one hand, fitting my chin over Bradley's little head under the coat. I don't know if he was crying then. I couldn't hear anything; I couldn't see very much. By memory and instinct I moved toward the corner where I could turn uphill toward the church.

When the water came rising, it was like nothing I could have imagined. Feet and swirling feet of water, rushing up around my ankles, around my calves. As if pouring out of the earth itself, as if the earth was making it. It was to my knees in no more than a minute and still it rose, dirty and cold and filled with unidentifiable shapes that knocked against my legs. The air smelled of salt; I could taste it in my mouth. I looked up and saw through the rain that the corner was just a few feet away.

The wind came up even higher then, shockingly fierce and insistent, as though something knew I was trying to get to safety and was trying to prevent it. The wind blew into my nostrils, into my open mouth, forced itself down my throat. I snorted and breathed, snorted and breathed, shallow sips of air. I don't remember having any coherent thoughts; I wasn't thinking of anything except getting to the church that lay somewhere beyond the dense wall of rain. Solid and safe, its carved wooden door a gate to Heaven. Heaven being a place without wind, without water, without this terrible noise in my ears. I was almost swimming now in the rushing flood; I held Bradley higher on my chest to keep his head above the surface. I turned the corner. The church was now only half a block away. I might have been crooning to Bradley, some panicked attempt to comfort him, something like *It'll be all right, Mama has you, Mama has you.* I don't know if I spoke in French, or English, or a mixture.

At last my foot, shuffling forward, struck the bottom step that led up from the sidewalk to the church gate. These were the same steps I had mounted so many times, going to Confession, to catechism, to Mass. The gate would be just beyond the steps, the church door just a dozen yards more.

When I reached the top step I was for a brief, brilliant moment out of the water, and at that instant, as if forfeiting the battle, the wind dropped. I staggered through the open gate. Then had to stop: a tree had fallen across the path inside the iron fencing and lay wedged there against the metal. I would have to climb over it somehow. I looked at the tree, reckoning the best, shortest way over it. There—where two branches were spaced widely apart. I could clamber onto the trunk and drop down to the other side.

I quickly opened the flaps of the coat to check on Bradley. I had been holding him awfully tightly. I took just a second to see that he was breathing, although sodden and quiet, and hitched him up in order to resettle him against my body. A terrible mistake, a terrible, terrible mistake. In that moment of shifting, that small movement, I loosened my grip on him.

And then. The wind roared up like it had been waiting. It took his little wet body from my arms. My clumsy hands closed a moment too late onto empty air. Like the umbrella, the pram hood, like all the objects that had been tossed and dancing along above my head during the journey, my baby was snatched up, torn away in the space of a heartbeat, leaving me with my arms still cradled, still feeling his weight there, the warm spot against my breastbone suddenly gone cold. I turned my head up to the slanting rain.

Something came out of nowhere and slammed into me, and all was black.

I AWOKE IN a dark room filled with what seemed to be sleeping people. Looking back, I know that they were actually dead, or in the process of dying, and someone must have carried me there with others found after the storm. There was probably moaning and breathing around me, but I don't recall it. All I knew was that it was cold and dark, and that Bradley wasn't with me.

My limbs were stiff and my clothing wet and heavy. With some difficulty I got down off the hard surface I was lying on, a table of some sort, and made my way toward a faint light at one end of the room.

The light, it turned out, was spilling from the crack beneath a door at the top of a flight of stairs. I took hold of the stair rail and stepped up. The light fell across my body, and looking down, I saw my injury for the first time. You couldn't blame whoever it was who'd brought me to that room for thinking I was beyond saving, with the great big piece of wood sticking out of my chest, and me cold as the water I'd been floating in. No one could survive such a wound, but miraculously, I had. I didn't feel any wonder about it, not then. Without hesitation, I put both of my hands around the spike, tore it out, and flung it away. It clattered down the stairs, leaving a quarter-sized hole but no pain; I pressed my hand there to staunch the bleeding as I climbed the stairs.

The door at the top opened onto a long corridor pierced along its length by windows, gray oblongs that told me it was morning. I'd been in that basement all night. I went down the corridor, found a door at the end, and pushed through it to the street.

I didn't recognize any landmarks in the devastated scene before me. I turned and looked at the building behind me, read the words carved over the doorway. The Methodist girls' school; I'd never been inside before, but I knew it from my childhood bedroom window above the bookshop. It was on the other side of the river from home.

The water still surged in the street knee high, a glittering, tinkling crust of broken glass moving on its surface, banging together with a sound like chimes. Cars were slewed in random patterns, where they'd floated sometime during the night. Houses had emptied into the wind. A lidless porcelain toilet stood beside the crushed remains of a dining room set, one delicate, Queen Anne leg angling away from the heap like the limb of a wounded animal. A tea tray balanced on a louvered section of clapboard, pot and sugar bowl and creamer quite intact. Tree limbs, heavy with leaf, were showered over the landscape. Things fluttered in their boughs: clothing, paper.

I kept to the middle of the street, as the sidewalks were largely blocked by debris. I retrieved a floating plank and used it to push a path through the glass, sliding the flat pieces apart like ice floes and wading through as quickly as I could before they came banging back together again. Beneath the water, unknown objects bumped up against me like curious fish. A group floating on a makeshift raft pulled up to a broken storefront window, and a fellow hopped off into the building. He passed things out to those waiting, adding to their pile of booty.

I crossed the bridge that arced up to a dry point in the middle and then turned onto Wickenden Street. This was the lowest point of Providence; it was like a wide bowl full of water. The tops of motorcars, submerged above their windows, were like giant stepping stones, and I used some of them that way, hauling myself up, walking over the metal, then jumping or swimming to the next. A man coming from the opposite direction jumped onto a car just after I did; he grabbed me around the waist to help me steady myself, and then without a word leapt away again, onto the car behind me. When there were no more cars, I swam. There were rats with me in the water, little heads with ears laid back and V-shaped wakes behind. I looked at them without disgust: they were no different from me. They had also somehow survived, and also were heading home.

I reached a corner and recognized the building that was still standing there: somehow, I had passed the bookshop without knowing it. I turned to look behind me: the whole block was a smash of wood, roof tiles, bricks. No distinction between buildings, just a long mass of wreckage with a chimney poking up here and there. I walked back, against the force that was pulling me toward the church, to the place I had last seen Bradley. Had my mother somehow gotten to safety before the walls came down? The bookshop was a mountain and I scrambled up its slope of splintered boards, stones, tiles. Digging where the kitchen would be, tearing my hands, finding at last a muddy ruffle of apron. The shadow girl turns away before seeing the rest.

WHEN I FINALLY got to the church, I saw that people had been at work there already: the tree that had blocked my path had been sawn apart and moved in pieces to one side. The building front gaped, doorless; some of the stones around the entrance had come out. I turned slowly in a circle, in the place where I had stood that terrible minute, face upturned. I began walking.

It never occurred to me to go to the apartment I shared with Hugh. I didn't give a thought to the potential damage there, or to my husband. I suppose I was thinking of the tea set I had seen, that had blown through the air on the tray and come to rest unscathed. A trivial rescue, but still miraculous; why not a miracle for Bradley?

The air grew warmer as the sun rose above me. I knew these streets well, yet I hardly recognized anything. So many of the buildings were smashed to pieces, or gouged like sandcastles kicked by an enormous foot. I passed people, some in groups working together to lift wreckage into a pile or to shore up a sagging front porch; others wading, as I was, grimly along. We didn't speak. The silence was overwhelming, like another presence among us.

The street continued to slope upward; soon the water was just at my calves, and then at my ankles; then it was only in the gutters. I was now on streets I didn't know. I passed another church, its steeple cracked off and plunged into the earth in front of its narrow entrance; there was a small crowd standing around it, and a man under the cloak of a camera, taking a photograph. Farther along, I saw a car tilted up onto someone's front lawn, only two of its wheels on the ground, the other two held up by shrubbery. I was listening hard. I heard plenty of crying children and babies, none of them mine. A mother knows the sound her child makes, can distinguish it from among an orphanage of wailing.

As I continued, the houses became more intact, but I hardly noticed. I scanned the treetops, looked hard at every cluster of humanity I passed. That was the new thought that had come to me while walking: a frail hope that maybe he had been taken in, by someone who found him caught by his little sweater in the branches of a tree. Yes, I can see now that it was ridiculous. I was half-mad, I suppose.

I finally stopped because I could not walk anymore. I was in a field, very far from where I had started. There were no trees here to have caught Bradley, no people here to have found him. I had been moving mechanically, propelled by an unthinking purpose, and now, my thickened senses returning, I began to doubt. The wind had been so changeable—it could have carried him in any direction. He could be in one of the homes I had passed and left behind. For the first time, I considered the possibility that the wind had dropped him quickly, that he could have been one of those unmoving shapes in the basement of the Methodist school. That he might have been on one of the tables beside me in the dark. And that I had left him there.

WHEN I AWOKE again it was bright day and I was in a clean bed in a large room. My legs felt very heavy, and every part of me was howling with pain. I was wearing a man's plain white nightshirt, the placket partly open. From beneath the fabric, the corner of a bulky bandage peeped out. With effort, I held my arms up before me; they were scratched and swollen.

"Are you hungry?" asked a man coming over. I didn't realize at first that he was a monk; I thought he might be a hallucination, maybe even Death, in those robes.

"*Soif,*" I said, the French coming to me first. If he was the Devil, if this was Hell, he would pour sand into my throat. But he brought me water and tipped the glass to my lips so I could drink. When I'd had enough, he put the glass by the bedside and went away. He returned carrying a metal basin and took a seat by the bed.

"Where am I?" I said, in English this time.

"St. William's Priory," said the man. Or boy: I could see now that he was not much older than I was. "I'm Brother Silas." He took a scroll of bandage from the basin, unrolled a length and cut it, folded it into a thick square.

"What town?" I said.

"The nearest town is Waite," said Silas. Seeing my blank expression, he explained, "Hope County. Where did you come from?"

"Providence."

He looked surprised. "So far on foot?" I nodded. "You just appeared in one of the fields. We didn't know what had happened to you at first. We didn't have the storm here."

That seemed impossible, that there had been a place in the world outside the storm. "How long have I been here?"

"A week." He reached toward my chest, then hesitated. "I have to dress your wounds."

I nodded, and lay back.

"This may hurt a little," he said.

He pulled the bandage away quickly, ripping the flesh. A burst of pain and then the warm trickle of blood. Then a strange pulling feeling as he drew more bandage out of the depths of the wound.

"This goes very deep," he said, inspecting the place when all of the bandage was out, pressing a clean cloth against it. "It seems to be healing, though. You're lucky there's no infection." *Lucky*. It hardly hurt; it didn't feel like part of me at all. He took the cloth away, turned it to find a clean spot, applied pressure again. Then he poured water from a jug into the basin and washed the area gently. His eyes fiercely focused on his hands; my breasts were plainly within view. "We wanted to contact your people," he said, patting the skin dry and packing new bandage into the wound, smearing the area around it with unguent. His movements were sure; it was clear that he had done this many times while I was sleeping. "But we didn't know your name." He finished his work and covered me up again.

"Thank you."

"I'm not finished," he said, and moved down the bed to remove the blankets from my legs. I looked down and saw why they felt so heavy: they were wound with gauze from thigh to ankle like two stiff bolsters. He lifted one foot and started unwinding the bandages. A blaze of pain as the gauze pulled away. A welcome pain, a cleansing pain.

I laid my head back, and was asleep before he finished.

THOSE DAYS ARE muffled, a long dirge moaning in my memory. I was mute, stony. Sleeping, waking. If I had felt enough to want anything, I might have wanted to be dead. Brother Silas ministered to me every day while I lay like an already dead thing. I allowed him to wash me and feed me and lift me to a chair by the window, where I sat unthinking, unmoving, until he put me back into bed again.

I was sitting in that chair by the window, my freshly bandaged legs propped up on a little stool with a pillow, when someone new appeared in the doorway. Silas was reading to me from the lives of the saints. Today's story was of the saint who had burned to live a humble life for Jesus. She'd run away from home, given up all her worldly goods, cut her hair off, worn rough cloth, and lived without money. She'd died happy, telling her followers, *Can a heart which possesses the infinite God be truly called poor?*

When the man entered the room, Silas stood and excused himself, leaving the book open on the little table beside me.

"I'm Prior Washburn." He was much older than Silas, and shorter, with fine silver hair. He stood the way they all did, his hands clasped before him, his arms swallowed in his sleeves. "Silas tells me you've been up and walking."

I nodded. I had walked the length of the room the day before for the first time.

"He also says that you won't tell him your name," he said.

I looked down at the book Silas had left, then out the window.

"There must be someone looking for you. Someone worrying about you." He unclasped his hands; in one of them he was holding a folded newspaper. "I have the list of the missing and dead from

Providence." He held out the paper but I did not move to take it. "I'll read it to you, shall I?"

He pulled a chair over and read the list of the dead while I looked out the window. He read slowly, watching me. The Sullivans and Cabrinis and LeComptes and Coelhos, all mixed together in a list as they never were in life. Among them, my mother and Michel. My own name. Bradley's.

Outside the window, the sky was blue and innocent; the fields rolled out in all directions. I could see figures in one field, and a horse and cart. Harvesting something. I squinted: pumpkins? They were just orange dots from here. It was early for pumpkins. Maybe squash.

"That's all?" I said, when Prior Washburn had stopped reading. "No one else?"

"That's all."

The world turned around me, empty and breathtakingly large. I had no place in it. No warm fragment of home. I floated free. A terrible unwanted freedom, a world too large. *But hadn't I wanted it?* And of course I was not quite free: there was the remaining tether of Hugh. That thought was impossible.

The figures in the field were children, I realized. The landscape swarmed with their industry. We were on a high floor; the window let me see beyond the field and over the tree line, to a little hill in a clearing. There stood a tiny stone house, all alone.

"What's that?" I said, and lifted one of my battered hands to point. The prior rose to look.

"That's Roscommon. The old cemetery, and the keeper's house. It used to be in the center of town, long ago when there was a town there." How could a town just disappear? "The old church used to stand beside it. The cottage is very primitive. No one lives there now."

I have no one. I have no place in the world. I didn't realize that I had spoken aloud until the prior answered me.

"I'm sorry," he said. "Tell me their names. I can pray for them."

Just like a priest. Next he'd be offering Confession. I couldn't confess, though; a proper confession requires both contrition and a sincere resolve not to repeat the sin. The sin I was about to commit was one for which I would not feel contrite, and one I planned to commit for as long as possible.

"God already knows their names," I said.

"That He does. A little reminder doesn't hurt, though." He smiled. "God knows your name too, but I don't know what to call you."

There was a silence.

"You can call me Clare." The saint who had lived in poverty with God.

He looked at the open book, and out the window again at Roscommon.

"Fitting," he said, and I knew he wasn't fooled.

CHAPTER EIGHTEEN

Lucy

THE LAST TIME I LOOKED for an apartment, I didn't really. Joe scoped out all the possibilities and did the first-looks, and I went along for the second pass, viewing the two or three options left after he'd filtered by location, price, amenities. I'd teased him for sounding like a realtor as he drove us from place to place, describing each offering as we pulled up. The wedding-cake Victorian with the top-floor apartment featuring huge drafty windows and a spiral staircase to a cupola (no); the modern two-bedroom with a gym in the basement (tempting, but the place was very dark); the second-floor apartment in the funky historical-registry building close to the hospital, with a balcony (yes, despite the iffy neighborhood).

The coffee shop is quiet, one of those bare-bones establishments that provides good pastries and Wi-Fi and power strips in every outlet; when the doors open, the students flock in and settle with their laptops and books. The quiet conversation of two young women at a nearby table floats to me, the vocabulary catching my involuntary attention: *dysplasia, angiomyolipoma*. They're students, medical or possibly nursing, studying the genitourinary system, judging from the terms that trip out in their happy voices. They must be preclinical, from the mispronunciations: he-ma-tur-I-a, cysto-SCO-py, cryptor-CHI-dism.

The medical academic year runs from July to July, the under-graduate year from August to the end of May. Craigslist in March is a bath of remainders: crumbling South Providence walk-ups and first-floor apartments off the tatty northern end of Hope Street, all alike with their drafty double-hung windows and tiny rooms floored with hardwoods varnished to a sickly yellow gloss, the built-in china hutches wearing so many layers of paint over the hinges that the doors don't open all the way. I can't see myself in any of them. Or is it just that I can't see myself anywhere alone? Until recently, I'd expected my next address would be a home, not another temporary stopover. I can't keep living in a call room, though.

"Dr. Cole?" I look up to see a vaguely familiar face. Six feet, close-cropped hair. "It's you, right?"

This happens with embarrassing regularity. Providence is a small enough city that I am forever being hailed in the grocery store or while pumping gas, strangers striding toward me with great famil-iarity: *Hey, Doc.* Is it some kind of agnosia that I am not able to recognize them when they are fully clothed and free of the hospital stretcher?

"Hi," I say, striving for an all-purpose tone, wanting it to be appropriate to the circumstances of our previous encoun-ter. Did I pronounce your father dead, lance your suppurating groin abscess, splint your fracture, coddle you through a night of drunken excess?

His smile broadens. Failure: he can tell I don't know who he is.

"I'll give you three guesses." He nods with raised eyebrows at the chair across from me, then sits down at my return nod.

"Well, I'll need three hints." Glad we aren't going to play the usual game of me trying not to look blank while the mystery person chats away and I frantically mine the monologue for clues.

"I'll give you one." He peels back the plastic tab on his coffee cup and takes a sip. "You liked my shoes."

Shoes. It's a blank. Shoes. A hint of aftershave comes across the table, and then it swims up to me—the Found Down who smelled too good to have been lying on the sidewalk. It's none other than Coma Cop.

"Last I saw you, you were hightailing it down Trauma Alley butt naked."

"Not my finest hour," he concedes.

"So what was that all about?"

"It was an undercover operation." He sips. "We've had a lot of complaints from patients who reported thefts after an ER visit. They said they were picked up with a full wallet, and when their belongings were returned the wallets were empty."

"Drunks are always saying that." *I had two hundred dollars in here.* Our response was always some variation on *sure you did.*

"And you blew them off."

"They sleep on the sidewalk in South Providence," I say. "They're going to get robbed."

"Blaming the victim, uh-uh-uh," he says with mock reproof.

"Just pointing out the cold, hard facts."

"Well, we've always blown off those kinds of complaints too. Until our shift commander's kid was brought in after partying a little too hard. When he was released from the hospital in the morning, the cash was missing from his wallet. The possibilities were other students at the party, hospital personnel, or EMS. When we checked the run sheets for similar complaints on record, we found a common denominator. Always the same squad, and one name was on every single run sheet."

Some whaddyacallit designer drug, squawks my memory.

"Not Big Bill."

"Bingo. We waited until his squad stopped for coffee, and I went and lay on the sidewalk nearby while my partners called 911."

"Anyone could have picked you up."

"We knew their routine: always the same Dunkin's, around the same time. I lost the coin toss and had to play the patient. Two hundred dollars in my wallet for bait. Big Bill stole it from me in the van."

"So you had him right away," I said. "Why did you have to pretend to be comatose in the trauma room?"

"We had to keep up the game until Bill actually left the hospital with the money. Otherwise he could always claim that he was intending to turn it over to the nurse."

I absorb that. "Well, you did a great job. I mean, we did a *blood gas* and you didn't move a muscle."

"You did more than that," he says, and I recall with an internal *yikes* the rectal examination.

"That was Alice, not me."

"Good to know."

There's a short silence, but it's not entirely awkward.

"So you're the head doc over there?" he says. "You don't look old enough for that."

"No, just a senior resident. The head worker bee on shift. There's an attending for backup."

"The shit you must see."

"The shit *you* must see," I say, and we share a grin.

"I'm Dave," he says, putting out a hand.

"Lucy." I notice his warm, dry palm, wonder if the pinprick of his arterial puncture is still there on the inside of his wrist. I remember him naked on the stretcher, the sterile paper ringing his penis, Alice's hand poised with the catheter.

"Stop thinking about that," he orders.

"How do you know what I'm thinking about?"

"Am I wrong?" I say nothing. "Okay then. New subject."

"Okay. Um. Judging from the accent, you're not from here."

"Aha. That's where you're wrong," he says, stretching out *wrawng,* smiling at my surprise.

Not the hack *I pahked my cah in Hahvahd Yahd* you hear from tourists buying crimson T-shirts in Cambridge, not the basic subtraction of terminal Rs that you hear from actors in movies set in Boston, but the more subtle and complex distortion of vowels and consonants specific to the Biggest Little.

"You can just turn it on and off like that?" I ask.

"Now I can. A couple of beers and all that practice is out the window, though, right back to normal." *Nahmull.* His phone buzzes and he glances down at it. "Shit. I have to go, so I'll just ask. Wanna go out sometime?"

It's been so much less strange than I ever thought it might be, to flirt and be flirted with, but the question takes me aback. "I'm sorry, I'm—"

"Seeing someone," he says. "Of course you are."

"Well . . . it's complicated."

"Well, if it ever gets *un*complicated enough for a pizza"—he stands, slips a card from his pocket, and offers it to me—"I'm buying."

ALL THAT'S VISIBLE of my next patient from the door of Trauma 2 are the soles of his sneakers, the treadless deck shoes that are as much a part of the prison uniform as his orange jumpsuit. He's flat on his back on the stretcher, all four limbs pinned. The jumpsuit is code, and so is the extraneous shackling. In Rhode Island, an orange jumpsuit means *life sentence.* Four cuffs instead of two is correctional officer code for *we extra-hate this guy.*

The prison treats minor injuries and ailments on-site, but more serious afflictions come to us. I'm sure the inmates are very different people when at the prison, but they're usually nice as pie to me, almost absurdly soft-spoken and courteous. The hospital's like a vacation to them, the COs have told me; they'll do anything to get here. I've seen plenty of foreign objects in inmates, swallowed or inserted in hopes of the ER field trip. One of the radiologists has collected X rays from those cases into a teaching file: multiple

D batteries nestled against the greater curvature of the stomach, a ballpoint nudged under the skin of the forearm, an open safety pin in the small intestine. To medical students, they're shocking and even humorous examples of human behavior, but I can't help but see the message of desperation in them: How terrible must prison be, to make a person swallow an open safety pin?

As I come into the room, nodding *hello* to one of the COs at the foot of the stretcher, I hear a noise that sends me into high alert: a gurgle. It's the sound of liquid bubbling in an airway, and it signifies death for someone who's lying on his back.

"He needs to sit up," I tell the COs. "Unshackle his arms so we can pull up the stretcher."

He's been beaten to a pulp, I can see that at a glance, and he's struggling to breathe through his shattered face. I turn on the wall suction above the head of the bed and unloop the hose.

"Now," I say to the COs, who seem to be moving in slow motion, standing and fumbling keys.

I slip the tonsil tip of the suction between his lips and angle it around carefully in the oral cavity to find the pooling, choking fluid. Success: a rush of blood and saliva thuds into the canister on the wall, accompanied by a huge inward gasp of breath from the ruined face.

The COs release one wrist at a time, each gripping a forearm hard while I raise the stretcher. When the stretcher back has been ratcheted up to forty degrees, they immediately begin to refasten the cuffs.

"Can we leave the right wrist free?" I ask. "That hand looks bad."

They're not pleased but they comply.

"Don't try anything," one of the COs warns the still-gasping patient as they back away just to the foot of the stretcher.

I tuck the suction tip behind the stretcher pad. Gravity's taking care of his airway now, secretions drooling out of his mouth instead of back down into his windpipe. Breath sounds clear, good pulses at both ankles, and normal blood pressure. That's A-B-C taken care of, so I can move to the head-to-toe assessment.

"I'm Dr. Cole," I tell the patient, holding up my gloved hand in front of his face. "I'm going to put my fingers in your mouth. Don't. Bite. Me." His eyes are barely visible, two coffee-colored irises and bright red sclera peeking out of puffy ecchymosis. He hears me, though, and nods the tiny bit that the cervical collar permits. I tug at his two front teeth gently and stop immediately at the grating shift of his upper jaw. It's an alarming mobility in a bone that should be anchored to the skull.

This is not a small guy. He's muscular and tall, yet his assailants were able to hold him down and punch his face hard and repeatedly. There are contusions over his ribs and at least one fracture there; luckily no abdominal tenderness, so no damage to liver and spleen; the long bones are intact, but the unshackled hand is extremely damaged and swollen, like a glove full of Jell-O with fragments of bones rolling free inside.

As I examine him, the sequence of events comes to life: *here* he was pinned down while someone battered his face with a fist or a blunt object; *here* they kicked him as he curled up to protect himself; *here* they stomped on his wrist and hand. Someone armed with something sharp tried to stab him, but he brought his forearm up and the blade glanced off the ulnar surface, ripping through the skin and down into the muscle. The weapon must have come into play near the end of the attack; a second stab would likely have reached something vital, and he'd be dead.

"You've got significant facial fractures," I tell the patient. "You'll need surgery to fix them." *Jackpot*, murmurs one of the COs behind me. As if the man had beaten himself up as a ruse to get here. "Your hand's badly broken; it'll also need surgical repair. I can give you some pain meds. Are you allergic to anything?"

"No," he says. A single syllable, a deep voice.

"Okay. We'll get some X rays and a CT of your face and abdomen and see where we are. If your neck bones look okay the collar can come off."

"How long's he gonna be here?" asks one of the COs.

"Not sure," I say. "The specialists need to see him. He's definitely going to be admitted for surgery, and it could be a couple of weeks post-op before he can go home." The last word lingers mockingly in the air. Prison is hardly home.

I put consults in to three services: Trauma, Face, and Hand. Ear, Nose, and Throat is covering Face today, and Plastics is on Hand; they'll do his surgeries, but by protocol Trauma will have to accept him to their service for the first twenty-four hours. After that, there'll be a little hot-potato skirmish between the ENT and Plastics service chiefs.

"I'm writing for Ancef and tetanus," I tell Stacey, his nurse, who's appeared in the doorway. Where has she been? I go over to her and add sotto voce: "Listen, this guy almost choked to death. They had him in four points with an unstable airway."

"Sorry," she says, but her tone says she's not at all sorry. The orange jumpsuit can have that effect.

After X rays have ruled out cervical spine injury and his collar has been removed, after Trauma and Neurosurg have consulted and Plastics has splinted his left hand and ENT has booked him into the OR, there's still the long slice on his right forearm to be repaired. It's nearly dawn, and all the consulting surgeons have vanished to upper floors in the hospital to make their morning rounds. I don't feel like fighting with them about whose responsibility it is to repair the lac. Trauma will argue that everything below the elbow is considered Hand, but Hand will argue that a simple laceration, however deep, doesn't need subspecialty repair. They'll both be sort of right and sort of wrong. It's easier just to do it myself.

I sweep through Triage, make sure everyone in the urgent area is stable, then with a mental fingers-crossed against an influx of new patients, gather all the materials I'll need from the Clean Utility Room. As I load up a deep plastic bin with bottles of sterile saline, a big syringe for irrigation, four-by-four gauze pads, and antibiotic ointment, the charge nurse, Brenda, pushes open the door.

"You gonna sew up Trauma Two?" she asks.

"Yup." I add two rolls of gauze and an adhesive dressing to the bin. "Listen, I don't know what's going on with Stacey. She left him alone in Trauma with a compromised airway. You might want to check in with her about that."

"She was helping in Trauma One," Brenda says, in that same *sorry-not-sorry* tone. "The guards were with him." Her eyes fall onto the bottle of local anesthetic I'm taking from the drawer. "You could do him without any lido. He deserves the pain." She sees that I'm not following. "You know who that is, right?"

"No." I drop sterile packets—needle driver, toothed forceps, mosquito clamp—into the bucket.

"That's the guy. The Birthday Party Killer. The one who murdered those kids." She watches comprehension sweep across my face. "See what you can do."

She lets the door fall closed.

Vigilance has waned in Trauma 2. The original adrenaline-taut pair of COs is gone and the single CO that replaced them is seated on a chair outside the room, chat-flirting with a tech; he nods to me as I go by.

The four-point restraints have become two-point ankle shackles; the fractured hand is splinted and the other arm, the one I'll be suturing, is free. His eyes, glinting slits in the swollen face, watch me put the bucket on a bedside stand and roll a stool up to the stretcher. I run water into the bucket and squirt in some amber disinfectant. With wadded four-by-fours, I scrub and rinse the skin, then adjust the surgical light over the field and punch it on. Under its heat I irrigate the wound, jetting sterile saline through the big syringe until the tissue is clean and soft and waterlogged, all clot and dirt and foreign matter removed.

"This is going to sting a little." I pull up lidocaine into a five-cc syringe, attach a twenty-five-gauge needle, and slide it into the tough white layer of dermis.

"They told you," growls the patient, his voice nasal from the blocked nostrils but no gurgle in it now. He's breathing without difficulty because I saved him from choking to death a few hours before.

"Told me what." No expression, redirecting the needle under the skin, injecting, injecting. I have not looked him in the eyes since I reentered the room, and I don't look up now.

"I know they told you."

I've doctored countless murderers before him and sutured miles of swastika-tattooed skin, all with professional detachment. This shouldn't be any different. I drape the arm, peel the instruments and sutures out of their packaging so they drop onto the sterile field, then pull on sterile gloves and study the injury to plan my repair. Muscle is difficult to sew, like wet tissue paper: too much tension and the suture cord pulls right through. Maybe a horizontal mattress will spread out the tension. I clamp a 4-0 chromic gut suture in the jaws of my needle driver.

"You should be numb now, but tell me if you feel anything," I say, and slide the curved needle into the muscle.

Suturing is considered a menial task, one usually consigned to junior residents, but it can be deeply satisfying. You begin with a bloody mess and end with a neat row of black stitches, working by instinct to get there, matching uneven layers by the slant and placement of the needle, restoring the anatomy as closely as possible to its unviolated condition. Like turning back time.

"You know, I did kill them," he says, conversational.

Startled in midstitch, I look up at him, then glance toward the doorway.

"He can't hear me," he says. A snatch of conversation and laughter drifts in. He smiles; a small star-shaped tattoo beside his eye crimps and flares against the bruised, shiny-swollen tissue there. "And you're my doctor. You can't tell him anything I say."

I use the toothed forceps to approximate the next section of torn muscle and pierce first one side, then the other with my needle, pulling the suture through smoothly, watching the flesh draw together. Perfect.

"The kids were easy." Another good stitch, just the right angle. "I did the big one before the other two even knew what happened." Another knot snugged down the length of cord, five throws to keep it from loosening, clip the ends. "They barely made a sound. The women put up a fight, though."

My head is buzzing and light, my vision a tunnel around the tableau of gloved hands, needle and suture, half-closed muscle. I could leave, just lay my instruments down and stand up. Leave the room, leave the wound open. But it's already been open for hours; it needs to be closed or infection will set in. I begin the subcutaneous layer.

"They won't convict me," he says. "It was the perfect crime. And you'll never guess," he continues, in a *just-wait-it-gets-better* voice, like we're laughing together over an anecdote, "where I hid the clothes I was wearing." He stage whispers, "*Septic tank*. So even if they find them, they're covered with other people's DNA."

I shouldn't answer of course, but it's impossible not to; his smugness is too disgusting.

"You left evidence behind in the house," I say. A cell, a hair, a fiber. *A witness.*

"Nope." The syllable is plump with satisfaction. "And doesn't matter even if I did. I installed new carpet in that house a month ago. I was all *over* that house for that job."

Maybe he doesn't know about the boy. Had Ben been hidden?

"I don't want to hear any more," I say.

The laughter grates out of him. "You can't fool me," he says. "You're the kind of person who wants to know everything."

I concentrate on knotting the last subcutaneous stitch.

"You want to ask me a question?" he says. "Go ahead."

He's right that I can't repeat anything he says; the Tarasoff exception to doctor-patient confidentiality applies only to knowledge of future crimes. I can't share anything he tells me about the past. So I could ask him the obvious question, *Why did you do it,* and he could answer me. Even if he told me the truth, though, what answer could possibly matter?

I lift my eyes to his; I'm jolted by the loathing that boils up.

"This isn't your story," I say. My head feels hollow; my voice sounds loud, as if I'm speaking into a cavern. "It belongs to the people you killed. Just because they aren't able to tell it"—jaw clenched, I'm biting the words off now—"because you took that away from them—doesn't make it yours." His face doesn't change; expression is not possible with his injury. "Now shut up and let me do my job."

The two layers of repair have brought the wound together well. Everything's tucked inside demurely now, leaving just a thin red river on his skin. All that's left is to close the small gap between the banks. If this were a child, I might forgo suturing at this point and Steri-Strip the final layer of skin closed. Children heal beautifully. But adult skin is less elastic, it needs the strong pull of nylon in most cases, especially with a large wound like this. So I'll have to sew the final layer. How many stitches will it take?

"You know what I enjoyed most?" he says in a pleased, confiding whisper. It's as if I haven't spoken at all. "Saving the boy. I liked making him lucky."

One, I decide; I clamp the nylon monofilament into the jaws of my needle driver and start whipping in a continuous baseball stitch. Tightly spaced short diagonals, a lot of stitches, but just one knot at the beginning and end. Closing the wound like a zipper, the skin coming together to lie flat under a long seam of black. It's a good repair. There won't even be much of a scar.

"You know what I mean. You know what it's like to save people." The needle piercing, then piercing again, unclamp and reclamp, pull the suture through. "I gave that kid a miracle."

Done. I clip the knot, drop my instruments onto the Mayo stand, strip the gloves from my hands and drop them also, get up and leave the room. Leaving a mess for the nurse to clean up, the way they complain that *those dickhead surgeons* do. I can't care about that. All that matters is that I'm done. Not another stitch or another minute in that room.

IF ANY SHIFT should give me nightmares it would be this one. But when I do fall asleep, I don't dream about Karen, nor about her murderer. Instead I dream of my mother. I wake up at some point suffused with happiness, and I close my eyes and try to go back into it, but she slips away and I am left awake. I look up at the call room ceiling as the joyful glow ebbs and let my mind drift, trying to find a pleasant thought to lull me back to sleep.

The café banter with Dave from earlier in the day floats up. He'd been nice, but I recall our pas de deux now with a kind of weary bleakness. Just the thought of having to explain myself, of telling my story to a new person, seems exhausting. I know it's Death Month and on top of that I've just had a terrible shift, but a voice within tells me that part of my life is over. This is how it will be, now and forevermore: navigating a world of strangers, a world without landmarks or history, no one knowing me, not really knowing me, ever again. I miss Joe. I miss my mother. I turn onto my side and cry a little bit. Quietly, although there's no one nearby to hear.

CHAPTER NINETEEN

Leo

"M AY I TALK TO BEN?" asks Dr. Jellicoe. He asks that every time.

When I don't reply, he says, "You're doing a really good job of protecting Ben. I know Ben had a scary experience. But it's safe here. Leo, can you let Ben know that it's safe to talk to me?"

"Did you find Clare?"

A sudden sharpening of interest: he looks up from the folder he's holding.

"Is Clare here now?" he asks. "May I speak to her?"

Sometimes he doesn't make sense at all.

Disappointed—Confused—Worried.

Dr. Jellicoe, scrutinizing the charts of my feelings, isn't listening.

GO BACK TO *a good day. Maybe a summer day? Feel the sun on your skin. Blue sky. It's so bright you have to shade your eyes. Look around you and see what's there.*

"UGH, I GOT a mushy one," says Bedrick, spitting.

"They're all mushy," says Austin.

The berries are warm from the sun. You can tell the overripe from the sweet by both look and feel. I pull a handful from a branch, sort through them, drop the bad ones to the ground.

Bedrick spits a new mouthful at me. I haven't spoken, but I moved and that reminded him I am here.

"It's hot," says Jimmy.

"Hotter in the laundry," Bedrick says. "You wanna go back? Go on then."

"I don't want to go back," says Jimmy.

I saw them sneaking away and followed them up the hill. The others didn't say anything when they first saw me, for fear of making noise as we walked by the outbuildings, which might get all of us caught. Once we were a good distance away from school they ignored me, except for the occasional tossed handful of dirt in my direction. They didn't run me off, though. I think Bedrick likes having me around to torment.

"Look at the lady," taunts Austin, mimicking the way I am poking through the berries and pushing the bad ones out of my hand. "Afraid you'll swallow a bug?"

"No," I say, but of course I shouldn't have said anything at all. They are all on me in a minute, Austin with his knees on my chest and Jimmy cramming his hand against my mouth. Something with legs squirms against my tongue and I shake my head back and forth, spitting.

"He bit me," says Jimmy.

"I didn't mean to," I say, but he doubles up the bitten hand and punches my stomach.

"Let's see if he's really a lady," suggests Bedrick.

I writhe and struggle but they have me pinned.

"Stop," I say.

"Stop," mimics Austin in a falsetto.

Jimmy yanks my trousers down to my ankles, and then suddenly the game is done. They release me and I lie panting, the sun hot on my face; the places where their fingernails scratched make stinging trails across my skin.

"You gonna cry?" says Bedrick.

"Crybaby," says Austin.

I pull up my pants and sit up.

"I'm hungry," says Bedrick. "Gimme the stuff."

Austin hands him the bag he has been carrying. We've all missed lunch, but they prepared for that. Bedrick rummages through the things in the bag and brings out something wrapped in a napkin. Biscuits, from breakfast. He hands them around to the other boys. Another bundle is a soft wedge of cheese, which he slices up with a penknife and distributes. They sit down a little distance away from me to eat.

Bedrick makes himself a sandwich of the cheese and biscuit. I know he is enjoying my hunger, my envy, as he draws the knife through the cheese and then carefully scrapes the blade clean between his teeth. The bush nearest to me has a crop of healthy berries on it. I want to reach out to them, but I don't. Instead I put a hand in my pocket and finger the box of matches I stole from the chapel, when Brother Patrick left them unattended after lighting some candles. I don't know why I took them; I think I just wanted something in my pocket, something of my own.

I take the box out and slide the little drawer open. It's full, the matches packed in tight. I bring it to my nose: the clean sulfur whiff has an unexpected cooling effect, like a tiny breeze. I extract a match and roll it between my fingers. The other boys are lying on their backs now, ignoring me.

Such a perfect thing, this match. The slender wooden stick, the red head like a hardened teardrop of blood. You can't tell by looking the power that it contains, or its potential for transformation. I put the match head against the striking patch on the bottom of the box and draw it slowly along. Not pressing at all, but the match blooms with a soft *crack* and there is fire in my hand. I hold the flame under the cluster of berries; the shiny surface of the largest one clouds up but it doesn't burst. I want it to burst, I want something to happen. I move the flame under the branch; it darkens and rolls out a small amount of smoke. I hold the match there until it burns down to my fingers.

"Jesus Christ." Bedrick has sat up and is staring past me. I look where he is looking, and see that the bush is on fire. Real fire, licking orange and hot, leaping up in points, running like liquid along one branch, setting the next one alight.

Bedrick stamps the fire with his feet, scoops earth from the ground and shovels it onto the flame. The other boys jump up and join him, and in a minute or two the fire is out.

"Did you do that?" says Bedrick, panting. The bush is charred and smoking. He clouts me hard across my ear. "The whole hillside could have gone up."

"We better go," says Jimmy. "Before someone sees the smoke."

"No one lives around here," says Bedrick. He gives me a kick. "I don't want to go back yet."

"We could go see the witch," says Austin. "Maybe we'll see her naked. I almost did once."

"You did not," says Bedrick, but I can see that the idea has caught his fancy.

They head down the hill and I get up, tousle the dirt and dry bits of grass out of my hair, and follow. We reach the forest and walk through it. Its shade is a relief. Things live here, not like on the baked top of the hill: there are chipmunks and squirrels and birds. A snake slithers over a root, and this provokes a discussion of how to tell if it's poisonous; Bedrick dares the others to pick it up. When they don't, he bends toward it. I am afraid he will throw it at me, so I am glad when the thing eludes him, sliding away under some leaves.

"There she is," says Austin as we come out of the woods. He points to the middle of the cemetery.

You can tell she's a woman, although she has her back to us and she's dressed in overalls like a man. I am walking automatically, thinking about how women move differently from men, when Bedrick pushes me and I crash to the ground.

"Get down, stupid," he says.

The stone wall is twenty feet away; we crawl toward it. I can hear the ring of metal against rock as we approach.

"She's digging up dead bodies," whispers Jimmy. "She makes soup from the bones."

We all know this must be a lie, but it is exciting, more exciting than anything else we have done today. Maybe we'll see her pulling human bones from the grave. And what if it's not a lie? What else is there to dig for in a graveyard?

"Give me the bag," says Bedrick when we reach the wall.

Austin hands him the bag again, the one that held their lunch, and Bedrick upends it and shakes out some small apples, puckered and spotted with brown.

"Each of us gets two tries," he says. We're all sitting with our backs to the wall. He rolls one of the apples toward me. "You first."

I take the apple and slowly rise to my knees, peek over the wall. The woman is about ten feet away; as I watch she swings the shovel and drops some soil into the wheelbarrow. She's wearing a wide hat and her hair is piled up into it; there are curls on the back of her neck.

I drop again, flatten myself against the ground.

"She nearly saw me," I say.

"I'll do it," says Austin, and he gets up on his knees, throws the apple hard, then falls onto his belly again. "I got her," he says.

"You did not," says Bedrick.

We scramble to a new place, and this time Bedrick looks over the wall.

"She's gone," he says.

We all rise to our knees to look. Just the wheelbarrow and the shovel leaning against it, no lady.

"That's because I got her," says Austin. "Got her right in the head."

"She's coming back," says Jimmy. We drop down again and listen for the ring of the shovel, but it doesn't come.

"What's she doing?" says Jimmy.

"Leo, you look."

I peek over the wall. "She's washing the stone with a brush."

"Is she facing this way?" asks Bedrick. "Or does she have her back to us?"

"This way," I say, although she isn't. She's in profile. Her face is really pretty, actually. Delicate; it doesn't go with the drooping overalls.

When we hear the shovel again, Jimmy rises and throws his apple as hard as he can. The sound of the shovel stops abruptly.

"I got her," says Jimmy. He didn't have to say this; we all heard the thud. We scuttle along the wall and sit again, pressing our backs against the stone. "What's she doing now?"

"It's your turn, Leo," says Bedrick.

"You didn't throw yet," I say.

"Saving the best for last. Go on."

I rise slowly into a crouch and twist, one hand on the ground for balance, and my heart nearly stops when I see her so close. She is poised with the bucket lifted, right above Bedrick's head. I could say something, I could cry out a warning. But she looks straight at me and her eyes are clear blue, and even if she is wearing overalls and a witch and older than my mama, she is beautiful.

"What's she doing?" hisses Bedrick.

The last syllable is a *glug*; he has his face turned up toward me, and the stream from the bucket catches him full in the mouth. It gets Austin and Jimmy too, but just on the tops of their heads and their arms. They are all on their feet spitting and cursing. They run toward the trees, but I don't move. The lady hasn't said a word; we're still staring at each other. I think of a story I read once to Sally from a library book, about a princess who smeared mud on her face and dressed in animal skins and went among the commoners. The prince was the only one who recognized her, royalty calling to royalty through the disguise. Finally the spell breaks, and I drop my apple and run after the others.

When we get back we are punished for sneaking away from work, made to kneel before the prior himself in evening chapel and pray for forgiveness, then sent to bed without supper. After lights-out, the other boys hiss promises of retribution at me from their beds in different corners of the room. No matter what they choose to do to me tomorrow, no matter the empty hole of hunger in my stomach, I am not sorry for any of it. Today brought me two new precious things: the princess, and the knowledge that there is something in the world under my control. Fire is powerful; it frightens even Bedrick, who doesn't seem afraid of anything.

WHERE ARE YOU? says Dr. Jellicoe, the voice dropping to me in the dark. And the word breathes through me, before I even think: *Roscommon*.

CHAPTER TWENTY

Lucy

THE SOCIAL WORKER IS BRISK, professional to professional, just the facts.

"You know how the world is," she tells me. "A normal white six-year-old could have trouble finding a healthy foster placement. A six-year-old with mental illness? From a murder house?" Her mouth is a grim line. "He's going to be tough to sell. Add in possible Axis I, and he'll be landing in one of the marginal homes. That's if he gets a placement at all."

Axis I: thought disorder. So they're holding on to the dissociative identity disorder diagnosis, or something like it.

"He can't just stay in the hospital forever," I say. Ben's already been an inpatient for two weeks. Hospital wards are under enormous pressure to discharge patients before insurance stops paying for the bed. Maybe it's different, though, when the head of the department has taken the case. "How about Clare? Has anyone found her?"

"The no-last-name babysitter who lives on a hill? That lead went exactly nowhere." She signs the note she's been writing and snaps the chart closed. "Maybe he'll be put with one of those batshit martyr types; they come out of the woodwork for kids like Ben. A story like his is crazybait. I guess he could do worse."

Have I ever sounded that callous? I wonder, knowing beyond doubt that I have.

She flicks a look of interest over me. "You married?"

When that answer was easy, it seemed like no one ever asked that question. I shake my head.

The spark snuffs out.

"Too bad. He likes you."

"Let me know what happens to him, okay?"

"Sure." She walks away without a good-bye, having dismissed me for what I am: a looky-loo, a bystander. I won't save Ben and she's too overworked to spare even the effort of judging me for it. She's moved on, and the message is clear: I should too.

"Are you consulting on Ben?" A young Indian woman has come up behind me. Her badge identifies her as Preeti Chaudhary, medical student; she must be a third-year doing her required psych rotation.

"I admitted him through the ER," I say. "I sort of knew his mom."

"I did his intake." That's what they call an admission on Psych, *intake*, as if they're swallowing the patient whole. "What happened to him was tragic."

"Yes." That's going to be Ben's life from here, isn't it, his first six years replaced by one terrible day. No one will mention him from now on without thinking or saying *tragic*.

"You know about Dr. Jellicoe's diagnosis?" she asks.

"Yes," I say. "Is the hypnotherapy working?"

"He's remembering some things," she says.

She teeters on the brink of her next sentence. There's something she wants to say. I can guess at her internal calculations: I'm a resident, but I'm not visiting Ben in a professional capacity. Also, I've said I knew his mom, which might color me as family in medical-speak.

"Dr. Jellicoe thinks that Ben created Leo as a new personality to protect himself from what he saw," she begins.

"But you don't agree?" A medical student contradicting the chairman of the department; stunning in its audacity.

Again, that measuring moment, her scrutinizing gaze before she replies. "I believe that the trauma caused retrograde amnesia. And now the wrong memories are coming back."

"The *wrong memories*," I repeat.

She seems to come to a decision.

"I had a cousin," she says. She keeps her voice low, her eyes on mine. "From the time he could talk he spoke of his village, which was not the place we lived. He said he'd been killed in an accident there."

"What?" I say, but she talks over the syllable as if I haven't spoken.

"He was very angry at his brother-in-law, who'd stacked bricks improperly on a cart; the bricks had fallen on him and broken his neck. He demanded to see his wife. He worried about his children." She pauses. "He was three years old."

As she speaks, scenes flurry in my mind: crowded unpaved streets, ragged children clambering on a heap of trash. I can't connect any of it with Ben.

"What exactly are you saying?" I ask.

"I think Ben *is* Leo," she says. "Or that he used to be called Leo, in a life before this one. Just as my cousin was also the man who died from the falling bricks." She puts a hand to the side of her neck. "My cousin was born with a scar here, where he said the bricks cut him. Ben has a place on his ear."

I know the place she means. The divot in the flesh where the auricle joins to the head, just a tiny flaw on that side and not the other, which I'd noticed under the penlight beam during my initial exam.

I have the most extraordinary feeling, as if the surface of everything is lifting, the world peeling back to reveal a deep complicated beauty.

"What happened to your cousin?" I ask. My voice sounds far away, as if someone else is talking.

"We took him home," she says. "To the other village, so he

could talk with his children and his wife. It was what he needed. In time, the memories faded. He was able to be present in his new life only after making peace with his old one."

For a breath Preeti and I stand looking at each other.

A white-coated resident goes by, her heels ticking on the hard surface of the corridor. The sound reorients me. High heels are worn by office doctors, the kind who work easy daylight hours, far from the raw landscape of the Emergency Department. Like a compass needle swinging back to true north, I am brought back to myself, from wherever I have gone during this conversation.

"It's a nice idea, Preeti," I say. Her face falls. "I wish it were that simple for Ben."

I unclip my badge and slide it through the security sensor. The electronic lock releases with a *chunk*. When the doors swing closed behind me, Preeti is still standing there, looking determined but helpless, like a widow abandoned on shore.

CHEST PAIN IN a seventy-year-old, chest pains in a twenty-year-old, twisted ankle, "drank too much," vaginal bleeding, "stepped on a broken tile and cut my foot," cold symptoms for one week, penile discharge, pinkeye.

Surgical team to Trauma 1.

William Barber, eighty-two, scalded in the shower.

"Now why do I need all this fuss?" He holds his arm out co-operatively while Brenda knots the tourniquet around his biceps. "It's just a little hot water."

"You're going to need some intravenous fluid," Brenda says, wiping an alcohol swab over the blue ladder of vessels in his ante-cubital fossa.

"If I was home I'd just put a little aloe on it and go about my business." He looks up, sees me. "We're from Texas." He pauses as if he's a comedian expecting a crop of *Yeah!*s from the audience.

Brenda tapes down the IV catheter and dials open the occluding wheel with her thumb; the Lactated Ringer's solution chases the blood from the tubing. "It's the first time in my life I ever had one of these, can you believe it?" says Mr. Barber.

"What happened?" I ask him.

"My wife was in the shower. One of those tubs with the old ball-and-claw feet? I was all for the Motel 6, but we're being fancy." I know what he means. The cobblestoned downtown historic district called Downcity has a boutique hotel on every block. "Here's a tip for you, honey: after sixty, *unique* means *uncomfortable*."

His wife had slipped getting out, clutching at the tap as she fell, turning the water to boiling. He had been helping her navigate the high step over the tub side; while she lay under the spray he had put his own body into the steaming blast to protect her. He'd managed to turn the water off, but not right away.

My heart squeezes when I pull back the sheet. It's worse than I expected, the front half of his torso red and bubbled, chalky white in places. The anterior thighs and perineum. Most of the left arm. I calculate rapidly: over 40 percent of this man's body surface area seriously burned, a life-threatening proportion even in a young person.

"Can't be too bad," he says. "It barely hurts at all."

His lack of pain is the opposite of reassuring, signifying that the skin has been destroyed to a depth below the layer containing the sensory nerve endings. Second degree hurts; third degree does not.

"Two-fifty bolus to start and let's give him two of morphine," I tell Brenda, and set about calculating his fluid requirements.

"I'll call for a bed in the burn unit," she says.

"Can you find out how my wife is?" he asks me. "The ambulance brought her in too—she had some pain in her leg after the fall. You won't have any trouble finding her. Just look for the most beautiful woman you've ever seen." Do men really talk like this?

The computer reveals that she's in bed 5, out in the urgent area. I punch up her films and review them.

"She's all right," I tell Mr. Barber. "Nothing broken."

I expect him to smile, but instead he closes his eyes.

"Praise Jesus," he whispers. When he opens them, he's blinking tears away. "We've been married fifty-nine years. I know it can't last forever, but I'm not ready." I feel answering tears start in my own eyes and turn to Brenda, who's wheeling a Mayo stand to the bedside.

"Central line," she says.

Burn protocol requires aggressive intravenous access—two large lines in the arms would suffice, but this burn involves the left arm, so that can't be used. To get adequate access we'll need to go central, into the largest vessels in the body at one of the points where they travel with least obstruction: the neck or chest or groin.

"I'll need to put an IV right here," I tell him, touching just below his clavicle. He nods.

I'm always surprised how calmly people take that information: *I'll need to put a needle into your chest.* The chest is a horrible, unthinkable place to put a needle. When I was an intern, it seemed an impossible task: sink this needle into this chest to find the deep invisible vein, and avoid puncturing the lung that is *right there,* or the huge artery that is *right there,* or any of the ropy important nerves that run *right there.* I learned it the way I learned every other medical procedure, segmenting the challenge into a sequence of steps, blotting out the instinctual horror of the whole. By now, I've done it so many times that it's almost routine. Mr. Barber has never had this done, though, so by rights he should be terrified. He's not—because he trusts me. Joe doesn't see this part of my job; if he could, would it change things? I tell him in my mind, *this is the purpose of all the training: to be worthy of such trust.*

The procedure goes smoothly; less than ten minutes after nudging the first needle under the flare of collarbone I am finished and suturing the subclavian line into his skin.

"Tell me, Doctor, are you married?"

Talkative Mr. Barber has stayed quiet under the sterile paper as long as he can.

"Sort of." I clip the nylon suture, squiggle some antibacterial ointment over the place where the catheter tunnels under the skin, apply an occlusive dressing. "I mean. Separated."

"I'm sorry to hear that." *Me too.*

"All done." I tear away the sterile paper and turn off the overhead surgical light.

"Will you accept a little advice from an old fogey?" he says as I pull the stretcher back up to a sitting position. His white hair is damp, standing up like flame; it gets hot under the strong light.

"Sure."

"Is he a good man? Don't think about it—yes or no?" I nod yes. "Then *un*separate." His blue eyes are like an oracle. "Put aside the wrongs and go forward. We're none of us made perfect for each other. We have to grow to fit together. That growing—that's marriage." I've kept nodding while he speaks: *Okay, I'll do that.* As if it is that easy. As if any of it is my choice.

His face lights up as his gaze moves to fall on something behind me. I turn to see Mrs. Barber being wheeled in, a small nondescript woman in a zippered flowery gown.

"You look like a mummy," she says, reaching up and touching just her fingertips to his where they protrude from the gauze.

"Hey there, punkin," he says.

The joy of reunion is palpable in the room.

This couple married during the Eisenhower years. Surely their time together has contained intermittent dissatisfactions, petty grievances and irritations, as well as deeper, more important rifts. But they've weathered it all and come through. My husband and I didn't even make it to our fifth anniversary.

I step out to speak with the son, a lantern-jawed man in his fifties wearing a button-down shirt and khakis.

"Is it bad?" he asks.

"It's an extensive burn," I say.

"They're supposed to be going on a cruise next week," he says, and leaves it there, the silence a kind of negative space, making the question for him.

In a week, I know with heartbreaking certainty, Mr. Barber will be on life support. His elderly body can't withstand the loss of so much of its protective covering without dreadful consequences. When that cruise ship sails, he will be swollen beyond recognition, the fluid weeping from his skin, the intravenous replacement building up in his lungs and escaping into his tissues. He'll be unconscious from sedatives given to prevent him from resisting the ventilator breaths, and he'll be multiply catheterized: his heart, to measure his body's delicate fluid balances and assess the squeeze of his ventricles; his bladder, so that his urine may be precisely quantified; his rectum, so that fecal matter will not seep out and infect his perineal burn. He will be beset nonetheless with infections: his skin, despite all efforts, and then his lungs and urinary tract. His stressed heart will fail, a series of infarctions necrosing a patch here, a patch there; his kidneys will falter. His wife will keep vigil at his bedside. Because she's been told that the last sense to leave is the ability to hear, she'll talk to him. In her soft voice she'll comfort the ballooned caricature of her husband, taking his tight swollen hand into hers, wiping away the beads of moisture forcing themselves out onto his skin. He may feel fine now, but he's doomed. In the next few hours, the siege will begin.

"You'll need to cancel the cruise," I say, watching the son's face change as he takes in my meaning. "I can write a letter to the cruise line if you need, to avoid a penalty. You should call your brothers and sisters. Anyone who needs to say good-bye. Tell them to come as soon as possible."

His face is vague; he reaches one hand up to his collar, puts his hand down again.

"I'm so sorry," I say.

He nods. He puts his hand up again, grasping something invisible between thumb and first two fingers, and I realize he's used to wearing a necktie and must have a habit of fussing with the knot.

"I'll be here all night, if you have any questions or need anything."

Before he parts the curtain to go into the trauma room, he rearranges his face into lines of reassurance; when he greets his parents his voice is robust with cheer.

Such mundane things have the power to unmake us. Six decades of affection and compromise and care brought to an end by a trendy bathtub and a hot-water heater set too high. Ben marooned forever by a birthday party. No one can save this family gathering now under the trauma-room light. No one will save Ben. The world doesn't work that way.

CHAPTER TWENTY-ONE

Clare

Y OU CAN'T LIVE HERE," SAID Prior Washburn. "There's no electricity. No plumbing."

"A lot of people live that way."

"Not a woman alone. Not by choice." He looked at my hands. "Have you ever farmed before?"

"I'm not looking for luxury. Give me a year. If I can't manage, I'll leave."

"A year. Where will you go then?"

There was no answer to that.

"I can bring those roses back," I said. It was a stray thought, but his expression softened as he looked toward the cemetery and the struggling roses.

"They're beyond hope, I think," he said.

"Maybe not. My mother's roses were famous." Mentioning her was like swallowing a lancet of glass. I was lying again. It was true that she'd espaliered roses on the back wall of the bookshop, and that I'd been pressed into caring for them sometimes, but I knew nothing of bringing roses back from the dead.

"It's autumn now, and no crops in." His reckoning tone told me he was weakening. "You'll have all you can do to get the house habitable again. It's been a while since the last tenant." The state-

ment finished a bit abruptly, and I knew he'd left off the word *died*.
"We can give you some supplies to get you through to spring. But
you have to promise that you'll come to me if you fail. Clare"—I
looked up at the command in his voice—"please don't lay a suicide
on my conscience."

"I won't."

"You must not let your pride lead you."

"I'm done with pride." And added another lie to the pile that I
wouldn't be confessing. "I will come to you if I fail."

THE FIRST ORDER of business was the house itself: it was a two-
room structure, with walls of stone and a roof of rough square tiles,
and a short wooden porch in front that creaked as I walked across
it. The front door was ajar; when I pushed it open I could see that
the opening had been wide enough to admit raccoons or possums
or foxes, judging by the calling cards they'd left behind.

The main room, filled with piles of animal waste and dirt and
leaves, was sparsely furnished: a stove and a worktable in the kitchen
area, another sturdy table near the front window, and a settee beside
the hearth that had been home to a mouse family, judging from
the cotton stuffing bubbling out of a large hole in the cushion.
Luckily the door to the bedroom had been closed, so it was dusty
and cobwebbed in there, but not actually filthy. It held a single
bed, a night table, a tall wardrobe, and an empty trunk. I started in
that room with a broom, pulling down the cobwebs and sweeping
the floor, taking stock of the few possessions. A Bible and a rosary,
both of which I put into a drawer; a figured bowl and pitcher on
the night table that would be useful for ablutions. When I swept
beneath the bed I found another wide bowl, and it took me a moment to understand its use. When I did, it brought me up short.
My childhood had never included a chamber pot. Was I really
going to do this?

What other options did I have? My parents were dead, my child was dead, I had no means. I might have an older brother or two left somewhere, but Hugh had the greatest legal claim on me. That reminder solidified my resolve. I put the chamber pot aside to wash; it would go back under the bed when the room was clean.

Clean. That was going to take a lot more work, and a good deal of water. There was no sink in the kitchen. Had I seen a pump outside? I went out the front door and stood on the splintery porch.

Weeds had taken over the front yard in a waist-high, waving sea. Later I would know all the names—dock and pigweed and goosefoot and sorrel—but on that day they were anonymous, an undifferentiated invading mass of green. I stood on my toes to look beyond the wall and down the hill: there lay the overgrown cemetery ringed by the scruff of moribund rosebushes. How long had the property been unoccupied? Nature was obviously determined to drag it back into wilderness.

But the weather was fine, sunny with a light breeze, much more cheerful than the gloomy, dusty cottage, and I decided that I'd resume work inside later. In a corner of the yard, surrounded by a forest of pokeweed that drooped purple berries from stems ten feet tall, I found a toolshed. It had been immaculately kept and was as full as the house was empty. I chose a hand scythe and a wooden-handled hoe and a whetstone and honed the blades of the tools, noting how well they'd been cared for: not a speck of rust. My mother would have approved. Again that pang at her memory, and for the first time questions crowded after. Had there been a funeral? Where was she buried? Michel's name had been on the list the prior had read aloud. How had he died? For a moment the burden of loss buckled me, and I staggered.

Swinging the scythe pulled painfully on my wound, but it wasn't unbearable. The rhythm was soothing, anesthetic; after just a few hours I'd reduced the green sea in front of the cottage to a wading pool, ready for the hoe. I'd found the pump in the middle of the yard, an enameled-tin mug tied to its handle, and I pumped until the water was clear. While I stood drinking, the sun went behind a cloud and the fabric of my dress grew clammy against my back. My second-best dress. The monks had laundered and mended it while I convalesced. Suddenly I couldn't bear its gritty, sweaty tightness and returned to the shed, where I'd seen a pair of denim overalls and a holey plaid shirt. I changed right there, hanging the dress on the nail that had held the overalls, and went back to work. I kept at it all day; at sundown I opened my sack of provisions and made a meal of cheese and bread before crawling onto the dusty bed, asleep as soon as I closed my eyes.

I awoke the next day almost too stiff to move, my body screaming in protest when I tried to sit up. I had to sidle out of bed, the way I had from my childhood bed under the dormer. I wrestled the mattress outside, a clumsy business, and used a spade to beat it, raising a gratifying cloud. When I tired of that I propped the mattress against the wall in the sun and pumped a bucket of water, taking that back into the house to resume cleaning in there.

Prior Washburn arrived in midmorning, carrying a basket. He raised his eyebrows at the sight of me.

"You must be hungry," he said, stepping up the path that had emerged under my scythe and hoe. I accepted the basket eagerly, peeking in: eggs, fruit, butter, more cheese and bread. "We expected you back last night."

I gave him a tour of the little cottage and the land around it, pointing out the sunny place I planned for the garden.

"You can't mean to stay here," he said, looking around. Through his eyes, I saw how paltry was my progress. The house interior might be free of the piles and drifts of dirt, but the windowpanes were still black. The tall weeds in the yard had been hacked down and removed to a gigantic wilting mound outside the wall, but that had only revealed a tough carpet of chickweed and bittercress and dandelion that surged, springy and dense, in all directions. The lumpy mattress sagged in the sun. I'd need to repair the porch. I'd need to find, or dig out, a cellar. Everywhere I looked, a different massive project waited.

I felt a stab of panic, then closed my eyes and quelled it. I'd pick the seams of the ticking and wash it, and restuff the mattress. I'd dig each weed out of the earth, root by root, and I'd turn the soil. I'd wash the windows. One square foot at a time, it all could be done.

"It's been one day," I said. "You promised me a year."

"So I did. Although that was probably not wise."

"I can do this." Gritting my teeth, ignoring the cacophony of need calling from every corner of the landscape.

"It may not be possible," he said.

"Then I'll find that out," I said.

THAT NIGHT I was simply too tired to pull the mattress back into the house. I pushed it down from its slant against the wall to land on the weeds with a giant puff of dust. At that point I was almost more dirt than skin, and beyond caring about such niceties as bed linens. I crawled onto it and fell asleep immediately.

I awoke sometime later, under a dome of stars. There was no wind. Something walked in the grass nearby, but I felt neither curiosity nor fear, and I had no urge to move. Flat against the earth, I felt a deep sense of belonging. No past or present, not even a person but a soul, liquid and blank. Unmoving, I was yet moving with everything on the earth, no boundaries between me and the stars and the ground and the grass and whatever roamed or hunted nearby. No sorrow, no hope or fear. I felt Bradley, gone and also with me, against my chest and slowly leaving, evaporating from my grasp. *My sweet boy.* The tears were for the joy of him, back in my arms to tell me not good-bye, but the opposite—that I could join him if I wanted. I closed my eyes, released my hold on the world. *Wait for me.*

I AWOKE AGAIN in the wee hours. It was as though I'd had a fever that had crescendoed and left me weaker but well. It was more: as though I'd had an invisible companion, one who'd accompanied me my entire life, and who was now gone. Leaving me alone, but also relieved of the worry and care that comes with love. Now the world was emptier, less rich, but also simpler.

I heard a distant crack, like a twig breaking under a footstep, and was instantly alert. I realized that I had never actually been alone at night. Now I was more alone than I had thought it possible to be, totally vulnerable, at the mercy of any passerby. I thought of the shotgun I'd seen in the shed; even if I had it with me, I wouldn't have known how to use it.

I lay stiff and listening while the predawn splashed a rim of amber above the distant trees. I didn't move until the sky was cobalt and the ball of sun was molten behind the tree line. I rose then with a fresh determination: I would get the bedroom habitable and pull the mattress back in there. No more sleeping in the open. And I'd learn how to use that gun.

I hauled water into the kitchen, bucket after bucket to fill the deep tin tub I'd found in the shed, and washed my filthy self in water so cold it turned my arms numb. I put the flannel shirt and overalls on again, emptied the black water from the tub and left it upside down to dry in the yard, then fetched kindling to make a fire in the woodstove and boil myself an egg.

In the afternoon a wheelbarrow arrived, pushed by a redheaded St. Will's lad with a freckled face. It bore a set of bedsheets, a bar of soap, a hairbrush and comb, a lantern, and a container of lamp oil. There was also a wide-brimmed hat with a note pinned to it. *Your nose is sunburning,* it said, and *Keep the barrow.*

AFTER TWO WEEKS, the house was reasonably clean, the soil for the garden was turned, and the roses had been pruned and fed with a compost tea I'd brewed in a bucket, following what I could remember of my mother's recipe.

I took the shotgun and the box of shells from the shed and went a good distance into the field behind the cottage, setting some cracked jars on a stump for targets. My first shots went wide and wide and wide, wasting shells and raising a bruised place on my shoulder. I pushed the hat from my face, let it hang by its ribbon against my back while I aimed carefully, closing one eye. At last! One of the jars flew into pieces.

Through the ringing in my ears, I became aware of a new sound, repetitive and distant. I looked around for its source and saw a flash beside the stone cottage, then the sound again. Who was at Roscommon, and what was he doing? I walked swiftly in that direction, carrying the gun.

As I got closer, I could see that the flashing was the sun reflecting off an ax blade, rising and falling. Someone was chopping wood. Not one of the schoolboys from next door as I might have expected, but a grown man. Perhaps thirty, clean-shaven, with dark wavy hair.

"Hello," I said.

He brought the ax whistling down.

"Was that you shooting on my land?" he said, not looking at me, rocking the blade out of the wood.

I was confused. Was this man making claim to Roscommon? After all my work?

"This is your land?"

"I own the farm next door," he said, indicating the direction with his chin. "That big rock over there is the boundary." He raised his arms high again. *Crack,* two quarter logs jumping apart and falling on either side.

"I didn't mean to trespass," I said. He nodded. *Crack.* "What are you doing?"

"Firewood," he said. *Crack.*

"Why?"

"It'll be winter before long. You'll need a lot of it." Now he looked at me, holding the ax and waiting, to see if I had more questions.

"Oh. Yes," I said. "Yes, of course. Thank you."

He split logs every afternoon for a few days, until the firewood pile stretched the length of the building and all the way up to the roof. In time, I'd teach myself to chop my own firewood, and I'd be a tolerable shot too. But that was my first year at Roscommon, and I wouldn't have had any chance to make it through the winter without that wood. The farmer had asked nothing from me. I didn't know who sent him, or why he might have wanted to help, but I accepted the kindness as something given, human to human. From now on, I would leave God out of everything.

CHAPTER TWENTY-TWO

Leo

J ENESSA, THE AIDE, TAKES ME to the library. It's the first time I've seen her smile. She walks me around the corner and down two blocks.

"Shoot," she says, puffing, when we come into view of the place. She is pretty fat. "I thought libraries had to have like stone lions and shit. That's just a house."

It does look like a house, yellow clapboard, a long set of steps reaching down from the white front door to the parking lot. A small sign stuck in the grass at the foot of the steps says Public Library.

I'm almost to the top of the steps before I realize Jenessa's not with me. She's seated herself on a bench near the sidewalk. She looks up and sees me waiting.

"You go on in," she calls, bringing a pack of cigarettes and a lighter from the pocket of her patterned smock. "Gonna get some fresh air."

IT LOOKS LIKE just one room at first. There are rolling carts of books against the far walls and I head toward those.

"Well, hello there!" A voice drops from somewhere I can't see. "Are you all by yourself?"

"Jenessa's outside," I say as a lady stands up behind the counter. She's got a frozen-looking puff of light yellow hair and square glasses.

"Are you looking for anything in particular?"

I can see now that this is just the middle room, with wide doorways on either side. The room through the doorway to the right has a long table and the room on the other side is bigger and filled with bookshelves. There's a long line of television sets on desks with chairs in front of them, and a huge stuffed dragon in one corner.

The library lady is looking at me with a thinking expression on her face.

"I sense a discriminating reader," she says. She beckons, and I follow her into the dragon room. "Here," she says, handing me a book with a boy's face on the cover, pine trees and a wolf in the distance behind him. "Have you read this one?"

I shake my head.

"And if you like that," she says, reaching to another shelf and handing me another. She pulls a third book out and considers, holding it. "Is that too many? You'll have two weeks to read them."

"I don't have a card," I say.

"Oh, you do need one of those." She looks really disappointed. "You can still read the books while you're here, though. You just can't take them out."

I point to one of the televisions.

"Can you show me how to use that?"

She raises her eyebrows, as if surprised. "Certainly."

She pulls out one of the chairs and I climb up. The screen is blue, with a box that says Log In.

"The log-in information is on a sticky here." She points to a yellow flap of paper stuck to the frame of the screen. "First, use the mouse to put the cursor in the box."

The *mouse*. I shake my head.

"This is the mouse." She moves a plastic oval on the desk with a freckled bony hand. "You move it like this, and it moves the cursor." She makes a click and there's a thin blinking bar in the Log In box.

"Now you can type," she says.

I press the keys for the letters and numbers and then Return when she tells me; the Log In box is replaced with a white screen.

"You got it," she says. "Now, is there a project that I can help you with?"

"I thought this was television," I say.

Again, that faint surprise washing from her. "Well, you *can* watch television on it," she says. "But in the library, we don't do that."

"Can it play games?" I am thinking about the big boy and the Nintendo.

"It can, but in the library people mostly use it to look things up," she says. She moves the mouse again, clicks it. "To learn more about something. You type in what you're looking for." She has a thought. "Are you homeschooled?"

"I don't think so," I say.

We share a puzzled moment before she puts her hand lightly on my shoulder.

"Okay, well. What would you like to look up?" She leans close over my shoulder, reading the screen as I type. "Hmm. I think you might need a spelling adjustment." She taps the Delete key, then taps another letter into the word and clicks Go. The screen flashes white before new text furls down.

"That's a long way from here," she says.

I hadn't considered that.

WHEN I COME out of the library, Jenessa is sitting on the bus-stop bench next to the street, looking intently at her phone. I jump down the steps. She doesn't notice me until I am right beside her.

"You don't have any books," she says accusingly. Tobacco reeks from her in a sweet musk. "What were you doing that whole time?"

"I can't take books out 'cause I don't have a card. If you bring me back, I can finish the book I was reading."

"Fine with me," she says, gathering the cigarette box and lighter from beside her on the bench and standing up. "Beats emptying bedpans."

CHAPTER TWENTY-THREE

Lucy

IT IS THE SAME DREAM I have had many times before. There's an intruder roaming around the apartment. In my dream, I slip out of bed; as I go from room to room he is just ahead of me, a dark shape passing through a doorway or in front of a window. In the last room, I am alone. Suddenly there is a noise behind me. I whirl and he is there, not more than a foot away.

Usually this is where the dream ends, but this time he lifts his hand and I see the gun in it. There is nothing but air between its muzzle and my chest. I can feel the burning of the place where the wound will open in my sternum. I am not looking at the gun, I am looking at the face of the intruder, waiting for the explosion.

Lucy. A man's voice, but it's a little boy who runs toward me. Ben? *Don't be scared,* he says. He reaches up, slips his hand into mine.

I awaken with my heart pounding. The call room is dark, filled with looming unfamiliar shapes—is that a person there, by the window? My chest squeezes; I turn on the flashlight from my phone and see that it's my white coat on a hanger, unalive, unfrightening. It's just past midnight. I've stayed up all day, trying to turn my schedule around for the day off tomorrow. Which is actually today.

I touch the screen of my phone, once and then again; it collapses into blackness *Connecting . . .* Is the phone ringing beside the bed? Perhaps he's not in the apartment. At the thought, I almost end the call, but then he answers.

"What's wrong?" A whisper. So as not to wake the woman beside him?

"I had a bad dream." It is a familiar statement, one with which I awakened him several times over the years.

"Oh, sweet pea." There's rustling from his end. Is he getting out of bed and going into another room? Already the burning in my chest is fading, the images are sinking away from my memory. "It was just a dream," he says. "It wasn't real."

I close my eyes: I could be home, he could be beside me, about to draw me into an embrace, my brow against his collarbone, his chest hair tickling my nose. Both arms solidly around me.

"Are you home?" I ask.

"Yes."

"Are you alone?"

"Yes."

We are silent for a minute.

"How are you?" I ask.

"I'm okay. No, I'm not. I miss you."

"I miss you too."

The cover of night, it seems, or maybe just the disorientation of disturbed sleep, has peeled away our shells of anger and disappointment, and freed the softer truths.

"Sweet pea. What are we going to do?" he says. And then, "Come over."

Voices crowd into my mind: Giles's *What an ass* and my stepmother's gentle *Maybe you two just need to talk, honey.* Then the Texas twang of Mr. Barber: *Is he a good man?*

I wash my face and brush my teeth. The uncompromising rectangle of mirror in the bathroom reflects me back in all my hollow-eyed glory. My hair is brown but my lashes are blond, invisible. I used to wear mascara and lip gloss. That was then, this is now.

When Joe opens the door, candlelight flickers against the apartment walls behind him. He's been lighting the candles while I've been driving.

"I'm glad you came," he says, stepping back so I can go past him into the apartment. Dark, tidy. No sign of the mess I made when I was here last time. "I opened some wine. I wasn't sure what shift you're on."

"It's Death Month. I have the day off tomorrow."

I can barely speak for the rushing in my ears, my thoughts so loud it feels that he must hear them: *how I love you, how I've missed you.*

He pours and I take the glass. We bought these when we lived in New York, full lead crystal and so beautiful, but only two left on the clearance shelf. I'd said, *Who buys two wineglasses?* and he'd said, *That's all we need,* and put them in our basket.

I sit on the desk chair, the only other place to sit besides the bed. He sits on the end of the bed and puts the wine bottle on the floor.

"I almost called you a thousand times," he says.

"Why didn't you?"

"I guess I didn't know where to start."

"Just start."

He looks into his glass. "She was there, you weren't." *She.* It's a jolt to hear the pronoun. "I know that's no excuse," he adds, although I haven't said anything. "It's just been—" He shuts his eyes, opens them again. "Waiting for you all the time. Tiptoeing around while you're sleeping. Do you know how long it's been since we had fun?"

Were we ever fun? We were intense. We fell headlong into each other, it was destiny, it was passion.

"Is *she* fun?" I ask.

He looks at me sharply, but he sees that I'm really just asking, there's no antagonism in it, and he takes a sip of wine and then says, "She's a good listener." Thinks for another moment. "She's nice."

"*I'm* nice," I say, and I hear the comedy in it, the cartoon character shouting *I'm not angry!*

He smiles just a little.

"Well, I used to be nice," I say, and correct myself again. "I used to be nic*er*."

I remember gunshot Mrs. Ortiz cursing, her husband's insistence: *she doesn't even know those words.*

"You can be nice," he concedes. "But you're not nice all the time."

The word is starting to sound like nonsense. *Nice. Nice.* Repetition is crushing the meaning out of it. Who's *nice all the time*?

"I'm not trying to make it sound like your fault," he says. "But it started to feel like we were enemies."

"I never felt that way." But if I'd had all that time alone, maybe I would have. "But this is just the *for worse* part. You know, for better or for worse?"

"Those are just words," he says. "Like the Pledge of Allegiance. No one actually thinks about what they mean when they're saying them."

"I did," I say, shocked. "It wasn't the Pledge of Allegiance to me."

"It's every day," he says, impatience breaking in his voice. "You coming home, saying, *What did you do today?* I collated the quarterly report, what about you? *I brought a dead person back to life.*"

He's talking, finally we're talking. I want all the details, I want to know everything. But another part of me doesn't want to know any of it, and wants him to stop telling me about how terrible it's been to know me.

"I don't want to feel this way when I'm forty," he's saying. "I want things to be easier."

We started in our twenties, at a party as he was coming in and I was leaving, and something about the way our eyes caught as we passed each other made me turn around and stay. That minute was the beginning. Minutes accumulate into hours and days and months and years. All those minutes have brought us here. Was there one minute among them that could have turned us onto a different path? He's right, we did have fun once upon a time. We used to laugh a lot. When had our lives become such a terribly serious business?

"I know it's been difficult," I say. "I don't want it to be. I just—" I grope for the right words. "It's been like standing so close to a mountain that the mountain is all you can see. You can't see over it or around it, or even the sky above it. Just the mountain all the time." He's listening, eyes on me. "And the person you're closest to, the person you love most, doesn't even see the mountain."

"I think I've been on a different mountain," he says.

I put out my hand and he takes it. His guitar-callused fingertips, I'd know them anywhere. Our separate pulses beat against each other where our fingers lace together. He puts his wineglass down.

The rest is very easy. We have done this so many times before. The sameness is overwhelming. The same body, the same smell. The same shoulders, the same furry chest, and the same knees knotted with football scars. This is the back I remember, the banks of muscle along the deep trough of spine, the mole just below the neck. It is all quite dizzyingly the same, and I close my eyes and let our hands, our skin, re-create us.

When we are lying together afterward, I have a sudden cramp of ravenousness.

"I'm so hungry I could die," I say.

"Don't move," he says, dropping a kiss onto my shoulder. He rises and goes into the kitchen. I lie on the sofa under the blanket and watch the patterns of light on the walls, listening to Joe clatter around in the kitchen, opening drawers and cabinets, then the *tick-tick-tick* of the gas igniting on the stovetop, the hum of the microwave. It all feels so right, so familiar, just the way it should be.

I wrap the blanket around me and walk toward the window; the low bookcase under the sill is strewn with objects. It had always been a sentimental surface; Joe used to put mementos there, ticket stubs from concerts and wine corks from our meals together. They are still there. I am briefly warmed by this, until I look more closely, see the date on a pair of ticket stubs: just last week. The wine corks are less readily identifiable; maybe they are also new. He is a creature of habit; have I been that easily exchanged?

I find my clothing in the nest of bedsheets, pull on my underwear, and drop my T-shirt over my head.

"Brave is the man who cooks naked," Joe asserts a minute later, putting a tray down on the bed. There are two bowls of pasta, some bread, and a little bowl of olives. He retrieves his boxers from the floor and pulls them on.

For a while we eat, nothing more complicated than putting food into our mouths and chewing, the vacuum at my center filling slowly. I watch him eat. Is it possible that in this short time apart I've forgotten how he chews? How he lifts his fork? Everything looks strange yet also deeply familiar, as if I'm a castaway newly returned to civilization.

"What?" he says, seeing that I am staring at him.

"What did you do with the stuff in the drawer?"

"What stuff?" he says, but then says, "Oh." He puts his empty pasta bowl onto the tray with mine, moves the tray from the bed to the floor. "I threw it away. I'm sorry."

I had never considered that. Images play out behind my eyes: the drawer pulled out and held over the recycling bin, the stack of postcards falling with a solid thump and the Post-it notes fluttering after. The bin at the curb, the wind pulling out a few pieces and distributing them around the block before the recycling truck comes.

"We can make more." Putting his arms around me.

"It won't be the same." We won't be young like that, naive like that, new to each other or to anyone else like that, ever again.

"It will be better," he whispers. He pulls the blanket over both of us and snugs me little-spoon against him, his hand over mine. I close my eyes and try to climb up into sleep, against the backward schedule I've been on the last three weeks.

"You're not sleeping," he says after a couple of minutes.

"I've been on nights," I remind him. He sighs and turns onto his back, pulling me with him so that my head is against his chest. "I'm thinking about this kid from work." I've let my thoughts float free, and that's where they've gone.

"Mmm-hmm."

"His doctor's trying to diagnose him as dissociative disorder. You know, multiple personality. He doesn't have anyone to advocate for him. No family." I swallow past the next words. "His mom was murdered." A throb of pain in the center of my chest, a memory of the fear in my dream.

"Which doctor? Aren't you his doctor?"

"No, his psych doctor. I saw him in the ER and admitted him to Psych."

"Does he have multiple personalities? Did you see that?" A perk of interest.

"I don't know. He's amnestic from the trauma, he's calling himself Leo. He doesn't seem psychotic, though."

"Amnesia, is that really a thing?" says Joe.

"It can happen."

Light flares around the curtains in the window: headlights from a car cresting the hill on the street below. A pale panel of illumination travels the ceiling as the car makes a turn. I'd forgotten that Australia-shaped stain on the plaster.

"Mmm." Joe's drowsy again. "He's not your patient anymore, right?"

"No, but." But what? I'm not a psychiatrist. Maybe Dr. Jellicoe is right, maybe it's traumatic dissociation. Maybe hypnosis will help. Maybe they'll try medication. I hear Karen again, *I told them no fucking way.* "He's only six."

The half moon shows in the space between the window curtains; its light falls through the gap and glazes the things on the top of the bureau. We're balanced right here, the two of us, between our past and our future. Joe's measured breaths tell me that he's asleep. I try to force myself to relax and follow. Listen to his breathing, inhale, exhale. *I don't belong here. I do belong here. I don't.* Like pulling the petals of a daisy, but with a real daisy the outcome is certain: always five petals, so you know you'll end up back where you start.

CHAPTER TWENTY-FOUR

Clare

A FEW DAYS AFTER THE APPLE incident, the boy they'd called Leo came back, walking up to the wall in plain view and climbing up to sit. This time I was tending to the Conroys, not ten feet from the wall; I could hardly pretend not to see him, but I paid him no attention. I listened for sounds of approaching compatriots, but it seemed he had come alone. He stayed there, facing my way with his legs dangling, for nearly a quarter of an hour with the only sounds in the air between us the varied trill of birds calling out their territory markings, and the *scrape, scrape, thunk* of my blade.

I knifed some weed-bristled sod away from Nuala Conroy, wife of Treacher, 1863 to 1897. Died in childbirth, most likely. Left five live children behind, and as many dead ones, their little stones in a row stretching out to the side of hers, like ducklings following their mother. Her surviving daughters and sons had married and reproduced and come to rest in their own clusters in other places across the field. No sign of Treacher, though. Either he married again and settled with his new wife in another place, or he'd done something unspeakable—suicide or Protestantism—and was barred from St. William's. Or there simply hadn't been room for him in the end, what with all the children in the Conroy plot. I brushed some dirt from Nuala.

"You're not supposed to be here," I said finally.

"I'm supposed to be in the laundry," he agreed. "They threw me out because I scorched a sheet. Not on purpose. I held the press closed too long. Brother Nicholas told me to get out. He doesn't believe in caning." His tone made it clear that not all the brothers agreed with Nicholas. He swung his feet, his hands tucked under his thighs. "I think he's going to send me back to Folding."

I hadn't heard so many words in a long time. It was like a wall of sound coming at me, the syllables tumbling past almost faster than I could understand them. During that period in my life, there were whole tracts of time—weeks, months—where if I hadn't had to speak to the grocer on my biweekly visit to town, I wouldn't have uttered a single word to anyone, nor heard a word in return. I moved over to Catherine, age three.

"Where are your friends?" I asked.

"They're not my friends. Why do you do that?" he asked, watching me step on the metal crescent with one foot, driving it into the sod.

"Keeps it neat," I said. *Scrape, scrape, thunk.*

"It's a lot of work. If you do all of them."

"Yes, I do all of them," I snapped, straightening up and looking him full in the face. "Just because some folks don't have anyone living to remember them doesn't mean they don't matter."

He absorbed my irritation without flinching, leaning forward from his perch and pointing to the headstones below his swinging feet.

"They look like teeth."

I said nothing.

"Why are they crooked?"

I said nothing.

"Why are those ones so little?"

I said nothing.

He read the lettering on the Conroy stones aloud: *Catherine,*

Sadie, Willie, Susan, James. The front curtain of his brown hair had a tendency to fall down over his eyes, so that he had to keep tossing his head every few minutes. He was wearing the St. William's laundryworks uniform, the dark-blue serge trousers and the round-collared shirt; both were too large on him.

With him watching, the movements I had made unthinkingly so often seemed more discrete. Foot on the edger blade, step hard to push it in up to the eye; slide it out, reposition at an angle, step again. Lift the wedge of sod, swing it over to the wheelbarrow, deposit it with a soft thud. After a few minutes, I stood back to admire the Conroys. Even if their stones were leaning this way and that, they looked better. I moved on to the next plot.

"Why are those ones so little?" the boy asked again.

I said nothing.

"They're baby graves, aren't they. They're dead babies."

I straightened up.

"Don't you have anything better to do than bother people while they're working?"

"Not really. What did the babies die of?"

"How would I know?" I said.

"If you had to guess."

I bent to resume my work.

A minute or so passed.

"If you had to guess."

I gritted my teeth, said nothing.

"If you had to—"

"All *right*," I said, cutting him off. Ignoring wouldn't work on this boy, evidently; he would repeat himself at two-minute intervals, the same five words, until the sun went down or I answered, whichever came first. "They might have died of . . ." I paused, as though I'd never thought about it. The sweat was trickling down my forehead, a drop collecting on the tip of my nose. I lifted a hand and swiped my forearm across my face. "Diphtheria, maybe, or pneumonia."

"Dip-theria," he said. "What's that?"

"A sore throat so bad it chokes you."

"I had a sore throat last month. Brother Silas put a bad-smelling scarf around my neck and I had to gargle. What happened to those bushes? There's no flowers on them."

He was pointing to the rosebushes I was coddling after the previous winter's killing frost. The others were in full flower, but these three had been slow to recover.

"You should pull these up and get new ones," he said.

"And *you* should get back where you belong. Go on, shoo."

"Shoo isn't something you say to a person," he said, reproachful. "It's something you say to a bird."

Scrape, scrape, thunk.

"Or a bug. Not a person."

"Well, apples are for eating. Not throwing at people." I wheeled the barrow a little distance, to the next plot.

"A boy got eaten by the wringer last year and died. Is he buried here?"

"He's not here." If he ever existed. "I know everyone here."

"Why does that one have a buffalo?"

"That's not a buffalo," I said, looking up briefly to see where he was pointing. "It's a horse." Now that I looked, I saw that the carving on the top of the tombstone did look like the humped shape on the back of a nickel. Time had worn the ears and tail away.

"Why does he have a horse?"

"I don't know."

Would Bradley have done this, I wondered, if he had grown up to be this boy's age? Would he have pestered me with whys until I went mad?

He jumped down from the wall and read from the headstone: "1813 to 1824. He was eleven. Same as me." He interpreted my look of disbelief correctly. "I'm small," he said, pushing his fists into his pockets; the movement bunched the fabric of his trousers and created a gap at the waistband, as if to emphasize his statement. "That's the way God made me."

My blade sliced through a stand of dandelions. The Meehans tended to grow particularly nasty dandelions, with big, thick stalks that bled milk from their hollow centers when they were snapped.

"Make yourself useful," I said. "Pull that up."

He knelt, and I could see right away he'd never pulled a dandelion before: he put his fist around the stems.

"Let me show you how," I said.

"I can do it."

I said nothing: live and learn.

"Shit," he said, falling backward onto his rear end.

"*What* did you say?"

"I mean shoot," he said, showing me the sunny head of a flower on his palm.

"Pulling the stems will never work. You have to get down to the root. The bigger piece is underneath. Here, use this." I gave him the trowel from the loop on the side of my overalls.

He knelt again, his forehead folding up between his eyebrows, his fingers creeping into the splay of toothed leaves at the base of the plant, gathering them up before pushing the trowel point into the soil. I edged Zed Meehan for a while, buried with his nameless wife.

"Ha," the boy said finally, showing me a clump of root-choked dirt. I inspected it.

"You need to get the whole taproot. See how it's snapped off at the bottom? You need to dig that out."

He crouched again, his tongue poking out of the corner of his mouth, and a minute or two later brought out the wormy root. I nodded approval, and he dropped it into the wheelbarrow.

"There's another one over there," he said, and ran to it.

We worked for a while in peace, just the grate of tools on earth and stone and our separate panting in the heat. We tidied Zed and wife, daughter Anna, son-in-law William.

"Why isn't her name there?" the boy asked, dropping a dandelion cluster into the barrow. "She's just called Wife." He squatted by the headstone, put his hand out to the letters there. "If nobody knows your name after you die, is it like you never were born at all?"

I chunked out the last bit of weed encroaching on baby Roger, and upended the edger with a harsher movement than I intended. He looked up at the noise.

"That's enough for today." I ran my fingers over the metal, freeing the bits of dirt and grass that clung there.

He looked around at the families of stone spreading out in every direction, his cowlick dancing on his damp-darkened head, the rest of his hair beaded with fragments of earth. How had he gotten so dirty?

"There's a lot more," he said. He wiped his nose on the back of his hand, leaving a streak of mud above his upper lip.

It was true; the day's work had made but a spot of calm in a sea of chaos. A field a hundred feet on each side looks small, except in its caretaker's eyes.

"Their turns will come." I saw a peek of white flesh through the navy fabric below one knee. "You tore your pants."

He looked down at the rip and his face closed, like a curtain coming down.

"Will you be punished for that?" I asked.

He nodded, a tight movement up and down, not looking at me.

"Well. Come on with me."

I wheeled the barrow without looking back, threading my way between the headstones toward the gate. He got ahead and was there to open it for me as I passed through. He closed it with a soft *clang,* then followed me up the path to the yard in front of the cottage.

I pulled the pump handle up and down a few times to loose a warm cord of water and rinsed my hands.

"Fill that bucket," I told him.

I went inside and got my mending basket, a bar of soap and a towel, and the three-legged stool from the kitchen. When I came back outside he had his head under the pump, taking a drink.

"Give me your trousers," I said, placing the stool on the grass and sitting down. He hesitated. "Oh for goodness' sake." I swiveled myself around on the stool so that my back was to him.

A few moments later, the trousers came flying over my shoulder; I bent and picked them up.

"Have a good wash while I see to these," I said, and heard the squeak-rattle of the pump handle behind me. "Use the soap." I turned the trousers inside out and stretched the torn leg across my lap. "I've been wondering," I said, taking a spool of thread from the basket and pulling a needle from the pincushion. "Why didn't you warn the boys I was going to dump the bucket on them the other day? You had plenty of time."

"I guess I thought they deserved it" came through the splashing.

"More than you did?" I licked the thread and pushed it through the needle's eye.

"I didn't throw anything."

"But you watched them do it. You went along." Whipping stitches along the rent, holding the fabric taut so it wouldn't pucker.

"But I didn't throw any. Even though they told me to."

"You think that makes you better. Because you only watched, and didn't throw." The squeak of the pump again and more splashing while I stitched back the other way, making a row of neat Xs. "They were pretty angry at you."

"They peed in my bed that night." A shrug in his voice: he accepted the boy justice that had been dealt out.

I took the scissors from the basket and clipped off the end of the thread close to the knot, then turned the trousers right side out again.

"Done," I said, and held them up. A small damp hand came over my shoulder and snatched them away.

The mended place didn't even show when he'd dressed.

"Thank you," he said. His face was shiny and red in places from the rough towel.

"Well, go on," I told him, getting up from the stool. "I have to put things away before the rain comes."

"How do you know it's going to rain?" he asked.

"I just know." I poured the basin out onto the grass, collected up the towel and soap. He stood and watched me. I went to the house, climbed the two steps up to the front porch, turned around. He was still there. "What?" I said.

"Some of the boys say you're a witch."

"I know." He jerked his eyes up to mine, and I laughed at his look of surprise. "There are boys who called me that who are men now."

"But you're not."

"No."

"But you're not a *normal* lady either."

"No, I suppose not."

He fingered the mended place on his trousers, flexing his knee back and forth.

"I did burn the sheet on purpose," he whispered.

"All right," I said.

He appeared taken aback. He'd probably expected a scolding— for the act, or for the earlier lie.

"I hate the press," he said. "It steams big hot clouds up in your face." He sighed. "I'll have to confess it."

"Why?"

"So God knows," he said, clearly a little shocked that I didn't understand this.

"Shouldn't God know already?" He looked thoughtful. "And anyway, to my mind pulling dandelions out of dry ground on a hot day is penance enough for just about anything."

That's when he smiled. I hadn't realized until that moment that he hadn't smiled once during the whole afternoon.

"I'm Leo," he said.

"You can call me Clare."

"Not Missus something?" he asked.

"Just Clare."

"Clare. I'll come back."

He waited, through a long uncertain moment.

"All right," I said.

"When I get thrown out of Folding." That smile again. "Maybe tomorrow."

IN THE DAYS after Leo's visit, I felt an agitation, like a person with an event on a mental calendar—a feeling of *something to do*. I had plenty to do, of course. I always did in summer, but all of it was so familiar by then, my body moving through the motions without thought, that it was easy for my mind to slide away from my physical activity and reveal the waiting underneath.

I found that deeply annoying. Waiting? Waiting for what? For a scrawny, naughty child who was no relation to me and no concern of mine? Who talked endlessly and who clearly had discipline problems. A child nobody wanted.

It had been nearly two decades since I had had regular contact with anyone. Three-quarters of the year I was servant to my garden, which provided me with much of my food. I kept chickens for eggs; I got dairy and sometimes meat from James, the taciturn farmer next door, in exchange for jams and pickles and pies. His wife, I gathered, wasn't much of a cook. Staples, like soap and salt, sugar and flour, I got from town. I visited there every couple of weeks during good weather, traveling on foot and carrying little; I had the heavy items delivered, whenever it was convenient, by James when he visited town in his truck. I'd go weeks without speaking more than a sentence to anyone.

I had fit my life to the seasons, and lived without company or surprise. Spring brought torrents of rain, beating harmlessly on my roof and turning the garden to mud while I started my seeds in pots indoors. The waters' retreat ushered in the long, busy time of planting and weeding, harvesting and canning, clipping and mowing and edging, which lasted throughout the rest of spring and summer. Autumn brought late harvest, leaf burning, preparing the garden for frost. Harsh winds scoured the hill in winter even when the daytime temperature was not severe; usually there'd be a spell of deep cold in February, and a blizzard or two to snow me in. Hard to imagine some days that spring would ever come again, but it always did, everything starting over. Apart from a few early miscalculations, when I hadn't preserved enough to carry me through the winter and the thaw found me eating pickles for breakfast, I had done well. I'd hammered out a self-sufficiency in the little stone house on the hill. If I did ever long for human companionship, there was no time to dwell on it. My body kept busy and I slept well without dreaming. How could one small boy change all that in an afternoon?

I slashed at the Grady family plot, and later in the garden my impatient fingers left bruises on the tomatoes. I couldn't stop the wondering that ran along underneath everything: Had Leo been reprimanded for sneaking away, for coming back in a wet uniform? And what was he doing now—was he praying, or eating, sitting in a classroom, being punished? Was he thinking right this minute about stealing back here? Was he perhaps walking up to the cemetery wall right now? I'd hold off as long as I could, then turn . . . and see no one.

After a week, it seemed clear that he wasn't coming back, and I had to accept that unlikely as it seemed, he must be doing well in Folding after all.

I WAS RAISED to believe that God holds each of us in His hand, and makes all the choices according to His divine plan. Now I believe that even if God provides the choices, we make our own destinies, even when we don't know we're doing it. Every choice we make carries us along toward our fate: one act, one moment, can swivel a life right around. But I wasn't thinking any of that on that late summer day sixty years ago, a week and a half after Leo's visit. I was engaged in the simplest, the most ordinary and womanly of tasks: I was looking for something to wear.

Over the years, I'd abandoned any pretense at femininity. The wardrobe in the cottage bedroom held two pairs of overalls and three blouses that would more honestly be called shirts. In a trunk scattered with mothballs were a couple of roughly knitted sweaters and a single dress. I lifted out the dress and shook it by its shoulders. My Second Best Dress. I hadn't worn it since the day I'd come to Roscommon. Despite the mothballs, the bruise-colored fabric was peppered with tiny holes. I held it up against myself. I was stringier now, but I could take it in with a quick basting and mend the larger holes. No time to air out the mothball smell.

An hour or so later, I walked down the long path toward the cemetery, past the garden with its beckoning weeds, feeling the tickling of the wind on my legs. It felt indecent, almost as if I were naked; I had gotten used to the weight and coverage of overalls. Through the cemetery, passing the Brennan plot, the Cahills and the Flynns. I opened the far gate and stepped through into the no-man's-land between Roscommon and St. William's Wood. The turf was springy underfoot, the air cooler under the roof of branches, a good ten minutes of brisk walking before I broke back out of woods and into the sunlight. All the while feeling that strange absence around my legs, kicking the skirt out with each step to feel the cloth and dispel the alarming sensation of nudity.

In the distance to my left, I could see a long green line of vegetation, the tight points of cornstalks working their way toward the sky. Beyond them were the pastures and fields and outbuildings, and the giant structure that contained the laundry works. I passed the springhouse where the path curved. In front of me was the dark-gray priory building with its peaked doorway, looking exactly as it had the last time I had seen it.

Even then, I could have unmade the pattern of what was happening. I could have turned around. Even after I was up the path and lifting the door knocker, I still could have eased the knocker soundlessly against its brass rest and gone back through the woods to Roscommon. There was nothing to stop me from doing that. But I brought the knocker down with a loud sound, not once, but twice. I heard the boom of it in the hall within.

One of the brothers answered, his eyebrows climbing toward his hairline at the sight of me. I held one arm awkwardly against my side to cover a cluster of moth holes at the waistline and asked for the prior. The man glided away without a word, closing the door in my face, leaving me alone with the sounds of the wind and a distant booming noise from the laundry, the lowing and bleating of livestock.

When the door opened again, it revealed another stranger.

"I'm here to see the prior," I said.

"I am the prior." This man was younger by decades than Prior Washburn. His robe embraced his stout form closely, hanging shorter in the front because of his belly, and he had a long, fleshy face, like a satisfied horse.

"I mean Prior Washburn." Could a monastery have two priors?

"Prior Washburn passed on in the spring. I'm the new prior. Charles."

"But I just—I just saw him." It had actually been months, I realized. He'd come to Roscommon for a visit; we'd had tea and he'd spoken of the frenzy of lambing. "In April."

"He was already ill then. Although no one knew it."

He'd brought up topics long put to rest between us. *Hasn't it been enough, Clare? Isn't there anyone missing you?* I'd been annoyed and short with him. *Not anyone that matters,* I'd said. *Everyone matters,* he'd said in his gentle way. Had he been trying to tidy things up before he passed?

"He was very kind to me." Shame at the memory of my ingratitude. I realized that Prior Charles was waiting. "I'm sorry; I haven't even introduced myself."

"We've met," he said, smiling. "The first bad winter after you came. That terrible blizzard."

I remembered the blizzard well. My second winter at Roscommon. I had had to shovel every few hours during the worst of it, to prevent the snow drifting against the door and windows of the cottage and sealing me in. It had been a strange time, sleeping in snatches, going out into a white world in my never-quite-dry clothing. A world filled with the noise of the wind and of my breath, made loud by the scarf around my head.

"We thought you might have run out of food or firewood," he said. "Or that the snow had bound you in."

Yes, there was a monk who'd come that winter. He'd knocked at my door; I hadn't heard him over the wind. It was not until I happened to pass the window and saw his thin, anxious countenance pressed up against the glass, startling me, that I had known he was there. Looking now, I could see that same young man in the older one before me.

"It took me a good hour getting through the drifts," he said, "and I didn't know what I'd find at journey's end. I expected the worst. But then you opened the door and—well." He made a dry sound of laughter, apparently remembering the cozy scene that had greeted him: soup in the big iron pot, the crackling fire in the hearth. "Prior Washburn said he knew we didn't have to worry about you after that."

I'd fed him a bowl of soup, I recalled, his fingers almost too frozen to hold the spoon. He'd stayed just long enough to thaw out, and then he was gone, declining my offer of a makeshift bed by the fire with something like terror. I would never have expected that stammering lad to grow into this confident cleric, the years fattening his speech as well as his body.

"It was kind of you to come that time," I said.

"Prior Washburn asked me to." Of course. I felt another stab of sorrow.

"Where was he buried?"

"He went to Swan Point," he said.

Naturally he'd have gone to the new cemetery. Only a hundred years old, it was nonsectarian, but many prominent New Englanders were interred there. I couldn't have expected loyalty to Roscommon to withstand the beckoning prestige of Swan Point.

"I should have come to tell you when he passed on," said Prior Charles. "I'm very sorry. It's just—" He lifted his hands, as if to say: *we forget about you over there.* How could I take offense? That had been my whole intention, after all. "What brings you here today?"

"I thought you might be able to spare a boy." I just blurted it out like that, still thinking about Prior Washburn. Not at all the way I had planned.

His face recorded confusion, and a hint of alarm. Too late, I realized how it had sounded: as though I wanted a little meat for some stew, or was planning a human sacrifice.

"I mean—" I thought back to what I'd prepared to say. "I have need of some help at Roscommon. Keeping the cemetery and the garden."

"It's a big job," he agreed.

"It hasn't been a problem before. But this summer's been so dry—a lot of water hauling. I was thinking—"

"It must get lonely there," he mused, on his own conversational tangent. "Such a lot of work. I don't know how you've managed it this long. Maybe a young man would be better able to handle it. Perhaps a couple, husband and wife."

"There's no room there for a family," I said after a shocked moment. I hadn't expected this. "There's hardly room for me." Perhaps I should beat a hasty retreat before this conversation went much further. Get back to Roscommon and be forgotten again.

"That land belongs to St. Will's," said Prior Charles. "We can reassign it at any time."

"But—I had an agreement with Prior Washburn. Rest his soul."

"Rest his soul," he echoed. "You know he didn't expect you to stay so long. We could find you a little house in town. With a garden. You could make those cakes year-round; Mrs. Massey would be happy to sell as many as you give her. It could make you a tidy living."

"I'm not ready to leave Roscommon," I said. His expression hardened at my tone. I took a breath, and with effort made my voice meek. "It must have been a nice Mass for Prior Washburn," I said. "I suppose there was a large attendance."

"There was." Apology crept into his voice; he hadn't thought to invite me.

I let the silence spin out.

Looking back on it now, I can see the humor in the situation: me so obvious and clumsy, so out of practice at manipulating men; him bewildered, so unused to being manipulated. I had been alone too long, and he had not been among women.

He gave a heavy sigh. "All right. I don't intend to break Prior Washburn's promise. If you think you can manage over there—"

"Oh I can, I can." Then added, "with just a little help."

"Some of the older boys are good workers." He pondered for a moment. "I suppose Gregory might do, he's strong, and once lived on a farm."

Gregory wouldn't do at all.

"I was thinking." I cleared my throat. "I met a boy on one of my mushroom walks." Hoping this monk didn't know anything about mushrooms, for it had been far too dry for fungus this year. "I thought maybe—"

"The boys don't go into the woods unsupervised." Fat lot you know, I thought. "What did he look like?"

I pretended to consider. "Brown hair. Pale. Short. He told me he was eleven." What else could I tell him, to make him think of Leo? "He asked a lot of questions."

"That would be Leo," said the prior immediately. "I don't think he would be a good choice."

"Why not? He seemed energetic enough."

"He's undisciplined," he said. "We've already tried him at out-side work; that was a dismal failure. We put him in the laundry; another catastrophe. He doesn't follow instructions. Always has his own ideas." As if ideas were a bad thing. "I think Gregory would be better. He's a bit slow, but tractable. He'll be ready to hire on to a farm in a year or two."

I shook my head.

"You're set on Leo." With real curiosity, he added, "Why?"

That was the question, wasn't it. I couldn't think of any answer but the truth.

"I like him."

"You like him," he repeated as if nothing I could have said would have surprised him more.

Perhaps that was actually the moment when my life turned, once again, on its hidden fulcrum. Through the open door behind the prior the gong of a case clock struck the hour.

"He'll never make a farmer," warned Prior Charles.

"No."

"He needs discipline."

"I can provide that."

"He's too clever for his own good. But I suppose you'll find that out for yourself." I nodded, not quite believing that the thing had been settled. "You'll keep an eye on him." A final admonition. "He tends to wander."

"Yes," I said, a single breath.

We agreed that Leo would come to Roscommon the next Monday. Prior Charles stepped back and closed the door, and I retreated down the path toward the trees and the cemetery beyond them, eager to take the dress off and fold it back into its slumber in the trunk.

WHEN LEO CAME to the cemetery the next week I almost didn't recognize him. I was weeding around the rosebushes at one end of the wall as he vaulted over the other end.

"What on earth happened to your hair?" I said.

"Lice." When I shrank back he added, "Not me. One of the other boys. They shaved us all though."

Who would sit for hours and fine comb the hair of reform-school boys? Easier just to shear them and be done with it.

"Did they boil your clothing?" I looked him over. Perhaps this whole idea was a mistake.

"Yes," he said. He stayed where he was, as if knowing I was teetering on a decision.

"Well, all right then," I said, sounding more certain than I felt. "You'll be cooler without all that hair anyhow."

"Why are you working on that dead bush?" As he came closer I saw the shadow of stubble on his scalp, like ashes. "What was it?"

"It's a rosebush." It did look dead, stunted and budless, reaching out of the ground like a skeleton hand. But a lower branch on the same bush had put out a tiny leaf, just a wee green fold, like a leprechaun's ear. "Look at that," I said, showing it to Leo.

"That's just a leaf. Not a flower."

"It's a sign of life," I said. "These rosebushes were deader than this when I came to live here, and I cared for them and they came back to life." It had taken three years. "They're not just any rosebushes. They were brought over here on a ship more than a hundred years ago. Each of them was just one little branch once, and a ball of dirt. The people who brought them left important things behind so they could bring these."

"Why would they do that? They could just get new bushes when they got here."

"These roses were home to someone." He looked skeptical. "And they need water. Do you remember where the pump is? Take that bucket, fill it up, and bring it back with you." He took the empty bucket and trotted off. I called after him, "Get some gloves from the shed." They'd be too big, but better than nothing.

I could always send him away at the end of the day, tell Prior Charles I'd take Gregory instead, or more likely no boy at all. Who needed a boy around?

As I was thinking this, I looked up and saw Leo coming back down into the cemetery with the water. He looked like nothing so much as a miniature convict, in the striped cotton outfit the school provided for outdoor work, with that bald head. He was walking quickly but carefully, watching his feet so as not to trip or spill, and was humming a tuneless tune that might have been intended to be "Clementine."

Maybe it was the humming broken around his breathing, or maybe that shining white vulnerable skull. That's all it was, perhaps, the kind of charity you feel for a puppy at the door, or a cat once you've taken the fatal step of feeding it. Put down a bowl for a stray and it's your responsibility, my mother always said, even if it never pays you back with love. Even if it scampers at the sight of you and hisses if you get too close. I knew at that moment, watching him coming toward me, that I wouldn't be sending Leo away. The deed was done.

CHAPTER TWENTY-FIVE

Leo

First the soft lump of butter in the bowl, then a whole twin-kling cup of white sugar; mash them together with a wooden spoon until they become a grainy-fluffy substance. Two eggs, cracked one at a time on the side of the bowl and beaten in, then a spoonful of brown fragrant liquid from a tall bottle. Into a separate bowl goes the flour, the cup dipped into the sack and a finger swept across the top, and a spoon of baking powder sprinkled over; the whole thing sifted twice. Clare shows me how to combine the dry with the wet, pulling the whisk through and shaking the batter off the wires. *You don't want to bruise it.* She tosses a cup of plum chunks into a big spoonful of flour and sprinkles them over the batter, takes the bowl from me and folds the fruit in with a few strokes.

When the batter's been scraped into two greased and floured tins we start again, with a clean mixing bowl and more butter-sugar-eggs-and-flour.

"We could make more than two at a time," I suggest. "We have six pans. We could use a big bowl and make enough for six at once."

She shakes her head. "Some recipes can't be multiplied."

Why not? I ask, and she says, *There's little forgiveness in baking.*

So we wash and dry the bowls and start again, do it all over until we have six pans each three-quarters filled with airy yellow plummy batter. She takes a jar from the cupboard, offers its wide mouth to me to smell: *last summer.* She presses a design into the top of each cake, a heart made of cherries.

Six pans fit into the oven side by side, and while they're baking we have a sandwich outside on the porch in the cool dirt-smelling air, a blurry curtain of rain between us and the green world.

At Roscommon, I eat my fill. After a few weeks I notice that the pail of water that had seemed impossibly heavy is no longer so difficult to carry. And it's quiet here. At St. William's, the machines working in the laundry shake the ground all day and most of the night, and boys, even when they are sleeping, are noisy. In Clare's cemetery and garden, there's real silence. I tell that to Clare and she says, *You're not listening.* I hear what she means: the birds' singing and the distant noises of the cows and horses, the chuckling of the hens in the coop. Still, all of it so much quieter than St. Will's.

After lights-out I lie awake as long as possible. When I judge that all the other boys are asleep and am reasonably sure that there'll be no surprises, no manure slipped under my pillow or honey dripped into my hair, I close my eyes and allow my mind to wander back to the little yellow house. I go up the path to the front door, the tulips on either side that Mama and I planted two years ago. But as I reach the front step the door transforms, the white with three square panes near the top darkening and thickening into Roscommon's glassless cottage door. And when the door opens it's not Mama there, but instead the tall woman who feels less like a stranger every day. She smiles at me and there's no worry in it, only welcome. I wake with tears slipping from my eyes down into my ears, hot tracks of betrayal.

CHAPTER TWENTY-SIX

Lucy

M Y PHONE VIBRATES ON THE mattress. I clutch at it with sleep-clumsy hands and it slides off the bed and drops onto the carpeted call-room floor. When I look over the edge of the bed, the screen shines up at me:

Are you asleep

I retrieve the phone and tap in:

Not anymore

Was that too snarky? I watch the dot triplet begin on the other side. After a couple of minutes it becomes:

There are buds on the lilac

The bushes outside our apartment building, no taller than your knee. They leaf out quickly each year, within a week going from bare branches to full green with cascades of tiny purple blossoms. They don't last long, and we always leave our windows open during lilac time, to enjoy their powerful fragrance.

The next frost will kill them I type, then erase.

I can't be *nice all the time,* but I can make an effort to be nicer *some* of the time. I hear my mother in my mind suddenly: *slow down, Lucybee, take your time.* Definitely her voice; she was the only one who used that nickname, I can't believe I forgot it. I can't believe I've remembered it now.

Spring is coming I type, and press Send.

The pulsing dots on his side appear again and eventually turn into:

I'm writing a new song

I type That's great! and reconsider—does it seem condescending? I delete it, put in What's it about and delete that too. Who can explain a song in a text? And will he feel pressured to say it's about me, or about us? What if it's about the Good Listener?

Finally I type I'd like to hear it and let that linger for a few seconds, before pressing Send. And fall back to sleep.

CHAPTER TWENTY-SEVEN

Clare

L EO WAS FULL OF QUESTIONS. He drove me to distraction with them. Why did I live here? Where had I been born? What was my favorite day of the week? Why did I keep watering the dead roses instead of pulling them up? If I could live in one season permanently, which would it be?

I live here to care for the cemetery, I told him. I'd been born in a different part of Rhode Island. Weekdays were all the same to me. And the roses might come back, we'd have to wait and see. Definitely spring, the world reborn, a celebration. He liked Wednesday, and he didn't think he'd want one season all year-round, but if he had to, he'd choose spring too.

In his interrogations, there was an element of restraint. He didn't press once I'd given some sort of answer. And he didn't ask the questions anyone else might, such as why I lived alone, or where my people were. In turn, I didn't ask him if he remembered his parents, or how he'd come to be at St. Will's.

That didn't mean we didn't find other things to talk about. A thousand topics interested him, and he was forever posing questions I could answer, like what the stars were made of, and if the earth really turned like a top like Brother Angus had said, why we didn't all fly off; and things I couldn't, like how a magnet worked and what was in the bomb we had dropped on the Japanese two years before he was born. Fire, I told him, stars are made of fire, and it's gravity that keeps us all anchored to the spinning world. When I didn't know something, I told Leo to ask the brothers; but he sighed and said they always gave the same answer: everything happened because of God.

"Where do you go to church?" he asked one day when we were pinching up small weeds from the asparagus bed. We had dug the trench the week before, built a long mound of earth in its center and laid the crowns there, draping the bare-knuckle-white roots to either side and sprinkling soil over them. During this tender time before the plants settled in, hoe and fork were too rough. There wasn't anything to do but squat and pinch with bare fingers.

"I don't," I said.

"Never?"

"I used to go to a fine church, with a big stained glass window and an oak door so heavy it took two men to open."

"Was it Catholic?"

"Of course it was Catholic. You need to keep your mind on what you're doing. See there, you've missed some."

He backtracked to pull up the offending shoots.

"If you don't go to church, won't you go to Hell?"

"I don't know."

He was startled by this; he sat back on his heels and stared at me.

"Fear of Hell shouldn't be what drives a person to do right," I told him. "And besides, why would God create all of this"—I swept a hand around at the vivid green, the trees vibrating with birdsong—"and then wait for us inside a dark building?"

His eyes followed my hand, then came back to meet my gaze.

"Brother Angus says we can't know the mind of God," he said.

"That means my guess is as good as anyone's."

He was still looking around, as if seeing the place for the first time.

"You could grow honeysuckle," he said. "It smells good."

"Honeysuckle is hard to control," I told him. "And strong. It's really just a big weed."

"My mother likes honeysuckle," he said, surprising me. So he remembered his mother?

"Well, it is an honest flower," I conceded. "It tastes as good as it smells."

I felt a twinge in my chest and slipped my hand behind the strap of my overalls, rubbing the scar just above my heart. The sun had made its way to the fringe of trees on the horizon behind us, leaving a rimless bowl of blue.

"It's going to rain tomorrow," I said. "And none too soon."

"How do you know? You always know."

"I feel it," I said, taking my hand out again. There was dirt from my fingers on the blouse. I'd have to rinse it out tonight.

"Like Brother Michael. He feels it in his gout. Do you have gout?" He directed an interested gaze at my foot.

"No I do not," I said, getting up and going over to the wheelbarrow that stood at the ready, filled with earth from the digging, enriched with manure from St. William's livestock. I slid the spade into the rich mixture in the wheelbarrow and spread a thin layer to either side of the central raised mound in the trench. Two inches a day and plenty of water, and the trench would be to ground level in a month. Then a full three years of care after that, to be ready to pick and eat. Asparagus is a commitment. Maybe my impulse purchase of these crowns the Saturday before had been a stab at Prior Charles. A statement: *I'm not going anywhere.*

Inside the house, I took a jar of strawberry jam down from the cupboard, made sandwiches, and sliced them from point to point while Leo filled two glasses from the pitcher of sun tea. We sat on the front step, in the shade of the porch overhang. In wintertime, a taste of this jam could bring tears to my eyes, but the evocation of spring's balm is not so powerful in summer. I noted merely that the fruit was oversweetened, and decided I'd use a little less sugar next year.

"If it's not gout," Leo said.

I didn't know what he was talking about for a moment. Then I sighed.

"Leo. It's none of your business."

"Well, nothing is really."

There was that naked look on his face, when it seemed that the bones of his mismanaged childhood were rising up through the skin of his general good nature. I understood his statement immediately: he had no business, nothing private, no secret that he did not share with his dormitory mates or the monks. Nothing in this world could be said to belong to him, to matter to him and him alone: he had no business. In that moment, I made a decision, to give him my secret, or at least part of it, to keep. It's our secrets that make each of us different from everyone else. Our secrets, and what we choose to love.

I reached for the glass and chased down my own mouthful.

"I have a splinter," I said with the exhale. "It aches when it's going to rain, and itches before snow."

"Where?" Leo asked, fascinated. He sucked jam and butter from his fingers. His hair had partially grown back, and stood out from his skull in a velvety pelt; he no longer looked like a little convict, but he had a convict's manners.

"Use your napkin."

He rubbed his hands perfunctorily on the cloth. "A splinter where?" he said again.

"In my chest."

He looked incredulously at the place where the overall apron lay against my breasts, and then blushed and jerked his eyes away. He'd already finished two of the four sandwich triangles I'd made him, and now he took up the third. We chewed for a while in silence.

"Were you born with it?"

"Of course not. Who's born with a splinter in their chest?"

"How did it get there then?"

"That's a long story," I said, swallowing the last of my tea and standing up, stretching out my backbone *krik-krik-krik*. "You'd best be getting back." We always said *back,* never *home.*

He wolfed the remaining sandwich, drank down his tea, wiped his hands carefully on his napkin. Then rose to his feet, his young spine limber and soundless.

I took up the plates, now empty but for a smear of red and some small light fragments of crust, while he went down the path, heading into the cemetery. I had tried to get him to use the gate, and sometimes he remembered, but not this time. He put his hand on the wall and vaulted over the bare rosebushes, then dropped down onto the other side. I stood there watching him go. Not until he had disappeared beyond the tree line did I notice that my hand was against my chest again, a firm pressure, as though to protect the secret burrowed there under the skin and the bone.

DOES IT HURT?

Sometimes. When it's going to rain. And some other times.

It's been in there since—

Since that day, yes. It was the root of the spike that I pulled out after the hurricane. The doctor says it was actually lucky: if I'd pulled the whole thing out, I would have died on the spot.

That's luck all right.

WE SETTLED INTO a routine: Leo came in the midafternoon every weekday and stayed for supper. As the sun was sinking, he'd go back through the woods.

When I scraped our supper plates one evening, I noticed that there was only one chop bone in the scraps. I said nothing about it, but when Leo went through the door, I waited just a minute and then followed.

I found him in the shed, kneeling just inside the door. He looked up when my shadow fell over him.

"What do you have in here?" I looked into the space. "It had better not be a raccoon."

He clucked his tongue softly, and a tiny shape unclotted itself from the shadows and ran to him. A kitten, so young that his fur made a fuzzy halo around his form; no markings yet.

"I found him in the rain barrel," said Leo. The kitten wound around and around in front of him, pushing his cheek against the boy's fingers with each pass.

"Did you leave the lid off again?"

"I'm sorry." His voice was small, ashamed.

"If he'd drowned in it, all that water would have been poisoned."

"I think he's lost," said Leo. "He should be with his mama."

His mama was probably dead; there were plenty of predators around to have made a meal of her. The kitten raised his head as if he had heard my thought and blinked his yellow eyes at me.

Leo brought out a napkin from his pocket and unfolded it, revealing the half-eaten pork chop. He scraped meat from the blade of the bone with his fingernails and put the scraps down on the floor. The shed filled with the sound of purring.

"He purrs and eats at the same time," said Leo, proud as if he'd taught him to do it. He added, "He'll be useful. He can catch mice."

"He's too young yet to catch his own food. A mouse would probably eat *him*."

"He won't be any trouble," said Leo. "He can sleep in here."

"He's a wild thing. He doesn't need us."

"He does," said Leo. I knew he was trying not to cry. "You said. He's not old enough to catch his own food."

Other boys mistreated cats, I knew, out of evilness or boredom. They tied their tails together or set them on fire to watch them try to outrun the pain. There had to be something deeply good in a boy who'd known a cruel life not having turned to cruelty himself. A boy who responded tenderly to weakness, instead of exploiting it as a pitiable exercise of power. I watched Leo petting the little creature I'd told him he could not save.

"Well, he'll need a name," I said.

Leo looked up at me, surprised.

"I don't want him in the house," I warned.

"I promise," said Leo.

Two days later, I woke to tiny needling sensations on my calf. The little cat was curled up behind my leg. How had he gotten inside? I reached down, felt the chittering breath of his purr on my fingers, disengaged his claws from my skin, and brought him up to sleep in a ball near my chest with a sigh.

During the daytime, the still-nameless kitten followed Leo and me from chore to chore, jumping to bat at the cabbage moths where they hovered over the cauliflower heads, or lying on the dirt and giving himself a bath in various odd positions—one hind leg stuck high in the air while he worked on the soft fur of his inner thigh—or simply curled on his side, watching us through half-closed eyes. Leo fed him table scraps. Before long, he was big enough to eat a mouse, and massacred them happily at night. More mornings than not, I woke with the furry bloody-mouthed lump of him on my bed and a ravaged carcass on my doorstep.

He earned his keep, I told myself, stroking his silky back in the dark. And it wasn't like I'd taken on a pet. Not really.

I DIDN'T HAVE any animals by the time I came to Oak Haven, but Gloria had had a bird, a parrot named Carlo, who'd been with her since her childhood. He'd been trained to sit on her shoulder, and she even took him to work with her sometimes. He chuckled into her ear as she typed, startling her colleagues by bursting into commentary from time to time like a raucous sidekick. Gloria swore his conversation was intelligent, not just mindless repetition. He had a long memory: once when she was in her forties, he suddenly sang out in a strong, clear voice, "Elbows off the table!" She recognized the voice of her great-aunt, who had lived with her family and helped raise the children, and who had been dead for more than twenty years.

"It was a shock," Gloria said when she told me the story. "I hadn't heard that voice for so very long. The most amazing thing was, I *did* have my elbows on the table when he said it."

When Gloria couldn't live on her own anymore, something had to be done about Carlo, whose life expectancy might be more than a century. We aren't allowed pets at Oak Haven. A sensible rule: animals are a lot of work and noise and mess, and who would care for them after we die? Still, the message stings: it is not our choice anymore. It is that shrinkage of a life that truly makes a person feel old, the pruning of all the small branches of possibility until one is left with just the nubbin of what is, and no more of what *might be*.

Gloria belonged to a parrot-fanciers' group on the Internet; before she came here one of them offered to take Carlo. The stranger drove from two states away to collect him while Gloria was still recovering from her latest coronary event, and by the time she was out of critical care, Carlo was gone.

Carlo's new mistress emails updates from time to time. Apparently he is still up to his old tricks, bellowing out the ABCs at dawn and murmuring nursery rhymes in Portuguese. Gloria loves to receive these messages, but they also pain her.

"She's asking What does *Florzinha* mean? Carlo says it all the time." Gloria taps a response and presses Send. "It was my family nickname, Little Flower. No one knows me by that name now but Carlo." Despite the tears in her eyes, there is a smile touching her mouth.

My own nickname, chou-fleur, had been overheard by my Providence schoolmates and immediately corrupted in translation. Perhaps there is another very old lady even now, somewhere in Rhode Island, whose muddled memories include an adolescent shadow, that gangly, bookish Shoofly? And I have to wonder what kind of world it is that we live in when the only souls who know your true name are too far away for you to hear them if they choose to speak it.

CHAPTER TWENTY-EIGHT

Lucy

BY 3 A.M. MONDAY, THE urgent patients have been taken care of, the Tank is full and snoozing, and the chart rack is nearly empty. I'm jotting the procedure note after a shoulder reduction, my own shoulders aching pleasantly from the task. Some nights are busy all through, without a moment's pause. But tonight has been more typical, a storm that has thrashed itself out by the wee hours. The pitch of the evening is behind us; the night shift is sloping toward dawn.

"It's so quiet," says a tech.

Everyone looks up: the secretary, the nurses. Even I stop writing.

"I need a doctor here!" The shout comes from bed 8, a curtained cubicle on the opposite side of the big room.

"You *see* what you did?" the charge nurse calls to the tech while running toward the source of the outcry. I follow, and by the time we get there, I've mentally ratcheted through the possibilities and settled on the most likely: a patient actively seizing, and at bedside a panicked family member.

But when I pull back the cubicle curtain, it reveals not a family member but Alice the intern, and the patient is not seizing but dead. The monitor hanging above the stretcher shows a quivering line where the spikes and notches of heart rhythm should be.

"He just stopped talking." Alice's voice is high.

"Get him to Trauma," I say, and a small crowd of nurses and techs surges around us, popping the monitor leads off the patient's chest, twisting the oxygen tubing from the wall, pulling the stretcher away and shooting with it in a tight cluster through the doors to Trauma Alley.

In Trauma 2, I yank the patient's trousers down and put a gloved left hand to the groin, feeling for a pulse. This ignominious stance is the command post of a Code. Stand *here,* hand *here,* watch the monitor, give the orders.

No pulse, not breathing.

"Bag him." The mask is already over his face, a nurse squeezing breaths from the Ambu bag, and a respiratory therapist is lubricating the endotracheal tube for me and snapping the laryngoscope together, testing the light. "Chest compressions. Get him on the monitor." A tech hauls himself up to stand on the bottom stretcher rail and begins CPR. Hands snake around his, pressing monitor lines onto the leads mapped across the patient's chest wall. "Hold CPR." The tech pulls his clasped hands up; all eyes look toward the monitor, where an undulating line of static appears: V-fib, ventricular fibrillation. Inside his chest, his heart is at a quivering standstill, the electrical impulses moving chaotically through the muscle. "Charge to two hundred. Alice, get ready to shock." The defibrillator whines, the paddles are pressed into Alice's trembling hands, the sound tops out, and she says, "Clear."

We all take our hands off and lean away, and the body on the stretcher convulses slightly, never the enormous jump that one sees on television, then we all rush back toward him and take up our positions again.

No change on the monitor.

"Charge to three hundred," and the process is repeated. This time, success: the thin orderly pattern of sinus rhythm peeps happily across the monitor screen.

And we're swarming again, but it's different now, the room awash in cheer: another one pulled from the brink. The nurse hangs a bag of heparin and the respiratory therapist dials in settings on the ventilator while I slide the endotracheal tube into the dark diamond of space between the vocal cords at the back of the patient's throat.

"Aspirin and morphine and beta-blockers," I tell Dennis. "Call the Cardiology fellow for admit to CCU."

All is calm efficiency in Trauma 2 now, the patient's chest rising and falling with ventilator breaths, the IV pump ticking the heparin in. A tech undresses him, shakes out a hospital gown over his naked body, folds his clothing into a bag. I tap orders into the computer and read the chart Alice had started. Thirty-eight years old, no cardiac history. He'd gotten a clean bill of health from his primary doctor just last week. He'd come in complaining of indigestion.

"Let's get a postcode ECG; he may need stat angioplasty. How's his heart rate?" I turn to check the monitor again, and see the patient's arm move. "He's waking up. We need to restrain him."

Too late: he is already sitting, eyes open. His hand comes up, reaching for the tube in his throat. A tech pulls his hand down, pins it; a nurse catches the other hand. He shakes them off.

"Sedate him," I say, but in that blink he is standing, literally standing upright on the stretcher stark naked, the hospital gown sliding down his arms and puddling at his wrists. He has the endotracheal tube in one hand and the IV tubing, squirting a clear stream of heparined saline, in the other. He roars at the wide-eyed staff.

Just a beat with him balanced there; then we all leap toward him.

"Lie down," I plead as I grip his calf with both hands. "Please lie down." His brows are drawn together into a mask of incomprehension and rage as he stares down at me. I try to make my voice calm and professional, commanding. "Sir, you need to lie down or you'll fall." For an instant his gaze unclouds and I think he's understood, but then he kicks out, almost jerking me off my feet. I grab again, my hands slipping on his sweat-slick skin, and end up winding both arms around his leg in a kind of hug. I reach around myself, clutch the fabric on the back of my white coat, and hold tight. "Someone get some Valium." My cheek is pressed so hard against one hairy thigh that the words cause me to bite the inside of my cheek.

The stretcher bucks against its wheel brake as we struggle to bring him down. The monitor leads spring free and flail, and the tube in his hand whips, spraying heparin into the air. Blood streams from his open IV site. I can feel the *taptaptap* of drops on my scalp and a warm trickle through my hair.

"Is someone getting Valium?" I yell. "Goddamn it."

My fingers are losing their purchase on the fistfuls of fabric, my nails making little ripping noises on the cloth as they slide, when suddenly the seething knot of humanity on the stretcher comes loose and the patient drops.

Breathless, my fingers numb, I lean across his inert body, fumble for the monitor wires and snap them back into place, look at the screen: a straight, lifeless line. We swing into a second code, all of us still panting. I slip another endotracheal tube into position in his throat, squirt epinephrine into it, and bag it in while Dennis places another IV line. Then back to the groin, new gloves squeaked over my damp hands. Giving orders: *continue chest compressions* and *more epi*, again and again, the ampoules twinkling in midair as they are passed from nurse to nurse toward the stretcher and depressed steadily into the new IV in his arm. Nothing on the monitor except the coarse, unpretty waves of CPR.

"Change the lead," I say, but the second lead shows the same.

We're grim now, no talking except the essentials, my orders and the brisk answering of the nurse pushing meds, *epi in*. Every few minutes the CPR provider changes, a new person stepping up as the one before steps down.

It might be twenty minutes, it could be an hour. I push it through round after round of meds, changing leads again and again, but never get anything on the monitor except that flat green unshockable line. Gradually I become aware that the tech stepping up to take over CPR is not on his first, or second, or even his third turn: large stains show under the armpits of his scrubs as he locks his arms together to begin chest compressions.

"Doppler," I say, and it's in my hand. "Hold CPR."

I squiggle gel over groin and neck, run the transducer over the femoral artery, then the carotid. Nothing but white noise. I dial up the volume, straining to hear any syncopation of pulse. Finally, I take the transducer away from the cooling skin and switch it off, quieting the ocean rush. The room is absolutely still. I look at the big clock on the wall.

"Time of death zero three fifty-one."

The respiratory therapist disconnects the oxygen bag. Someone clicks the monitor off. The sweating tech steps down from the stretcher, pulling his CPR-locked arms apart. They all stream out into Trauma Alley, leaving only me and the charge nurse in the room.

I write his death note. *Code: V-fib successfully converted to sinus with 300 joules; patient reverted to asystole. Second code, ACLS protocol followed, unsuccessful.* The words hold nothing of the Frankenstein moments between the codes, the patient standing on the stretcher with hospital personnel hanging from his limbs. *Cause of death probable myocardial infarction. Discharge to morgue.*

No CCU now, no stat angioplasty or cardiologist. Instead, calls to the medical examiner and the primary doctor. And to the family: another chance for me to plow that unwelcome divide between before and after into a stranger's life.

"Did he get three rounds of epi or four?" Dennis asks without looking up from the chart where he is documenting.

"Five," I say from the scrub sink. "I think." I wash my hands, then wet a handful of paper towels and wash my face, crouching a little to look at my reflection in the paper towel dispenser.

"Can bed eleven have more morphine?" Maureen, one of the urgent area nurses, puts her head around the trauma room curtain. "He says his pain's eight out of ten." She looks at the naked, blood-slicked body on the stretcher, the sprays and smears of red on the floor. "Yikes."

"Bed eleven." Mr. Blythe, kidney stone. "Yeah. Give him another six. Thanks. How is it out there?"

"Under control," says Maureen. She's been a nurse for twenty years; she knows better than to say *quiet* or *calm.*

I toss the clump of towels into the bin. "I'm going to do a ramp check." A bit of ED slang meaning *I can't be in this fluorescent box of hospital for one more second, I have to step outside and pretend I have the option to walk away.* "Back in five."

"All righty," says Dennis.

The glass doors at the end of Trauma Alley sense my approach and whish open. For once, there are no ambulances chugging out carbon monoxide in the roofed space just beyond the sliding glass doors. We'll have another deep snow or two before winter is done, but it's just bearably chilly in my long-sleeve shirt under scrubs under white coat. I sit on the loading dock, take a deep lungful of the night air. Somewhere in this city, there are flowers; I can smell them.

It was a good code: we did everything right. *I could have given him sedation right after we got sinus rhythm back.* Sometimes things go unexpectedly, some alchemy of circumstance, no one to blame. *The morphine during the code hadn't been enough, one good stiff dose just two minutes earlier might have made the difference.* This one was young, only five years older than me; he'd come in walking and talking. Usually if they're going to die, they're more than halfway there when they get to us. I see his eyes again, confused and furious. There aren't a whole lot of ER patients who look at you and then die; if they are well enough to look at you, they are usually well enough to save.

In extremis, people do not resemble themselves. I'd coded him and pronounced him dead, but I wouldn't recognize him now if his ghost were to walk up to me. His life had ended in a room crowded with strangers.

One ER shift can swing from a beautiful satisfaction—a dramatic save, a neatly made diagnosis—to a dismal failure. Underneath the hubris that keeps us moving, always a churning river of worry: *Could I have done that better?* Strange that an impulse at eighteen—*I think I'll be a doctor*—translates so many years later into this dark moment. I remember again that aphorism that's been haunting me lately: *it won't love you back.*

I jump as a long shadow wavers on the ground beside me. I turn and blink up into the floodlight beam from the ambulance bay, see the bright orange hat. It's the homeless frequent flyer with the worms in his knees.

"Freddy, you scared the hell out of me."

"Sorry." He stops walking. "What're you doing out here? You're supposed to be in there."

"Just taking a break."

"That's okay, that's okay," he says, as if reassuring himself. He comes a little closer. "Is it all right if I smoke?"

"Aw, Freddy. What am I supposed to say to that?"

He sits on the other end of the loading dock, slides a crinkling packet from some hidden pocket in his camo vest, and scrapes out a small flower of flame. He puts the cigarette to his lips and sucks in deeply.

"You've got blood in your hair," he says in a tight, breath-holding voice.

"Yeah." I remember the boy, Karen's son, drenched in blood, his button eyes.

"Somebody get shot?"

"Heart attack."

"Right, right," he says, nodding so hard that it rocks his body back and forth. "People die from those all the time."

They don't, actually. Heart attacks are generally fixable.

"Even if you do everything right, you still die," says Freddy on a long exhaled plume.

A flash of screaming for Valium with my face squashed against the naked haunch of the man whose name I didn't even know, his genitals bobbing inches away from my ear. It had been a disaster. What will I tell his wife? Platitudes I can't truthfully rely on this time: *he wasn't in any pain* and *he died instantly*. What is left to say? Only *I'm very sorry*.

"My heart's good," says Freddy. He coughs.

During the day this street throbs with traffic and the sidewalks are thronged with people walking urgently, talking into cell phones. At night the population evacuates to the nicer neighborhoods and homes, leaving shuttered storefronts and abandoned houses. I look at the yellow oblong of a fourth-floor window in the research lab building opposite, wonder who is toiling there so late, and why.

Freddy turns his face up to the sky. "Look at all the stars," he says.

I look up.

"Where?" The patches of sky between the buildings are too light, the glow of the city besting the universe. "I can't see them."

"The point isn't to see them." Freddy has his head tilted far back. "The point is to know they're there."

I HEARD THE best thing tonight I type into my phone when the shift is done and I've been restored somewhat by a large light coffee.

from a philosophical hobo and wait.

Then I think, maybe he's asleep; but the dot-dot-dot pulsing ellipsis appears on his side of the conversation. I type it in exactly as Freddy said it, all ready to send. Then Joe's message comes through.

I can't do this i'm sorry

I'm trying to interpret that when the next message comes, the *whoop* of the alert sound bringing the words to me.

I know I may be making the worst mistake of my life

I backspace back through Freddy's words, erasing them forever, while the inevitable next message is being created.

I'm sorry

I type in what happened and erase it, then why, then erase that. Then Can we talk about this and press Send, just as his next message comes through.

I'm done

The two discordant bubbles hang there on opposite sides of the phone screen until the screen blinks to black.

I HAVE BEEN in the habit of framing my life into stories, pouring them out to Joe after work, letting myself interpret on the second pass what I cannot take time to appreciate as it happens. My life has been made real by its retelling. While Joe and I have been separated, that valve has been closed and the stories have drained off as if into an internal vault, to meld together, never quite processed or true. Now I realize that somewhere inside I have been waiting, expecting the valve to open again, and that it isn't going to happen. And the biggest, most intricate story of all will go unreported. He will never know the details of my heartbreak; that story will stay within me, forever untold.

CHAPTER TWENTY-NINE

Clare

I HAD HAD SOME CONCERNS THAT with the waning of summer Leo would be reassigned to the laundry, but each afternoon the figure jogged into view beyond the wall and went to the shed to change. I had taken scissors to an aged soft pair of my own overalls, suspecting that Leo was allotted only one set of clothing and might be punished if it wore out too quickly. The side gap of the overalls hung to his thighs and the legs were so wide they met in the middle and looked like a skirt. I bit back my smile at the sight, for I had nothing better to offer.

On a windy day in early October I made a trip to Waite with a load of cakes packed into the wheeled wagon behind me, getting to town when the shadow-dappled main street was just waking up. The door of Massey's Dry Goods pushed inward with a sound of tinkling bells. Mrs. Massey's smile curled above her triple chin as I approached; she stood on her tiptoes to look over the counter at the load in the wagon.

"How many do you have today?"

"Twelve."

"Well, we'll sell them all by this evening. I can't keep up with the demand. Honestly, I could eat them all myself."

I piled the cakes onto the counter. Six cherry and six plum.

"You sure you won't share the recipe?" she wheedled.

"Sorry." They were my mother's cakes, down to the fruit pressed into the top in the shape of a heart. Each one felt like a song to her, love passing from my hands into the batter.

"Do you want it all in cash? Or in goods? Maybe some fabric for a dress?" Did her smile broaden as she glanced down at my overalls?

"Do you have boys' clothes?"

"Of course. Any particular size of boy?"

"Eleven years old. On the small side. A pair of overalls."

I followed her to the back of the store, where a supply of clothing lay folded on shelves.

"This here's a nice pair, strong seams. Riveted." She shook them out. "They can get passed down from brother to brother."

I skimmed a hand over the front bib with its wide, flat pocket, thought about Leo's pale scratched legs. These would do fine.

"Perhaps a few shirts too, for the same boy?" She turned to another shelf. "We have navy blue and white, three for a dollar."

"Two white, one blue."

She laid out a sheet of brown paper to make a package for me, folding the overalls into a stiff rectangle of dark blue cloth, tucking the buckles inside. "You know," she said, shaking out the shirts and snapping them into folds. "I'm thinking about your boy." *My boy.* A warm spot started in my chest. "In his nice new shirts and overalls. He might be wanting some socks?"

"Socks, shoes, of course." Why hadn't I thought of that?

"Now, you'd have to bring him in for shoes. Feet are the most unpredictable parts of a person." She produced three pairs of cotton socks, hesitated a moment, then went back to the shelves. "He'll also be needing these, I think." She put a small white bundle on top of the rest.

Cotton briefs, boy sized. Judging from St. Will's stingy clothing rations otherwise, no doubt he could do with some of those. I nodded.

"That's a lot of white. You've got bleach?" she asked.

"You're a good saleswoman," I said as she fetched a bottle and a cube of bluing.

"Just a mother." She laughed.

How nice she was. All this time I had been coming into Massey's I had never gone out of my way, never said an extra word. Maybe her smile all along had been friendliness and not mockery.

"I've never shopped for a boy before," I confessed as she tied up the parcel with some string.

"I have three. Of course, they're men now."

I was grateful that she wasn't overly curious about the sudden addition to my household. I had been buying from her for years, and never a word about a boy. Perhaps she assumed he was a nephew or cousin, come to visit. That was a good idea, I thought. In case anyone asked.

But no one did. Not Mrs. Massey, nor the grocer who bought my preserves, giving me a thin wad of bills in exchange. I pushed through the grocery door onto the sidewalk, and after a moment's hesitation, turned left and went down the street to the bookshop.

"I'm looking for a science book," I told the middle-aged man who was reading behind the counter. In my mind I browsed the shelves of my childhood, the cards bearing their curlicued legends in my father's hand. "Something general, with both earth science and basic botany."

He nodded, headed into the stacks of shelving, and returned a minute later. "Will this do?" he asked, holding out a book.

I felt its solid weight in my hand, admired the title embossed on the front cover and the pages of text illustrated with line drawings, each new section headed with a half-page photograph and a title. Meteors, I read, Volcanoes. Gravity and Inertia. *A body at rest will stay at rest until acted upon by an outside force.*

"It's up-to-date," he said. "Very current."

I looked down at a picture of a glacier. "Has the earth changed that much?"

"The earth hasn't," said the man, smiling. "But our understanding of it has."

I went back through town with my parcels behind me in the wagon. The journey uphill was slow going. The wind smelled of rain; I didn't need the twitch in my chest to warn me. I wanted to make it home before the downpour, but I stopped to tie a cloth around the gatepost of the farm, the signal to the farmer that I'd put a note into his mailbox. He came out of an outbuilding while I was tying it, so I waited while he walked over, and handed him the note.

"Meat again. So soon?" He blushed after saying that, as though it had been unbearably intimate.

"Apple or cherry pie?"

"You choose."

I took up the wagon handle again and resumed my trudge up the hill. The science book would make a nice Christmas present. Not too soon to think of Christmas. I had gotten sugar and raisins and ginger from Mrs. Massey, and had a spree of holiday baking planned. There'd be plenty of time for it, now that the summer was past; the harvest would soon be dwindling to squash and second-crop broccoli and lettuces. The roses still needed to be protectively mulched and there would be mowing until the end of the month, for the cemetery grass continued to grow after the other plantings were exhausted. Leaf raking to add to the mulch pile would be necessary for a month to come, and after each windstorm dead branches would need to be cleared and chopped for kindling. There would be enough work to occupy Leo and me through November. And then what? Well, I wouldn't think about that right now.

That evening, the farmer brought four paper-wrapped packages and four bottles of milk.

"This is far too much in exchange for one pie," I said.

"Growing boy needs meat," he said. So he'd noticed Leo at Roscommon.

"But surely your family—"

"It's just me now."

"Oh," I said. Hadn't there been a wife? I hadn't ever seen her, just heard a feminine voice across the fields sometimes. I realized now that I hadn't heard it in a long time. "I'm sorry."

"Chops and ribs and a hock and some sausages," he said. I noticed what I hadn't before: his shirt collar was frayed, and a button was missing.

"One pie isn't a fair trade for all this." I wished I'd made both pies. But how much pie could one man eat on his own? And I'd be needing ever more meat and milk, as long as Leo came here. "I could help you with your mending," I suggested. "Put a new collar on that shirt, replace the button. It could be as good as new. Look there, you're going to lose another one." I put a hand out to the loose button. His eyes followed my hand, and I pulled it back.

"Well, thank you," I said, taking the packages and the milk inside to load into the icebox, as he turned and went back down the front path.

The next morning, when I opened the door, there was a basket just outside. I lifted the covering cloth and saw the frayed shirts within. Evidently, we had struck a deal.

I MEANT IT as a sort of early Christmas present, I suppose. Just after Thanksgiving, after we had come in from raking leaves and were drinking cocoa by the fire, I told him.

"I've been to see the prior," I said. It was still strange to refer to Brother Charles that way.

Leo looked at me over the rim of his mug. There was a touch of chocolate on his nose.

"I was telling him, since you're here every day anyway—" I was having trouble getting the words out for some reason. "He's agreed to let you live here, with me." Leo brought the mug down;

his face was unreadable. "You can sleep here, on the settee. It'll be comfortable. I've slept on it myself."

"Live here?" he said.

"You'll still go to school over there. But yes, this will be your home, with me and Kitty." Leo still hadn't given him a name.

He turned to face toward the window. Was he crying?

"You really have to come up with a name for him," I said, looking down at the cat on my lap. "We can't keep calling him Kitty." Trying to josh him out of his joyful tears. A bit tearful myself, thinking, *You'll never be caned again, I'll see to that.*

But when he turned from the window, his eyes were dry.

"You can't make me."

I was wounded, and surprised. I had been so filled with munificence. I hadn't imagined that he felt such an affection for St. Will's; I'd stupidly presumed that he'd prefer my little house, and me.

"Of course I won't *make* you," I said.

He put his mug down on the table, took his coat from the peg, and thrust his arms into the sleeves. He opened the door; the chill wind filled the room and blew the flames sideways in the fireplace.

"Leo," I said.

He slammed the door behind him and it bounced against the latch, opening again; Kitty sleeping on my lap jolted awake. I went to the doorway, the cat in my arms. It had gotten dark while we'd been drinking our cocoa, and the moon had risen. It lit the world in silvers and grays and I could see Leo through the leafless trees, already into and through the cemetery, standing on the far wall. He yelled something, his words carried away by the wind.

"I can't hear you," I called.

He turned his face to the sky and yelled it again, to the trees and the wind and all of those lying under the earth listening, and this time I understood. He stood for just another moment, before dropping down on the other side of the wall and disappearing from view.

I shut the door, put my forehead against it. The cat scrabbled his way over my shoulder and jumped down. The painful points where his claws had gotten purchase made an appropriate accompaniment to the echo of Leo's words in my head.

You're not my mother, he'd cried, to the sky, to the field of listening families. To me. *You're not my mother and this is not my home.*

HE MUST HAVE come back in the wee hours. Must have crept out of his dormitory, careful not to wake the other boys slumbering in their cots, and back to Roscommon in the dark. Where did he get the matches? I never found out.

I smelled it right away when I awoke early that morning, and I leapt out of bed. The wind had blown all night, rattling the bedroom window in its frame; perhaps it had come down the chimney and scattered embers across the hearth rug? I dressed quickly and went out to the main room, which was blessedly not afire. The screen was in place, and the ashes in the fireplace were cold and dead. Yet *something* had been burning.

When I opened the front door, the smell was intense, assaultive. I clutched my coat around me and ran down the path, turned to look back at the house to see if the source was there. Maybe a spark from the chimney had caught some leaves on the roof—I circled the cottage, saw no evidence of fire.

I followed the scent down the path toward the cemetery. There was nothing to burn in there; still, I went through the gate, sniffing like a bloodhound.

I was nearly to the middle of the cemetery before I lowered my eyes enough to see it. I had been looking for plumes of gray in the sky, but the smoke was low, curling out from the far wall.

I walked the path between the silent graves toward the smoldering bushes. As I got closer, I could see that he hadn't started with fire; he'd started with his hands. One small boy's anger had been no match for a hundred-year root system, the hard winter ground, all those thorns; only two of the rosebushes were partly pulled up. Of the others there was nothing left but a long row of char, and thin black stubs reaching up through the ash like cremated fingers. An ember blew along the ground toward me.

They were just flowers. I knew that. They weren't people, or even animals. They didn't have souls and they couldn't love. I didn't know why their destruction mattered to me so much, but it did. He had known it would.

Heat was still coming from them: I could feel on my cheeks the memory of the blaze they must have made. They'd survived an uprooting in a faraway country, a long ship's passage, replanting in alien soil, many hard frosts. I had believed that all they'd needed was loving care. I'd been a fool: they had been more fragile than that. One dose of cruelty had killed them.

I sank to my knees on the cold ground and looked directly at the pinpricks of orange nestled into the long row of destruction, letting the tiny angry messages burn into my vision. Keeping my eyes open until they began to smart. *That'll teach me,* I thought, staring as the breeze whipped up and scuttled a leaf along the path behind me with a rasping sound like something tearing in half. The sun was climbing the sky now, sending a thin warmth over Roscommon. Still I stayed staring, not turning, not looking away. *That'll teach me.*

Finally the last speck of fire guttered and went out. I got up from the ground, my knees numb, my feet bloodless and tingling, and stumbled up the path toward the house without looking back.

That'll teach me to cherish signs of life.

WHAT DOES THAT *noise mean? I'm calling the nurse.*
It's nothing. Happens all the time. Keep going.

Mrs. Pereira, are you having chest pain? Open up, lift your tongue. Okay, close.

It's just the afternoon conga. Nothing to worry—Oh!

I'll come back tomorrow.

Just need to maybe close my eyes awhile.

CHAPTER THIRTY

Leo

IT'S A GOOD HIDING PLACE behind the bakery. The vents push out warm air from the basement ovens and the alley is a dead end, so no one comes through here. There's a nook behind the garbage cans just big enough for me to lie if I bend my knees a little. I sleep there all day, and wake when one of the cans jolts. Someone's loading up the day-olds that didn't sell. I don't breathe until the lid goes back on with a clang and I hear the back door slam. I stand, cautiously peek out—no one there. I lift the lid and pick out two pastries, crouch and wolf them down. When the bakery lights finally go off, leaving the alley in the dark, I stand up and stretch.

The people I pass on the sidewalks have their heads down, going toward their suppers, coat collars turned up against the chill breeze that's started. No one looks at me.

When I get to the house I march right up the path. Same cracked stone on the front walk, same screen door with the scuff mark where Tad kicked it. But the rip in the screen has been fixed and there's a new set of iron numbers screwed into the wood beside the front door. I can hear music as I creep across the front porch: the plinking of scales, then the beginning of a song. "O Come All Ye Faithful." Then a discordant noise in the middle of a stanza, someone pounding the low keys.

I look through the window and see Sally slapping Tad's hands away from the piano. She is seated, but I can tell she has gotten taller; slimmer too, not such a baby anymore. Her hair is in barrettes; she's wearing a dress I've never seen. She scowls at Tad with the crease between her eyebrows that I know means she's about to cry. But instead of crying, she gets up dignified from the bench and leaves the room. Tad sits and crashes a few more sounds into the air, then without his sister there to annoy, he leaves the room too.

When did we get a piano?

"Enough," cries Mama, loud enough to hear through the glass. She comes into the room, both children following her. I take in my breath at the sight of her. She looks younger than I ever remember her looking, and her hair is smooth and styled. She's wearing lipstick and a dress with a skirt that stands out around her legs like a bell. She speaks to Tad, then Sally, then closes the lid of the piano over the keys. Sally's face brightens in response to whatever my mother is saying; the warmth of her joy radiates from her like heat. I can almost feel it through the windowpane.

They've decorated for Christmas: there's a big tree in the corner of the room, with tinsel and colored lights on it, a star at the top. A store-bought star, not the one I made last year out of tinfoil. Last year Clyde drank the money for our tree, drank the money for all of Christmas. I put my clumsy star on the mantel, and we put our homemade presents under that. Sally believed in Santa then. The next day, after Santa brought nothing, I told Sally the truth. Clyde whipped me when he found out. I'd known he would, but how could I let Sally believe that Santa was punishing her?

"You said by Christmas," I say in a low voice. The glass stops my words; no one hears them. "You said."

And that's when my mother turns in profile to me, and I can see that under her skirt is a baby, pushing her stomach out. Like Tad did before he came; like Sally.

I still have the matches. I strike a flame, hold it licking against the shutter. It makes an oval dark spot, growing until the heat reaches my fingertips, the paint bubbling up. I shake out the match, light another. I hold this match for a long time, letting my fingers burn too. It almost feels like more cold; it doesn't bother me at all. The fire doesn't catch; a house doesn't burn as easily as a rosebush. A muffled boom of regret deep inside at that thought. I drop the dead match from between my blistered fingers. My greatest power proven weak and foolish, a small fist against the chest of a giant who doesn't even notice the blow.

I HEAR A *voice rising and falling. I am not at the house anymore, I am somewhere else. My heart pulls toward the voice.* More than sequins, *it says.* More than kangaroos and twilight. *It is an answer, to a question I didn't know to ask.*

"YOU'RE WAKING UP . . . you're feeling refreshed." Dr. Jellicoe's voice narrates me up and away, back to the hospital and the squishy blue chair. My eyes unstick slowly, like they did the time I had pinkeye; I scrub at the lashes with a finger but there's no gumminess there, just the hard crumbly stuff my mom calls sleep. *My mom*: a fuzzy pang, but then it's gone.

"You need to try to describe more of what you're seeing," says Dr. Jellicoe. He taps the pad of paper in his lap with the point of his pen. "The only words I understood clearly were *piano* and *cold*. I need more to help you process."

If you look closely at the poster in my room, you can see the ghosts of my previous Xs, faint lines where the marker didn't get completely wiped away. Nothing is perfectly clean; there's always a trace of what came before. If the poster were in this room now, I would X over all the faces. All of them, over and over again.

CHAPTER THIRTY-ONE

Lucy

ANTIBIOTICS OR NO? I CONSIDER as I carry a throat swab to the tube station in Trauma Alley. The rapid-strep test was negative, and sore throat without fever is most likely viral, meaning antibiotics would be pointless. But the patient told me she's convinced it's strep, and after waiting two hours to be seen she'll want something more than a list of instructions.

I load the bagged specimen into one of the capsules and press one for the lab. A rumble of suction starts deep in the building, the machine shuddering as the pressure builds. I decide: I'll write for three days of antibiotics and then the primary doc can extend the prescription if the two-day culture is positive. As if in agreement, the valve in the tube station opens, and the capsule is sucked away.

There's a tweedy man lurking just inside the double doors to the ambulance bay. A plainclothes detective?

"Are we getting more vics?" I ask him. We had a shooting earlier in the night. With gang violence there's always the possibility of a retaliative second round.

"Are you Dr. Lucy Cole?" he asks.

I've barely said yes when he hands me an envelope and says the words I have dreaded for my entire professional career.

"You've been served."

And he's gone, leaving me to rip open the envelope, every nurse and tech in earshot eyeing me, while trying to appear not to. They want to know what case it is, did they work on that patient, will they be named too.

I pull the sheaf of paper from the manila enclosing it, enough to read the front page: REIDY vs. COLE. Confusing me for a minute. My husband's suing me for malpractice?

Of course not.

CHAPTER THIRTY-TWO

Clare

A SPELL OF MILD WEATHER BLEW in from somewhere, an Indian summer. It was Roscommon's slack season, when even the squash plants were done and the cemetery needed little care. The garden patch had already been sown with winter rye to protect the soil from the long chill ahead. If Leo had been there, he'd have found a dozen things for us to waste time on, pestering me to teach him more French or to let him try to fix the broken radio. He had been talking about making a kite.

I gave the cottage a thorough airing, opening all the windows and the front door and dragging the furniture out onto the grass. I deep-cleaned the rooms from top to bottom, poking with a dust-cloth-wrapped broom at the cobwebs in the corners of the ceilings and boiling gallons of water to scrub a long season's dirt out of the floors. While the floors were drying, I turned my attention to the pathetic assembly outside, the bed frame and settee and nightstand and kitchen table and rocking chair jumbled in the front yard.

I was lying on my back under the bed frame, ruthlessly disrupting the home of a spider with my dust cloth, when a pair of legs appeared to my right. I put my head out and peeked up to see the underside of the mending-basket, and far above that, the farmer's face.

"Have you been burning leaves?" he asked, sniffing, with a slight frown; bonfires were inadvisable in a dry spell.

"Just leave the basket on the step," I told him. "I'll have the mending for you by day after tomorrow."

He didn't move, despite the dismissal in my tone. His face was puzzled.

"Do you need help getting any of this inside?" he asked.

"No, thank you." I went back under the bed frame, and after a minute or two I heard the basket placed on the step and footfalls moving away.

Moving the furniture back inside, I caught a glimpse of myself in the window glass. With my face streaked with soot and the leaves caught in my hair, I looked like a madwoman. No wonder the farmer had been bemused. The embarrassment I felt was followed quickly by defiance: I could look as I wished; that's part of the luxury of living alone.

After three days I stood in the middle of the house, with nothing left to do. The place was clean, even the insides and outsides of the windows. I had waxed the kitchen drawer that had squeaked for half a year; I had scrubbed and polished the cutlery and glassware and put it back onto freshly washed cupboard shelves. I'd even poked a broom up the chimney to knock the soot loose. I had mended and laundered and folded my entire meager wardrobe; the farmer's clothing was laundered and mended and folded too, and was stacked neatly in the basket waiting to be collected. Outside, the woodpile stood taller than my head. I was clean too, having taken a long bath and washed my hair, combing it out and letting it dry in the sun before pinning it back up again.

The little house seemed much emptier and quieter than it ever had before; the hours ahead stretched empty. The cat was dozing by the fire; the sun was low in the sky. I was exhausted. I should go to bed. But instead I bundled myself up and hurried outside as though I had an appointment.

A quarter of an hour later, I stood on the front step at St. William's, waiting for a minion to fetch Prior Charles.

"I've come about Leo," I said when the door opened again. But then I didn't have any next words: Why *had* I come?

"I'm not surprised," Prior Charles said. "Well, send him back then."

"He's not with me," I said. "I thought he was here."

He sighed. "I expect he's run away again. I thought all that had stopped." I remembered what he'd told me: *he tends to wander.* Was that what he'd meant?

"He's been gone days. You didn't notice?"

"I thought he was with you." His voice was casual. Perhaps having charge of so many boys made a person relaxed about having misplaced just one. "I'll send someone to Waite to get him tomorrow."

"He could have gotten to Boston by now."

"Oh, I doubt that. We'll find him where we always do—at his mother's house." I must have looked surprised, because he went on: "Leo's not an orphan. His mother gave him up to the state earlier this year. But he keeps going back there. We even shaved his head at one point, to make him easier to spot in town." He paused, thoughtful. "Maybe we should have kept it shaved."

I had a sudden sharp memory of Leo, squinting in the summer sunlight, telling me that story about lice. The truth shamed him. Of course it would: his mother, his *own mother,* had given him away. And she was nearby enough to tantalize him, but always out of reach. No wonder he'd been so angry when he thought I was trying to replace her. I felt sorry for the woman I didn't know; it must have been a desperate thing to give up her child. I wondered what dire circumstances had forced her into it.

"I don't know why she hasn't brought him back yet," said the prior. "We'll go get him tomorrow, and send him on over to you. After suitable punishment, of course."

I shook my head. "I don't want him."

He raised his eyebrows.

"I've given it more thought," I said. "There's not enough work to be done in winter. And the cottage really is too small for two." The bells rang from the chapel: Vespers. I had no idea it was that late. "I'll let you get to your praying."

The time with Leo had been only an interlude, I told myself. It had been a brief passage, now closed, like a set of parentheses, in the life I had made for myself. I had chosen an isolated road deliberately; the deviation to take in Leo had been a misstep. I did not need to look again at the carnage of the roses to tell me that.

I could still smell them as I walked in that singed air up the path to the cottage. I slammed the door behind me, too quickly; the little wooden bar that fit into the latch hadn't fully dropped, and it hit the iron bracket so hard that it split, a chunk like a large tooth falling to the floor. I knelt to collect the fallen piece. It was old wood, brittle, cleaved along a diagonal. The remaining point of wood just barely reached into the bracket; one good gust would break it and swing the door wide open.

"*Damn* it," I said.

"Are you all right?" I heard from behind me. I wheeled around: James, the farmer, was standing by the hearth.

"What are you doing here?" Surprised into rudeness, and embarrassed that he'd witnessed my cursing.

"I came for the mending—"

"It's right there where it always is."

"—and I heard your cat crying from inside the chimney." That silenced me. He made four legs with the fingers of one hand, put the other hand, flattened, beneath it. "He was on top of the flue."

"He likes to climb things." I had left the fireguard ajar after washing the hearth; Kitty must have pushed past it and, ever curious, climbed up through the flaps of the flue and then they'd fallen closed below him. "Is he all right?" It must have been a job getting him out. I noticed the soot on the farmer's sleeves.

"He was a little scared, but he's fine now." He took a step to the side; I could see the fuzzy, exhausted curl of black-orange on the cushion of the settee, sides heaving slowly in sleep. I looked up and saw telltale smudges of soot on the thighs of the farmer's trousers: he'd taken the cat onto his lap.

On a farm, dogs and cats had their uses, but they weren't viewed as companions; they weren't indulged and they certainly weren't cuddled. I hadn't expected that a farmer could spare pity for a small frightened cat, would take the time to comfort him.

"That was very kind of you," I said. "Thank you."

He nodded; he took the basket of mending from the table and carried it outside, shutting the door behind him so gently that the frail latch fell into place, the sliver of wood just long enough by a hair to keep the door closed.

"Kitty," I said when the farmer was gone. I went over to the cat, put my hand on his back. He twitched his ears in his sleep. "You do have a talent for focusing the heart."

THAT NIGHT, TURNING over in bed, I heard a *mew* of protest, felt a set of warning claws against my foot. The cat was under the blankets. "Sorry," I said, pulling my foot back. My breath made a cloud of fog that hung in the air. The temperature had dropped precipitously since the sun had gone down. I lay awake most of the night despite my weariness, with the cat warm and soft against my shins and the darkness pressing like a frosty hand against all the windows and the roof. I couldn't stop the thought: where was Leo?

THE MONK APPEARED when I was outside adjusting burlap over the charred rosebushes in the crisp bright morning. They wouldn't survive; I knew that. But I wasn't able to bring myself to leave them naked and alone in the cold.

The monk loomed over the wall, his shadow falling across me. This is what it is, I reminded myself, to know people. They know where to find you to bring bad news.

I pulled the rough cord around the last bush and snipped the end with my shears, looping the two pieces together in a double fisherman's bend. This wouldn't be easy to untie again; it would have to be cut apart in the spring. But simpler knots often don't hold.

"It's about Leo, isn't it?" I said.

The monk nodded, the top of his shadow bowing back and forth over my hands.

Quickly, I forced the images through my mind again, the ones I hadn't permitted myself to linger on before. As if freshening them now would prepare me. Leo beaten, or trampled under the wheels of a motorcar. Frozen to death in an alley.

I looked up: it was Brother Silas. He'd been an oblate when I first met him, when he'd nursed me back to health. He was only a little younger than Prior Charles, but the years had changed him much less. He still had the thin frame and unlined face of a boy.

"What happened?" I asked. Steeling myself.

"He's in the infirmary. He's asking for you."

Not dead? Not dead! And asking for me. My heart, which had felt stopped in my chest, was beating again. I got up without another word and followed Silas.

The infirmary had curtains tacked around the bottoms of the windows. All the beds were empty.

"Quarantine," said Silas. He handed me a cloth from a bowl just inside the door. He took one also and placed it over his nose and mouth. I did the same and followed him across the room.

I could see that what had appeared to be a solid wall jutting into the corner of the room was actually a bedsheet, strung from a line along the ceiling to meet another sheet perpendicularly, making a rippling white box against the wall. Silas pulled at one of the sheets, making an inverted V opening for me to slip through.

There were no windows in the stone walls that made up two sides of the enclosure. A bedside table held a lamp and a ceramic pitcher and basin; in the dim light I could see Leo's dark head against the pillow. His body made a tiny lump under the bedclothes and his hair was matted against his forehead. His eyes were closed. There was nothing else here: just the boy and the bed and the little table.

I went to the bedside, put my hand on Leo's forehead. There was a rough quality to his skin, like sandpaper.

"Clare," he said, opening his eyes. His voice was a croak.

"Shh," I said. "Don't try to talk."

"I killed your roses."

"Never mind," I said.

"They were a hundred years old," he said with a glassy insistence. "From all the way across the ocean."

"I made that up," I said. "I don't know where they're from."

"You loved them," he said. He closed his eyes; the tears streaked down his cheeks.

There was a rustling noise behind me. I turned to see the upper part of Prior Charles's long face, a cloth covering his nose and mouth, poking through the opening in the sheets. He motioned; Silas and I followed him out and across the room, into the hallway.

"I want to ask your help," he said, taking the cloth down from his face. "I'll understand if you refuse."

"What is it?"

"He has scarlet fever. As you must know, it's contagious," said the prior. "We're taking the usual precautions, but it could be a long ordeal. Weeks in bed."

I wasn't sure what he was proposing. Did he want me to come to the priory and nurse Leo?

"I'm not a nurse," I said. "I don't know what to do for scarlet fever."

"There's nothing really to do," said Silas. "I'll give him penicillin injections, but other than that, he just needs rest and basic care."

"He can't stay here," said Prior Charles. It was not unkindly said, and I did see the sense in it: a hundred boys' lives could not be put at risk for the comfort of one. "We could send him to the contagious ward in the hospital in Providence."

I imagined Leo alone in a hospital. No visitors, no familiar faces. The nurses wearing cotton masks to tend him, only their eyes showing, no one breathing too deeply or touching him more than she had to.

"What about his mother?" I asked.

"She has other children," said the prior.

She had other children? Whom she had kept with her, while sending Leo away? I revised my opinion of her at that moment; my previous sympathy for her maternal sacrifice evaporated. *This is not my home,* Leo had cried the last time I'd seen him. He must have been thinking of his mother, believing that he had a home with her. Apparently he'd been wrong.

I closed my eyes, called up the memory of the burning roses to remind me: this is what you risk. This is what he's capable of. Instead I saw bald Leo, humming down the cemetery path with the sun behind him. I opened my eyes.

"I'll take him."

"It's very good of you," said Prior Charles with relief.

"I want to be sure you know what you're taking on." Silas's brown eyes stayed on me as he spoke. "What could happen."

"I'm willing to risk it." I thought he meant the contagion, but as I looked from one grave face to the other, I understood. "You mean he could die."

Both men nodded.

"Well," I said, looking back into the room, at the sheeted corner. "Then he'll die at Roscommon, with me."

NOWADAYS, AS YOU may know, scarlet fever is nothing. A gnat among illnesses, a mere pebble on the path of childhood. A few days of rash and fever, some antibiotics, and it is done. But it was not so in 1958.

Brother Silas brought Leo over to Roscommon, bearing him in his arms like a bundle of laundry. We put him in my bedroom, into my bed, which I had stripped and covered with rough St. Will's linens. All the bedding he used would have to be burned later; everything he touched, and everything that touched him, would have to be burned. I made up a bed for myself on the settee in the main room.

He was sour smelling from the streets and the fever-sweat. He didn't flinch as I washed his chest and arms and neck and dried them. I sat him up like a doll and washed and dried his back. Put a nightshirt on him and laid him down again, layering blankets over his torso and leaving his lower half outside the covers so I could pull off the filthy trousers and wash the rest of him. He was so pale in the lamplight. When I got the dirt off his feet, the bluish veins there were like dark lace. When I was done I tucked his legs back under the pile of quilts. He'd never awakened.

What to feed a sleeping person? I boiled down bones for broth and fed the thin fragrant liquid to him in slow dribbled spoonfuls, hoping it wouldn't choke him as it went down. He swallowed automatically without opening his eyes. The quick frost after the fine weather had made icicles along the eaves; I chopped one down and hammered it into chips that I fed to Leo one by one, slipping them between his lips and pressing a cloth against his chin to catch the melted water that seeped back out.

It was like caring for a gigantic baby. Leo weighed very little—he must have starved the whole time he was away—but it was dead weight. It took an hour to change his bedclothes; an hour to change his clothing; another hour to get an ounce of fluid down his throat. I would finish a task only to begin another; feeding him necessitated washing him and changing the bedding; then it would be time to try to feed him again, and when that was done he'd be shivering, having soaked his sheets with sweat. Every four hours it was time for another dose of crushed aspirin. I wasn't very successful at that; he drooled it out of the corners of his mouth, pill fragments clinging to his chin. I wiped them away. Who knows how much got into him? His fever was unrelenting, and he tossed and moaned.

One night, the metal spoon I had been using for a makeshift latch on the front door fell out of its place with a clatter. I was in the kitchen pulverizing more aspirin and looked up to see the farmer standing in the doorway. I strode over and pressed the door closed in his face. There was a grunt of surprise on the other side.

"Scarlet fever," I said through the wood. "You don't want to come in."

"You're ill?"

"Not me. Leo."

"Oh." Then, "Do you need anything? Can I help?"

"No," I said. Then, "I don't know."

There was a long silence.

"Are you gone?" I asked.

"No," he said.

I put my forehead against the door.

"I don't know what I'm doing," I whispered. "He's getting sicker."

"Have you had the doctor?"

"Brother Silas comes every morning. He says there's nothing really to do." *God's will will prevail* was what he'd said. "I can't get him to swallow the aspirin."

"There's always something to do," said the farmer with an uncharacteristic vigor. "Do you have any books?"

"What?" I said.

"Children like to be told stories when they're ill. It comforts them."

"He's sleeping. He can't hear me."

"There's comfort for the reader too," he said. His voice was sad; I wondered how he knew this. "Also applesauce."

"What?"

"Crush the aspirin tablets into applesauce."

I stayed like that against the door for a long time, listening to the crunch of his boots going away through the snow.

Leo was talking to himself when I went back into the room, an uninterrupted slush of sounds, no words that I could make out. I took the cloth from his forehead and freshened it in the basin of water by the bed, brushed the hair from the ivory skin above his eyebrows, laid the cool cloth back down. He didn't seem to notice any of it; he was still dream-babbling. After a moment I went to the trunk at the foot of the bed and took out a parcel. *For Leo from Clare,* I had written on the paper. *Merry Christmas.* I tore the paper and ribbon off and went to the chair beside the bed. I opened the heavy science book, tilting it so that the lamplight fell onto the page.

"Any body completely or partially submerged in a fluid is acted upon by an upward force." Leo continued to mutter and I raised my voice. "Which is equal to the weight of the fluid being displaced by the body." This was no good: I needed a story. I flipped through the pages. "Listen, Leo," I said.

I read about the mathematician who got into his bathtub and observed how the water level rose. I added details that weren't in the book: the long curly beard of the man, how it floated on the surface of the bath, and how when he leapt from the tub with his famous cry, *eureka,* he'd slipped on the water that sloshed on the floor. How his youngest child, putting his curious head around the doorframe, had been just in time to catch his father's arm and steady him. *If not for the boy,* I invented, *the discovery might have been lost.* I was not sure Leo was hearing any of it, but he definitely grew quieter while I talked, his chest rising and falling more slowly.

When I got to the end of the story, my throat was dry and Leo was asleep, the kitten curled at his feet. I tiptoed from the room.

The next night, I made up another story from a different chapter, about a seed dropped by a bird, then inadvertently buried by the paw of a passing squirrel, lying asleep for a season before pushing up and bursting through the soil, unfurling its leaves wide to drink the power of the sun.

"See the layers inside?" I said, holding up a picture of a botanical cross-section. Of course he could not see; his eyes were closed.

I had forgotten the power, the beauty, of words. I savored them as I sounded them out, naming things I hadn't even known existed: *cambium, xylem, phloem.* So much intricate design went into something as simple as a stem. If God took that much care with even the humblest piece of each living thing, it seemed evidence that He must know, and have a hand in, every thing that happened to every bit of creation. For the first time in a long time, I found comfort in the thought.

"THE INFECTION HAS moved into his joints," I told the farmer through the door a few days later. "Both knees are swollen."

How much I anticipated this half hour each day, his visit the only light in the long, grim hours. As the sun went down my spirits lifted, knowing he'd soon be trudging up the hill after his chores were done. Today I had put a chair outside. When I saw him coming up the path, I opened the door, set a steaming mug of cocoa on the seat, then closed the door again.

He said nothing about the chair, but I heard the creak as he sat down.

"Silas says he could be crippled," I said. "But the real worry is injury to his heart."

"His heart," repeated the farmer.

It *was* inexplicable: what had started as a sore throat was now creeping into his knees, and from there might marshal an attack on his heart.

"Silas gave him another injection." Leo's thighs were mottled with bruises.

"Good cocoa," said the farmer.

"It's your milk," I reminded him. "How's Evangeline?" One of his cows had mastitis; he'd been up hours the other night, massaging out the blockage.

"Better," he said. "I won't use her milk for a while yet, though. Best to be safe."

He had only six cows; Evangeline was a great producer. I knew this was a significant loss to him.

"You don't have to bring me milk if you can't spare it," I said. "Leo's not eating anything anyway."

"You need to keep up your strength. You can make it into butter or cheese. I make a nice soft cheese with pepper. I'll show you how."

"After Leo gets better." Or after he died. In any case, there would be an *after*; these visits reminded me of that. This long, difficult time would come to an end.

There was a silence, and for a moment I thought he'd left.

"You've, ah, left something outside here," said the farmer.

"What is it?" I asked, and then when his answer didn't come, I realized what it must be. "Sorry," I said, horribly embarrassed, and also trying not to laugh. "It's just the most convenient place."

The bedpan had been one of the most difficult things to manage. Leo jumped each time he rolled back onto the unyielding shape and felt the cold ceramic kiss on his buttocks. I had tried keeping the thing by the fireplace in order to warm it up, but the cat took an inordinate interest in it. Finally, I had settled on leaving it outside in a snowbank and dousing it with hot water from the kettle right before I took it into the bedroom. I would bundle up while the kettle hissed, stand on the porch and pour, then watch the steam rise from the smooth white shape for a minute before bending to pick it up, throw the water out of it, and carry it back inside. All of that three times a day, and usually for nothing. Leo hadn't much in him.

Now the farmer must be staring at it where I'd left it, jammed into the snowbank beside the porch, not four feet from the leg of the chair he was sitting on.

"Are you all right?" He sounded concerned. My laughter must have sounded like tears.

"Yes," I said. I couldn't stop laughing. How long had he been staring at the bedpan, wondering if he should say anything about it? I put my arms around myself and laughed until the tears ran down my face.

"I'm sorry," I said when I had gotten control of myself. "I haven't been sleeping much."

"You have a nice laugh." He was probably blushing out there at his forwardness. His voice became businesslike. "I have to get back to Evangeline. What should I bring tomorrow?"

"Just yourself," I said, a little forwardness of my own. "Thank you."

I heard the chair creak as he got up. I stayed seated, waited a full five minutes until he was surely away and out of risk of contagion, before I opened the door. When I did there was a package on the seat of the chair, wrapped in brown paper. Books. I took them, and the chair and the bottle of milk and the empty cocoa mug back inside. I left the bedpan where it was.

SPEAKING OF WHICH.

Hm? Oh! Let me call the nurse.

What can I do for you, Miz Pereira? Oh. All righty. I'm going to put the bed down a bit, and then we'll roll onto our side.

I'll be back in a while, all right, Gloria?

Take your time.

I'll come get you when we're done, Miss Clare.

THOSE OF US who have reached a delicate age have dispensed with modesty; it's a pleasant frippery, like cut flowers. With time, both wither and die. Not a one of us here has not known the indignity of a bedpan or a nurse's efficient washcloth. Gloria's in the nursing unit now, and has a catheter in; the bedpan is reserved for her more solid efforts. She was moved to the unit a week ago; the staff delivers my trays here, so we can have meals together.

It is my long life's greatest surprise: I have found best friend-ship again, in that holding-hands-on-the-playground, save-a-seat-beside-me, choose-each-other-first-for-games way. I would have said it couldn't happen, a meaningful connection at my age, much less with Gloria, considering the difference in our ages and experience. Maybe it has been partly the sharing of my life, the hours that I have talked and she has sat listening, the recording device between us drinking up the things I've never said to anyone. But it's not just that; we don't record every day, and after shutting the recorder off we linger and talk, both of us, about anything.

When the aide calls me back into the room, Gloria's in good spirits.

"That was like childbirth," she says.

"How would you know?"

"Extrapolation." She aims the remote control at the screen bolted up near the ceiling. "Guess what time it is."

I find television slightly overwhelming; many of the programs seem to concern themselves with extremely unpleasant subjects. Gloria likes the program that has people bringing their old things to experts to be valued. Objects they have cherished as heirlooms turn out to be cheap copies, while the neglected item that has been serving years as a doorstop or paperweight or moldering away in a closet is revealed as a priceless wonder. How reverently people regard their old doorstop when they've been told it's valuable. Gloria likes to guess what the expert is going to say.

Her intravenous line disappears under the top of her bed-clothes, and from the foot of the bed another tube snakes out. I am grateful for the anonymous medication that is keeping her alive. She has an infection in her leg, a red angry tumescence that started as a scratch.

"I *knew* it," she tells the screen. "That thing was too darned ugly. It had to be worth a bundle. Just look at that woman's greedy face. Beloved family heirloom my rear end. She can't wait to hear how much she can sell that thing for." She lies back against the pillows, a bit breathless. "Do you ever wonder where all that stuff goes? Those things we had in our houses all those years?" She spreads her arms to indicate the room we are in. "And now we're here, and there's nothing left. Where does it go?"

"Well, at least some of it ends up on the television." I am trying to joke.

"But everyone had a pitcher like that," she says, indicating the screen, where the man in the jacket is turning an enamel jug to show the mark on its bottom. "*Everyone*. And only one shows up on TV. Where did the others go? How did they all disappear?"

"They didn't disappear. They wore out, got damaged, were thrown away. There are probably lots in attics and basements."

When the program is over, Gloria puts her thumb on the remote to shut off the power. Then she fiddles with the tray table until the top slides back, revealing the drawer inside.

"Goodness," I say. "It's as bad as your purse in there." I see a comb and a denture case and a box of tissues and at least three rolls of mints before she finds what she is looking for and slams it shut again.

"Happy birthday," she says, placing an envelope flat on the surface. "You don't look a day over ninety-five."

"It's not my birthday."

"It will be sometime. The way things are going here, better safe than sorry." She nudges the envelope toward me.

I take it up. It's bulky; something other than a card is inside. I tear open the flap, then turn the envelope over and an object falls out onto my palm. It's a Monopoly piece: the car.

"I've hired you a driver," she says. "Two hours, to go to Roscommon and back. Saturday at 9 a.m. You're gonna put your feet on that ground one more time."

I stare at the car. "Gloria."

"I hoped to go with you, but—" She lifts the arm with the trailing IV. "You'll have to tell me all about it."

"It's a lovely thought," I say.

"You should see your face. What's the problem?"

I turn the car over between my thumb and index finger. It's the style from my youth, the open touring car.

"You'll have to give that back," she says, putting out her hand. "I stole it from the common room."

CHAPTER THIRTY-THREE

Lucy

I SLEEP FOR A FEW HOURS after my shift, then pop awake at 10 a.m. as though an alarm has gone off. I shower and dress in regular clothes, jeans and a long-sleeve shirt, and take the elevator down to the psych floor. I badge myself in, nod hello to the unit coordinator.

"How is he?" I ask.

"Not great," she says. "Honestly, I think this hypnosis is doing a number on him. It must be bringing up some stuff."

"He's remembered the murders?" What a terrible burden. It might be preferable to have no memory at all. "Does he still want to be called Leo?"

"I don't know. He's kind of stopped talking." The phone rings and she puts her hand on it. "You can go back." She lifts the receiver. "Six West, this is Connie."

He's in his room, coloring in a book. He looks up briefly when I come in.

"Hey, buddy," I say. "How are you?"

He doesn't respond.

His room is so spare, not like any of the other rooms I passed coming down the hall. Those rooms are filled with color: toys on the beds, cards and posters on the walls. The anorexic girl sitting on her bed texting had been doing so from a landslide of stuffed animals.

"What are you coloring?"

Still nothing.

I'm used to the silent treatment from pediatric patients, but with them I have a guiding purpose, an acute problem to solve. I'm not here to examine him; I have no medical goal. I'm not quite sure what to do.

"Are you okay?" I ask. I sit on the end of the bed. He pulls his feet up so they aren't near me, but otherwise he doesn't acknowledge my presence. "Are you mad at me?"

He stops moving the crayon but doesn't look up.

"You *said*," he tells the paper with little-boy rage. "You said you'd tell them to find Clare."

"I did. I did, Leo. Ben. They couldn't find her."

He looks up then, his face pinching around the mouth. He's trying not to cry.

"I don't want to stay here," he says. "I want to go home."

Is he finally remembering Karen?

"Home with your mom?"

"With Clare." He tells the crayoned picture in his lap. "I hate being here. He's making me remember the bad stuff."

Is Jellicoe actually getting information from him about Karen's murder? At what cost? The boy is clearly miserable. The cops want his testimony, the attending physician wants a publication, the social worker wants to get him off her to-do list. All of them doing their jobs, but none dedicated to his interests alone.

"What do you remember about Clare?" I ask. "What can you tell me about her?"

His face gets an interior look, as if he's holding something in his mind to describe it. "Her house is really little," he says. "The walls are made of stones. It's up a hill and there's a graveyard." He looks up at me. "I help keep the graves neat."

Surely Karen hadn't let her son hang out in a graveyard. Young children can conflate fantasy and reality; maybe that's the explanation for what's been going on with Ben.

"Honey, is Clare maybe someone from a story?" I ask. "From a book, or a movie?"

His hopeful expression dissolves. He shakes his head and curls onto his side facing away from me. And no matter what I say, he won't turn over or look at me or speak again. After half an hour or so, an aide comes to get him. *Time for therapy,* and he wriggles down from the bed, careful not to brush against me, and goes away without a backward glance.

CHAPTER THIRTY-FOUR

Clare

IN THE THIRD WEEK OF his illness, Leo was barely responsive, just skin over bone; his hair was plastered to his scalp. I'll wash it tomorrow, I thought. If he lives. The image of tipping his head back and pouring the warm water over his scalp called up a memory so powerful that it loosened something in me. *Careful. Careful not to get soap in his eyes. Careful that the water isn't too warm, or too cold.* All that energy and love and care, come to nothing.

Silas visited, gave him extreme unction, left again. I swayed a little on the doorstep watching him go. Day and night was mixed up by then; was the gray sky morning or twilight? I couldn't tell. The snow glittered across the fields, made a blanket over the sleeping plants. In time, they'd awaken. Driven by the Creator, or by their own deep hearts? The God who loved His creation enough to make every piece of it beautifully intricate, who loved each leaf and each worm—how could that be the same God who had chosen to give Leo a hard, short life? Who had taken Bradley from my arms, who had let my mother die alone. Which was worse: an all-powerful divinity that exerted such cruelty, or a total absence of any meaning to the world?

I lay down *just for a moment* on the settee by the fireplace. When I awoke the fire was low and the room cold, and someone was shaking my shoulder.

I swam up out of sleep to see James bent over me.

"You didn't answer my knock," he said.

"How long was I asleep?" I leapt up, pushed past him to go to Leo.

The bedroom fire was also low; the cloth on Leo's forehead was freezing. How could I have fallen asleep and left him? I fed the fire and rearranged the blankets, dislodging Kitty, who'd been sleeping among them.

The farmer was still there when I came out of the sickroom. He'd tended to the guttering fire; flames were now dancing behind the screen.

"You shouldn't be here," I told him. "It's not safe."

He followed me to the doorway, but when I reached to slip the spoon from the latch he put out a hand to stop me, clasping my wrist.

"This is no place for a person alone," he said.

"It's my home."

"You could choose a different home." His fingers were warm. "You and I, we're not young, but we're not old. We like talking to each other, and that's more than many marriages have." He cleared his throat. "I could teach the boy to farm. It's not always an easy life, but it's a good one." He brought his eyes to mine, waiting.

For a moment I could see it: Leo a young man on a tractor, acres of land spreading around him that he would one day inherit. Myself on the porch of James's fine white house, looking over those same acres. Laughing together in the evenings. What I'd never had: true friendship in a marriage.

And of course that word stopped my foolish daydream: I was already married. And then another harsh truth: Leo wouldn't live to ride that tractor.

"I'm sorry," he said, taking my silence for an answer. "I've clearly misunderstood. I won't embarrass us both anymore."

He let go of my wrist and pulled open the door. Nearly through it, he turned back, took something out of his pocket, came two long strides into the room, and put it on the table. Then he went out, his shoulders shrugged up against the cold. I shut the door and slipped the spoon through the latch to keep it closed.

The small bundle he'd left was about as long as my hand, wound around with cloth and tied with a bit of ribbon. I took it over to the fireplace, sat with it in my lap. The ribbon was threaded through a small card that said *Merry Christmas, From James, To Clare.*

Today was Christmas. All those plans I had had for baking and presents had evaporated during Leo's illness, and I'd lost track of the days. It had been years since I'd received a Christmas present. As a child, how I'd lingered over each one, loosening the paper without tearing it, keeping the gift inside hidden from view until the last possible moment. A brush with infinity: until the item was revealed it could be anything. I held James's present a little longer before slipping off the ribbon, the object spinning in the unwinding cloth until it fell out into my hand. A piece of wood, just the right size, with a hole in one end for the bolt. I turned it over: he'd carved a rose into the face of it, the petals rising out of the wood. It jumped and blurred in the firelight as if a real flower was trapped there and being blown by the wind. It was better than anything I might have imagined. A new latch for my door. Something I needed; something I wanted; something beautiful.

I could feel the hot ovals where the farmer's fingertips had grasped my wrist. I felt ashamed; how cruel to let him go away without a word. But what could I tell him? *I have a husband.* It might not even be true. If I was thirty-nine now, Hugh was fifty-two, and people didn't always live so long back then. He might have died while I'd been at Roscommon; I could be an unwitting widow, bound to no one, instead of a fugitive.

What I would have told James, if I'd been honest: *I don't deserve a happy ending.*

I went into the bedroom again. Leo didn't move when I opened the door. Had he slipped away? But when I felt his forehead it was neither cold nor feverish, and as I watched he took a slow breath of natural sleep. I poked up the fire again and then bundled up to go outside for water. I'd be washing his hair after all.

"He's turned the corner," confirmed Brother Silas when he visited the next day. "He might have some residual heart weakness, but I think he'll live."

Heart weakness. Well, who didn't have that?

EVEN AFTER THERE was no more need for quarantine, Leo stayed. And after he was well enough to return to school, he stayed. His legs eventually overhung the end of the settee but he stayed, pulling up a chair for his feet and sleeping crosswise. Through harvests and plantings and snowfalls, he stayed. Nothing formal was ever drawn up or decided, but he went through the woods to St. Will's every morning and returned to me in the afternoons. In the summers, we worked together in the garden and the cemetery, the roses blooming around three sides of us, while the cat moved from napping spot to napping spot in the warm grass. We named the cat Archimedes, after the scientist in the bathtub, and called him Archie.

The earth along the one wall of the cemetery stayed barren. I planned to replant someday with cuttings from the living bushes, but it didn't ever seem time. I watered and fertilized the soil sometimes when Leo wasn't there to see me do it, but nothing more.

ONE DAY LATE in the summer after Leo turned sixteen, we were out in the garden harvesting tomatoes.

"It's a bumper crop," I said. "I think tomorrow will be a squirreling day."

It was Leo's word, invented when he was about thirteen, for the process of storing up food against winter. He said that while I was doing it I looked like a happy squirrel burying a nut. It was true that I enjoyed it, even in the height of summer, when the cottage got terribly hot from the big boiling pots of jars and lids. Although I'd begun reading again after Leo's illness, getting books from the library every time I visited town, I still liked things I could do with my hands.

Leo brushed the dirt from a tomato and scraped at the surface gently with his thumbnail. Sometimes slug bites hid under a patch like that. It must have passed muster, for he put it into the bowl he carried.

"Whatever happened with that farmer?" he asked. "The one you used to do mending for."

"I'm sure he's remarried," I said after a surprised pause. "And has someone else to do his mending." Ever since I had declined his proposal, I had seen the man only from a distance. Leo did most of the shopping now; he had a crate on the back of his bicycle to carry packages. Whenever I passed the farm, James was not near the fence; he was on his tractor or driving his combine, or nowhere at all in sight.

"He's not. Mrs. Massey told me."

"You shouldn't pry into other people's business."

"I didn't ask. She just told me." That was probably true; Mrs. Massey was a gossip. "You can't just stay alone here forever."

"I'm not alone. You're here."

He shrugged, and I understood: he wanted to leave.

I knew that he must be restless, tucked away in Roscommon the way we were. He had taken a part-time job delivering for Massey's Dry Goods the year before, bicycling around Waite on his second-hand Schwinn. The town was small, but the world was suggested there, in the magazines and the newspaper headlines, and on the curved black-and-white screen of the television in the hardware store window.

"You haven't finished school," I said.

"I'm older than anyone else in my class."

"You were ill. You missed almost that whole year."

"Clare," he said softly. "That was a long time ago." As he said it, of course I could see it was true: he was nearly a man now, his arms muscular and brown. It had been a long time since he had had to tilt his head up to talk to me.

"I don't want to sit in classrooms anymore," he said. "I want to do something."

"I always thought you'd make a good teacher. Or a scientist."

He walked down the row of tomato plants, turning the fruit expertly without releasing it from the vine, inspecting it for blemish or rot.

"I'm thinking of joining the navy," he said.

"The navy?" Almost nothing could have surprised me more. He hated the water, unfortunate for a lad born in Rhode Island. There'd been a fishing excursion sometime when he was small that had not gone well, sunburn and seasickness at least, perhaps other miseries he didn't mention. He'd grown up without interest in swimming or sailing.

"It's not just boats," he said. "They have naval pilots."

He wanted to fly.

"You don't have to join up to fly airplanes." I heard how foolish the words were as I spoke them. How else would a boy like Leo get the opportunity to learn how to fly? "Anyway, they won't take you for two more years."

"They will if I get permission." He muttered this with his back turned to me.

We hadn't talked about his mother, ever. She was still legally his mother, would always be; he and I had no official or legal relationship. She could sign the paper to approve his induction, and I would have no say in the matter.

I'd reached a heavy-burdened plant whose vines were hanging almost to the ground. Leo put his bowl down and came over to do the restaking while I knelt to reach the hidden fruit.

"You know, they may not take you in the service, with your heart," I said.

"My heart's fine." He lifted a trailing vine and knotted it to the wooden upright with a soft strip of an old undershirt.

"They'll do an examination to check."

A pause, a hitch in his movements.

"They already did one," he confessed.

I sat back on my heels and looked at him, my knees cold in two patches from the damp earth.

"You already joined up."

"I didn't know how to tell you." Contrite.

With the sun behind him like that, he could be any grown man. He *was* grown. And that was part of it, wasn't it, part of what I'd taken on. The letting go. I would have had to do it with Bradley, if he'd been lucky enough to live that long. If I'd been lucky enough.

"Well, you've told me now." My chest twinged hard, and I looked up at the sky. "We'd better finish before the rain comes."

HE CAME HOME after basic training looking both frighteningly adult and terribly young in his uniform. He'd be gone again in three days, to a place I'd never heard of. I made him repeat the name. He'd rolled his eyes and pulled the atlas from the bookshelf he'd made for the front room, paged to Asia and put his finger on the country that ran along the edge of the landmass, pinched and narrow in the middle and bulging at top and bottom, like a drop of honey coming off the spoon.

"Clare," he said. "You have to read the papers. We're at war."

"We're not." I'd lived through a war.

But apparently, we were.

I'm a gunner, his first letter said. It didn't say—didn't have to say—how disappointed he was. A gunner, not a pilot. Still, he was flying. Leo was flying—and he was shooting at people. Leo, who didn't like killing pests in the garden.

They name everything here. The plane's called Victoria, and the gun's Caroline. Were they named for sisters or sweethearts or mothers? He didn't say. He sat in the side of the plane, he reported, but the rest of that paragraph was blacked out by the censor. It picked up again with *The pilot's a guy from Wyoming called Ticky.* The next sentence stuttered with censored bits: *He's ▆▆▆▆▆▆▆ and I don't know if ▆▆▆▆▆▆▆▆▆▆. It'll probably be all right, but ▆▆▆▆▆.*

I held the paper up, tried to see his words through the censor ink, but it was thick and did its job well. His letters gave me only the barest sense of how he was; they focused on concrete details, about the food and the men who were flying with him, their habits and their silly nicknames. The men who were holding his life in their hands.

"How's he doing over there?" said the postmaster when I pushed through the post office door. "Mine's infantry. He doesn't write much, though. Not like your boy." I took the stack from him: three letters, a bonanza.

He wrote every week. I didn't get all the letters, and sometimes they arrived in a clump and I had to sort them by the postmarks to read them in order. He didn't tell me enough of what I longed to hear: how he was, what was really happening, when he might be coming home. *You need to get out of your hidey-hole, Clare,* one letter told me. *You need to go back into the world.* Why was he wasting words talking about me when he knew I wanted to know about him? *Don't worry about me,* I wrote back. *I'm fine.* But he did write every week. Until he didn't.

CHAPTER THIRTY-FIVE

Leo

Ticky's in a fouler-than-usual mood on the airstrip, jamming his sunglasses on against the breaking dawn, sucking from a cup of what I hope is coffee. Probably up all night drinking *ba muoi ba* and whiskey, and then a handful of uppers to jumpstart the day. Not a person you want to trust your life to. But his double chevron tells my blank shoulder what to do, so when he snaps, *Move your ass, Cherry,* I ignore the sore pit of fear under my breastbone and climb into the plane.

Clare asked me for the names of the boys I fly with. *What boys?* I wrote back, *We're all men here.* But that wasn't true. We are boys, reckless, testing ourselves and cocky. We have to be. I can't write her the way we really talk, the language we use. I'm called FNG and Cherry, and sometimes Rhoda. No one uses my real name. I can't write about how I wake every morning with my heart beating so hard I can feel it in my throat. Reading about such things would frighten her. Writing it down would frighten me.

Sometimes, coming back from a mission, knowing I'm as far from the next one as I can be, I feel something surge up in me like a wave, so intense I can barely contain it, something like joy or love. Not love for a sweetheart or even a brother, it's like nothing

I've felt before, and I feel it for all the men with me in the rattling ship, our airborne sanctuary. It's a feeling born of this time that will not come again; it draws a circle around us and makes us one forever, and no one who has not been here with us will understand. The feeling lasts in me until we land. It sometimes lingers into the evening, but by morning it's always gone. I have thought more than once, while the feeling fills me, that it is worth all of the rest, all the terror and sorrow, all the unspeakable horror, just to experience these moments, so alive and filled with feeling. I think nothing will ever feel so real again.

I can't write any of that either. My letters have gotten shorter and more meaningless with all that I have to leave out. I still write as often as I can, filling in the space left by what's unsaid with questions: how is Archie, how are the crops, did Mrs. Massey ever get that color TV she'd been talking about. While I'm writing, I'm crawling through the words back home.

"Taking the scenic route?" calls Peach up to the cockpit. I'm glad he's the one who said it. He's older than me, and not afraid of anything, not even a superior officer. "Where's that fucker going?" he says, maybe to me, maybe to himself.

The Snoopy ahead is hovering along the treetops like a metal dragonfly, a lure to draw fire from hidden VC. If they take the bait we'll pick them off. We haven't had a nibble and the sun is fully up now. We'll have to turn back soon. I am glad; I don't like the shooting. I hate how the people run and scatter. I know about the things they're capable of—the punji pits and the tiger traps and the other hundred brutal ways they have devised to torment and slaughter us. But when I see them up close they're just people. Some of them are just kids.

Today there won't be any of that; either we're in the wrong place, or the snipers below are too smart to go for the Snoopy. The engine drones on, the blue above, the green below. With the breeze coming in the window, it's much cooler up here than on the ground, and no mosquitoes. If I close my eyes, shut out the noise and the gasoline fumes, this could just be a nice ride in the country.

A folded map hits me in the face, thrown back from the cockpit.

"Since you're so smart," calls Ticky over the roar of the engines.

He wouldn't have thrown it at Peach.

I unfold the map and compare it to the view from the open window, try to match anything on it to the anonymous vista of jungle canopy below. There is a blue line of water bending on the map; a river, surely large enough to see from the air.

"We need to go west from the river," I say.

"What river?" says Peach, leaning out his window. "Ain't no river down there."

Ticky's heard us, apparently; there is a jolt and then he is taking us down and down, in a deep descent. He does this occasionally, intentionally, kind of a midair tantrum. I wouldn't ever do that. I wouldn't leave the Snoopy without cover, or expose us this way. But I'm a gunner, not a pilot, and I don't make the decisions.

"There's your river," says Peach while my stomach is straining to come up my throat. "Turn right," he yells to Ticky.

We're turning right, cresting in the air with the dragonfly doing the same beside us, when the new noise comes. A tiny noise. Just a *ping* on the skin of the plane. By now, I think I know all the noises this airplane can make. I have never heard this one before. I look out the window: no dragonfly.

Another *ping*.

"Jink it, jink," yells Peach. "Go up."

"Shut the fuck up," cries Ticky. "You wanna come up here?"

Maybe those seconds he takes to scream this are our downfall. There's a tearing sound, and a *pop*, and then the motor cuts out and we are plummeting. No frighten-the-kid about this; nobody's playing. I am on my back, then on my face, then on my back again, and then I am hanging from my harness, belly down over the world. The green rushes up at me. Peach is yelling something but I can't make out the words, and when I look over he is not there. There's a smoggy space of air where he just was, his unmanned gun jerking crazily on its pivot.

I scrabble for the hook that clips my harness to the side of the plane, release the catch. And though it is the most frightening thing yet, I dive out of the open window and into freefall.

CHAPTER THIRTY-SIX

Lucy

No one conjectures aloud, but it might turn into a good night. A *good night* is something that can be decreed only in retrospect; everything can change in a minute. A little medical Zen: we accept the peace we are given. Only a few days in the ER year are predictably, almost-without-exception slow: Thanksgiving morning through afternoon (before the surfeit of postprandial belly-aches); Christmas (pretty much all day); and Super Bowl Sunday (only while the game is being played). A thick snowfall will impede shenanigans too, at least while the snow is falling and before the snow-shoveling heart attacks start coming in.

And then there are nights like this one, random jewels. The stream of injury and illness is steady and manageable, the trauma bells going off only rarely. There's time for luxuries like legible documentation and chatting with the patients, time even for teaching the medical student something more useful than *hold that* and *get out of the way*.

Next chart in the rack: Kayla, a four-month-old whose triage note says *won't stop crying*.

"I know exactly how she feels," quips her nurse as Bryan, the medical student, and I go into the room. But it's a sham complaint, delivered with a smile.

The patient's mother is sitting by the stretcher, her hand on the infant's belly as it wails up at the ceiling. She's a slender girl with long hair parted zigzag, who can't be more than sixteen. *Teen mom* dings a warning bell in my head—it's a risk factor for child abuse.

"I've changed her, fed her, burped her," she says over the baby's cries. "Maybe I'm not doing it right. She just won't stop."

Kayla has some lungs on her; we have to half shout the interview. Two days of almost nonstop crying but no fever, no vomiting, no cough, no change in appetite or diaper contents, no rash, no trauma. Not left in anyone else's care for any period of time. No obvious explanation for Kayla's distress.

"So what do we do?" I ask Bryan. The best way to teach, the best way to learn: the Socratic method applied to a real patient.

"Rule out sepsis," he says. "Blood culture, urine culture, spinal tap." The mother's eyes widen at *spinal tap.*

"Keep in mind that she's four months old." Which, thank goodness, puts her out of the age range where rule-out-sepsis would be mandatory. Four months is practically elderly for an infant.

Bryan looks blank, and I relent.

"First we examine her." His face says, *Damn it, I should have said that.*

I show him how to go over a baby head to toe. How to examine the infant retina: hold the ophthalmoscope still and let the roving eye scroll a carpet of vessels and optic disk through the path of the light. How to check for common problems like ear infection, and for more occult ones like hair tourniquet. Toe tourniquets in particular are easy to miss, hard to spot if one plump, pea-sized toe is redder than the others.

We get a urine sample to check for infection and toxicology, and even though there's no outward sign of injury we order a babygram: a one-shot X ray of the whole infant to look for new or old fractures.

Everything is completely normal.

"There's no other tests?" her mother pleads, her eyes panicked, when we tell her. "She's gonna start up again when we get home, I know it."

Kayla's not crying now; she's fascinated by a yellow finger puppet Bryan has produced from his pocket. Medical students' white coat pockets can be a treasure trove.

"You said you live with your mom," I say. "Has she been able to help?"

"She works a lot." The tears spill. "She stays with her boyfriend."

So this teenager has been alone and terrified in an apartment with a screaming infant for days.

"I think we need to evaluate Kayla overnight." Bryan looks up, surprised, when I say this. "Just in the ER. You can stay in this room and we'll keep her in a monitoring room for the night. Will that be all right?"

"Okay," says Kayla's mother, her features flooding with relief. She suddenly looks her age, which I remind myself is not old enough to vote.

I take Kayla into my arms and her mother climbs onto the stretcher, turns on her side away from us, and pulls up the sheet. I shut off the light and close the door.

"Is this legal?" asks Bryan. "I mean, she's not medically ill." He's a modern doctor-in-training, filled with admonitions about door-to-discharge timing and cost-benefit analysis.

"We don't need the bed right now," I tell him. "The tests we already did were the major cost. What's a few more hours?" Kayla's begun to whimper again and I pat my hand against her back. "In the morning, we'll get them plugged into whatever support systems are out there. In the meantime, the baby's safe."

"You think she's in danger? Should we call CPS?"

"There's no evidence of neglect." Actually, the opposite is true: even after days without sleep, Kayla's mother made a good choice and brought her here, instead of shaking her or dropping her out a window.

I don't have to explain to the nurses; most of them are moms. They tuck a warmed blanket around Kayla's mother and she sleeps behind the closed door of bed 8 while the baby is carried around the Big Room by various staff. I jog her on one hip as I check on patients' test results or the effect of administered medicines or fluids. She works baby magic: every patient smiles at the sight of her. She falls asleep in my arms after a while, bubbling spit into the lapel of my white coat, her springy hair tickling my neck.

We could never, ever do this on a normal night. It couldn't have happened last night; it's unlikely to be possible tomorrow. But tonight, it is something we can do. Bryan is right—it's basically very expensive baby-sitting, and it's not a permanent solution, but it worked for tonight, and who knows? Maybe that will be enough.

There is nothing magical or mysterious about the medicine I practice. We save or don't save, we reassure, we comfort, all our efforts successful only insofar as they lay the groundwork for knitting together the damaged body, the damaged life. There are always going to be things we can't fix, and it will never stop being terrible to see them. Healing has only its merest beginnings here.

"I'M GOING TO take off early," says Bryan just before dawn. "If that's okay with you. Can you sign this?"

It's the standard evaluation form that will go into his academic file.

"I've really enjoyed working with you," he says. It's the last day of his rotation. This is good-bye. "Do you have any criticisms for me? Anything I can improve?" It's a routine question.

"No criticisms," I tell him. "But I do have some advice." He waits at attention. "You're on a long road. I think you know that." Kayla whimpers and I put a hand over her curly head. A sudden stab of regret: the warm head of my own child under my comforting palm is something I will never know. "Medicine will take everything you give, and some days you will have to give it everything. But not *every* day. Guard something in your life, Bryan, something that you love. Keep it safe from all the sadness and madness. Because no matter how much you love it, medicine will not love you back."

He nods, but I can tell that he has heard it before, and that it doesn't resonate this time either. I suppose he'll need to learn it for himself.

CHAPTER THIRTY-SEVEN

Clare

WHEN THE LETTERS STOPPED COMING, it didn't worry me at first. But when three weeks passed in a row with the postmaster's head shake *no,* I felt a clutch of panic.

"Don't think the worst," said the postmaster. "He might be whooping it up on leave, forgetting to write. Boys will be boys."

Yes, I could hope for that.

"No news is good news," he added. "Bad news comes in a telegram."

A telegram. I hadn't thought of that. But if there had been a telegram, it would have been sent to Leo's mother, not to me. She could have it already, along with his personal effects if they had been found, his dog tags and the pocketknife I had given him and whatever else he'd carried in his pockets. She could be smoothing out one of my letters right now, puzzled, thinking, *Who's Clare?*

Five weeks; six.

It was easy to find out where she lived. Only a few blocks from the center of town, in what seemed to be a nice neighborhood. I didn't know why that surprised me.

Wilson, said the mailbox; wrong name, but it was the right street number. I went up the path and knocked at the door. Instantly there was an eruption of barking, high yips accompanied by scrambling toenails.

"Get back, Taffy," said the woman who opened the door. "Sorry. Can I help you?" She smiled up at me. She was petite, dark-blond, with a high forehead. I couldn't see anything of Leo in her. A little dun-colored dog leapt about behind her.

"I'm looking for Mrs. Dutton," I said. "Someone told me this house."

Her face grew sharper, a little suspicious. "It's Wilson now. Do I know you?"

She was wearing an apron over her skirt, the picture of a middle-class housewife. I was glad that I'd chosen to wear the dress I'd made over the winter, from fabric Leo had given me for Christmas.

"I'm a—friend—of Leo's." There was no mistaking the recognition in her eyes when I said the name. "He's your son?"

"Yes, but . . . He was fostered out years ago."

"I—I'm the one who fostered him."

She hesitated, then unhooked the screen door. "Come in."

The dog backed up against the wall as I entered, then turned tail and ran out of the room. We went into the parlor. Mrs. Wilson motioned me to the sofa and took an upholstered chair across from it. I looked around the room. Modest, very neat. An upright piano against one wall with a metronome on the top, and a child's lesson book on the music stand.

"You have other children," I said.

"Three," she said, and blushed. "I had Leo—before." I nodded: I'd always suspected that he was born out of wedlock. "And then I married Clyde, and we had Tad and Sally and Matthew." She jumped up. "What am I thinking? Let me get some lemonade."

She came back in a few minutes later with a pitcher of lemonade and a plate of cookies. She poured me a glass and sat down; her hands smoothed the apron over her lap.

"It was hard with Clyde and Leo," she said. "They didn't get along." As if they were quarrelsome peers, as if Leo had not been a child. "Leo talked so much. He was always asking questions. You know."

I didn't say anything, but perhaps she read my expression, because she looked ashamed.

"What else could I do?" she said. "I couldn't leave my husband. I had the other children to think of." Her hands smoothed and smoothed. "I knew he'd get a good Christian education at St. William's."

"It's a hard place," I said.

"He didn't like it at first. He kept coming back here. It broke my heart every time. And then he stopped." She added in a whisper, "That broke my heart too." She looked into my face. "But it got better, didn't it?" Her voice was beseeching. "When he came here to get his join-up papers signed, he was all grown up. He seemed happy."

"I think he was," I said, watching the relief relax her features. Thinking sixteen was not *all grown up,* not by a long shot. "Have you had any news of him? He hasn't written to me in a while."

"Oh," she said. "I—wait a minute." She left the room and returned with an envelope. She gave it to me. "I thought you knew." She watched me take the paper out and unfold it.

Missing, presumed dead. My eyes went straight to those words.

"I thought they'd tell you," she said.

I could barely speak. "Your name was on his papers."

"His plane was shot down," she said. "Over enemy territory."

"Presumed," I said. "Only *presumed.* Maybe he was captured."

We looked at each other dully. Then the clock on the mantel chimed, and she started.

"The children will be home from school any minute," she said. "I'm sorry, but it's better if you go."

As I went through the door, she reached out and touched my arm.

"You did a fine job raising him."

Then she stepped inside and closed the door.

The walk back to Roscommon was slow and long. I kept my head down as I walked, waited until I was out of town before I let the tears come. Up the hill toward Roscommon, making the end of the same walk I'd made all that time ago, trying to follow Bradley. Another boy taken from me in the air, gone without a trace.

James waved at me as I passed the farm. He hadn't acknowledged me for a long time, but I wasn't up to a conversation; I just waved back and went on.

Presumed wasn't *certain*, I told myself. I had to believe I'd see him someday. Maybe only in Heaven, if I could ever believe in all that again. For a moment the thought of it was so delicious.

When I saw the long burgundy car parked on the curve of the road before the cottage came into view, my first irrational thought was *Leo?* and my heart leapt before I came to my senses. It had a fancy convertible top and shiny hubcaps; hardly a military vehicle. No one bringing news of Leo would come in such a car, nor would they come to me. I turned the bend, and now I could see up the path to the front of the cottage. There, sitting on the step of my stone house, my sanctuary, looking irritated as hell, was Hugh.

DAMN CONGA HEART *again. It'll calm down in a minute.*

I'll come back tomorrow.

Thanks for the cliff-hanger.

CHAPTER THIRTY-EIGHT

Leo

"O H NO," SAYS JENESSA WHEN we're nearly at the library. "You did *not* come here."

She's not talking to me. She's looking at a man across the street who's leaning against a car with his arms crossed.

"No," she says. "Uh-uh."

"Baby," he calls as we get closer.

"You get out of here," she yells back, and puts a hand up as if he's a car and she's stopping him at an intersection. "I'm working."

"Well, work it on over here," he says with a mock pout that spreads into a wide smile. "Come on, baby."

"Oh Jesus God," she says, and turns to me. "I have to talk to this fool. You go on in. I'll meet you right outside like always."

I run up the steps as she crosses the street.

"I WAS HOPING to see you again," says the library lady. "Something popped into my mind a couple of days after you came in last time. When you get old, your memory can be unpredictable." She smiles and taps her head. She puts down what she is holding, a newspaper on a long wooden rod, and I follow her to a computer.

"We didn't dig deeply enough," she says, typing.

The search results furl down on the screen: the same ones from last time, as far as I can tell.

"See, these all say Ireland," she says, putting a fingertip on the glass.

"It's not in a different *country*," I say.

"Well, I think you're right," she says. "And it occurred to me . . . I'm not an authority on local history by any means, but . . ." She's paging through the results now, clicking *next . . . next . . . next*. Finally on page sixteen, she scrolls down and clicks on a block of text. "Could that be it?" she says, standing back.

At first I am not sure what I'm seeing, but then she enlarges the image and there's the curving road on the hill, the church, the road to town.

"That's it," I say.

"I *thought* so." Triumphant. "And . . . print," she says. The printer beside us starts humming, and a paper slowly pushes out. One page, then a second. "Only about twelve miles away," she says, squaring the pages on the tabletop before handing them to me. "Is this for a school project?"

"Kind of," I say.

WHEN I GET outside, I can see Jenessa sitting in the car across the street. The man who'd been leaning against it is inside the car with her. The sun flashes off her hair clip as she turns her head. I look away quickly, as if that will help her not see me. A bus pulls up to the stop, blocking her from view. I walk around the corner.

A few other kids pass me, hands in the straps of their backpacks, walking home from school. They eye me—they know I don't belong—but they don't say anything, and no one else notices me. Only a couple of cars go by. After a few blocks, the sidewalk is gone and I'm walking on tired-looking grass filled with glass pieces and cigarette butts. I look at the map. The way I'm supposed to go on the map starts as a thick blue line, but I don't see a road like that anywhere. I'm going toward the sun, so I know it's the right direction. There aren't a lot of street signs, just tall poles where they should go. The buildings are different here, nearly all shops of some kind, with ripply metal roofs and chain fences. There are hardly any houses.

It takes me a while to realize that the blue line from the map must be the big road that's below the one I'm on. I can look down and see it like a river of moving cars, the waning sunlight winking off them. I can't possibly walk on that busy road; I'd be spotted in a minute. I'll stay instead in the tangle of small streets that nestle into the curves of the map's thick blue line. They'll get me there. It'll be smarter to walk after dark; I'll find a place to hide until then.

CHAPTER THIRTY-NINE

Lucy

A RED BLOOD CELL LIVES 120 days and then dies, part of the natural senescence happening all over our bodies all the time. Everything about us is constantly dying and regenerating. Even while we sit quietly we are humming with activity, making and remaking ourselves. In 120 days all my blood will be new; not one blood cell that has known my husband will remain. The thought of my fresh, unbetrayed blood comforts me. I can wait 120 days— four months—I can wait that long. And while it's not complete renewal —we're more than blood, we're a panoply of organs, we're skin and bones and muscles and sinew and nerves and fat and lymph and miles and miles of gut—the solid fact remains that red blood cells live 120 days and then are replaced with brand-new cells. And that seems a good enough place to start.

CHAPTER FORTY

Clare

BELINDA IS THE ONE TO tell me.

"I'm so sorry, Miss Clare." She sits down on the bed. "Miss Gloria passed last night."

"She was doing so well yesterday." My tears surprise me. I've outlived everyone I've ever known; I naively supposed I'd outlived my capacity for grief as well.

Belinda pats my hand. "You know it can go like that."

I do know. Haven't I seen it many times before? Sudden improvement often is a harbinger of doom. Gloria had seemed so much better yesterday, and I took it as a good sign, a sign that she was getting better. Hope can make a person blind.

"She wanted you to have this."

A small box about the size of a pound of butter. Beautifully wrapped in paper printed with lilacs and a narrow ridged ribbon curled into a profusion of ringlets.

"Gloria didn't wrap that," I said. She would never have had the patience for all that ribbon fussing. She was the lumpy-envelope-plastered-with-tape type of gifter, all substance over style.

"I wrapped it for her," admits Belinda. "She gave it to me last week. I think she knew her time was coming."

She had. She'd tried to tell me, but I hadn't been listening.

"I didn't say good-bye," I tell Belinda. My voice cracks on the last word.

"Oh Miss Clare." Belinda puts her arms around me. She has a scent like clean linen. "You'll see each other again."

"Do you really believe that?"

"I really do." She leans over and pulls a tissue from the bedside box, pats it against my cheeks. "She also gave me a message: *You're going or I'll come back and haunt you.* She said you'd know what that means. Are you going somewhere?"

I suppose I am.

CHAPTER FORTY-ONE

Leo

THEY WALK SO SOFTLY BEHIND me that I can't hear them, and I start to wonder if they've gone away, if I'm walking blindly on alone. I slow, and immediately there is a poke in my back, jolting me forward. So they are still close behind. I resume walking, straining to see, to hear, but I see only darkness, hear only my own breathing and my heavy boots crashing through the jungle.

We have been walking for hours, ever since they found me and cut me down from the tree my parachute was tangled in. The white silk must have looked like a signal flag. I was dangling and dazed and grateful at first to see them.

I've been trying to work my bonds loose while I walk, a slow-motion escape. Pressing outward with my wrists as far as I can, bringing them back together and then putting my hands against my hip, trapping the loops and rolling them just a little higher than they were, just where the wrist starts to widen into forearm. Keeping my movements as subtle as possible, not sure if I'm making any progress at all.

I consider my options. I can't get far on my own; I don't know where I am. Without moving my head, just using my eyes, I look up and see that the dark is infinitesimally less dark in patches: sky between treetops. I was always good at climbing. If I could get up high enough, wait for dawn, I could look around and try to get my bearings. I could stand with my feet on a branch, my back against the trunk, motionless until night comes again. *Bark on the tree,* like the training instructor used to say. Luckily we haven't dropped chemicals here and there is still foliage to hide me.

Another hard poke: I quicken my pace, although my legs feel like concrete tubes swinging from my hips. I take only a few more steps before I am jerked backward by a hand on my shoulder. So that last poke must have meant Stop.

There is a scraping noise, unmistakable: a Zippo. Tears in my eyes at the friendliness of the sound, or maybe just the sudden light. The jumping flame on the ground frightens me more than anything else so far. It tells me how hopeless this is. If we were close to any ARVN or Americans, they wouldn't make a fire. There's a kick at the backs of my knees; my legs buckle and I fall heavily onto one shoulder with an *oof,* provoking a rough clatter of laughter from the direction of the fire.

They are ignoring me now, crouched around the fire, going through the things they have taken. Eating while they inspect the goods, flicking an occasional item into the flames. They must have found others before they found me: one of them unwraps a small sheaf of GI belts, snaps them to test the fabric, then coils them up again.

They notice me looking; one of them gets up and stands in front of me, blocking my vision. He speaks down at me, a harsh chain of meaningless noises.

"I don't understand." My voice is hoarse, clogged.

He speaks again, staccato, imperative. I shake my head.

He bends down, slaps me so that I fall over onto my side again; there's a sudden pain in one bound wrist. No laughter this time. He crouches beside me, the speech like machine-gun fire. He is so close that his saliva makes wet drops on my cheek; I squeeze my eyes shut.

Now a hand grasps my ear and pulls it away from my head. The new pain brings tears to my eyes but I am almost grateful for the fresh sensation, crying out louder than the dull powerful ache everywhere else. It focuses me: all I am is ear. I am the line where the tender flesh joins my skull, I am nothing but that hot line and the heartbeat shaking my body, and the rasping sound of my own breath.

He is shouting now, jerking my head back and forth by the ear between his fingers, grinding my cheek in the dirt, and eventually I understand. He wants my eyes open. He wants me to watch.

AND I'M TUMBLING *back toward the beginning, wherever that is. I am at the beginning, then before the beginning. The beginning is all around me.*

A SWEEP OF light wakes me, glaring through my eyelids. It's very cold. Everything is white before the light moves away again and I realize that it was headlights, a car going by. I wait.

When my eyes have adjusted, I emerge from the place I've been sleeping—a cardboard box flattened on the ground behind a row of bins—and set off. I may not be able to walk on the blue-line road, but I can walk on the streets beside it and follow it as it curls west. I just need to walk as fast as I can before the sun comes up.

Past parking lots and fences, it's all pavement here, no grass. A redbrick building with tall dark windows takes up one whole long block. When I get to a big street, I stand outside the cone of streetlight until I'm sure there's no traffic before I try to cross. I count while I walk, get past a thousand before I lose track, sing every song I know. The alphabet song, "You Are My Sunshine," then hymns that float to me from somewhere. *For all the saints* makes a good marching song, and I sing that a few times over, all the verses I can remember, then, *A mighty fortress is our God.* I have to stop when my throat is dry.

The street I'm on gets winding and narrow, the walls of buildings rising high on either side. Someone unseen coughs and calls to me from the shadows. *Hey kid, hey kid c'mere*—making chills spread down from my shoulders like a cape. *Leave him alone,* says another voice.

In the distance is a sign with lights shining on it, a picture of a hamburger and a glass of Coca-Cola. It's very high; it must be on the roof of a building. It hangs in the dark sky like a promise. The hamburger would be wonderful, but I stare at the glass of Coke, the ice cubes in it. Maybe there's a machine at the bottom of the sign. No money needed, just reach in and take out a bottle; don't I remember a machine like that from somewhere? I can almost feel the cool scalloped glass in my hand. Now I'm thinking of the red iron handle of the pump standing in the yard at Roscommon, and now of the drinking fountain in the hospital. I imagine stepping on the metal lever and putting my mouth over the upside-down U of cold water; the thought of it makes my throat hurt with longing. It starts to rain and I put my head back to let it rain into my mouth, but the drops mostly hit my eyes and my cheeks and my forehead, hardly ever my tongue.

It surprises me when the street I'm walking on ends. I stand between the arms of an untidy bush and unfold the map. The rain taps the pages and flutters them in my hands. I look at the wrong place in the dim light for a long time, trying to match it up to anything, before I finally find the corner I'm standing on.

It can't be, it just can't. I've been walking for hours but I've barely gone any distance at all from where I started. I measure with my thumb and forefinger pinched apart: I would have to make this walk another ten times, another twenty times, just to reach the white spur of road that runs from the blue line west toward

Roscommon. I can't do it. I know I can't do it. I close my eyes and hot tears slide down my face.

My thirst returns, urgent. The map doesn't matter anymore, I have to have something to drink. I turn away from the big windowless buildings into a warren of streets, and walk until I'm in a neighborhood, houses on either side, shabby and maybe some not even lived in. I cross the dead grass of a lawn and push into the bushes in front of a house, rubbing my hands over the clapboard, feeling for a spigot.

"What are you doing?" The voice makes me jump. I try to turn around but the bushes are too tight; I have to back out the way I came in. I stand up in front of a skinny man.

"You live here?" he asks, and then answers himself. "You don't live here."

"I'm thirsty."

He nods, as if that's a perfect explanation.

"I know a place you can get a drink," he says. "Free. And a sandwich. Sound good?"

"Yes," I tell him, a single syllable filled with all my failure, the blue line that defeated me, Clare waiting—I know she's waiting— and the impossibility of getting to her.

"Come on then," he says.

He's not used to walking with a kid; he takes long steps and doesn't look behind him, and I have to hurry on my cold-stiff legs to catch up. The sky turns orange in front of us. I don't know where we're going. I'm just walking, nothing but walking, the promise of water, warmth, food pulling me on.

CHAPTER FORTY-TWO

Lucy

I LEAVE THROUGH THE AMBULANCE BAY, stepping out into the world. The sun's barely up. White coats are streaming past me through a misting, cool rain: the day ranks coming to work. Death Month's over. A little celebration is in order. No cafeteria food today. I'll get breakfast somewhere and go back to the call room for what I hope will be the last time—and when I wake up later today, I'll rent one of the apartments I looked at. It doesn't matter where; it'll only be for a few months. Residency will be over soon, and the rest of my life will begin.

"Hey, Doc," says a voice, very close, when I am halfway to the far lot where residents park. My heart lurches. Haven't we all been told a thousand times, pay attention when you leave, don't look at your phone, stay aware of your surroundings?

"Jesus Christ, Freddy." It's our frequent flyer, the philosophical hobo. "You have to stop doing that." And then I see that he's not alone. A smaller figure steps out from behind him, looking dirty and wet and exhausted. *Ben*. I can't make the connection between them. "What are you doing out here?"

"He's thirsty," says Freddy.

"I'm going to Clare," the boy says in a small, determined voice. He produces a limp square of folded paper, holds it out to me.

I've been up all night, I'm off duty now. I could return him to the psych floor and let them take it from there. Or take him into the ER: my training shouts that he needs hydration and electrolytes. But something inside me recoils at what that will entail: stripping him down and putting a needle into his arm, then calling Psych and Social Services, plugging him back into the system that has clearly failed him.

We took him home. Preeti's voice comes into my mind.

I take the paper, peel apart the damp pages.

"You good?" Freddy asks the boy, who looks at me.

"Yes," I say. "Thanks, Freddy." He salutes and goes off in the direction of the hospital. I turn to the child. "First, what you need is a good breakfast." Something better than rubbery hospital eggs and sugary juice. "Okay?" He nods. "Then I'll take you where you need to go."

CHAPTER FORTY-THREE

Clare

IT'S TOTALLY DISORIENTING. FIRST GETTING the driver to understand where I want to go, and then knowing if I am really there at all.

Is this Roscommon? I see nothing I recognize. There is no field. It's a sea of cement, with flame-shaped pear trees marooned at orderly intervals in strips of grass. The driver thinks I want to go shopping—I didn't contradict him when he said so—and he drops me in front of a fancy kitchenware store. He gives me a phone and shows me the button to push to call him when I'm ready. He points out a shop with a green sign above it, across the parking lot. "I'll be right in there having coffee," he says. "They have a bathroom if you need one." He helps me out of the car, tells me to take my time, drives off.

There's music coming from somewhere; I can't locate the source but it follows me as I walk by the long shop windows. I should have known it would all be gone. I spent sixty years here. Somewhere under this concrete the gallons of sweat I dropped into the earth, the seeds I planted and nurtured, charred petals from the roses that never bloomed again. My life. Swallowed up. They must have moved the graves, dug up those families and carted them off somewhere else. Nothing is sacred.

I sit on a bench and set the small box down on my lap. The ribbon is beautiful. Is that why I'm crying? For a ribbon? It's the care, perhaps, of Belinda, who selected and curled the ribbon, thinking of me. It's not as small a thing as it might seem.

I open the box. Inside, nestled in lavender tissue paper, is the tape recorder. *Push the red button,* says Gloria's cursive on the Post-it note attached. *Finish it.*

IF YOU'D ASKED me the day before, I would have expected to have trouble summoning Hugh's face. But that was a story I was telling myself, because of course I knew him instantly when I saw him.

"It *is* you," he said, standing up. "I didn't really believe it." He was smoking a cigar; he dropped it to the earth and ground his heel onto it. "That farmer down there is an idiot. He said your name was Clare."

"How did you find me?" I stood on the path, a wary fifteen feet between us. Twenty-five years had wrought the expected changes to his face and body—less hair, more girth—but there was something else very different about him; I couldn't put my finger on it.

"It wasn't easy," he said. "What is this place?"

"This is where I live."

"You raised our son here? In this—hut? Where is he?"

"No. Bradley died, Hugh. In the hurricane."

He sat down on the step again as though someone had pushed him. I hadn't meant to be cruel, speaking so bluntly.

"I'm sorry to tell you that way," I said. "The papers published our names among the dead. Whatever made you think otherwise?"

He spoke into his hands, which were cradling his face.

"One of my workers brought cake with his lunch."

"Pardon me?"

He lifted his head. "I work at the electrical plant now. One of the men brought in a cake. With the"—he moved his hand—"on top."

My mother's cakes, the ones Mrs. Massey sold out of her shop. One of her sons worked at the electrical plant in Providence. Hugh had recognized the cherry heart on the top, my mother's signature. What a twisted chain had led him here.

"I knew your mother was dead. I went to her funeral." He gave a little laugh. "It was your funeral too." So we'd been laid to rest together; I found that oddly comforting. "Still, that cake. I knew it had to be yours. I thought I was crazy to think it." He looked around again. "Have you been here all along then?"

"Yes."

"All this time. In this little place."

"Yes." I watched as he took in the message telegraphed by the stone house and the lines on my face, the calluses on my hands: I'd chosen to live without earthly comforts, rather than return to him.

"Who is he?" I'd forgotten the dramatic transformation that anger could bring to his features.

"There isn't any man, Hugh. I live here alone."

"Nonsense. You wouldn't be able to fend for yourself out here for one day." He leapt up from the steps, covering the space between us in a few strides, and took my arm. "Do you know what you've done? You've made a bigamist of me." His fingers dug in above the elbow. "I have children."

I cringed just for a moment before I realized: the hand on my arm wasn't getting purchase. My muscle there was firm. And then I understood what the change was. It wasn't a difference in Hugh; it was a difference in me. I shook easily out of his grasp.

"You need to go home, Hugh."

He looked at his empty hand as if he'd seen a magic trick, a woman sawn in half.

"Our marriage was a lifetime ago," I told him. "It barely happened. We might have found a way to make it real, and we might even have found a way to be happy, if—" I stopped. "But that's not the way it went." I looked him in those bright blue eyes, feeling only sorrow.

"Is everything all right?"

It was James, coming up the path. His voice was casual and his expression pleasant, but something about his bearing spoke to Hugh, man to man.

"This isn't any of your business," Hugh said to James.

"No one has to know about me," I told Hugh. "I can stay dead, and you can go on with your life. We don't have to be enemies. We shared a tiny, sad bit of our lives. Just leave it in the past. Leave me here."

His eyes moved as I talked, to the house behind me, the tidy garden, the tall woodpile. They all spoke for me: *I'm not the girl you knew.* Maybe they even said the rest: *I never was.*

"How did he die?" he asked.

"I don't know," I said. The truth. I didn't know what had happened to Bradley, just as I didn't know what had happened to Leo. I had told myself a story of wind carrying the baby through the air, and that may have happened, but my clear memories stopped after the pram blew away, and I was never sure whether or not I'd dreamed the rest.

"Just go," I told Hugh. "I'll never bother you, I won't shame your wife or children. You can just pretend you never saw me today. Go back to your life, and leave me to mine."

"I was well rid of you." His voice was bitter. "This is what you deserve."

In silence, James and I watched him walk back to his car and get in, navigate the turnaround on the narrow road and drive away down the hill.

"I didn't know about the child," James said finally. "I'm sorry."

I nodded, watching the cloud of dust left by Hugh's car twinkling as it settled back onto the road.

"I don't want to marry again," I said. "I don't want to be a wife." I turned to James. "That doesn't mean we can't have a life together."

He didn't follow at first.

"We can make the rules," I said.

I took his hand in mine, my rough fingers between his rough fingers.

He looked shocked. Then he smiled. Then he laughed and said, "Why not?"

We had thirty-three years of *why not* after that, thirty-three years of working our side-by-each lands and going to one or the other place to sleep. Not every night together, but most. We put in a long line of fruit trees along the border of the two properties, sour cherry North Stars and sweet Pippin apples and a hardy variety of peach. In spring they littered the landscape with fallen blossoms deep as snow, making a white avenue between his house and mine. It was a good thirty-three years, the best of my life, before cancer took him and I was alone at Roscommon again.

SEE, GLORIA, YOU *were right. It is a love story after all.*

I FIND THE button and click the recorder off, sit for a few minutes watching the people go by. This place was never mine, just as Leo wasn't mine. We have things for a while, and then they're gone, and we're lucky to have had them at all. How Gloria would smirk at that, how she would carry on in that terrible faux-southern accent she would sometimes perpetrate. *Miss Clare, I do declare you are full of wisdom today.*

And then there's a catch in my chest, and all the shadow girls in the back of my mind hesitate. All of them—naughty chou-fleur up past bedtime, arms folded on the windowsill looking over the city; the arrogant girl watching the ink bloom from the nib like a rotten flower; the skinny drudge in the weaving room; darling mouse; the sad, silent wife watching her mother's hand hovering over the tea; the overalled Witch of Roscommon with hoe between callused palms; the awkward figure in the Second Best Dress lifting her hand to the priory door knocker; the woman walking up the stairs inside the white farmhouse, sliding the pins from her hair—all of them stand still. They stop their motion-loops, they cease what they are doing, they drop their hands to their sides and they turn toward me, in a long chain like accordioned paper-doll figures, cocking their heads as if listening.

Another twinge in my chest. I automatically look upward, but there's not a cloud in the sky. My eyes fall again to the crowd hurrying along the sidewalks. A woman among them, coming toward me. Thirties maybe, wearing scrubs and those clogs that all the Oak Haven doctors and nurses wear. She sees me too, and her face looks concerned. Maybe an off-duty nurse, worried about the old lady sitting alone on the bench.

I don't see the boy until he runs toward me.

CHAPTER FORTY-FOUR

I'M SORRY I DIDN'T COME back," says the boy. "I wanted to. I tried."

"That's all you could do," says the old lady, looking down into his face. "I did hate not knowing."

"Were you happy anyway?" he asks.

"Yes. Always a little bit sad, though." She sighs, a long wind of unspoken history breathing out between them. "It was very hard sometimes, wondering how it was for you. Did you suffer?"

"Yes. But not for very long." He climbs right onto the bench with the old woman and puts his arms around her. "I never thanked you."

"You didn't have to."

"I'm sorry," says the woman in scrubs. "Ben, get down, what are you doing? Ma'am, are you all right?"

"I never forgot you. You should know that," says the old lady.

"I know," says the boy.

"It happened, and it mattered. We know it happened. Even though there's nothing left." She gestures around at the outdoor mall, then puts a hand to her chest. "Oh."

The woman in scrubs dials her cell phone and speaks quickly: *Elderly female at the outdoor mall on Route 44. Just across from the Starbucks.*

"I'm here now," says the boy. "I'm here."

"Oh. What's happening?" says the old lady. There's a tearing sensation, not totally unpleasant. It feels something like an internal itch is being scratched. Finally.

The woman holding the phone to her ear fumbles at the old lady's wrist, presses two fingers against her neck, then turns away to speak more quietly into the phone. "No sirens," she says. "She's got a No Code bracelet."

It's a tiny knot of humanity on that bench, the morning crowds drifting past, no one taking notice. If they did look, it would appear to be just a family outing, three generations. A boy hugging his grandma, his mother on the phone, on the first day of April, almost spring.

AT FIRST IT seems that he's sleeping. Lucy hates to disturb him, but he can't keep embracing the dead stranger. She puts her hand on his back, and he opens his brown eyes and blinks.

"Where's my mom?" asks Ben, and he starts to cry.

"It's okay," says Lucy. She crouches in front of him. "You're okay."

He turns from the old lady on the bench and draws into himself, his legs bent up.

"My mom died. The star man hurt her and she died," he says.

The star man. She immediately sees it: the star tattoo beside the murderer's eye. So he remembers. Lucy lifts her phone again and scrolls down her contacts to find the number for the detective who'd been in charge of Karen's case.

"She's not coming back," Ben says. Lucy looks up.

"No," she says. "She's not. I'm so sorry."

He's crying so hard now that the snot is running onto his lips. He gives a lurching hiccup.

The man has got to be in the hospital still, recovering from his injuries. He isn't going anywhere. The call can wait. She drops the phone into her shirt pocket; her arms aren't even fully raised before Ben falls into them. She gathers him against her, pulling his damp wailing head against her shoulder.

"I know," says Lucy. "I know."

He's saying something, almost unintelligible through the sobbing. It sounds like *How much?*

"How much what?" says Lucy. What is he asking?

"How much?" he cries into her chest. "How much?"

"So much," she says, helpless, guessing. She feels a change in him at that; he's still shuddering with sobs, but attentive.

"More than what?" he says. Mandating, hopeful, like someone asking for a password.

"More than . . ." she says, her palm against the wet curve of his head, the curling tips of his hair licking back around her hand. He smells of mud. He needs a haircut. "More than anything."

EPILOGUE

THE AIRPLANE IS LIKE A tube, rows of seats all facing forward, windows set deep into the curved walls. After the roar and whine of takeoff, everything settles down into a mild vibration. No engine smell, just a stale chilly dryness with all the flavor taken out. It is only when I look out the window that I can tell we are in the air. I know I've been on a plane before, but I can't remember exactly when.

"Where are the birds?" I ask.

"We're too high for birds," says Lucy, brushing at the front of my shirt. "Do you want my pretzels?"

Too high for birds; that seems impossible. The ground, where it peeks through the fluffy white below, is incredibly far away. Pressing my face against the thick plastic over the window, looking straight down, I can see the shadow of the airplane slipping across fields before the cloud bank intervenes again.

"If it rains," I say, leaning back from the window, "will we be above the water?"

She nods.

I put my fingertip into my mouth, and then into the empty pretzel bag. Capture a dozen tiny cubes of salt, let them melt on my tongue.

"Who will be there?" I ask.

She has told me this already, but she tells me again. All the things that will happen. I put my head against her arm as she talks. Out the window just blue, no clouds.

"Your new grandma and grandpa will be there," she says. "They're so excited to see you. You know, your grandma wasn't my first mom. She started being my mom when I was a little bit younger than you."

I know now more clearly how things sort out. Here, I had Mom, and now Lucy; before, there was Mama and then Clare.

"The house has a porch with a swing, and a big backyard. We can put in a jungle gym."

"We can plant things," I murmur. "Roses."

"We'll plant roses," she agrees. "Your bedroom can have constellations on the ceiling. Would you like that?" I nod. "At bedtime you'll put on your pajamas, the green ones or the Superman, and you'll brush your teeth." I can hear her voice both through the air and also a deeper, lower echo through the ear that's pressed against her arm. "I'll read you a story. Or you'll read to me. And we'll talk about your mom. You'll always remember her." She bends toward me, puts her mouth against the hair on the top of my head. She stays there when the kiss is done, her lips against my skull. "You'll have good dreams," she says, and her words spread out against my scalp, raising gooseflesh.

Before, there were so many gaps; now they are filled, right to the smallest warm corners. Nothing important is missing.

ACKNOWLEDGMENTS

Thank you first to my agent, the tiny and inimitable Laura Gross, for your long forbearance, unwavering trust, and matchless zeal. I am very grateful to my editors, Nan Graham and Kara Watson at Scribner in New York, for taking on my rough work and wisely, patiently guiding me to make it better, and to Susan Sandon at Penguin Random House UK, a kindred spirit if ever there was one; you can't know how much your enthusiasm has meant to me.

Heartfelt thanks to Emily Greenwald, Katie Rizzo, Michelle Marchese, Jaya Miceli, Rosie Mahorter, and the rest of the team at Scribner; and to Emily Griffin, Laura Brooke, Celeste Ward-Best, Amber Bennett-Ford, Cara Conquest, and the rest of the team at Penguin Random House UK.

Great appreciation goes to Will Morningstar for cluing me in to some awkward bits, to Kristina Trejo for helping me fix them, and to Kate Miciak for early encouragement.

I am fortunate to have brilliant friends: Spike Lampros, Danielle Teller, and Emily Scott, who each blessed a struggling draft with dazzling insight; Carol Dysinger and Diana Spechler, who encountered portions of the protobook and were firm but gentle with my nonsense; Pamela Friedman, Annalee Harkins, Elizabeth Branch, and Mary Huey, my cheering section; Bobby Rogers, who walks the walk better than anyone; Ilse Jenouri, to whom I am bonded as if by war; the marvelous Alyson Denny, who sees things others don't; the delightful Eric Friedland; and Natalie Wolcott Williams, who, with wit and poise and cheer, embodies what we all might hope to be in our next lives if we are very, very good in this one.

It's impossible to thank Marghi Barone Fauss enough—your spectacular generosity is not even the tenth most remarkable thing about you. To Jillian, Jocelyn, Jonathon, and Aidan, thank you for making *Aunt* seem such an illustrious title. Thanks also to Tim Buckley, who really puts the *brother* in brother-in-law.

I am deeply and permanently indebted to Richard Bausch, who lifted his lamp high for me and who shows us all every day how it's done; to Catherine O'Neill Grace for taking me seriously from the very start, and to Phyllis Sidorsky, dear "Mrs. Sid," who curated the books of my childhood.

My very special thanks to Carla Buckley, sister and author, who's been there for this book's whole damned ride; you were there before the ride, urging me onto the horse. Hell, you were making horsey sounds at me when there was no horse in sight. It's been fun to share this with you. Let's never stop.

And thanks to you, whoever you are, for having read this book. Perhaps you've gotten to this part because you're the kind of reader who reads past the finish line; that would make you, as my mother would say, *a person after my own heart*.